LOST CROW CONSPIRACY

ROSALYN EVES

LOST CROW CONSPIRACY

BLOOD ROSE REBELLION

VOLUME II

ALFRED A. KNOPF · New York

THIS IS A BORZOI BOOK PUBLISHED BY ALFRED A. KNOPF

All rights reserved. Published in the United States by Alfred A. Knopf, an imprint of Random House Children's Books, a division of Penguin Random House LLC, New York.

Knopf, Borzoi Books, and the colophon are registered trademarks of Penguin Random House LLC.

Visit us on the Web! GetUnderlined.com

Educators and librarians, for a variety of teaching tools, visit us at RHTeachersLibrarians.com

Library of Congress Cataloging-in-Publication Data is available upon request.
ISBN 978-1-101-93607-8 (trade) — ISBN 978-1-101-93608-5 (lib. bdg.) — ISBN 978-1-101-93609-2 (ebook)

The text of this book is set in 12.5-point Bembo.

Printed in the United States of America
March 2018
10 9 8 7 6 5 4 3 2 1

First Edition

To Evelyn—because she is brave and bright (and because she asked me to)

*Red is the colour of blood, which will
flow in streams, and of fire, which will
consume cities and villages; green is the
colour of the grass, which will grow on
the graves of the slaughtered people;
white is the colour of the shroud in
which Hungary will lie. . . .*

—PROPHECY ON THE FLAG OF HUNGARY,
FROM M. HARTLEY'S *THE MAN
WHO SAVED AUSTRIA*

*. . . her heart was full
Of passions which had found no natural
scope. . . .*

—ROBERT SOUTHEY,
THE CURSE OF KEHAMA

Anna

CHAPTER 1

Vienna, May 1848

There is a feeling a hunted creature gets: a prickling of fine hairs at the back of the neck, a sense of unseen eyes crawling across one's spine, a shift in the air. A smell, perhaps.

I could not say what it was that night that struck me, only that between one turn on the ballroom floor and another, a sickness settled in my stomach. Someone—or some*thing*—was watching me.

My laugh turned brittle, my fingertips cold. I scanned the ballroom as I danced, searching for the source of my disquiet. Music swelled around me. Men in dark suits and women in jewel-toned gowns swirled past, gliding across the marble floor in time to one of Johann Strauss's waltzes. Frost and fire flickered up alternating walls, part of the night's illusions.

It was not so unusual, at a ball, to play at predator and prey: for women to hide behind their fans and fluttering lashes; for men to prowl the rim of the room in search of new game.

This was different.

Catherine would say I was being fanciful—or fretful. Maybe I *was* imagining things. Maybe the eyes I felt boring into me, the glances that shifted just before I turned, belonged to gentlemen whose interest in me was more flirtatious than feral. But most of those gentlemen owned their interest: their names crowded my dance card. And the thought of their attention did not make my skin crawl.

Perhaps it was one of the many military men, resplendent in their dress uniforms: white and red and green and gold. I had not missed how they turned away when I approached, how their mouths lined with distaste. The Austrians had not forgiven me for releasing Hungarian rebels in Buda-Pest in the middle of a battle their soldiers had lost. Only the Hungarian hussars, with their elaborately frogged and embroidered dolmans, smiled at my approach.

But neither the Austrian soldiers nor the Hungarian hussars knew the whole truth: that before I had freed the prisoners, I had broken the Binding spell, shattering elite control of magic and releasing the creatures held inside the spell. If they knew, they would do more than turn away. They would shun me entirely.

A particularly exquisite being floated past, as much light as solid form, bearing crystal goblets on a silver tray. I watched it pass, my gloved fingers curling. Of all the things I disliked about my new home in Vienna—from the overwhelmingly ornate buildings to the excessive formality—this new fashion of hiring inhuman beings distressed me most. I had not freed the creatures from the Binding for them to serve as ornaments for the nobility. *Praetertheria,* the scientists called them now. *Praetheria* for the nonscientists, for those who did not simply call them monsters.

"Do you make a long stay in Vienna?" my partner, a tall man with thinning hair, asked.

I wrenched my focus back. My inattention was rude, and he had done nothing—yet—to deserve it. "I am not certain. I am visiting my sister, Lady Gower, and her husband. He is attached to the British embassy here." I did not tell him that it had taken a month of wheedling, after Catherine's yuletide wedding, before Mama allowed me to leave England, and then only because Mama thought gentlemen on the Continent might not be so particular, and the money Grandmama had left me might sweeten the pill of my forward nature.

My *chimera* nature, the dual souls fighting for dominance inside me. But Mama knew nothing of that.

I shivered, wishing abruptly that I had not come. I did not want to dance with strangers, to make small talk with snobs. I wanted to be in Hungary, among my old friends, walking alongside the Duna River with Gábor. But this was part of the deal I had made with Mama when I left England: I could come to Vienna with Catherine *if* I made an effort in polite society.

My partner asked another question and I answered mechanically, my mental image of Gábor's dark eyes and warm smile dissolving.

I searched out the creature again, now on the far side of the room. I wondered what it was: vila or hundra or álf or something I had no name for.

A girl with hair so pale it looked white stood beside the praetherian, whispering to it. As if she felt my eyes on her, she glanced up. A cold shock flashed through me. Was *she* the source of that hunted feeling? But her eyes fell away, uninterested.

We finished out our dance with idle chatter: discussions of the weather (chilly still), speculations as to whether Emperor Ferdinand and Archduke Franz Joseph might appear (I doubted it), and gossip (on my partner's part) about people I did not know. Neither of us spoke about the real issue—the reason why so many outsiders had convened on Vienna in late spring, a season when the nobility should be preparing to leave for their country estates.

In the months since I had released the praetheria from the Binding, the question of what to do with them had grown increasingly vexing as they regained their strength and mingled more with society. What rights—if any—ought praetheria to have? Where should they live? A Congress to settle the issue was to begin in a little over a fortnight, on the seventh of June. Were it not for the Congress, Catherine and Richard might have stayed in England, and I with them.

My partner returned me to the corner where Catherine waited, her cheeks still flushed from her own turn on the floor. For a fraction of a second, some trick of the light and her profile made me see Grandmama, and I stopped, my heart aching anew with her loss.

Catherine turned at my approach. "Anna, can you not persuade Noémi to dance? I hate to see her buried among the dowagers and chaperones like this."

My cousin Noémi shrugged, her fingers flickering upward to brush the glimmering pelican of her soul sign and then linger on the filigree cross she wore. Mátyás's cross. "My brother is but eight months dead, ma'am. My uncle bid me come, but I do not wish to dance." Her hands dropped to smooth the lavender folds of her skirt, and my heart fell with the gesture. Noémi would not have abandoned the black of deep mourning without pressure from her family. "I am no longer certain of my steps."

Once, Noémi had loved a dance. As had I. The revolution and Mátyás's death had changed us both. Luminate magicians had smoothed her blistered skin to show no scar, but some of the deeper damage she had sustained when we fought to break the Binding remained. Even Luminate healers could not work miracles. At home Noémi wore spectacles that sharpened some of her dulled vision but could not correct the near blindness in her right eye. But her aunt had forbidden the eyeglasses at the ball.

"*You* certainly do not lack for partners." Noémi caught my wrist, where a silver charm dangled from a bracelet. It was cunningly engraved with the fire and ice of the night's theme, the pages of my dance card folded neatly inside.

"Money compensates for many faults."

Now it was Catherine's turn to frown. "You underrate yourself." Her own rose soul sign glittered, a reminder that she, like Noémi, was among the lucky Luminates who had not lost their magic when the Binding shattered and could still cast a soul sign for public display.

I had promised myself not to unduly aggravate Catherine, so I swallowed a tart answer and said merely, "Thank you."

Catherine peered over my shoulder, reading the fine print of the names to Noémi. "Zichy, Széchenyi, Peterffy . . ."

"You are still the darling of the Hungarians, and not for any of your wealth," Noémi said. "They remember what you did."

"What *we* did." Noémi had been with me the night I broke the Binding, and in the prison, during the terrible aftermath of fighting. I did not think either of us had forgotten the smell of gun smoke and blood, the keening of creatures in the street, the silence of an assassin moving through a dark prison. Besides Grandmama and Mátyás, who could no longer speak my secret, only four living souls knew what happened that night: Noémi, my uncle Pál, myself—and the praetherian with whom I had made my bargain, an army in exchange for a broken spell.

Catherine shuddered. "Please, Noémi, must you mention that *now*? Someone might hear you."

As if talk of a revolution were the worst thing that could happen to one. I sprang up. "I am parched after all that dancing."

"Richard has already gone to fetch me some lemonade. I'm sure he will bring some for you as well," Catherine said. "And haven't you a partner for this dance?"

"Please make my excuses." I did not wait for Catherine's answer before plunging into the crowd. Unwanted images from that bloody October day tumbled through my head. Though I pressed my fingers to my temples, I could not shake the pictures. I could not stay beside Catherine and pretend I had any interest in the dance. I could not sit placidly with Mátyás's sister and lie to her with my smiles and light words.

Noémi did not know all my secrets. She did not know that everything we had won that day—the broken Binding, the praetherian army, the revolution—had been bought with her brother's blood.

And I had held the knife that killed him.

I had not gone more than two dozen paces when fingers snagged me: long, rather bony fingers attached to the arm of a stranger. It was a girl who held me, a girl with hair like raw silk and granite eyes, and a grimness to her mouth that looked like death. For a brief second I knew the tight, frantic flutter of an animal caught by the thing that hunts it. But it was only the girl with grey eyes who had watched me earlier as she talked to the praetherian servant.

"Anna Arden?"

We had not been introduced, but her accented German betrayed her foreign origins. Russian, maybe? Perhaps she did not know our customs. "Yes?"

"Ah! I have wanted to meet you. I am—that is, you may call me Vasilisa."

She gave me no family name, but I did not press her. Like my sister and cousin, she wore a soul sign: an oddly boxy sort of bird with long legs. "I am pleased to meet you. Your soul sign—I don't recognize it. What sort of bird is it?"

Her smile slid oddly across her lips, as if it did not quite know what shape to take. "A Russian bird. You would not know it. But I do not want to talk of birds with you. Let us speak rather of the praetheria."

My face must have betrayed my shock, because her smile stretched and firmed. "Why?" I managed. "I am no expert in them."

Her eyebrows, so faint they were nearly invisible, lifted. "No? I had heard otherwise."

Hairs prickled on my arms. What did she know?

"Come." Vasilisa tugged me toward one of the French doors that opened onto the terrace. I hung back, unwilling to leave the security of the ballroom for the darkened gardens. A stir rippled through the crowd.

I craned my head to see the source of the disturbance. A small group had entered the ballroom: a well-dressed woman with dark hair, a young man only a little older than myself in a white uniform with medals glittering on his breast, an elderly man with thinning hair and a long nose. The royal family. I caught my breath: I'd seen them only once, months before, when Grandmama and I had stopped in Vienna en route to Hungary. Emperor Ferdinand, his nephew Archduke Franz Joseph, and Franz Joseph's mother, Archduchess Sophie. I'd heard Richard laughingly refer to her as "the only man at court."

Vasilisa pinched me.

"Ow!" I rubbed my smarting arm. "What was that for?"

"You do not attend me. I find it rude."

"Pinching people is not done either."

"Is it not? But it is so satisfying."

I crossed my arms. "What is it you wished to say to me?"

"I wish to know why you are hiding."

"What?"

Vasilisa leaned in close. Her breath was sweet, violet and mint, but beneath it ran something cloying that I could not place. "I know what you are."

"What I am?" I tried to laugh. Most of the people who knew I was chimera were dead: Mátyás, Grandmama. The others, Noémi and my maid Ginny, would never betray me. "I'm only a girl at a ball." Could this girl with her strange eyes see how the truth chafed me? Once, I had held a world in my hands, watched a sky shatter at a word. Now, I was trapped in ballrooms, confining my steps to the measures of a dance whose ending I already knew.

"Do not lie to me." Her eyes flashed, and I thought of lightning in a dark sky, rain on stone, and things rotting in wet wood. "I met a pale-eyed Hungarian in St. Petersburg. He told me about you. He said he was your uncle."

Pál.

Grandmama had given him as a child to the Circle governing Luminate magic, under pressure from her husband. As an adult, he had both helped us escape the Circle in Buda-Pest and then betrayed us, leading the Circle to us for a private revenge and letting Grandmama die in the process.

He knew I was chimera, able to break spells but not cast them because of my two souls: he was the one who had told me.

"Don't." I stepped away from her. "I don't wish to speak of him."

"What shall we speak of instead? The way a girl with power to break the world hides in a ballroom in Vienna, her gown and collar as empty of magic as if she were a maid? What you could be, Anna Arden, if you were not afraid!" As she spoke, her dress took on an illusion mimicking the theme of the room: a band of glittering frost encircled her hem, spreading until she looked like an ice maiden from a fairy story. Then a lick of yellow fire ran from her gold neckline down her gown, melting away the ice. Something about the effortlessness of her spell (no spoken charms, no gestures) hinted at a carefully leashed power that chilled me.

"Stop. That isn't who I am—that isn't what I want."

"And what do you want, Anna Arden?" She held my eyes with hers.

What did I want? Longing caught in my throat so fast and hard I nearly choked on it. I wanted impossible things: To be with Gábor without the tangle of social expectations. For Mátyás to be alive. And Grandmama. But my shadow self, my second soul, responded to her words, longing for the vision she painted: a girl with power to break the world. Yes. I wanted that too.

With a gasp, I broke free of her gaze. I knew this feeling, this yearning so strong it left a taste in my mouth like honeyed wine. I whirled around, spotting an impossibly beautiful man with golden eyes standing just before a column of illusory fire.

"Hunger." I ought, perhaps, to have offered him my hand, but I knew how his touch burned. "What a delightfully calculated pose. You look like an avenging angel, fire spouting all about you."

"Or demon." He grinned at me.

He must be here for the Congress that was to decide his fate and the fate of others like him. Yet I wished he were not. Hunger had been with me when Mátyás died; he had helped me drive the bone blade into my cousin's heart to break the Binding spell. He knew the darkest of all my secrets—and I did not know if I could trust him. "Have you been watching me?"

"No more than any other man here. Did you wish me to?" Hunger's eyes glinted with amusement, as if he liked the taste of my discomfort. "I've come to beg a favor of you."

My fingers tightened, the chain of the dance card snapping off in my hand. "Your favors cost too much."

Vasilisa laughed, water falling on stones. It was a graceful sound, but it grated on my ears. "We need allies in the Congress. Every nation in Europe has a right to representation here, even the states so small they are only a dot on a map. But we are excluded."

We. "You're praetherian," I said.

Vasilisa preened, sliding her shoulders back to expose her lovely, long neck. "Did you not guess?"

"In any case, I can't help you. I have no voice in the Congress."

"Oh, but you could. If you wanted to. If you were not hiding." People were starting to look, drawn by Vasilisa's rising tones.

A mix of irritation and fear prickled my throat. I was *not* hiding. But—

Unwanted, a memory bubbled up. The resistance then give of Mátyás's skin beneath the bone knife. Power filling

13

my body until my very blood burned, and a sky collapsing at my word. I did not regret what I had done in breaking the Binding: releasing the magic it bound to the upper class, freeing the praetheria held by the spell, bringing a praetherian army to defeat the Austrians, and liberating my friends who had been under a death sentence for rebellion. I could not regret it, as regret would negate Mátyás's death—but the scope of that power and the bloodbath that followed haunted me. No one should hold so much power, or be capable of such devastation. Perhaps least of all me.

Catherine scurried toward me, weaving through the crowd at the fringe of the dance floor. When she caught my eye, she stopped and beckoned.

"I must go," I said, trying to flatten the relief in my voice.

Catherine caught my arm as I drew near. "Someone wishes to be introduced to you."

Someone? The suppressed excitement in her voice worried me. A small knot of people watched our arrival with varying degrees of interest, curiosity, even hostility. Lord Ponsonby, the British ambassador; Richard; a couple of military men; and Archduchess Sophie.

I halted.

"Anna." Catherine urged me forward.

Though I knew one did not keep an archduchess waiting, I could not bring myself to move swiftly. Some animal sense whispered I was walking into a snare.

When I was close enough, Catherine curtsied and tugged me down with her. "Your Imperial Highness, may I present my sister, Miss Arden? Anna, Archduchess Sophie."

The archduchess bowed her head graciously. But the eyes that studied me were not gracious at all: they were a predator's eyes, cold and focused. I felt the invisible walls of a trap snap shut around me.

"It is an honor, Your Imperial Highness," I said, willing my face into my most neutral expression. In truth, I did not know how to feel about this woman, a member of the Hapsburg family I had always associated with the injustices Hungary suffered. And yet, when the Binding failed and the Austrian army had been routed in Buda, Emperor Ferdinand had caved to Hungarian demands for their own constitutional government. The archduchess had even built a school in Vienna for commoners to study magic.

Now this same archduchess smiled at me. The black eagle of her soul sign—doubtless a nod to the double-headed eagle of the Hapsburg crest—flexed its wings. "Come, you needn't look like that. We shan't eat you. We merely wanted to meet the heroine of Hungary." She was an attractive woman, her rich brown hair just beginning to grey, her amethyst dress fitted to a smart figure. She smelled faintly of lemon and bergamot.

I very much doubted that, but I returned her smile. "Your Imperial Highness is very kind."

"And you are an Eszterházy too, they say. One of our preeminent Hungarian families. The stories they tell of you are very romantic. You must be exceedingly brave."

What answer could she expect me to return? "I had help, Your Imperial Highness."

"Of course." She waved a hand. "Your humility is charming. You must know that there are many in our court who were not pleased to find our ancient connection with Hungary so summarily severed—some might, in fact, blame you." She held my gaze, her expression inscrutable.

Was that a warning? Or a threat?

She added only "We do hope you enjoy the ball" before sweeping away with her cortege. A dark-haired man in uniform remained, his gimlet-eyed gaze fixed on me.

Catherine turned to beam at me, murmuring something about a great honor. I could only stare at her, rattled by the encounter. When Lord Ponsonby, the British ambassador, led Catherine into a dance, I shook myself and headed toward the doorway leading to the refreshment room. I knew Catherine expected me to return to sit with Noémi, and ladies rarely fetched their own drinks, but I could not face the room or the dancing until I calmed myself.

I had just reached the fringes of the room when a voice called my name.

"Miss Arden?"

This was the second time in one evening I had been accosted by someone to whom I had not been introduced. Was this a Viennese custom—or merely bad luck on my part?

"I beg your pardon?"

A woman stood beside me, her short dark curls sleek against her head, a plain grey gown brushing the floor. If she was offended by my cool tone, she gave no sign but smiled disarmingly. "My apologies for not waiting for an introduction. I am a journalist, you see, and I must seize an opportunity when it presents itself. My name is Borbála Dobos, and I'm very happy to make your acquaintance."

I smiled back. "I don't think I have ever met a journalist at a ball."

"I may have bribed my way in. Balls are excellent places to gather information, if one knows where to look. Take yourself, for instance. No one seems to know exactly how you came to be in the Buda Castle district in the midst of a battle, just as an army of praetheria arrived, or how you managed to free those prisoners."

The dark eyes fixed on my face were entirely too shrewd by half.

I swallowed, wishing I had been able to secure some lemonade. If I made no answer, she would think I hid a secret. Best to tell the truth, if not the whole of it. "There is no great mystery. My friends were held in the prison, so my cousin and I climbed through the labyrinths beneath the castle and snuck into the prison while the guards were distracted. We stopped a man who was killing the prisoners."

"Hmm," she said as if she did not wholly believe me.

I changed the subject. "Frau Dobos, can you tell me who the dark-haired military gentleman is with the archduchess?" The man who had stared at me when the archduchess retreated watched me still, his frown pronounced.

"It's Fräulein, but call me Borbála, please." She followed my gaze. "That's Dragović, newly minted ban of Croatia, a bit like your prime minister. The Hapsburgs just made him lieutenant field marshal over Croatian troops— unprecedented rise for one not of royal blood. He does seem interested in you, doesn't he? I wonder why. He's not the type to show interest in a woman for her own sake."

I ignored her speculation. "You find his rise . . . troubling?" I asked, trying to name the emotion fraying the edges of her voice.

"Those honors are either a promise or a reward. Wish I knew which—and what they were for. I suspect the Hapsburgs want to make trouble for Hungary."

A chill crawled down my back, clotted in my throat. "But the Hapsburgs let us—I mean the Hungarians—go."

She laughed a little. "I suppose you could call it that. After the Binding broke, the emperor disbanded the Austrian Circle and granted Hungary her own parliament, but we are still part of the Austrian Empire, just as Canada has her own government but belongs to your British crown. We have greater independence, but we are not wholly independent. Emperor Ferdinand is still king of Hungary. And there are many here who grudge us even that much—they'd subject us again if they could.

"The current situation is difficult: Russia is looking to advance its borders, in Poland and in the Ottoman Empire, and Austria must present a strong, united front if it does not wish to be a target. The French are on the verge of civil insurrection, and the German states cannot unify. The praetherian question does not help: the presence of powerful creatures of uncertain loyalty only unsettles everything."

I buried my gloved hands in the folds of my skirt. I had thought everything resolved: the Binding broken, the praetheria free and safe, Hungary secure in her independence. During the long months since Mátyás and Grandmama had died, I had held those facts to me, a positive weight to counter my guilt and pain at their deaths. But if their deaths had accomplished nothing, the weight of what I had done might crush me.

There was no conduct manual for how to live with oneself after changing the world.

"You look pale," Fräulein Dobos—Borbála—said. "I apologize if I've frightened you with my bluntness."

I shook my head. "I prefer frankness."

"I suspected as much." She grinned. "Look there—see the woman in the dark gown beside that alcove? She's no Luminate, but I'd stake a year's income that she's controlling the illusions in the room. Everyone knows the Arenberg family all but lost their magic when the Binding broke. And they're not the only ones. Mark the soul signs. You'll see who still has magic."

I wondered at the shift of conversation. Was she trying to ease my discomfort with gossip—or unearth more information about me? It was an open secret that I could not cast spells. Though in theory one could ask a friend or relative to cast a soul sign to hide one's own lack, it was considered poor form to borrow someone else's spell work for a soul sign. "Perhaps some choose not to wear their sign as a kindness to those who have lost theirs."

Borbála's eyes flickered to my bare collarbone. "Perhaps. But the Austrian Luminate are not known for their kindness. Between you and me—"

Whatever she had meant to say was lost in the sound of shattered glass and screams cracking across the ballroom. The music stopped in a discordant jangle.

CHAPTER 2

Something big and lumbering climbed through the jagged French doors. It pressed toward the center of the floor, and the guests fanned out before it. The furred creature stood half again as high as a man, tangled hair springing like some kind of primitive ruff around its throat.

Sharp teeth splintered its face. But though women continued to scream around us, and more than one saber hissed as it was drawn, the creature did not look threatening to me: it looked confused, its great head lowering as it swept its neck side to side.

My new journalist friend had already lost interest in me, slipping forward into the room toward the creature. After a moment's hesitation, I pressed after her.

Weaving through the crowd was no easy task, as many of the gentlemen sought to escort fainting young ladies— and not-so-young ladies—to the safety of the halls outside the ballroom. I pushed against the current of bodies.

By the time I reached Borbála, the praetherian was ringed by a half dozen soldiers and gentlemen with swords, including the Croatian general, Dragović. The creature hissed and spat and batted at the nearest sword. The gentleman holding it danced backward, out of reach, then lunged forward, the tip of his sword sliding into the praetherian's arm.

It howled, an unearthly screech that I felt more than heard, and swiped at the sword. The sword clattered onto the floor, the ring of metal on marble unnaturally loud in the ballroom.

Borbála pulled a small notebook from a hidden pocket in her skirt and began scribbling.

Hunger thrust himself between the ring of men and the creature. "Let her go. She's frightened. She didn't mean to hurt anyone—she was drawn by the music."

"It's a beast!" Dragović said. "You've no idea what it's capable of. Who it may have already hurt."

"She's a living being, same as you. And she hasn't harmed anyone. Let me escort her from the building." Hunger stretched out his hand, and the creature swung toward it, her tiny eyes brightening with recognition.

"Let me try." The archduchess's voice was smooth, calming. She walked forward until she stood just behind Dragović. She began murmuring, her hands swinging together and then apart, and I felt the tiniest buzz of her Persuasion spell as it swept over the praetherian and enveloped the jittery bystanders. *"Pax,"* she said.

The edges of the spell snagged as they brushed past me, and I fought down a sharp stab of fear. I had not been near a spell-casting in eight months: Mama and Catherine had seen to that. And I admit, I had not fought them.

Unleashing my chimera self on a spell reminded me too much of the last time I had broken a spell, when Mátyás had died and the world had shivered apart. I could not panic now, not if I wanted the spell to work.

A long, tense moment, the air sharp and fragile like spun glass on the verge of snapping. Then the creature quieted. Her great shaggy head drooped, the razor teeth sheathed safely behind thick lips. Hunger put his hand on the praetherian and began to lead her back toward the shattered doors. Vasilisa joined them, twining her smooth arm through the creature's hairy one. She leaned in, her lips moving.

The room seemed to let out its collective breath. Some of the soldiers sagged visibly in relief. I discovered my hands were trembling and buried them in my skirts.

Then the praetherian halted. With a roar that hummed through my skull, she tore free. Vasilisa dropped to the ground with a small cry, and the creature whirled around. She stood for a moment in indecision, shoulders shaking and head swaying.

The soldiers moved swiftly, forming a protective barrier before the archduchess. The praetherian sniffed the air and roared again. She took a step forward, closing the distance between herself and the unflinching archduchess.

A crack, like the sound of a great stone breaking down its heart. I dropped to my knees, hearing again the echo of the Binding breaking, seeing Mátyás's blood on my hands. The room blurred around me.

Smoke and more screaming, and for one dizzying moment I could not remember where I was. Then my vision cleared.

Dragović stood with a still-smoldering gun and the body of the great praetherian on the floor, half a ballroom away. The blood beneath the creature ran black. My feet were moving almost before I realized it: I halted a dozen feet away and watched the light fade from her eyes like a spell run dry of magic.

⋊

"'Tis lucky no one was hurt," Richard said.

I stared out the carriage window and did not answer, watching the glow of Luminate lampposts flash past us. The gunshot still rattled in my head. I saw the dead praetherian on an endless repeating loop.

I could not help imagining the creature's sensations: hearing a whisper of music on the night wind, following it like a child might follow the smell of a baking cake, crashing through the unfamiliar barrier of glass into a room that was too bright and too hot and too loud. I should have roared too. And then coming out of the fog of a spell, angry and disoriented.

"I thought they had guards for this sort of thing," Catherine said. "It's too upsetting to have to witness."

Richard picked up her gloved hand and kissed it, murmuring the kind of nauseating nothings that newlyweds seem to find so necessary.

In the street outside, one of the lamps was dark: missed, perhaps, or snuffed. "Imagine how upsetting it must have been for that poor creature," I said.

"It could have killed someone," Richard said.

"But she didn't."

"Anna." Catherine spoke my name and hesitated, as if the silence might give her some answer as to how to deal with me. Mama often spoke my name with that silence too. "Your kind heart does you credit. But really, you must keep such sympathies to yourself. The beasts are not much favored here."

"Praetheria," I said, turning to look at my sister.

"Let's not argue, please." Catherine smoothed the pleats of her cranberry skirts. "I'm only looking out for you."

"But who's to look out for the praetheria?" I had told Hunger I could not help him, but that was before I had seen a creature shot down in a Viennese ballroom for nothing more than its unwanted appearance.

"Let others worry about them," Richard said. "You're only a girl, under our protection."

"I want to come with you when you meet with the Congress."

"I'm afraid that's impossible," Richard said. "There are already too many voices clamoring to be included, even if I thought you had some right to be there."

"Mama sent you to Vienna to find a husband, not a cause." Catherine's tone was mild, if her words were not. "I know it may not seem as glamorous to you, but truly, you can do more good in the world once you are married. Your husband's stature, should you marry well, will give you some voice."

I did not want the voice afforded me by this mythical husband. I wanted my own. "There are powerful women in society," I said, "women who think and act independently."

"Yes," Catherine agreed, and her voice was devastatingly gentle. "And they are all married."

St. Stephen's Cathedral hulked against the skyline like a dragon carcass: all blackened spires and knobs, the intricate carved details climbing like scales up its walls. Even the multicolored tiling on the roof seemed only an extension of the reptilian skin. In my weeks in Vienna, I had not yet gotten used to the sight, or the feeling, upon entering the vast nave, of being swallowed by some beast.

But the Hapsburgs were a religious family, and it was the fashion to be seen in church on a Sunday, never mind that Catherine and I belonged to the Church of England and the royal family were Roman Catholics who most often worshipped in their private chapel in the Hofburg. Or that Sunday masses were said in Latin, so that it was a difficult thing to prick my eyelids open during the resonant hum of the priest's recitation.

We arrived a few minutes early and took our seats in a pew to one side, where Catherine and Richard had a better vantage point of the congregants. They spent the time exchanging gossip about each new arrival. I listened absently and tried to ignore my scalp itching beneath my hat.

At once the entire congregation seemed to surge to their feet. This baffled me for a moment, as I couldn't remember this in any of the previous masses, and then my scattered thoughts caught up to me: one of the royals must have entered the building. I craned my neck, but I could see little over the women's hats springing up like mushrooms.

Eventually, the crowd settled and the priest entered with his retinue, resplendent in embroidered vestments. I listened, drowsing, through the recitations and woke during the singing, lovely and medieval, echoing in the bones of the building.

After the service, I followed behind Catherine as Richard greeted half the congregation. I was not attending much: the gleam of pale sunlight beyond the square door beckoned me. So I was caught off guard when someone grasped my arm.

"Anna Arden!" William Skala, revolutionary extraordinaire, beamed at me, his red hair springing wildly from his forehead.

"William!" I had not seen him since my father brought me home from Hungary. "I did not know you were in Vienna."

"Now that Hungary has won her independence, it's time for Poland to do the same. I've come to the Congress with the Polish delegation. We failed to win independence during the 1814 Congress, but by God, we'll win this time."

Typical William, always aflame with a cause. "I thought the Congress was to discuss the praetheria."

William waved his hand. "When did a group of politicians meet without arguing everything under the sun? In all the negotiations that are sure to happen, we'll find a way to plead our cause." He paused. "The Hungarian delegation is in town, with Louis Kossuth. Have you seen any of our friends?"

Something in me went very still. If Louis Kossuth, the anglicized name for Hungarian patriot Kossuth Lajos, was in Vienna, perhaps Gábor was too. I had heard nothing from him in the months I had been gone: as an unmarried woman I could not receive letters in either my father's or my sister's home from a man I was not related to. But I had seen the letter Kossuth sent my father, thanking him for my help in winning Hungary's independence. There had been a postscript too, written in a different hand, but my father had not noticed that.

Tell your daughter that her friend Gábor is come to work for me in a secretarial capacity. I find him smart and capable and eager to get on. The postscript had been in Gábor's writing, and I imagined him smiling as he wrote it.

I shook my head, already searching the milling crowd behind William for a slim Romani man.

William laughed. "I can guess for whom you search. He was here earlier—if I see him, I will tell him how *ardently* you sought him."

My face flamed. "You will do no such—"

Catherine caught my hand, interrupting me.

"What is it?" My voice was sharper than I intended as my sister whirled me around. I was hardly in the mood to be introduced to yet another Viennese doyenne, whose wrinkled face, pale hair, and permanently disgruntled expression would be indistinguishable from every other grand dame's. I wanted to abandon my sister and my dignity and search the crowd for Gábor.

But anything I might have said died on my tongue. The archduchess Sophie stood beside my sister. Just behind her, studying me with undisguised interest, was the heir to the Austrian imperial crown, Franz Joseph. When he caught my eye, he smiled, pink stealing into his cheeks.

That tiny betrayal by his circulatory system saved my

opinion of him: if he could blush, he could not yet be too toplofty.

Richard presented us, and I dropped the deepest curtsy I could muster without falling.

Franz Joseph bowed slightly in return, and I felt something that might have been fluttering in my breast—were it not that I categorically refused to be the kind of girl whose heart fluttered upon meeting a handsome prince. For Franz Joseph *was* handsome: dark gold hair with auburn tints, blue eyes, and a kind of fresh-faced openness I found appealing.

"The honor is mine," he said, smiling. "I've wanted to meet the darling of Hungary for some time. To hear tell, you stormed Buda Castle single-handedly and freed a regiment's worth of political prisoners."

"Rebels," his mother said.

"Patriots," came William's murmured voice behind me. The archduchess's face tightened almost imperceptibly.

I held up my gloved hands. "Not single-handedly, Your Majesty."

The archduke laughed, and pride flushed through me. I could already imagine Catherine composing a letter to Mama: *Anna spoke with Archduke Franz Joseph, and he laughed at her wit.* Though she might draw a line through *wit* and add *foolishness*.

From the corner of my eye, I caught a flash of a familiar face. And though I knew it was wrong to let my attention waver, even for a second, particularly with the archduchess watching so closely, I glanced away.

Gábor.

Light from one of the stained-glass windows fell on his

bare head and shoulders, transforming him into a medieval icon, all bronze and gold and stark lines. I watched his gaze flick from me to the archduke, and I tried, unsuccessfully, to hold his glance. With a tiny shake of his head, he stepped back, out of the light. The crowd closed around him. I gripped my hands together, unexpectedly bereft.

When I pulled my gaze back to the archduke, he waited with a mildly inquiring air. He had asked me something and I had no answer. I glanced to Catherine for help, but her pursed lips told me only that she would be speaking with me on our return home. The archduchess's smooth face gave me even less.

"I must apologize," I said. "I fear I was not attending as I should. The sermon was so overpowering—I'm still feeling its effects."

"I only asked if you enjoy riding."

"Oh!" I could almost feel Starfire beneath me, the pure joy of flying across the fields near Eszterháza. Before everything. "Yes. Very much."

The archduke beamed at me. "Capital! So do I. Perhaps you'd come riding with me—say Tuesday next?"

My brain had some trouble parsing his request. Had an archduke just asked me to go riding with him? How did one even *do* that? Where was I supposed to meet him? What would I wear? Or ride?

Catherine pinched my elbow. "My sister would be delighted."

Franz Joseph looked at me, his eyes uncertain. That flash of insecurity, in a boy who might with justice rate himself quite high, charmed me.

"I would enjoy that very much," I said.

"Wonderful. I shall make arrangements." Franz Joseph smiled and bowed, and he and his mother and their entourage drifted away from us.

Catherine slipped her arm through mine and steered me in their wake, toward the door of the cathedral. Leaning in, her lips so close I could feel her breath, she said, "Anna, how could you be so daft! I was quite humiliated by your inattention. Do you not understand what an honor this is?"

The honor I fully grasped. It was the why that eluded me. "I don't understand why they should seek me out."

"Do you not? I keep trying to tell you that you are an attractive young woman."

I laughed. "Are you suggesting he's courting me? Now it's you who's being daft: heirs to empires don't marry attractive young women, they make mistresses of them."

Catherine's shocked look nearly made up for the fact that I could not see Gábor anywhere in the remaining crowd.

He was gone.

CHAPTER 3

When one is the heir to an empire, a ride in the park is not nearly so simple as it might seem. On the heels of the archduke's invitation to go riding, a more formal invitation appeared a few days later, on paper so fine and thick that I held it for a long moment, admiring its heft and trying to ignore the sinking sensation in my stomach.

On the appointed morning, I spent hours in my room with my maid Ginny, under Catherine's close supervision, trying to achieve a fresh, natural look that would suggest I had spent no time at all. Then I waited in one of the salons for a quarter of an hour, afraid to move, my smart new forest-green riding dress brushed and fitted within an inch of its life, my riding cap pinned precisely to my curled hair.

When Archduke Franz Joseph arrived at last, he was not alone.

Nearly half the court had come with him, it seemed:

a brace of grooms and several ladies and gentlemen I did not know. My tongue was heavy in my mouth. I was not certain I remembered how to speak.

Catherine did all the necessary talking at the house, ushering me to the door after the butler answered it, thanking the archduke for the honor, and then walking me down the stairs to where a mount waited for me. Franz Joseph was an excellent judge of horseflesh: he'd chosen a pretty roan horse with just enough spirit to be interesting.

"A fine morning for riding," he said, cupping his hands so he could lift me into the saddle.

"Very fine," I echoed. It felt faintly blasphemous to set my boot, no matter how clean, in royal hands. Perhaps I should have insisted one of the grooms help me.

The morning was warm, but not unpleasantly so, and I lifted my face to the sunlight, hoping the radiance would give me courage to get through the ride without embarrassing myself—and to ask the archduke about attending the Congress.

We rode east through gates of the city proper, past the emerald sweep of the glacis, the band of grass surrounding the walls, kept bare for defense. We crossed an arm of the Donau on a stone bridge before reaching the leafy green expanse of Prater Park. The other riders rotated around us, and Franz Joseph introduced them all, though I'm afraid their names slid through my brain like water. The only name I did remember belonged to the archduke's personal valet, Count Karl Grünne, a bewhiskered gentleman twice the archduke's age, whose dour countenance suggested he had looked me over and found me utterly wanting. Gloom and Grünne, indeed.

I was not certain how to speak to an archduke in any circumstance, let alone when we were surrounded by the sharp eyes and pricked ears of a dozen courtiers. Anything I said would doubtless be repeated—with amplifications—to Franz Joseph's mother.

"Are you enjoying your stay in Vienna?"

I took a deep breath. An easy question; I could do this. "Yes, indeed. Such lovely buildings, and so much history."

Franz Joseph beamed, as if I had complimented him personally.

"And you—are you fond of the city?" I asked.

"I'm fond of Vienna; I've spent a great deal of time here, and the government is here. But I must confess I prefer the country: Schönbrunn and its gardens are much more my taste than the Hofburg. I have cousins in Bavaria, and it's beautiful there. My family has hunting lodges scattered here and in Hungary."

"So you hunt?"

"Yes. I enjoy it very much."

The remembered echo of the gunshot in the ballroom buzzed through my head. I changed the subject. "Have you traveled much? I confess, I envy that. I've really only been in England and Hungary, and now Vienna."

"Some. I was in northern Italy not long ago, with Radetzky's army. I saw the tail end of the fighting against the insurgents in Lombardy." Franz Joseph's face lit, and some of his exquisite politeness dropped away. "If I weren't— that is, had my life been otherwise, I would have chosen to make a career of it. My good friend the count"—he nod-ded at his valet, riding quietly alongside us—"is a military man through and through. In good moods, he consents to tell me stories of the fights he's seen." He grinned at me, betraying his youth. Mátyás and his student friends had been just as enthusiastic about wars and revolutions.

I swallowed and flicked my reins, blinking sharply.

"It would be lovely," I said, "to live in a world where the only expectations set for us by our families were that we be happy."

He laughed. "Lovely—but not very practical. Who should govern then? Or choose to work at all?"

His laughter stung a little.

We entered the long, leafy boulevard of the park, over-hung with white flowers as big as my fist. Other riders joined us, and the talk became more general, a peculiar mix of society and politics: the Congress, an upcoming lecture on the praetheria by an esteemed professor, a ball at the Belvedere, whether or not the fair weather would hold for a garden picnic.

I listened mostly in silence, speaking only when my opinion was solicited. I still could make nothing of the archduke's attention: why shower so much time on *me*? I had noble blood and money, but nothing remarkable in this company. My only claim to Luminate power was my dual-souled chimera nature, but that merely allowed me to break spells, not cast them. And just a handful of people knew I was chimera—a number that did not include Franz Joseph or his mother.

A pretty young woman was describing the pains her dressmaker had taken to procure the fabric for her most recent gown when Count Grünne stopped short with an oath. Franz Joseph dropped all pretense of listening to ride to the count's side. A mutinous pout clouded the young lady's features.

I nudged my horse behind the archduke.

"What is it?" Franz Joseph's voice was low.

The count scanned the bushes, his thick brows drawn together. "I thought I saw something. Praetherian."

"Dragović's Red Mantles have been patrolling the park religiously. If anything were here, they'd have found it. Probably a spooked deer."

"Best to be safe, Your Highness," Count Grünne said, rubbing his hands together and then weaving them through the air.

I backed up as the first buzz of the spell brushed against me, holding my breath. But the spell released safely, a set of tiny lights that arrowed between the trees and into the undergrowth. A rabbit bounded away.

The count nodded, satisfied. "It's secure, Your Highness."

Clouds scuttled across the sky, blotting out the sun. I wanted to ask about the praetheria, what it was the count feared and why, but I could not find the words to frame such a question. I said merely, "That was a pretty casting, my lord."

The count grunted.

"Count Grünne teaches at my mother's school," the archduke said.

"I saw a boy once," I said, "when the Binding was first broken, who killed himself with a Fire spell because he had no training. I am very glad your mother is doing something about it. Please give her my compliments." I wished briefly, impossibly, that the school taught courses in chimera.

"Gladly." The archduke smiled as he spoke, but there was something grim about the set of his smile. "Though I could wish there was no need for such a school. We're well rid of the Circle—my mother says a country ought not to have two governments—but the Binding . . . Well. I'd like to horsewhip the man responsible for the suffering he's caused."

My gloved hands tightened on the reins, and I stared fixedly at them. Would the archduke still want to horsewhip the accused if he knew it was me? If he understood the full extent of injustice the Binding maintained? But I could not argue without betraying myself. "Do you know," I asked, my throat dry, "who broke the Binding?"

"My mother thinks it may have been a Hungarian gentleman who worked for the Circle and disappeared after the spell broke."

Uncle Pál. I nearly sagged with relief. They did not suspect me. Yet. I fell silent and the conversation turned to more innocuous topics.

Eventually the line of riders attenuated, some far outpacing us, some falling behind. The sunlight returned, and I was drowsing in a warm breeze when Franz Joseph spoke to me in Hungarian. "I am trying to understand what happened in Hungary."

Astonishment nearly jolted me from my horse. The archduke's Hungarian was impeccable, if stiff. The count's lips pursed, as if he had bit something sour.

I answered in the same language. "I did not know you spoke Hungarian."

"One of my tutors spoke it fluently. I find it important to speak to people. I cannot govern a people I do not know. Will you tell me about the revolution?"

I shifted in my saddle. "What do you want to know?" There were too many secrets still bound up in that war: I did not mean to betray any that I did not need to.

Franz Joseph frowned and flicked his riding crop at a fly buzzing near his horse's ears. "I understand that some students tried to revolt and were caught and threatened with hanging. An army marched on Buda-Pest to release them, and the praetheria joined them." A shadow passed over his face, though it might have only been the dappled shade thrown by the trees lining the path. He cast a sidelong look at me and smiled. "I heard the prisoners were freed by a British girl. What was it like?"

The memory of smoke and blood and screaming descended like a curtain across my eyes. It was a moment before my throat loosened enough to speak. "It was not very triumphant. I had never been in fighting before, and the blood in the streets made me sick. I would not have gone at all, but I had friends in the prison, and I had to save them." I remembered the black, falling feeling when I had thought Gábor might already be dead.

"You are very loyal," Franz Joseph said, his tone warm with approval.

It had not felt as much like loyalty as desperation. "I do not have so many friends that I can afford to spare any of them."

"I hope you will count me as a friend."

Something about his words, uttered in hushed Hungarian under the shifting green branches, pricked the hairs on my arms.

"Thank you." I hesitated, already hearing Catherine's censure for what I would say next. "As a friend, may I beg a favor? I should very much like to be part of the Congress that is forming, but my brother-in-law tells me there is no place there for ladies."

Franz Joseph frowned. "My mother will be there, and surely no one would dispute her place. But—perhaps it is not suitable for unmarried ladies?"

"I miss being useful," I said. "I miss hearing people talk about ideas instead of clothes. I miss being part of things that matter."

His frown still lingered. "I understand. I will think on it—that is all I can promise."

Fair enough. I caught up my reins and shifted back into German. "Do you race?"

A gleam lit his eyes. *"Aber natürlich."*

I spurred my horse forward, driving her down the long stretch of pathway. Beside me, the archduke bent low over his sleek grey horse. The trees flashed past me, clumps of flowers perfuming the May air. The constraints and smallness of the last few weeks seemed to melt away, and there was nothing but me and the horse beneath me, the wind streaming through our hair. Franz Joseph's horse pounded along beside me, and when he looked across at me, he grinned. I grinned back.

By the time we reached the end of the straightaway,

Franz Joseph less than a length ahead of me, we were both flushed and laughing. The others, who had watched our race with varied expressions of amusement and contempt (directed entirely at me), joined us. A few of the young men applauded politely. The talk turned general, and we returned to the park gates and the more staid streets of Vienna.

At Richard and Catherine's flat, Franz Joseph dismounted and lifted me down from my horse. As he set me on the ground, his hands lingered for a fraction at my waist, firm and warm. He murmured, in Hungarian, "I understand now why the Hungarians adore you. You are quite charming. I think—yes—I will send you an invitation to the Congress as you ask."

I froze, heat stealing into my cheeks. Part of me thrilled at the thought of the Congress, of finding my voice. But a deeper part flinched away from the interest I saw kindling in his eyes. I knew myself enough to know I was not immune to such flattery. I also knew that such interest was dangerous—for him to indulge, for me to respond, and for Gábor, who would be unfairly hurt by it all.

All these thoughts flashed through my head as the archduke stood before me, his hands still warm at my sides. Then he backed away, bowing his head, and I dropped a curtsy.

"Thank you, Your Highness," I managed, and fled into the house.

CHAPTER 4

I tapped the glass face of the pocket watch on my dressing table. If Ginny did not hurry back with the walking dress she was pressing, I should be late to the praetherian lecture. Perhaps Catherine had put her up to this: my sister had not been thrilled when I announced I meant to attend the lecture, but she had grudgingly given me leave to go when I promised that Noémi would come with me (though I had not yet asked Noémi when I blithely committed her).

I could not explain to Noémi or Catherine why I was so desperate to attend. It was true I felt an interest in the creatures I had set free from the Binding spell. But it was also true that the Hungarian delegation to the Congress was likely to attend, and I hoped I might see Gábor.

My plan, however, hinged on a timely arrival. I tapped the watch again.

A scuffle at the door drew my attention. Ginny stood there, tears in her eyes, her freckles standing out against her pale cheeks. "Oh, Miss Anna, I am so sorry. I don't know how it happened." The grey walking dress was crumpled tight in her hands.

I bit back my annoyance. The dress would never do now she had mangled it like that. "Bring me the dress, please." When Ginny didn't move, I rose from my chair and took the dress from her. I shook it out, then gasped in dismay. Small black spots polluted the front of the gown. When I touched one, the tip of my finger came away ashy.

"How did this happen?" I asked, trying to stay calm. Ginny was my friend as well as my maid, and I was lucky she was here. The spots were too small and irregular to have come from the ironing press.

"I don't rightly know." Ginny's voice trembled. "There was a smudge on the skirt, but the more I tried to clean it, the more I brushed, the more the spots appeared. I felt like I'd swallowed a coal, I was that upset. Like tiny fires in my fingertips and everywhere I touched did *this*."

I stilled. "The spots happened when you *touched* the gown?"

She nodded. "You can take it out of my wages. It shouldn't have happened."

"Don't worry about that. The dress is not important." I brushed a finger against one of the burnt spots, my frustration gone, and looked across at Ginny. "I think you might have magic in you. Has anything like this happened before?"

A beat of silence before Ginny answered. She felt for

the chair at my vanity table and dropped into it. "I'm no Luminate."

"You needn't be Luminate to possess magic. Not since the Binding was broken." *Not since I broke it.* "The archduchess Sophie has founded a school for magicians who come from non-Luminate families. First thing in the morning we'll go by the school and have you tested. Come now, help me dress."

Ginny helped me button a lavender walking gown with navy frogging on the fitted jacket. Her actions were rather mechanical, and when I glanced in the mirror I saw her lips moving behind me. *Magic,* she mouthed, her eyes very far away.

Magic.

⚹

Noémi and I arrived at the lecture with just enough time to secure a pair of seats. As more and more people crowded into the room, latecomers ringing the walls, the temperature rose. Though someone had opened the wide windows into the square, the spring evening was still and the room was close. I scanned the audience, looking for Gábor, but mostly unfamiliar faces greeted me. Borbála Dobos stood near the wall on the far side of the room, dressed in men's clothes, her dark hair under a hat. She nodded at me.

Noémi scooted toward me, her new spectacles flashing. "The large gentleman beside me keeps winking at me. Remind me again why we have come?"

A faint movement in the back of the room caught my

eye—more newcomers pressing into the crowded area near the door. The gentleman tipped back his hat, revealing Hunger's golden eyes. Beside him, Vasilisa smiled as a young man sprang up to offer her his seat.

I curled my fingers over the edge of my chair. Why were they here?

Noémi leaned into me again. "You have not told me about your ride with the archduke. I want to know *all* the details. Did you like him?"

"He was kind," I said. "I did not *dis*like him. But I scarcely know him."

"That has never stopped you from forming an opinion before."

I laughed. "Very well. I liked him. Happy?"

Noémi grinned at me. "Very. Now tell me what he said, how he looked, what you did."

So I told her, breaking off only when a bearded gentleman rose to introduce the speaker, Dr. Helmholz, who proved to be a white-haired man with a narrow, ascetic face: exactly as one might picture a medieval scholar.

"The praetertheria," Dr. Helmholz began in a ringing voice, gripping the sides of the podium, "more colloquially known as the praetheria, are a great mystery to men of science. We know they were secured in the Binding and released on our world when the spell failed, though we do not know their origins prior to the spell. We do not know the extent of their sentience. Certainly, some of them are quite clever and work as servants in our best houses. But an orangutan at the royal menagerie can manifest a similar knack for simple tasks. Make no mistake, the praetheria are not our equals. Humans possess superior intelligence and a more sensitive moral organ. It is well known that the praetheria lack what, for want of a better word, might be termed a soul. Or conscience. They simply do not feel things as we do."

I thought of the lady who had blessed me before I broke the Binding spell, the majestic creatures who had come to our aid in Buda. The doctor was wrong. He must be. I glanced behind me. Hunger leaned against a wall, his face inscrutable. But Vasilisa's face glowed with an unearthly smile; I could not tell if it hid amusement or something more lethal.

"Folklore abounds with stories of the untrustworthiness of such creatures, though for many years scholars and scientists were inclined to dismiss such stories as tales invented to frighten children. Now it seems clear—"

"What evidence have you that the creatures lack a conscience?" Hunger's interrupting voice was smooth and tongue-curdlingly sweet as syrup.

I clenched my fingers in my lap, bracing myself.

Helmholz peered irritably into the crowd. "Surely you have heard stories of the violence wreaked by the monsters who attacked Buda Castle in the late difficulties. Men torn apart by griffins, their insides strewn across the street."

Hunger had been there. Would he say as much? Would he say, further, that I had let the praetheria out of the Binding? My silences were flimsy things: they would not protect me if my secrets came to light.

"Humans have been known to do the same," Hunger said. "Your own field marshal Dragović burned captives

44

alive in the Lombardy revolts. I do not see violence in wartime as conclusive proof of praetherian soullessness."

Helmholz pruned his lips together. Did he suspect Hunger was praetherian, or was he simply annoyed by the challenge? "Then perhaps you will accept this evidence? Three weeks ago, in the Croatian capital, a pair of vodanoj lured nearly half a dozen children to their deaths in a city well, for no purpose other than to see them die. That was no wartime violence."

"And Elizabeth Báthory, who set the Blood spell at Sárvár?" Vasilisa asked. "Your own empire's history is filled with human killers, women and men." She smiled as she spoke, and I wondered if it was only the lighting that made her teeth appear fanged.

Helmholz eyed Vasilisa rather grimly. "You take a keen interest in these monsters, lady. Such interest is not safe."

You *are not safe.* For a moment I thought Vasilisa had spoken aloud the words that hummed through my head, but her lips held their same brittle smile.

Helmholz blinked and waved his hand, as though dismissing her. He continued, sketching out some of the more common praetheria in the Austrian Empire and offering methods to categorize them, according to blood type (warm or cold), preferred environment (water, air, land), eating preferences (carnivorous or non), propensity for flight, and other characteristics. I must admit that my attention strayed midway through his lecture. This was not at all what I had hoped for. There was no sign of Gábor, and the lecture was only stirring up old doubts. *Had* I done right in freeing the praetheria?

I shook myself. Not all the praetheria were violent—and surely, violent or not, they *all* deserved a chance to prove themselves.

"How dangerous are the praetheria?" a broad-faced man asked as Dr. Helmholz began to wind down his taxonomy.

"Extremely." He brushed one hand through his white hair. "I do not propose their utter eradication, as that would be a severe cost to scientific knowledge. Much as we do not let wild beasts roam our streets, but keep them confined in a menagerie, so we ought to contain these creatures. We are too dazzled by the seeming beauty of some, and miss entirely their sheathed claws."

A sudden gust of air rattled the windows behind me; the evening had gone dark in the square outside.

Vasilisa stood. "I should think you'd prefer beauty to claws." She raised her hands above her head, then brought them down with a clap. Light radiated like shock waves from her clasped hands, temporarily blinding me.

When my vision cleared, the learned doctor was surrounded by a cluster of incandescent women. He attempted to continue his lecture, but as one of the women loosened his neckcloth, he faltered. As another took his hands, he came to a stop completely. A sound surprisingly like a giggle escaped him.

The women—were they vila?—began to sing, a wordless melody that held all the ache and wonder and longing of childhood rolled into one. Illusions sprang up all around us: a cool dappled forest with a sweet breeze running through it, a relief after the hot, cramped air of the room. Birds dipped and soared among the shadows. The walls appeared to melt into the trees, and when the vila danced out the door, most of the men in the audience followed them, including Dr. Helmholz.

I nearly followed them myself, pulled by a sharpness in my chest and the memory of the Binding. Before I had seen its secrets, that world had haunted me with its beauty. Noémi grabbed my hand, her nails digging into my palm, the prick of pain grounding me in the real world.

When the sounds of the vila faded, the illusions did too, and Noémi and I found ourselves blinking into a nearly empty room. Borbála Dobos scribbled into her notebook. Hunger regarded us steadily near the doorway. Vasilisa was gone.

I shook my head, trying to dislodge the lingering, dreamlike pull of the vila song. "She should not have done that." I could already imagine the fury of the assembly when Vasilisa's Pied Piper illusion ended.

Hunger smiled, and a thin thread of longing uncoiled inside me. "Perhaps she should not have been given such provocation. Don't worry—no one will be harmed."

Noémi blinked and turned toward his voice. "Not all dangers are physical."

"And do you find us dangerous?" He seemed amused.

"Us?" Borbála asked, joining Hunger near the door. "You are praetherian? Would you mind answering some questions about Dr. Helmholz's presentation?"

Hunger did not answer; his gold eyes fixed on my cousin.

Noémi was quiet for a heartbeat. "Oh yes," she said at last. "But not for the reasons the doctor suggests."

Hunger laughed. "I suspect you are underrated yourself,

my dear." He swung a glossy black hat onto his hair and bowed to us. "I ought, perhaps, to see that everyone is restored to their proper place." Turning to the journalist, he added, "I should be happy to discuss your questions at another time. I'll find you."

He disappeared through the door.

"Who was that?" Noémi asked. "His voice was familiar."

I heard longing in her words, and it drew ice fingers down my back. *No one,* I wanted to say. *No one of consequence.* But I had already lied to her once, about Mátyás, and I did not wish to add to that. *He helped me break the Binding.*

Borbála watched me with a bright, curious tilt to her head, so I did not answer Noémi's question. "It is good to see you again, Fräulein—Borbála—though I wish we could meet in less fraught circumstances."

She smiled and shrugged. "Peaceful times do not pay well. I won't complain."

I wished her good evening, then tugged Noémi through the doorway of the lecture room and down an arched hallway.

"Was that praetherian in the Binding spell with you when Mátyás died?" Noémi asked, shaking off my hand.

I kept walking, staring down at the tiled floor and listening to the *click click* of my heels. If Noémi asked Hunger to tell her about Mátyás's death, he would do so. Noémi scrambled after me, repeating her question. I reached the open front door. The cool breath of night bit at my face as I descended the stairs.

"No," I said.

CHAPTER 5

We had just reached the bottom of the stairs fronting the white-pillared university when someone called after us. "Miss Arden! Anna!"

I knew that voice. My heart dipped and then soared, a lark launching itself into the sky. I released Noémi's arm and spun around, my smile threatening to split my face.

Gábor emerged from the open doorway, his cupped hand held oddly before him, lamplight gleaming on his dark hair. I raced back up the stairs, my gloved hands reaching to grasp his.

"Careful!" he said, tucking his cupped hand toward his body.

Careful? I blinked at him, my outstretched fingers wavering. I had not spoken to Gábor in nearly eight months: perhaps his feelings had changed and he wished to spare me. But no—Gábor extended his hand and uncurled his fingers, and a small gold-and-black-furred insect lifted off his hand. "I found it inside the lecture hall, battering against the window. A creature that makes something as delicious as honey deserves better than death in a giant box."

"It might have stung you!" Noémi said, peering closely at his bare palm.

"But it did not." Gábor smiled, and I remembered why I had not forgotten him: the way kindness came to him as casually as breathing, the way a smile turned his face from a rather severe icon of an Eastern saint to a living boy, the way my whole self seemed to ease in his presence.

This time Gábor took my hand. I wanted to throw myself into his arms and smell the sunlight and grass scent of him. But we were in a very public square and Noémi was beside me, so I contented myself with squeezing his fingers in return. It was a very poor sort of substitute.

"Were you at the lecture?" I asked. "I didn't see you."

A pleased smile lit his face. "You looked for me? I came in late, and then when the vila . . ." His smile fell. "I was outside before I saw the spell for what it was. I went after Dr. Helmholz, but he would not be stopped."

I hoped Vasilisa knew what she was doing. This night may have only given the anti-praetheria crowd more ammunition. "How are you? Are you well?"

He nodded. "Well enough. And you? But I don't need to ask. Everyone at the embassy was talking of your exalted caller." Was that the slightest note of jealousy in his voice?

"The archduke is kind," I said. "But he was not *you*."

My heart beat hard and fast. It was very forward of me to say as much—suppose he no longer cared for me in that fashion? We had made each other no promises.

Noémi curled her arm through mine, a gentle reminder that we should be walking home.

I watched Gábor's face. For a long moment he looked at me solemnly, his dark eyes fixed on mine. Then he raised my gloved hand to his lips and kissed it. A pleasant buzz raced up my arm. "I am very glad to hear it." He lowered my hand, but did not release it.

"Will you escort us home?" I asked, heat rising in my face.

"Gladly," he said, proffering both arms. I slid my free arm through his and resisted the overwhelming urge to lay my head against his shoulder. Noémi, with only a small hesitation, released me and accepted his other arm.

As we walked, we chatted about unimportant things: Gábor's journey from Buda-Pest, the movements of the still-new Hungarian government, the unseasonably warm spring. Noémi described an opera she had recently attended.

When we reached the gate of the Eszterházy Palace, where Noémi stayed with her wealthy cousins, Noémi released Gábor's arm with a murmured thank-you. She stood waiting, her head slightly cocked, for me to follow her. "Aren't you coming in, Anna? I can have one of the carriages take you home."

"No need." I curled my fingers tighter into Gabor's coat sleeve. "Gábor can see me home. It's not far."

"But the impropriety . . ."

"Accepting a gentleman's escort on a public street? No one will pay us any heed."

She still looked doubtful, biting at the corner of her lip. Then her face softened. "All right. You know I only want you to be happy. Just—be careful." She disappeared inside the building.

I released a long sigh and let myself lean my head against Gábor's arm, as I had wanted to do since I saw him. His coat smelled of smoke from the lecture hall, but beneath it I caught the familiar notes of sunshine and growing things. I allowed myself only a moment, as the street was still too public for an actual embrace, then straightened, and we proceeded toward the flat near the embassy where I lived with Richard and Catherine.

"How is your family?" The last time I had seen Gábor's family, my uncle Pál had just cast a spell severing their connection to magic and their ability to speak. That moment haunted me, not only for the casual cruelty of the spell, but because it had been partly my fault. My brother and I had inadvertently revealed that the Romanies were using magic outside the Circle's law. My family's position had protected me, but Gábor's family had had no such protection.

"They are well," Gábor said. "After the Binding broke, the ban on magic dissolved. Izidóra and my grandmother were able to lift your uncle's spell with the help of a Romani woman living near Lake Balaton."

A wave of relief rushed over me. "I am so glad."

"As am I. I miss them, though. I have never been from home so long. I hope to see them again when the Congress ends."

"Please give my regards to Izidóra," I said. A warm breeze swirled around us, tugging at the loose curls over my ears. "I miss my brother too. And Papa." It was hard to miss Mama too much with Catherine at hand to remind me of her.

Gábor told me of his work, carrying messages and searching out information for the Congress, copying documents for Kossuth. It was not his heart's work—not the scientific experiments he planned someday to conduct—but it was important work, and he hoped to influence Kossuth to pass Romani-friendly laws when the Hungarian parliament convened. At length, he pulled away to study me, his eyes warm. "And you, Anna? Are you well?"

Because his question was genuine, I gave him a true answer, rather than the brittle society answer I gave everyone else. "I miss Grandmama. I miss Mátyás. Everything feels so uncertain. The praetheria are under attack, Hungary is not safe, and if their safety fails, then *I* have failed and Mátyás will have died for nothing." I did not realize, until I spoke the words, how much I had bottled up with them. Tears spilled down my cheeks, salt against my lips. Instead of drawing back in discomfort or disgust, Gábor shepherded me to the side of the street, handed me a clean handkerchief, and stood between me and the road, shielding me from the gazes of passersby.

When I had wrung myself dry, he took the handkerchief from me and dabbed gently at the tears still streaking my face. And though I knew I must look a fright, my eyes swollen and my cheeks blotchy, the only thing I saw in his face was concern.

"I miss Mátyás too," Gábor said, then added, "He still owes me money."

My hiccup turned into a giggle, then a decidedly

unladylike snort, and we both laughed. Gábor extended his arm again, and we continued on our way.

When we reached Richard and Catherine's flat, I asked, "When will I see you again?"

He pressed a kiss, featherlight, against my temple. "I don't know yet. As soon as I can."

I released a slow breath. Whatever was growing again between us was still new and fragile. It might be crushed in all the upheaval around us. But in that moment it felt like an island when everything else was at sea.

※

The archduchess's school for magic occupied a plain grey stone building near the walls of the city. A porter greeted Ginny and me in the clean, if spartan, lobby before disappearing to find one of the instructors. After we waited perhaps a quarter of an hour, a dark-haired young woman appeared.

"You're here to enroll?" she asked in German.

Ginny glanced sidelong at me. I translated for her, then said, "This is Ginny Davies. She has come to be tested for magic. If she does indeed have magic, then yes, she'd like to enroll." We had already arranged that I would pay any fees.

The young woman studied me a long moment before flicking her attention to Ginny. She smiled. "Very well. Follow me, if you please."

We climbed a narrow staircase and then passed down a long hallway, flanked on one side by windows opening onto a courtyard, and classrooms on the other. I dawdled behind the others, trying to steal a better look at the students. In one room, a group of mostly children, with a handful of older men and women, practiced kindling basic Lumen lights. In another room, a grizzled man stood in the center of the classroom, surrounded by men and women of all ages, a breeze stirring the hair at his temples and whipping through the room, though the air in the hallway was still. *Elementalists.* From the clothing styles and smattering of languages I heard, the school must hold a dozen nationalities, from social classes ranging from the poor to wealthy middle class. Nobility, of course, would have their own private tutors at home.

Inside the classroom, the students began to chant, echoing the instructor. The magic in the room, amplified by all the voices, buzzed along the base of my skull. A memory of heat hummed through me, the agonizing power of the Binding spell burning inside just before it broke. I retreated from the open doorway, my heart thundering in my chest, my palms damp. *Relax,* I thought. *Relax.* I did not break spells when I was calm.

"Miss?" the young woman called, waiting for me beside a door at the end of the hallway. Ginny rubbed her fingers, a habit she only adopted when she was anxious.

I scrambled after them. "It's a wonderful school." Though wonderful was only a step removed from terrible: all that power, all that potential for creation and for destruction. I hoped Ginny would find her gift less ambiguous than mine.

The woman's cheeks brightened. "Yes. Thank you, miss."

We were led into a large room, a table and three chairs

the only furnishings. The chairs were already occupied by two middle-aged men and a woman, so we stood in the center of the room.

The young woman who'd led us to the room turned to Ginny. "Please tell us why you think you might have magic, Miss Davies."

Ginny looked at me again. I translated, but before I could answer, one of the men held up his hand. In English he said, "Please, let the applicant speak. Has something happened? It's all right. There is no wrong answer."

Ginny took a deep breath. "I was pressing Miss Anna's dress and saw there was a smudge on it. I tried to rub it out, something I've done hundreds of times, but the stain would not come. I knew Miss Anna was waiting on the dress. A hot feeling started in my head and spread down my arms and hands, like I was standing too close to the fire. But I wasn't. And then these spots started to show— tiny burnt spots everywhere I touched the dress."

"Hmm." The man adjusted the neckcloth at his throat. "Has this happened before?"

"Only once. But it was an old dress and Miss Anna wasn't waiting on it, so I got rid of it."

"Why didn't you tell me?" I asked softly.

She shrugged, not looking at me.

"Have you been feeling differently?" the man asked. "Many of our students report that they began sensing something different soon after the Binding broke."

After a moment, Ginny nodded. "A kind of lightness in my head, or a humming, like a wind was blowing there all the time. I thought maybe I was sickening for something."

Ginny had felt this for *months*? "You might have said something. I would have helped you."

She shook her head. "It was nothing. And you were that upset about your grandmama and your cousin; then we came here."

"Well. It certainly sounds possible," the man said. "We'd like you to try a spell for us. Miss Meier will demonstrate." He nodded at the young woman.

"Wait!" My anxiety from the hallway rushed back. I had not broken a spell in months, not since the Binding, but that did not mean I might not do so here. That would not be fair to Ginny—and it could be disastrous for me, if the instructors of the school reported back to the archduchess that I could break spells. "I'm afraid I am sometimes . . . unwell around magic. Disgraceful in one Luminate-born, I know, but so it is. I'll wait outside."

I made my way back down the hall, darting past the classrooms. Once outside, I let the heavy wooden door thump into the frame behind me. I rested my head against the frame, breathing deeply. I hoped Ginny would do well. I hoped she might have the chance to study magic as I had not, as my younger brother James could not. After the Binding had broken, James, like so many other Luminate, had lost what little magic the Binding had granted him. But James did not seem to mind so much—his passion had always been for classics, not magic, and he was no longer the only nonmagical student in his class.

I traced runes over the stone wall beside me with my gloved finger: a leaf, a flower, a bird soaring into the sky.

Ginny emerged several minutes later, her cheeks flushed

and eyes bright. "You were right. I have magic! Elementalist, they said. They want me to study here."

Elementalist—like my father. Like Catherine.

Before the Binding had broken, the four orders of Luminate—Elementalist, Lucifera, Coremancer, and Animanti—had been strictly regulated, so no one could possess gifts of more than one order. (My uncle Pál had been an exception, granted access by the Austrian Circle to multiple orders on the strength of his gift. A mistake, as it turned out, since Pál had betrayed and killed the man the Circle had sent to stop me from breaking the Binding.) In the wake of the Binding, I understood that the orders were more relaxed, as someone with mostly Elementalist gifts—weather magic, fire manipulation, and the like—might occasionally manifest with prophetic dreams (Coremancer) or mild healing (Animanti). A Lucifera with the ability to fold the earth, as I had seen Lady Berri do, might also call wind. But the categories still proved useful, as most gifts tended to cluster around a particular ability.

"Should you like it?" A heavy, hard lump settled in my stomach. I should be happy for Ginny, for all the opportunities magic would open to her. And I was—only, I had seen what magic could cost, what *my* gift cost. But I could not project my ambivalence on her.

"I think so." Her face fell. "But will you mind? With you and James not doing magic, will your family think I am rising too much above my station?"

"Oh, pooh," I said, throwing my arms around her. "Who cares what my mother might think. This is why I—" I stopped, remembering where we were. "This is what we fought for last fall, so that anyone with aptitude might learn magic. It's a new world now." Or ought to be.

"And Catherine?"

I pressed my lips together. Catherine had abandoned her dreams to study magic after I had spoiled her debut, after she had met Richard. But Catherine would undoubtedly care.

"She doesn't need to know."

CHAPTER 6

"It's so lovely of you to join us, Noémi," my sister said, pouring steaming tea into the delicate Herend porcelain set she'd received as a wedding gift. She handed the cup to Noémi before settling into her blush-colored Biedermeier chair. "I am so glad Anna has a friend in the city. It can be lonely, else." She lifted one eyebrow. "I hear Anna is not the only one with prominent friends. The duke von Rohan has been calling frequently at the Eszterházy Palace."

Noémi had said nothing of this to me, which was unlike her. A new distance seemed to yawn between us, but I did not know why, or how to span it. "Who is he?"

"A friend of my uncle's." Noémi shrugged, her eyes downcast behind her spectacles.

"What of William?" I asked. "I saw him at St. Stephen's."

Noémi caught her breath for the barest moment. I

marked it, but I don't think Catherine did. "William has no time for anything but his causes. You needn't look so concerned. There is no longer anything between us." Her face was carefully neutral. Either she truly did not care, or she did not want to, and I would not press her in either case.

Catherine lifted a saucer and cup from the tray before her, hesitated, then set it down again with a soft *clink*. "I wish you both could bring yourselves to sever those old ties. It can do you no good to cling to an unpleasant past." My sister's eyes flitted from the tea set to Noémi to the window to the crowded mantel. Everywhere in the room but me.

"Catherine," I said. Her eyes flew to mine, then dropped. "What ties are you speaking of?"

"It's for your own good," she said.

The room seemed to pulse around me. "What have you done?"

"That Kovács boy came to the house. I sent him away, as was my duty as your sister and chaperone."

"Have I no right to invite friends here?" It hurt my heart to think of Gábor turned away at our doorstep, his pride snubbed.

"Proper friends, like Noémi, of course."

Proper. Catherine meant that he was Romani. "Gábor—Mr. Kovács—works for Kossuth Lajos as a secretary. He is smart and kind and honorable. Surely there's nothing objectionable in that?"

Catherine must have heard some betraying note in my voice, for she paled. "Of course not, in the ordinary way

61

of things. But you must think of your future—when the archduke himself has come calling on you, you simply can't have feelings for a boy like that. What future could you have? He can never rise to your level: you would have to sink to his."

I stood, fury burning through me. "In the qualities that matter, Gábor is more than my equal—he is far kinder and braver than I. And this is not your decision to make—it is mine. You had no right to send him away!"

"This is my home. I had every right." Catherine smoothed her skirts. "If you won't look to your own interests, someone must. And please consider my position—a closer association with the Hapsburgs would benefit Richard's career enormously, while the merest hint of scandal could crush it."

"Of course this is truly about you. When have you *ever* cared what I wanted?"

"I might ask you the same," Catherine said, infuriatingly calm. "But Noémi surely has no wish to hear our quarrels. Pray, don't be childish."

My shadow self stirred, pricked to devilry. So she thought me childish? I plucked up Catherine's cup, held it over the table, then let it fall. The china rang once before crumbling apart. I felt dangerously close to coming apart myself.

I braced myself for Catherine's attack—no, I welcomed it as an excuse to release my own temper. But Catherine merely pressed her lips into a thin line and said, "I'll send someone to clean this up." She stood and swept to the doorway. There she turned back to me. "We are to attend the Franz Liszt musicale at the Belvedere this evening. It is a very great honor—Liszt has come out of his retirement in Weimar solely to play before the Congress opens. I suggest you adopt better manners before then."

"And if I do not?"

"You will be gracious, Anna, or you will find yourself confined to this flat—if not sent back to England." She left the room.

I dropped down into the chair Catherine had vacated and put my burning face in my hands. Blood throbbed at my temple. A moment later, a weight settled across my back: Noémi's arm around my shoulders.

"I'm sorry, Anna." She pulled my hands away from my face. "It's no easy thing to love where your family disapproves. Or to despise where your family approves." She sighed. "I suppose one must be practical."

I sat upright, but Noémi continued to kneel beside me. I edged cautiously across the bridge she offered me. "The duke von Rohan?"

She nodded.

Frustration boiled hot inside me. "I thought when we broke the Binding that everything would change. But it's all still the same—anyone, any*thing* the least bit different is suspect and outcast. You and I are still trapped by social expectations. This isn't what we fought for." *This isn't what Mátyás died for.*

Noémi smiled a little. "One thing has changed. You are braver now than you used to be."

Was I? "I hope you are right. In any case, I must see Gábor."

"I will help you," Noémi said, rising to her feet. "Will you walk me home?"

Halfway between Catherine and Richard's flat and the Eszterházy Palace, Noémi said, "I had another dream last night."

A chill spring wind whirled around us, snatching at my hair. Since the Binding, Noémi had been plagued by dreams. Nightmares, really: blood and bodies and falling stars whose light winked out before they hit the earth. But Noémi believed they were something more. Visions, maybe—some latent, newly emerging Luminate gift.

I waited.

"It was Mátyás," she said, her fingers biting into my arm. "He slept in the shadow of a great tree on the *puszta,* wearing the white linen trousers of a laborer. He looked just as he did before, but hair covered his chin now too." She paused. "Usually, if I dream of Mátyás, it's to see him buried alive and screaming, or to find his head served on a platter with my breakfast."

We both shuddered, thinking of it.

"This was different. More real somehow. I'm nearly certain I could find that exact tree, if I were to go looking."

"Noémi . . ." Mátyás was dead. Hunger and I had driven the blade in together. "It was only a dream."

Her eyes were fierce. She brushed the cross necklace she wore—Mátyás's cross—with two fingers. "Did you see him die? Did you bury his body?"

No. The world had split apart instead. *Had* Mátyás survived somehow? Impossible. I could not bear her hope—I could not bear my own. I said, as gently as I could, "The Binding spell would not have broken without his death."

A man fell in step beside us. My heart stuttered. Had he heard me speak of the Binding? I turned to warn him off—no gentleman should accost a lady without invitation—but the words shriveled in my throat.

Hunger tipped the glossy black top hat he wore, his golden eyes glinting. "You ought to be more careful. Your longings"—he glanced from me to Noémi—"called me from half a city away."

"It's hardly decent," Noémi said, "to speak of our longings. Like airing a bit of gossip before its victim."

"Hasn't your cousin warned you? I'm not decent. But I thought Miss Arden should know that Austrian soldiers surprised a giantess and her children outside the city walls earlier today."

I swallowed something bitter. "And?"

"And they killed them all, though the giants were doing nothing more threatening than digging for roots. For this act of butchery the soldiers congratulate themselves on keeping the city safe. Because of this, and because of Vasilisa's prank at the lecture the other day, the city has established a new ordinance. All praetheria are to wear bells at their wrist, to warn humans of their presence. And any praetheria serving in a wealthy household are to wear enspelled silver shackles to prevent their casting spells."

"You wear no bells," Noémi observed.

"I can pass for human—and the soldiers have not stopped me yet." His gold eyes caught mine, held them. "I don't know how much room there is in this world for your kind and mine. Humans betrayed us once: we will not stand by to see it happen again."

Noémi shivered beside me.

65

"I do not think anyone wants war," I said.

"Then help us."

"I'm doing what I can. I've an invitation to Congress," I said.

"Attending the Congress is not enough. We need human allies to reiterate our words."

"We?" I echoed. "You—and Vasilisa? The other praetheria? I confess, I don't understand what part you play in this."

"Most of the praetheria in the city look to Vasilisa and me, as we can pass for human and have greater access to human society. But access is not enough. If your Congress knows we are praetheria, they will not listen to us. Even if they believe us to be human, they have no cause to heed us—yet. But you—the archduke has shown interest in you. Use that. Use your gift. I won't beg, but you know that I honor my debts. Help me, and I will find a way to help you in return."

I did not answer. I would gladly speak for the praetheria if I could, but I would not resort to seduction, or to abuse of powers I could not bring myself to touch. My voice would have to be enough.

"Mátyás," Noémi whispered. "If Anna helps you, can you bring my brother back?"

I flexed my fingers, cold with anxiety, and waited for Hunger to betray me. But Hunger only laughed. "You rate my powers very highly, my dear. Too highly, I am sorry to say. I cannot bring your brother back."

CHAPTER 7

The last notes of the Beethoven sonata hung on the air. The young woman who had performed the piece bowed to a light smatter of applause. As she left the floor, an electric energy settled in the red-marbled ballroom of the Belvedere palace. Beside me, Catherine shifted in her seat, her green satin rustling.

Then Franz Liszt walked in.

He was tall and slim, with jutting cheekbones and hair that brushed his collar. Not handsome, precisely, but he drew the eye anyway, and held it. Nearby, a young woman slithered to the ground, while her mama began frantically waving a fan over the girl's flushed cheeks. I knew the stories they told of him: how women would mob him after his public performances and fight over his silk handkerchiefs and velvet gloves, tearing them into scraps for souvenirs.

Liszt sat at the gleaming grand piano at the front of the

room and began to play one of his études, his hands flying across the keyboard with furious energy. There was no buzzing along my bones, as there often was with true magic, but it felt like magic all the same: the lilt and fall of the music, the curious ache around my heart as a minor chord sounded and died away, the rush in my head when the keys trembled together.

With a smile tickling the corners of his lips, Liszt launched into the "Rákóczy March," the very music Petőfi and his soldiers had sung that October morning, marching to the Buda hills to change the world. Someone shouted, *"Hajrá,"* and Richard leaned toward Catherine. "He might have chosen a less provocative piece!"

But I liked it. That small act of rebellious defiance seemed a sign to me, a reminder that, trapped as I might sometimes feel, I was not yet out of options.

After the march, Liszt launched into less fraught pieces. When the music finished and he stood to bow, the audience surged to their feet, the noise of their cheering sweeping through me, vibrating in my toes and ears. Most of the company pressed toward Liszt. I felt the pull of his presence, but I would not follow the crowd.

As I sought to extricate myself from my chair and Catherine's scrutiny, my sister caught my arm. "Be gracious," she reminded me. "You know the rules: smile, answer nicely, pretend you're a degree or two less intelligent than you really are."

I rolled my eyes and sought out the refreshment table. Sugar truly was the only appropriate response to my sister's nonsense. I was debating the merits of two different cakes when Franz Joseph found me.

"I'd take the chocolate," he said. "When in doubt, always choose chocolate."

I smiled and took the porcelain plate Franz Joseph held out to me. It would be much easier to be polite and distant if he were not so charming.

We spoke idly for a moment of the music and the company. He pointed out one or two dignitaries I did not yet know, including the dark-haired Russian tsar, Nikolai Pavlovich Romanov. He stood apart from the crowd milling around Liszt, his chin lifted a trifle disdainfully, his mouth stern beneath a curling mustache. Beside him stood a small knot of people, including a lovely red-haired woman and a man with golden hair—quite possibly the most beautiful man I had ever seen. I wondered who he was. Archduke Franz Joseph had not named him, so either he deemed him beneath my notice or he did not know him. I didn't ask.

"I am looking forward to the Congress," I said, a subtle reminder of his invitation.

"Does it mean so much to you to attend?"

"Yes," I said. "I want to see history being made—I want to be in the room where it all happens. I want to hear and be heard. And I care about the praetheria."

"Why do the praetheria move you so?" he asked.

I could not tell him the whole truth, that if the praetheria were to be confined again, it would cheapen Mátyás's death. So I gave him a partial truth. "Because I know how it feels to be dismissed for a trick of birth. I did not ask to be born a woman; they did not ask to be born praetheria—but we judge them for it all the same." I had said too much. Blood ran like ice beneath my skin.

"I did not ask to be born a royal," the archduke

murmured, so soft I was not sure I heard him right. The archduke's valet, Count Grünne, had joined us as I spoke, and he watched me now with cold, flat eyes. Other courtiers followed, claiming the archduke's attention. Under the cover of their conversation, I took my plate of cake and slipped away. I found an unoccupied chair at a safe distance and watched the archduke laughing easily with his company—some of the most powerful men and women in the world. What would it be like to assume such power?

I caught myself before my imagination wandered too far. I could not believe that the archduke was serious in his intentions—and I loved Gábor. Likely he was merely being kind. Even if he did, for some unfathomable reason, find himself drawn to me, I doubted I made his mother's short list of eligible wives.

I mashed my cake with my fork.

"Did the cake somehow offend you?" a voice asked in English.

I sprang up, handing the cake to a passing server before grasping William's hands. "I did not know you would be here! I thought you despised this sort of thing."

William made a face, his freckled nose wrinkling. "As a point of fact, listening to music—even that of the esteemed Herr Liszt—is not my favorite pastime. And there are too damned many Luminate in this room. But if Poland hopes to use the Congress to win back some of the rights lost her in 1815, when she was carved up among Napoleon's victors, I must at least pretend to like the people and the entertainment. They say at the last Congress, deals were made and broken on the dance floor—perforce, I must learn to dance and to deal."

I smiled at him. "Well, I am glad to see you in any case. At least this time I know your friendship is sincere—you can't possibly ask more of me than you already have." It had been William who had first tried to convince me to break the Binding spell to spur on a revolution in Hungary.

William laughed. "That is true. Though I was your friend then, you know."

"You incite all your friends to rebellion?" I asked.

"Well, naturally. Don't you?"

I laughed at the roguish expression on his face. "I should not have very many friends left if I did so." I found myself scanning the crowd as I spoke, looking for the Hungarian delegation, knowing that Gábor was not likely to be here. Still I could not stop myself from searching. I spotted Kossuth waiting to greet Liszt, but Gábor was not with him.

"While we are talking of friends," William said, abruptly sober. "I thought I might offer you a warning. I know the archduke has called on you. But you must know you cannot trust that family."

"Franz—the archduke has been very kind to me," I said.

"Then he must want something from you. Or his mother drives him to it. It is widely known that Archduchess Sophie heads a camarilla in Vienna of those who wish to see Hungary back under Austria's thumb. She's as charming as a snake, and as trustworthy."

"You make her sound a veritable ogre," I said, remembering only as the word left my mouth that there were real ogres in the world now, and perhaps I ought not compare the archduchess to one. It was disrespectful to the ogres.

"Would that she were. She'd not be half as dangerous."

"I shall be suitably wary," I promised, and after a few more minutes of light conversation, William left me for more promising political quarries.

I took a deep breath, the rising heat of the room surging around me. There were too many people, too many faces I could not place. Before Catherine or anyone else could corner me, I slipped away, aiming for the French doors that led to the garden.

Just before I reached the doors, I caught a murmur of voices from a nearby alcove.

"And you are quite certain, Your Imperial Highness?" I was nearly positive the low voice belonged to Dragović.

"I am certain. Though naturally you must be seen to be acting alone." Archduchess Sophie. "I could have borne the loss of one of my children more easily than I can the ignominy of submitting to a mess of students."

"I will make things right, Imperial Highness."

"I know. You have been a good and faithful friend."

I moved out of earshot, through the doors into the garden, puzzling over what I'd heard. What was it that Dragović was to make right?

The gravel beneath my feet crunched, and a cool wind slid around my bare shoulders, an invisible lover's touch. Overhead, a sliver of moon nestled in a black velvet sky. The air was full of the fragrance of flowers. The garden stretched, long and orderly, down a slope to a second, smaller palace belonging to the same estate. I began walking toward the far palace, glimpsing other figures in the garden. Mostly couples, but a few solitary individuals rambled through the geometric paths.

Gravel rattled behind me, and I glanced back to see Catherine gaining on me, a tall, sallow man with round eyeglasses just behind her. "I've been looking for you," she said. "The Russian ambassador wants to speak with you."

My sister made the introductions, and I curtsied. We stood for a moment, eyeing one another warily. Why had he requested my introduction if he had nothing to say to me?

"I wish you would tell me of Pál Zrínyi," Count Medem said in accented German.

A chill spread through me like an ice floe, a slow, steady creep from the base of my neck to my toes.

"He accompanied our delegation from St. Petersburg. He has been making himself indispensable to my tsar, but no one knows much of him, or of his friend Svarog, who has already been made count."

Pál is here. In Vienna.

"Oh?" I raised my eyebrows in insipid inquiry. Catherine frowned at me. Really, there was no pleasing her. If I looked grumpy, she frowned. If I looked sweet, she was equally displeased.

"All I can find of him are rumors. That he worked formerly for the Austrian Circle. That he broke the Binding spell. But I cannot find support for these stories. They tell me Herr Steinberg might know, but when I ask, I learn that Herr Steinberg is dead, and the men who were with him when he died do not know. Or have been instructed not to say."

I met his blue-eyed stare with a vapid gaze. Let him think me stupid, and he might not ask so many questions.

The chill spreading through me deepened. If someone accused Pál of breaking the Binding, he might betray the truth.

"Imagine my surprise, then, when I find that Pál Zrínyi had family. A mother, sadly deceased. A sister, living in England. And two nieces, right here in Vienna."

I glanced at Catherine, but her face told me nothing.

"Your sister says she did not know of his existence until a few months ago. She says you met him. What do you know of him?"

"I believe he is approximately forty years of age. He was born in Hungary. I think he likes dogs." *He is a Coremancer with unprecedented gifts. A man who deceived the Circle that raised him in order to help me break the Binding; a man who betrayed us in turn to the Circle to force a confrontation with Herr Steinberg, whom he hated. Whom he killed.*

But also a man who left a portal for me to return to Buda-Pest after the Binding was destroyed, allowing me to save my friends.

How could I describe the mix of betrayal, fear, and gratitude that filled me when I thought of my uncle? And why should I give that information to a stranger? Digging into Pál's secrets might expose mine.

The ambassador all but gnashed his teeth. "I meant," he said, speaking slowly, "what do you know of his personality? Is he powerful? Dangerous?"

"How should I gauge his power? I'm only a girl, and Barren, you know. He gave me a ring once. It was quite ugly."

A pained expression flashed across Catherine's face. The count, however, took me at face value. With a short nod, he thanked me for my time and stalked off, clearly wishing his job did not force him to waste time on silly debutantes. Had he but known it, I *had* answered his question: the ring Pál had given me was supposed to prevent me from entering the Binding spell. It had not done so—part of Pál's private plot against the Circle—but it had allowed the Circle to thwart and imprison my friends when they rose up against the Austrians. It had made me accessory to their betrayal, and was part of the reason I had fought so hard to see them freed.

"When I said act a degree or two less intelligent"— Catherine's voice was excessively dry—"I meant *only* a degree or two. There's nothing attractive in witlessness."

A gust of lemon and bergamot was the only warning I had before Archduchess Sophie was standing beside me, a measured smile on her face. "I wonder if I have perhaps underestimated you."

"Me?" I hoped my trick of camouflaging fear with feigned innocence worked as well on the archduchess as it had on the ambassador. Catherine dropped a deep curtsy, and a heartbeat later, I followed suit.

"Oh yes. You do that quite nicely, my dear. The open eyes, the rounded lips. Only, I'm not a man, and I see very well the intelligence you were at such pains to hide from our dear count. I wonder why." She tapped a fan against her lips.

The spot between my shoulder blades began to itch. I tried to smile. "I'm afraid you flatter me."

"Do I? After our first encounter I'd written you off as a charming young lady, but too impulsive to be much danger

to me or anyone I care for. But now, I begin to question."
She studied my face, and I wondered uneasily what she
saw. "My son tells me you have an interest in politics. How
very enterprising. So few young ladies care."

"I—" Some instinct prompted me to tread warily. "Yes,
Your Highness."

"Imperial Highness," Catherine hissed.

"And no doubt you think it an honorable thing to defend the praetheria. All creatures, you believe, deserve
self-governance. Even if they are dangerous. Even if their
freedom threatens the security of those around you. Those
you love."

Was she mocking me? "I believe all sentient creatures
ought to be able to govern themselves," I said carefully.
"But I don't espouse wanton destruction."

"Ah, to be young and idealistic." She folded her hands
together at her waist. "My son tells me he has promised
you an invitation to the Congress. Tell me why I ought to
let him grant it. You hold no great position in society; you
are no ambassador, though your brother-in-law is attached
to one. What right have you to be present?"

"I've the right of a concerned citizen."

"Then perhaps you should write a letter to the press,
signed 'A Young Lady of Quality.' "

"No one would take such a letter seriously."

Her eyes glinted at me in the moonlight. "Precisely."

I began to feel a little wild. My promise to Hunger drove
me, but it was more than that. Catherine's goads echoed in
my ears, that a young lady had no voice without a husband.
But she was wrong. I *would* have a voice.

"Surely the archduke is entitled to his own decisions."

"Naturally. But you see, he is a very *good* son."

Prickles crept down my spine. I had a sudden vision of my future: long months of empty balls and shallow talk while everything important happened in rooms that were closed to me. My throat went dry. I could not endure that. "I beg you will let me come."

"You beg, do you? How gratifying."

Fear made me reckless. "I'm not an ordinary young woman. You don't know what I have done. What I am capable of."

She raised an eyebrow. "Or so you believe."

The conversation was slipping away from me. I *had* to be part of that Congress—to prove something to myself, to Catherine. To salvage what was left of Mátyás's death. "If you do not let me into this Congress, you will regret it."

Catherine moaned. "Oh, Anna, the things you say."

The archduchess laughed. "A threat? How very unsubtle of you, my dear. Still, you intrigue me. I'm inclined to allow you to come. I shall look for you at the opening meeting on Wednesday. Perhaps you'll even learn something."

CHAPTER 8

Two days after the musicale, two days before the Congress was set to begin, Noémi called for me. To stroll along the ramparts of the city walls, she told Catherine, a common pastime for visitors and high society alike, as it offered spectacular vistas. My sister, who was "at home" that morning, receiving potential callers, merely waved us off with an injunction to enjoy ourselves.

I breathed a sigh of relief as the door closed behind us and tied the ribbons of my bonnet. I had feared Catherine would offer to come with us, and that should have ruined everything.

We made our way down the bustling streets of the inner city, Ginny trailing behind us.

Kossuth Lajos lodged in a neat, unpretentious hotel near the Hungarian embassy, along with his secretary and a half dozen other Hungarian government officials.

"Are you certain this is what you want, Anna?" Noémi asked. The wide brim of her straw bonnet cast the top of her face in shadow, and I could not read her expression behind her spectacles.

"What, are you afraid we're being improper?" I asked. "Nonsense. These are our countrymen. Besides, Ginny is with us."

Noémi laughed. "No doubt I shall regret taking advice on propriety from you. And as to being my countryman, well, Kossuth is in no great favor with the Hapsburgs. My uncle thinks Kossuth's radical views are a danger to peace."

"But your uncle is minister of foreign affairs. In Kossuth's own cabinet!"

"Well then, he should know."

I made a face at Noémi and marched up to the door. A uniformed porter admitted us into a lobby redolent of lemon.

"Would you notify Gábor Kovács that he has a visitor?"

The man escorted us to a private parlor and disappeared. Noémi dropped into a striped bronze chair beside the window, and Ginny hovered near the door, but I could not rest. I stripped off my gloves and peered out the window at the courtyard, watching the last-minute bustle of a carriage under way. A dull sky threatened rain. I drew back and circled the room, inspecting the rather insipid paintings of Austrian pastoral scenes.

A scratch at the door interrupted my perambulations, and I whirled.

I had expected Gábor, but the expressions of delight died on my tongue. "Uncle Pál!"

My uncle stood in the doorway, the unnaturally pale blue of his eyes blazing in the late-morning light. "I thought I saw you enter the building."

I eyed him as one might a snake, not certain if he would strike. The last time I had seen Pál had been at Eszterháza, as we confronted the members of the Austrian Circle that Pál had led to us. Grandmama had died that day, of injuries sustained fighting the Circle. Her blood was still on his hands.

I fumbled for the proper thing to say—how *did* one address a family member one would rather never see again?

Noémi stepped into my breach. "How do you do, Herr Zrínyi?"

He nodded at her—"Miss Eszterházy"—before turning back to me. "I would speak with you, Anna."

I crossed my arms. "Then speak. Though you might have called at my sister's."

"Here suffices, and my time is limited. This Congress is but the start of a great upheaval. The world as we know it is about to be rewritten, and you have a choice: side with those who hold the pens or be written over."

A touch melodramatic, I thought. "The Congress is meant to be peaceful."

"I do not believe it will end so."

"And you have chosen Russia as the winning power in this theoretical war of yours?" I knew Russia—or, more accurately, her tsar—harbored imperialist leanings, but I could not believe it would come to that.

"I have chosen myself," Pál said. My uncle had a lamentably underdeveloped sense of humor. "My alliance with

Russia is a means to an end. But I would welcome your assistance. Your skills could be useful."

My skills. A stone slab shattering, light fading from my cousin's eyes. There was always a cost—what price would Pál ask me to pay to build his world? *Or destroy mine?*

I shook my head. "Thank you for your offer." I had not lost *all* sense of social decorum, whatever Catherine might think. "But I must refuse."

Pál seemed unperturbed. "Think on it. You may find that I am not the worst of your choices."

"Well," Noémi said after he had left the room. "That was sinister."

I rubbed my bare hands across my arms, chilled despite the warmth of the room.

Gábor entered the parlor almost as soon as my uncle had exited. "What was Zrínyi Pál doing here? I thought he had gone."

"Why was he here at all?" I asked.

"He wants Hungary to support Russia in the Congress—Russia means to offer sanctuary to the praetheria, if the Congress will give them the rest of Poland, all of Galicia. But Kossuth refused."

"Sanctuary does not sound so bad," Noémi said.

"I am not sure the tsar's version of sanctuary is the same as yours, Miss Eszterházy. In any case, we don't want to increase Russia's power. Galicia sits on our borders, and Russia might view its acquisition as an invitation to expand further."

I had not come to talk politics, and Pál's vague threats had only added to the uncertainty roiling in my stomach.

It did not help that the mere sound of Gábor's voice sent all my ordered thoughts scattering awry like an autumn breeze through leaves. "Gábor, I must apologize. Catherine should never have sent you away like that. Had I been there, I would have stopped her."

His eyes caught mine, brown and warm. I tried to ignore the *thump* of my heart. Even after all this time, meeting his gaze seemed more intimate than the brush of bare hands, as though I'd peeled back the veils that shrouded my soul and he could see right into me.

"I don't blame your sister for sending me away," Gábor said. "She's only trying to protect you."

"I don't need protection from *you*," I said.

"Do you not?" The light in his eyes shifted, and the fluttering in my stomach increased.

I regretted my concessions to propriety and wished that I had not brought my maid *and* my cousin. It was difficult to flirt—or better yet, kiss—with an audience.

Perhaps Noémi sensed as much, because she drew Ginny away to the window and began talking to her about the city, and where the finest milliners were found.

"Are you feeling better?" Gábor asked me.

Warmth rising in my cheeks, I nodded. I was both charmed at his concern and chagrined that he remembered me weeping in his arms. "I am, thank you. And you? Does Kossuth keep you very busy?"

"Not so busy now as I shall be when the Congress starts. And even then I will have some hours off, to see the city." His eyes dropped to the floor, then flashed up to mine. "I might like company."

"I should love to see Vienna with you," I said, my heart already racing at the thought of a stolen kiss—or two—in some of the quieter paths in Prater Park.

"Kossuth wants me to speak with Dr. Helmholz about his findings on the praetheria, and I should like to talk with some praetheria myself. We need to know as much as we can before the Congress starts. You are friends with some, are you not? Would you ask them to meet me?"

I could not let Gábor speak with Hunger alone—Hunger knew too much about me, things I had not told Gábor yet. How Mátyás had died, and the bargain I had struck with the praetherian army. That I was chimera. I did not think it would matter to Gábor that I had two souls, but I had not yet found a way or time to tell him.

Vasilisa? She would eat him alive.

And yet. Hunger said they needed allies, and I had promised I would help. Gábor had access to Kossuth in a way I never should. Perhaps I could arrange to be present at those meetings.

"I'll see what I can do," I said, and turned the topic to other things.

※

Catherine stood waiting in the entrance to the flat, magnificent in a cherry satin evening gown, her hair tumbled around her shoulders. Clearly, she'd interrupted preparations for a night at the opera to confront us.

"How was your walk?"

"Uneventful," I said, which was true enough of the walk to and from the hotel.

Catherine brushed at a nonexistent speck on her skirt. "You were seen, if you must know. Imagine my surprise when one of my callers asked me what business my sister has at the hotel where Kossuth and the Hungarian delegation are staying."

"He is a countryman," I said.

Catherine nodded. "So I told my guest. But I remembered that the Kovács boy works for Kossuth. So I ask you: where did you go? Do not lie to me, Anna."

There was a note in her voice I had never heard before, a sweetness that called an answering note from me. A sweetness that reminded me of the Compulsion spells my mother used. But Catherine was Elementalist, not Coremancer as Mama was. Unless the broken Binding had changed that too.

I swallowed against the Compulsion and stiffened my spine. I would give Catherine honesty because she asked it, not because she tried to compel it. "I went to see Gábor. I owed him an apology. And I spoke with my uncle—would you forbid that as well?"

"Of course not." Catherine sighed. "I'm not a tyrant, Anna. I understand how heavy societal expectations can weigh. But you must see how impossible this is. You cannot simply consult your own will—you must be mindful of appearances. The least hint of scandal and I shall have to send you back to England, to Mama."

My corset seemed to constrict, until I could not draw a full breath. I could not go back to England, not now.

Not when so much was riding on this Congress. Catherine swung away from me, her long train susurrating across the rug.

But neither could I give up Gábor, not when he and Noémi were the only parts of my life in Vienna that were my own.

I should simply have to be more careful.

CHAPTER 9

The day of the first Congress meeting dawned sharp and clear. Richard had not believed me when I'd first told him the archduchess herself had invited me to attend.

"You?" he'd sputtered. "Ridiculous. No, it's impossible."

But then a thick cream card had arrived sealed with the crowned double-headed eagle of the Hapsburg crest, carried by a servant in the royal yellow-and-black livery. The card read simply: *Miss Anna Arden is cordially invited to attend the Congress on Praetheria, as a guest of Her Imperial Highness, Sophie Friederike Dorothea Wilhelmine, Archduchess of Austria.*

Richard's face, when I handed him the card in silence, was gratifyingly thunderstruck. He said nothing more about it, only adjuring me not to be late, as he would not wait for me.

As Ginny helped me dress that morning, in a sober brown

walking dress with silver trim, I was conscious of a delicious tingling along my arms, like a child awaiting some promised treat. But it was more than just anticipation. I felt, deep in my bones, that today's meeting and those to come would cement my future as breaking the Binding had not. Though I did not (much) miss the rush of power I'd felt as the Binding shattered around me, I missed the clear sense of mission that had driven me through the streets of Buda-Pest toward the prison where my friends were held. In those terrible, triumphant hours, I had played a pivotal role in the unfolding of events.

I had not known then how easy it was for a girl to slip unnoticed back into the obscurity of society.

Everyone else who had fought that day had risen on the wave of revolution to prominence. Kossuth led the government in Hungary. Petőfi Sándor might have taken an office himself, had he not preferred his poetry (and disapproved of Kossuth). Even Gábor had found a place in Kossuth's retinue.

My role alone was unchanged. I danced at parties and mouthed polite nothings, ostensibly in search of a husband whose career I might further, never mind my own aspirations. I might be popular, as Noémi had said, but it was the popularity of a mascot—a symbol—not the thing itself.

I was done with that.

Today at the Congress, I would find my voice. *Mine alone,* not that given me by someone else. I would forge my own place in the world.

)(

Richard waited for me in the entrance hall. "Mind you hold your tongue. If anyone wants your opinion, they will ask."

Catherine pressed my hand and kissed my cheek. "I hope this lives up to your expectations."

A short drive brought us to the Hofburg Palace, where the opening session of the Congress was to be held. Already, the streets were thronged with carriages trying to reach the palace, onlookers vying for views of arriving royalty and ambassadors, and entrepreneurs selling pastries and small commemorative prints.

I followed Richard up a long red-carpeted stairway to a vaulted antechamber, and then into a massive room with rows of chairs facing a central dais and podium. Elaborately carved pillars supported the walls, meeting overhead in a frenzy of gilt and scrollwork. I recognized a few of the already assembled guests: Lord Ponsonby, the British ambassador. Count Medem, the Russian ambassador. Kossuth Lajos and the Hungarian delegation were seated beside William and the Polish delegation on the far side of the room. Most of the high nobility wore soul signs, just as they might at a social event. Even here it represented a play for power, marking those who still bore magic from those who did not.

I couldn't see Gábor. Perhaps Kossuth had sent him on some other errand. Or worse, perhaps he was kept from the assembly because he was Romani. That thought made me, briefly and intensely, hate everyone in the room.

Lord Ponsonby raised his bushy eyebrows as Richard and I sat beside him. "This is hardly the venue for young ladies."

Richard sighed. "The archduchess invited her. I scarcely felt I was in a position to refuse."

When the room was full and humming with mostly masculine voices, the royal family arrived. Everyone stood, and they took their seats on the podium: the emperor Ferdinand; the archduchess Sophie and her husband, Franz Karl; the archduke Franz Joseph. Their soul signs, variations on the Hapsburg double-headed eagle, glimmered even in the brilliant light of the room. Franz Joseph saw me and smiled.

A blush burned up my throat at his public attention.

The meeting opened with a long speech in German from the emperor, welcoming each delegation by name, so many that I lost count: all the major and minor states of Europe, the Ottoman Empire, a confederation of Jewish businessmen, even a handful of Americans. It seemed everyone who could claim interest, however minuscule, was there.

Everyone—excepting of course the praetheria whose fate we were to decide.

As the emperor finished, he invited Dr. Helmholz to take the floor. The doctor argued that the creatures should be kept on a wildlife preserve. "Their glamour is reckless, dangerous, and unseemly," he said, his voice rising in fury. I remembered him blushing as the vila wound languid fingers in his hair. I heard he had been found some six miles outside Vienna's gates, half-naked and wild-looking.

A murmur of agreement swept the Congress, and members of various delegations began to rise, each proposing their own solution for the creatures, most droning on considerably longer than their proposal warranted. And then, of course, time had to be given for each proposal to be translated; Richard, who spoke multiple languages, translated for Lord Ponsonby. I wished the meeting could have been more like the debates at Café Pilvax—excitable students talking over one another, gesticulating enthusiastically and scribbling down fragments of ideas, or standing on the tables to shout down others.

Austria offered to house the creatures on a preserve within Austrian borders, provided the other countries offered monetary support and arms to patrol the preserve.

"Generous," Lord Ponsonby murmured, "did I not suspect they seek to strengthen their own standing in Europe by offering such."

Britain, with the support of the Polish delegation, proposed establishing a similar preserve in Poland, with the caveat that Poland be given the independence denied her in 1815. "We're looking to create a buffer between Europe and Russian aggression," Richard explained to me. William must be pleased, I thought, to see all of British might thrown behind his own plan. And indeed, when I looked across the room, I caught his smile blazing.

The archduchess, however, looked rather grim at this, as an independent Poland would require Austria to relinquish her territory in Galicia. And the Russian tsar was furious.

He sprang to his feet, waving down his ambassador, who had also started to rise. It was uncommon for royalty to speak their own mind at a Congress like this, though not unheard of: Nikolai's brother Alexander had wrought havoc in the 1814–15 Congress by insisting on presenting Russia's claims himself.

"What you ask is impossible, ridiculous," he shouted in French. "You do not seek to protect Poland, you seek only to ruin me and my country. It would be far better to give the praetheria to us. We will take them on as vassal subjects."

Richard's jaw went slack. "The man is mad if he thinks he can control the praetheria himself."

My glance fell from the tsar to the men at his sides: the golden-haired man I had seen at the Liszt musicale (what had the ambassador named him? Sarok? Svarog?)—and Pál. My uncle wore a tight, secret smile. He was plotting something, and he was pleased with himself. The combination did not bode well for anyone in the room, least of all the tsar. What was Pál planning?

When the tsar finished ranting, a stodgy gentleman with a droopy mustache rose from the Prussian delegation. "With all due respect, I think you are missing the obvious here. We know now that the creatures were held in the Binding spell. The Binding broke, and our magic has not been the same since. Most of our families are weaker than we have ever been. Meanwhile, we face rising threats from these creatures, many of whom draw on their own unholy magic. The solution seems simple: reinstate the Binding."

A smattering of applause broke out.

A cold horror gripped me, and I shot up. Richard grasped at my arm, but I ignored him. "Do you know how the Binding spell was cast? It took a blood sacrifice, all the best Luminate of a generation, to enforce that spell. How do you propose to do that in a civilized age? Will you offer yourselves, perhaps? Or your children? Which of you wants to die so that you can resurrect an archaic, cruel, horrible spell?"

A curl slid from Ginny's careful coiffure. I pushed it away from my eyes and took a deep breath, trying to calm myself.

The answering silence slapped me. Archduchess Sophie looked amused, Franz Joseph faintly awed. A few of the Hungarian contingent dared to clap, but most of the audience glowered at me.

Then the murmurs started, growing louder and more insistent until the rumbling words roared up around me like a tidal wave. "Who is that?" "She must be a lunatic; the Binding was nothing like that."

Richard, his face nearly florid, stood beside me. None too gently, he pushed me back into my seat. "Didn't I tell you not to speak?"

"But these men are wrong," I said. "They know nothing of the Binding. They know nothing of how dangerous it is. How unjust."

"And you do?"

I subsided in burning silence. I could not tell Richard how I knew about the Binding without revealing my role in breaking it. And though Pál might sit here calmly, defying rumors that he had broken the Binding, I felt certain that the court would not be so complacent if those rumors were confirmed as truth.

If these men knew *I* had broken the Binding, I would be driven from the city: back to England in disgrace if I was lucky; hurt or even killed if I was not.

A new voice cut across the buzzing. I did not immediately recognize it, but I recognized the feeling it carried with it—a yearning so intense it bent me nearly double. Hunger, skimming power from our desires, marched between the aisles to the front of the room, his gold-touched skin blazing under the light of the chandeliers.

"You speak of the praetheria as if they were animals, creatures of no sentience and no will to live life on their own terms. You did not even invite them to their own sentencing." He smiled, light glinting from his pointed canines. "So I've come myself, like the wicked fairy to the princess's christening, to spoil your pleasure. My young friend is right." He nodded at me, and I did not know if the thrill that ran through me was pleasure or horror at being linked with him. "You do not understand the magnitude of that spell. Nor can you honestly think that, having betrayed us once, we will let you do it a second time. We are willing to remain peaceable as long as you do—but if you bring war to us, we will return it to you."

He paused, looking across the frozen room. "We want what you want: a secure place to live, enough food to eat, a home for our children. A chance to grow old."

Hunger was no illusionist, but I saw his words play out in my head—a green estate, fresh fruit from the gardens, dark-haired children playing on the lawns. The Congress was silent, not from shock or derision, but from a kind of mutual daydream.

Dragović stepped forward from his post near the archduchess, his high forehead shining. "Stop that at once! Your demon magic isn't welcome here. And where are the bells the law requires you to wear?"

Hunger held out his hands, wrists upward in a gesture of submission. "No one has yet bound me, *sir.*" The contempt in his last word was so faint I wondered if I imagined it. "Perhaps your soldiers do not feel comfortable marking someone who looks and speaks like a human. Do you?"

Dragović started toward Hunger, as though he'd bind him there before all of us. The emperor waved his hand. "Let him be."

The Croatian soldier froze, one hand on the sword he wore at his hip, fealty to his emperor warring with outrage. Dragović turned back to the crowd. "Mark this. These creatures warp our minds and our hearts and make us forget that some of the most beautiful things are the most deadly. If even one of them is a threat to our safety, the whole lot are tainted. They must be driven from us, by force if necessary."

Murmurs of agreement washed across the room. Kossuth rose, a commanding presence with his thick chestnut hair and neatly trimmed beard. "Are we to condemn them all without due trial? Without full understanding? The church tells us all creatures are creations of the same God."

Hunger inclined his head toward Kossuth.

"How very like you," Dragović said, crossing his arms, "to consider the rights of creatures, but ignore the pleas of your brothers. When you asked Vienna to give you an independent government after your little revolt, your pleas were heard despite your treachery. Yet when Croatia asked Hungary for the same independence, you spurned us. I suspect your humanity now is inspired less by nobility than by self-interest. What did you promise the creatures in exchange for defending your armies?"

"I only ask that we consider the case rationally," Kossuth said evenly, though I could see temper working in his face. "And Hungary has no agreement with these creatures—what aid they gave us, they gave us freely."

Freely. I bit back a laugh at the irony. Mátyás's blood had been a steep price for their cooperation.

"You, of all men, preach reason? You are a traitor to your king and country," Dragović said.

The archduchess whispered something to Franz Joseph, who stood. "Enough. Nothing has been decided yet, and such squabbling ill becomes men of good repute. Please be seated."

Emperor Ferdinand merely looked on, his fingers playing a tune in the air that no one heard but him.

The discussion resumed as though my interruption had never happened. I hunched down in my seat, still smarting from my dismissal earlier. No one in this room took me seriously save Hunger and perhaps the Hungarians. And even I could see that their word carried little weight in this assembly.

I wanted to believe that well-spoken words mattered. I wanted to believe that a word could turn away a sword. But all I could see in this room was shifting alliances, men who sought their own self-interest by promoting the self-interest of someone else, at still another's expense. Money and position bought power, and though I had some money, I had no recognized position.

Catherine was right.

Alone, I had no voice. At least no voice that could be heard by those who mattered.

But I would not be silenced so easily. I would find a way

to speak—with words loud and sharp enough that even the dull men in this room would hear me.

I would speak for myself, for every woman who had held her tongue for fear of mockery.

I would speak with the praetheria, who were denied a voice in their own fate.

And for Mátyás, who no longer had a voice at all.

Mátyás

CHAPTER 10

This is not the story of my death.

That already happened, though it was disappointingly lacking in pearly gates or angels of any form. It's not as though I asked for much: I didn't need cherubim or seraphim. I would have been happy with a good German Valkyrie, devilishly curved and properly appreciative of my sacrifice.

This is not the story of my life either. As I understand it, "life" refers to that interval between birth and death. For me, that interval has passed. (On the whole, pleasurably.)

This, whatever it is, is something else entirely.

X

Here is what I remember: dying was not at all pleasant. I'd imagined a thunderclap, a conflagration, some flamboyant glory to spur me on to higher realms. Some pure moment of exaltation to purge me of my sins.

After all, I was giving up my life to break an unjust spell and rescue my friends. A moment's noble sacrifice seemed a fair exchange for an afterlife of peace.

My sister would tell you I strike poor bargains. This, apparently, was one of them.

I got all of the pain—and none of the glory.

Anna drove a knife through my chest, and I let her. We were trying to save the world. Pain burned through my body. Had it been real fire, I would have been a true inferno, a beacon seen miles around. Instead I just ached, damnably.

I died in the shadow of a rock, surrounded by roses. But when my heart failed and my vision went dark, Anna was already gone, fled through the crumbling walls of the spell-world. When I died, I died alone.

Was it too much to ask that she witness my death? Or at least see my body decently buried? I don't remember abandonment being part of our bargain—though in fairness, when I agreed to die on the tip of a bone knife, it never occurred to me to negotiate how my body should be disposed of.

I wish I had thought to dictate an epitaph for the monument I imagined Noémi would raise in a cemetery somewhere: *Here lies Eszterházy Mátyás: the right hero at the wrong time.* Or perhaps *the wrong hero at the right time.*

I'm not certain what happened after the Binding shattered.

I was dead for that part.

The next thing I remember was the wind.

It was gentle at first, only a whisper in my ears, an almost Valkyrie-like caress stirring the hair on my forehead. Then it grew louder, an endless bluster scraping across my skin, howling and pushing air into my nose so that my failed lungs creaked and expanded and remembered how to breathe.

I gulped in air like a man dying of thirst might guzzle water. But my lungs cramped and I gagged, rolling onto my side across some rough surface. As my stomach wrung itself out, memory returned, burning across my mind like feeling returned to frost-numbed fingers. I rather wished I were still dead. Oblivion is its own kind of bliss.

"You're awake." The voice floating on the air above me was gentle, pleasant. The kind of voice my mother had before my father died, before she let herself waste away.

I pushed myself to my knees, wiping at my mouth with the back of my hand and ignoring the dizziness that rolled across me. The woman facing me, her hands resting quietly in her lap, was no one I had ever seen before. Everything about her was bright: her eyes, the curve of her smile, the sun blazing on her dark hair. She was stunning—but for once, in the presence of a beautiful woman, it wasn't her looks that I noticed first. It was the bone-deep comfort she radiated, like a warm bowl of *gulyásleves* on a winter evening.

Limbs of some giant tree spread around us. The branches splintering away from us were as wide as buildings and so long I could not see the end of them. I'd never seen anything like it. Leaves rustled, sun glinting off them like new *kreuzer* coins.

"Am I dead?"

"No. That is . . . you were. But no longer."

"You revived me?" My sister was a healer. She had, once or twice before, revived someone whose heart had stopped, though she generally did not like to speak about it.

"Not precisely. After your body failed, I brought you here, to the Upper World, the uppermost of the three realms. You are *táltos*. Your soul can travel between worlds. It traveled between death and life and returned to you here, as I hoped it would. While your soul was traveling, I healed your body."

Traveling? Where the *hell* had I gone? And why didn't I remember any of it? Reflexively I reached for the small filigree cross I wore for luck. My fingers closed around air. With a stab, I remembered I'd given the cross to Anna.

"Are you telling me you're an angel?" Her gentle demeanor and the light that seemed to cling to her certainly fit, but I could see no signs of wings, a halo, or, thanks be to all the saints, a harp.

She smiled. "No."

I grinned back at her, encouraged. "A Valkyrie?"

Her smile thinned. "You are no dead German soldier, and I am not one of Odin's minions."

No dalliance, then. "Then who are you? *Where* are we?" She'd spoken of three realms and an upper world. I turned my attention back to the tree, vague memories surfacing of my nursemaid telling stories, until my devout Catholic mother had put a stop to them. Some of the stories spoke of a sky-high tree, sprung between heaven and earth, where heroes had climbed to rescue princesses from the seven-headed dragon-king who ruled there. In others, the tree was home to Hadúr, the god of war, and his brothers, the kings of the sun and the wind. The Upper World, at the top of the tree, was home to a pantheon of ancient Hungarian gods.

But those were only stories, born of a time before King István converted to Christianity.

This seemed very real, unless death was just some mass hallucination.

Now there was a cheerful thought.

A wind picked up, swirling through the leaves. As the branches waved back and forth, I caught glimpses of the world beyond us: whirling clusters of stars, as if the entire tree had grown up into the cosmos.

The Upper World.

Startled, I turned back to the lady. She smiled, serene as a Madonna. "I am the *Boldogasszony.*"

The joyful woman? "That must be very nice for you," I said politely.

She sighed. "I had hoped you, of all my children, might remember me. I was, once, mother-goddess of Hungary. After I was bound, that worship shifted to the Catholic Mary. You may call me the Lady. Your cousin does."

"Anna? You've seen her?"

"Not since the Binding spell was broken. But my birds tell me she is well."

A tightness in my shoulders eased. Anna was well. She

had made it out of the Binding, survived the Circle ambush at Eszterháza. The relief was followed almost at once by a prick of anger. If she was safe, why had she abandoned me? "And the others? Do you know what happened to the prisoners in Buda-Pest?"

"Freed by your cousin"—she smiled—"and an army of Hungarian patriots and praetheria."

Hála Istennek. "Prae—what?"

"Praetheria. What the humans call my kind, and the other uncanny creatures."

I scratched my head, trying to comprehend the stories made flesh before me. "So you are a . . . goddess? How does that work? Are you immortal? And how were you bound with the creatures in the Binding?"

She sighed. "I am not immortal. I am capable of dying, though it might take something extraordinary to kill me. I have lived for a very long time. I suppose I placed too much faith in the people I had nurtured for so long. I did not believe they could see me for anything other than what I was: someone who had loved them and sought to protect them. But your ancestors who agreed to the Binding were jealous of their power, and the Church disapproved of anything uncanny, anything outside their strict understanding. They bound everything with any power that did not appear to be human. We—Hadúr and I and the others, I suppose you would call us gods—were not prepared, and so we were caught up in the spell.

"The centuries in the spell did not kill us, though they have weakened us. The world tree"—she gestured at the branches stirring around us—"has always been our link to the human realm, and a source of some of our strength. It survived our long imprisonment, invisible to most human eyes, and I have spent these last months nursing it back to its old strength."

"Are there others like you?" For the first time, I wondered what we had released with the Binding. When I had agreed to die, I had only thought of Anna's need, of my friends locked away in a Buda jail. The creatures I had seen inside the spell—shy, almost wild creatures—might ease themselves into the existing world. But gods? How would they fit in a modern world?

"A few. There are powerful beings in all cultures. Some of us were gods, some witches, some monsters, some nameless. Most were never as powerful as the stories told of them, and they either died or faded away in the centuries in the Binding. Some of them do not care for their old glory. But the others . . ." Her voice trailed off and her eyes fixed on me. "The others may threaten everything Hadúr and I hope to rebuild."

Did those others have something to do with why the Lady had revived me? I rather suspected, from the earnest look she focused on me, that I did not want to find out. Anna had looked just as importuning—and I had agreed to die. What would I do for a goddess with ten times Anna's magnetism?

"Are you hungry?" The Lady stood, her gown rippling down like water. "You were dead for some time, and you have been sleeping much longer. Nearly eight months, as they tell time below."

Eight months.

For six months Noémi would have worn heavy mourning—by now she might have graduated to the subdued greys and lavender of lesser mourning. Did she blame me for leaving her? Where was she now? Still with our uncle János in Hungary, or had our Eszterházy cousins dragged her back to Vienna? My fingers reached again for my missing cross. I prayed she was happy.

I tried to stand, but the muscles in my legs seemed to have forgotten how to hold me. The Lady's arm was around me almost at once, lifting me effortlessly. She led me down the immensely wide branch until we came to an intersection with a vast trunk shooting upward. How long would it take a tree to grow this size? Millennia? And what did it feed on—sunlight and water like normal trees? Or something more macabre, like blood and bone? I glanced down between the branches, but all I could see was the green of more branches. A door opened into a hollow carved from the trunk: a high, airy space lit by tiny bits of light that spun back and forth in the air like fireflies.

While I stood beside the Lady, gaping, a great golden falcon dropped from the branches above to land on the Lady's shoulder. She murmured something to it, and the bird launched itself back into space. I frowned after it. In all the time I'd spent in crow form, I'd never seen anything like it. It gave off the faint electricity most living things did to my táltos sense, but its thoughts, if it had any, were closed and remote.

"My turul bird," the Lady said, seeing me watch the bird.

The same bird of legend that had led Álmos and Árpád into the Carpathian Basin. I shivered, unnerved by the sense that my world had somehow gone beyond any reality I had previously understood.

The Lady helped me into a chair that looked as if it had grown from the living wood of the tree. She glided across the floor to where a pair of greyish women no higher than my waist buzzed back and forth before a ceramic stove. The Lady returned with a tray bearing a single cup of steaming broth.

All at once I was ravenous. "Eight months and all I get is one measly bowl of broth? I didn't think heaven was so stingy."

"You cannot eat too much. You have been mostly dead for months. Your body will need to remember its functions."

I took the wooden cup in both hands. "And how do I know you don't mean to poison me?"

She lifted one fine eyebrow. "I would not have gone to the effort of bringing you back if I meant to kill you."

Why *had* she gone to this effort? I drained the cup, refusing to let unpleasant thoughts spoil my first food in ages. The hot liquid lined my throat and settled in my stomach. I had almost forgotten how deeply pleasurable food could be. Not that I intended to show the Lady that.

"Don't you have anything else?" I asked.

One of the grey women appeared beside the Lady with a tray. The Lady glanced down at the flaky, golden pastry, then at me. She sighed. "Very well. You may have this one, since Csilla made it just for you."

I bit into a pastry stuffed with sweetened cheese and moaned. "Now this," I said, closing my eyes in ecstasy, "was worth dying for."

Had it not been beneath her dignity, I would have sworn the Lady rolled her eyes.

After I had licked the last of the pastry crumbs from my lips, the Lady rose to leave. "You need rest," she said.

"Wait," I said. "Tell me why you've brought me here. What you want from me."

She shook her head. "There will be time for that later, when you've rested."

"I don't need to rest. I've just slept for eight months."

As we spoke, the grey women wrestled a mattress onto the floor. One of them brought another mug of liquid— not broth this time, but some kind of herbal concoction.

"Drink it," the Lady said.

"Tell me why I'm here first. The longer you avoid my question, the more horrible I suspect my fate must be."

"Drink," the Lady said again.

I took one sip, hoping to placate her, but the liquid was so bitter I spat it out again. "What *is* that?"

"Something to help you sleep." And then, as though I were a recalcitrant child, the Lady took the cup from me and pinched my nose until I gasped for breath, then poured the hot tea down my throat.

Almost at once a pleasant kind of haze fuzzed over my mind, dulling my anger before it could take root and setting my vision swirling. I sank down, and the grey ladies carried me to the bed, where I slept.

)(

I woke sometime later, woozy and faint, spots of light dancing outside my vision. When I managed to pull myself from the mat, I found I was alone. I dragged myself across the floor, pausing by the chair to catch my flagging breath, and peered out one of the small windows. The leaves still gleamed from the light of an invisible sun. Beyond them, caught in fractured glimpses as the wind stirred the branches, the stars still tumbled through the sky. How high *was* this tree? And how far should I have to walk to reach the end of the branches, or fall to reach the ground?

Questions whirring through my head, I leaned back against the wood of the wall, my fingers absently tracing the unnatural smoothness. Almost, I could imagine a slow heartbeat of the living tree thrumming against my hands.

Then memory descended, and my hands slammed against the wood: the Lady had resurrected me—and then drugged me rather than tell me why I was here.

I'd be damned if I'd stay under those conditions.

I started across the room, then froze. Perhaps I *was* damned. This did rather smack of some cosmic joke.

Then I shrugged. Damned or not, I couldn't stay here. I needed to get home to Noémi and János.

The easiest way down from a great tree, I reasoned, was flying. I closed my eyes, reaching inward for the memory of a crow, my favorite of all the forms I took. I started to shift, imagining my bones thinning and lightening, feathers sprouting from my fingertips, my legs rejointing to my hips. Shifting well took practice and concentration—I had to hold the shape and feel of the creature firmly in mind. The first time I shifted, I had sent Noémi screaming back to our nurse: I had tried to take the form of our family dog but had wound up as a mass of fur and teeth—I'd forgotten to imagine the bones.

This time I stopped midshift, my fingers only just beginning to fuse into bird wings. Something was wrong. The memory didn't feel right. Or rather, the memory was right enough, but I couldn't quite access it. Like an invalid trying to walk after months in bed, I could only grasp the recollection of shifting, not the deep-down muscle memory that powered my movement.

My stomach began growling: one downside of shifting was the tremendous energy it took. I was always hungry.

I paced the confines of the small room, wondering if the weakness were my own, a side effect of dying, or if it had something to do with the bitter tea the Lady had made me drink. I supposed it did not much matter—either way, I would need time. Time for the effects of the tea to wear off; time for my body to finish healing.

Meanwhile, what could I do? Already, restlessness stirred through my blood, making my legs twitch.

I examined the contents of the room. Aside from the mat I had slept on and a pair of chairs growing from the floor to one side of the room, there was only a little iron stove, a cupboard with plain earthenware plates and cups, another cupboard with eating utensils and a few knives. I ate what little food I could find—a half dozen pastries—and entertained myself for twenty minutes by rearranging the contents of the small kitchen, imagining the shrieks of dismay from the grey ladies when they discovered my work.

Then I strolled out the door of my new cage. Seven different branches split off from the main trunk, circling around the room where I slept. I chose one at random and began walking, slowly at first, then more confidently as the last of the tea-induced dizziness receded. But when I had walked out so far I could no longer see the main trunk, and the branch still extended endlessly before me, a wave of lightness prickled across my scalp. I'd always had a good head for heights (a necessity, if one makes a habit of taking avian shapes), but this—this was beyond anything in my experience, and I had the disorienting sense of a world turned upside down, my entire perspective wrong.

My legs trembled beneath me, and I realized I had been unwise to come so far, so soon. What would happen if I fell? Could I die more than once? Or would I simply lie beneath the tree, crushed and burning with agony? I'd rather not find out.

I took a few more steps and my legs buckled, dropping me to the bark below, my muscles contracting in pain and exhaustion. I don't know how long I lay on the branch before the Lady found me: the sun did not seem to shift, but the wind played endlessly across my face, whispering maddening secrets I could almost grasp. The Lady picked me up as easily as she might a child, and this time, when she pressed the bitter tea on me, I didn't fight it.

Now that I had awoken from my death-sleep, my body had more or less accustomed itself to night and day rhythms. Four more days—at least, four more periods of extended wakefulness punctuated by sleep—and I had regained most of my strength. In the hours when the Lady was gone and the grey ladies were not twittering about the small room, I took to walking down the branches. I never did reach the end, but I no longer collapsed in the middle either. Birds wheeled and shrieked along the branches: a pair of turul birds, a flock of cuckoos, a banded hoopoe like the ones that had so entertained Anna when she had first seen them near Eszterháza. I broke off a twig and threw it at the hoopoe, which flew away in a burst of color.

On the fifth day I had gone some distance out when I heard ringing overhead. Not the light tintinnabulation of bells, but a heavier clanking, of iron striking iron. A forge, I thought, though building a fire-fed forge in the top of a tree seemed like willful self-destruction.

Curious, I tried shifting again. I'd tried several times since first discovering I couldn't—each time I seemed to make it a little further. This time my arms formed nearly entire wings, and my face narrowed into a familiar corvid shape, but my bones were still solid, and no amount of beating my wings managed to lift me off the branch.

I shifted back, shaking my wrists and fingers (the after-effects of bone fusion were never quite comfortable). My heart shuddered, readjusting to its new size in proportion to my own body. My stomach tried to eat itself again.

The grey ladies had returned, murmuring to each other in their own language. They flapped their hands at me when I came in, but I ignored them, rummaging through one of the cupboards for the remains of my breakfast bread. The bread was dry in my throat and light in my stomach, but it would have to do.

When they had gone, I collected four small but sturdy kitchen knives. I used twine to attach a pair to the bottom of my boots, and pulled on thin leather gloves I had found in one of the cupboards, wondering as I did so what use a goddess might have for them. Grasping a knife in each fist, I stabbed the knives into the tree, alternating as I climbed and using the knives on my boots to help stabilize myself. The tree made a strange kind of groaning noise as I did so.

My arms were still not back to their full strength, and my legs ached from the unfamiliar posture. I gained enough height that the fall back to the previous level might break my neck and stopped, arms trembling.

This was absurd. I peered into the foliage above me, but a profusion of small branches obscured everything, and I had no idea how much farther I would need to climb to reach the next level—if there was a next level.

The wind shifted the branches again and I caught a glimpse of something gleaming like copper.

Curiosity giving me added strength, I pulled myself up-ward. Just when I thought I could go no farther, when I would have to risk sliding back down the trunk because my arms would no longer hold me, I reached another branching of the trunk.

I hauled myself up onto the branch and collapsed, aches pulsing through every part of my body. I took three long breaths, pulled off my boots with the knives attached— then stared. The green leaves of the lower level gave way to coppery leaves that shimmered as the wind shook them, as though summer had abruptly turned to fall. But when I touched the nearest leaf, it was not the dry, brittle husk I expected. It felt, in fact, like a thinly pounded sheet of metal.

Something about this tickled my mind, like I ought to

remember why there was copper at the top of the world tree. But nothing in my life had made much sense since awakening after dying, so I shrugged and circled around the trunk of the tree. Here, as below, seven branches sprouted off the main trunk. But unlike the level below, there was no room cunningly carved into the living wood.

A steady pounding sounded nearby, the ring of metal against metal, punctuated by intermittent silence. Since caution has never been one of my operative virtues, and curiosity my besetting sin, I followed the noise to a low, sturdy building set in the fork of three branches.

This close, the sound was distinctly that of a forge, though only a fool would operate a forge in a flammable tree, miles away from any buyers.

I stepped forward and rapped at the door.

The pounding stopped. A moment later the door swung outward, and I had to scramble backward to avoid getting whacked in the nose.

A man stood in the doorway, built like an old tree himself: his powerful, broad chest forking into equally powerful limbs. His face had the dark, craggy look of a weathered oak. He wore his black hair long, a pair of antlers snarled into the hair like a crown.

"I'm not selling," he said, and yanked the door shut.

I knocked again.

He opened it. "Do you have a death wish, boy?"

"I've already died."

He blinked at me, his eyes seeming to focus. He scanned me, taking in my bare feet and the rough shirt and trousers the Lady had left for me. "You must be that boy the *Boldo-gasszony* rescued. Come in, then."

I followed him into the forge, where a sword lay half-finished across an anvil, the tip still glowing red. While I watched, he thrust the tip back into the coals until it burned yellow-white, then set it on the anvil again. Plucking up a blunted hammer, he began tapping along the flat edge of the sword.

When he'd reached some unspecified point in the process, he looked at me. "Know how to wield one of these?" he asked.

"I know the basics." I'd never held anything heavier than a rapier for fencing, but really, how hard could it be?

The man set down the hammer and lifted a pair of swords from the wall. Nodding at the door again, he said, "Let's see what you've got."

I walked out onto the relatively flat area before the forge, stripped off my gloves, and took the sword he held out to me. The weight nearly pulled my arm from its socket, and I narrowly escaped dropping the blade on my bare foot.

The execrable smith was grinning openly at me now. He'd called my bluff, and he knew it. "Tell me again how much you know about swordplay."

I cursed him, dredging up every insult I could think of. He only smiled.

"Well then, show me." He held the sword out before him as though it were a natural extension of his body.

I lifted my sword and brought it screaming down toward his. Before I could even connect, he'd whipped his sword away and smacked me on the cheek with the flat side. I reeled back, my left hand flying instinctively to cover my cheek. A trickle of blood ran from the corner of my mouth. I twisted to look behind me: I still had a meter or so to spare before I'd topple off the branch. Good.

We sparred for a couple of minutes longer—just long enough for me to feel precisely how much better (and stronger) my opponent was. He whacked my other cheek, presumably so my face could be uniformly red and stinging, then disarmed me.

"I suppose you enjoyed that?" I asked.

"No," he rumbled. "You're a pitiful excuse for a swordsman, much less a táltos."

I froze. When I was alive, before, I had told only a handful of people what I was. Even among the Luminate, true táltos gifts were rare—rarer still in the last century and a half since the Circle had begun limiting Luminate gifts to a single order. No one had ever been able to explain to me why my gifts worked as they did, and after a while I had stopped asking. People looked at me differently when they knew what I was, like they expected something of me.

Like they expected a hero.

My mouth twisted. I wasn't a hero. Whatever I'd done for Anna, dying for her to break a spell, it had been the impulse of a moment. Something I'd thought vaguely would save my friends and redeem all my failures.

I had not expected to wake up from it. What *did* you call a martyr who lived? A lucky bastard? Or a sucker?

"Why do you care?" I asked. "What does it matter to you that I am pitiful or not?"

"You're táltos. You have a gift powerful enough that not

even the Luminate Circle could constrain you. Dying and being reborn has only made you more powerful, a true shaman."

"I didn't ask for this." My hands clenched.

"You were born with a destiny. As táltos, it is your duty to warn in times of danger, to protect your country."

He would not be telling me this unless he wanted something. They always did. "And Hungary is in danger? I thought that was the whole point of my dying—to break the Binding and help free Hungary from Austria."

He shook his head. "Austria is only a small part of Hungary's worries. Already the Croatian armies mass against her. The Romanians and Wallachians will not be far behind. Then Austria will sweep in, like a crow searching for carrion, and the Russians will come. All these are only human worries—Hungary has survived such before. But the Four are waiting for these human armies to destroy each other."

"Who?"

"Four leaders who emerged among the creatures who were bound. They want to reclaim their former glory."

A fene egye meg. Maybe Anna and I should have thought things through a little more. I remembered the golden-eyed man who had helped Anna stab me. Was he one of those four?

"Why do you care? Such petty human battles won't touch you here."

"I am Hadúr—the *Hadak Ura*," the smith said.

The Lord of Armies. The ancient Hungarian god of war. My frustration evaporated, giving way to something irritatingly like awe. I squashed an impulse to drop to my knees before him. Whatever he had once been to Hungary, he had been imprisoned for nearly a thousand years. I did not owe him worship, or fealty.

The smith continued, "Hungary was given to my brothers and me to protect, and we failed when we were bound. My brothers did not survive the Binding. Only the *Boldogasszony* and I remain." A ripple crossed his face that might have been sorrow—or humor. I didn't really speak deity. "If Hungary does not exist, who am I?"

The pieces began to fall together, like a pair of dice joining in exquisite unity. "And you think somehow that I can stop this?" I shook my head. "I'm no fighter." I was a shapeshifter. My gifts lay in misdirection and animal wizardry.

In any case, I was better at disappointing people than delivering them. If I managed to do something heroic once, it was by dying. The odds of that happening again were about the same as landing a royal flush when you'd staked your entire fortune.

As a betting man, I couldn't take the bet. I'd wind up broke. Or broken.

"I can teach you," Hadúr said.

I shook my head. "I'd sooner die again."

Never one to waste a good exit line, I spun around and began shifting to crow form. I couldn't quite finish the transformation—the bones were still too heavy, and something about the shape of the wings seemed off—but I flung myself off the branch anyway, my wings flapping wildly.

CHAPTER 11

What followed my abrupt launching was more a fall than flight, but my wings caught enough air that I didn't break anything on impact with the level below, though I suspected I'd have some pretty bruises. Branches whipped at my face as I fell, copper and crimson giving way to green. I took a moment to catch my breath on landing before shifting back, then stumbled naked into my room.

The grey ladies buzzed around the kitchen when I returned, sifting through drawers in some distress.

I pulled on some trousers before speaking. "If you're looking for the knives, I left them at Hadúr's doorstep." This was the first time I'd said anything to them—they'd never spoken directly to me, and I was not certain they'd understand.

They must have caught something, because they left abruptly, and I was not surprised when the Lady showed up a few moments later.

"Well, you have managed to upset everyone you've encountered today."

"I aim to please." I rubbed at a welt on my cheek, wondering at the magic that allowed me to reshape every cell in my body but still carry injuries with me into a new form.

"Hadúr says you've refused to help us. May I ask why, when we've gone to so much trouble to bring you back?"

"You did not ask me if I wanted to live."

"Everyone wants to live."

"My father killed himself."

"Were you trying to die, then, when you flew into the Binding after your cousin?"

"No, I—" I stopped. There was something holy about those moments before I died, before Anna abandoned me, that I could not talk of, even to the Lady. I had never felt so sure of anything in my life as I had then, when I knew I would not die my father's death: a failure and a disappointment. My death had meant something—and the Lady had taken that away, no matter how well-meaning her efforts. "It was for a good cause. I wanted my friends to live, for Hungary to be free."

Those grave, deep eyes studied my face. "We, also, want Hungary to be free, for your friends and family to live. The Four are watching Anna—they will use her if they can. Destroy her if they cannot."

"Is she still in Hungary?" I'd thought her parents might have fetched her back to England by now.

"In Vienna. Your sister is there too. The Four have converged on the city, along with the heads of most of the states of Europe, for a Congress to determine the fate of the praetheria."

"Hadúr mentioned the Four. But I don't understand their aim."

"The Four were already powerful inside the Binding. But since its breaking, there has been a great deal of unrest among those who were bound. Some wish to live their remaining days quietly, as they did before the Binding. Others wish to resume their old places of power, worshipped and feared by humans. And still others, including some of those who lived peaceably with humans before they were trapped, taught their children to hate those who bound them."

She paused for a moment, her narrow hands at her temples as if her head hurt. "After so many years in the Binding, feeding our energy into human magic, we are much weakened. Our connection with this world is tenuous at best. Hadúr and I have come here, to the world tree, which was our origin site and our ancient home. As the roots of the tree grow firmer in your world, our strength will return.

"But not all praetheria have an origin point, a place that links them to the human world. And grafting roots is a slow route. The Four and those who follow them are not so patient. The fastest ways to reground ourselves in your world are blood-born: baptized by death, or baptized by birth. War—or marriage. Humans have shown themselves disinclined to marriage, so the Four have chosen war."

"Do they have names, these Four?"

She hesitated again. "Naming gives things power I do

not like to give. But you might know them by their roles: Death, Conquest, Hunger, War."

I heard echoes of catechism in those roles. "But that's apocryphal. What can they mean by it?"

She made a face. "They have an abysmal sense of humor. They mean to bring on an apocalypse. To grow strong on human blood and human death, and remake the world for their own. I want you to stop them."

I held the silence between us for a long beat. "And what if I do become this táltos? What will this cost me? The people I love? Breaking the Binding spell cost my life." I thought a moment, then amended, "*Should* have cost my life."

The Lady's Madonna face was grave. "People will die in your name."

My blood ran cold. "If what you claim is true, suppose I try and fail. What then?"

"Then a great many people will die. You cannot fail."

My anger mounted, white hot. "Why are you laying this all on me? I already *died*. I gave my whole damn life so that you could be free of the Binding spell. I didn't ask to come back. That was supposed to be my redemption—and now you want me to earn it again?"

"It is much easier to die a hero than live one." The Lady's eyes were heavy and sad.

"Do you think I do not know that? But this—I'm not the person you want. I'm not particularly smart, nor courageous, nor strong. My magic allows me to shift, but generally only into creatures my own weight or smaller, and the animal persuasion I have hardly seems enough to stop an apocalypse. You want someone like William, who can inspire an army. Or Gábor, who has the brains to lead them."

"You would not be entirely alone. Hadúr and I will help you, train you."

My anger, never very enduring, sputtered out as quickly as it had flared. I knew the Lady meant well. But why wouldn't she see that I couldn't do what she asked? The best gamblers know when the cards are against them, when to lay their hand down and walk away. And my inner sense of risk was screaming at me—the odds were too great for the cards I held. I could never hope to match creatures like the Four, even with help. All I could offer would be false hope that would make my inevitable defeat that much worse, because the hopeful have more to lose. If I did what she asked, I would only lead thousands of people to their deaths.

I could not do it.

"I'm sorry." I turned on my heel, feeling the Lady's eyes on my back.

There was nowhere else to go in that small room, so I tromped along a branch outside, burning the miles of bark beneath my feet. I wished I could be the hero the Lady needed. Damnation, but I wished it.

I had no great illusions about myself. I could be charming, but charm is no substitute for conviction. My sister had charged all my life that my great failing was want of fortitude: I lacked the stomach to stick with things. In my life I had only ever succeeded at dying—and now I had not even succeeded at *that*.

And on this frail hope two ancient gods hoped to build their resistance? They must have lost their wits along with their strength in the Binding.

Perhaps the Lady was wrong. Perhaps she had misunderstood or misrepresented the aims of these Four.

I clung to this faint spark of hope as I walked. If I were William, desperate for a fight, I would take on her offer gladly. If I were Anna, sure in my own convictions, I would also answer yes. Noémi, my staid, practical sister, would urge caution. But my friends did not have to answer the Lady. I did.

※

For two days the Lady held her counsel and did not press me. I concentrated on improving my shifting and continuing to heal. If I did not mean to help the Lady, I could not stay. And if there was any truth to her stories, the least I could do was make sure Anna and Noémi were safe, and pass on the information to someone more responsible than me.

I think the Lady must have suspected what I planned, because for the next few days she was almost never absent from the tree-room, and when she was, it was never for long. On the third day she said, "Hadúr wishes to train you."

My bruises had not yet faded from the last time I spoke with Hadúr. "No, thank you."

She smiled. I did not trust her smile. "I will not force you, but I think you can be persuaded. Follow me. We have something to show you."

My curiosity piqued despite myself, I followed her. If I died again, my epitaph would read: *Here lies Eszterházy Mátyás. It was his own damn fault.*

Outside the door, the Lady put her fingers to her lips and whistled, loud and sharp. A pair of falcons appeared, their gold-burnished wingspan broader than I was tall. Turul birds.

The Lady extended her arms, and the birds closed their claws around each one and lifted into the air. "Come join us. Shift."

My last attempt at shifting had not gone well—and I'd never taken on a turul bird. I closed my eyes, picturing in my head the sharp beak, the proudly turned head, the immense sweep of the wings. But something about shifting into a holy bird felt faintly blasphemous, and I preferred crows anyway. They were smarter than falcons or eagles. I melted, my bones hollowing out, my fingers becoming feathers, my nose and mouth fusing into hardness. There was a rightness to the shifting that told me this time I'd succeeded.

Finally. A fierce satisfaction seared through me.

I launched myself into the air after the turul birds. For a moment, hanging suspended on the air, miles of nothing dropping away below me, I thought of escaping. But I did not think I could outfly both birds, and besides, I was still curious. We landed just outside Hadúr's forge.

Hadúr was already waiting for us. As my wings settled into place at my sides, the corners of his mouth turned up. That should have been my warning.

Without a word, he launched something at me, a tiny

pointed star still glowing red from the furnace. I squawked and fluttered upward, narrowly avoiding it.

Then Hadúr's hands seemed to be everywhere, sending tiny stars flying after me like an ice storm, relentless and sharp. Cuts grazed my wings, my back, the sides of my head.

I shifted back into human form so I could find my voice. "Stop! If this is how you—" A pause while I dodged another star. "Mean to persuade me to help you, I don't think you're clear—" Another pause. "On the difference between persuasion and force."

A star scored my side. I pressed my fingers against the stinging cut and dodged a pair of stars.

The Lady stood watching me impassively, her turul birds perched in a branch above her head.

"Stop! You're going to kill me. Again."

Hadúr's grin widened. "I am not so poor an aim."

This star caught me at the top of my thigh, entirely too close to my groin for comfort. Abruptly I was no longer bemused or afraid. I was angry, an anger that rooted itself in my gut and burned upward, like fire in a bush.

I shifted again, almost without thought. Black like a crow, but larger, swelling and splitting and stretching into a form as deadly as it was vast. If I had not been so angry, I might have been terrified: I'd never before been able to take a shape I hadn't seen. I'd never taken the shape of a creature larger than myself. But there, in that moment, something about the world tree sang to me.

I could feel the humming along my bones, a force external to me nudging my body into a new shape, heads sprouting from my shoulders like mushrooms.

When the new shape settled, I shook and knew myself for the first time. A seven-headed dragon, like the one that guarded the world tree in my nurse's stories.

The throwing stars continued to fly at me unabated, but they glanced off my hide and dropped harmlessly. I felt, dimly, that if I continued to grow I might eclipse even the tree itself; I might soar up among the skies, and the heavens themselves would not hold me.

I stared down at the tiny specks of the Lady and Hadúr. From this angle I could see up into the silver and gold levels of the higher realms.

A deep hunger filled me. I wanted to open my mouth and devour the Lady and Hadúr, and beyond them the tree, down to its roots. I wanted to swallow the world, though even that would scarcely begin to touch this endless aching.

A cool, almost minuscule hand brushed my flank and brought me back to myself. I ratcheted back into my own body, pushing away the memory of that hunger as if it burned me. It had only been momentary, but it had been so endless, so all-consuming.

It terrified me.

When my eyes refocused, the Lady and Hadúr were smiling at me. Hadúr held no craft this time: his hands hung loose and empty before him.

"You see?" the Lady said delightedly, as if celebrating the accomplishment of a child. "Your power as a táltos has magnified immensely. Let us help you. Let us train you, and you can stand against anyone."

But who should stand against me?

I could not meet her smile. That craving still reverberated

in my bones. The shape I had taken was nothing I could have conjured before I died. My death had changed me, though how and to what extent, I didn't fully understand. If becoming a monster is what it meant to embrace my táltos power, I would not save the world; I would slaughter it. It wasn't the Four we needed to fear—it was me.

"No." I took two steps back from them. "I won't do this."

I whirled around and flung myself over the edge.

The ground screamed upward. The shadow of the turul birds draped across me as I fell. No doubt the Lady had sent them to wrench me up at the last minute if my own stupidity prevented my shifting.

Stupidity was an unsatisfactory vice, and one I tried not to indulge in. I shifted midfall, my body narrowing down to that of a peregrine falcon, an occasional visitor to the Hungarian plains who could outfly even the wind. At some point in my plummet, the stars spinning around the world tree gave way to an ordinary sky: wisps of cloud and a pale wash of light betokening sunrise. The Lady had said the tree connected the Upper World to the human one, and a táltos could cross between worlds. Already, the air felt denser. My falcon shape drew in a full breath, and the familiarity of ordinary air sent new energy through my body.

I screamed once in defiance at the great birds still tailing me, then shot off. I didn't look behind to see where the turul birds went: I could feel the distant trail of their life force as they winged back to the Lady. I soared across the *puszta,* my sharpened gaze snagging on a horned skull at the base of the great tree.

The Lady had said the tree was invisible to most humans, and from my nursemaid's stories I remembered that only the most pure of heart had ever found the vast tree sprouting from a cattle skull. What did it mean, then, that I could see it now? Not, certainly, that my heart was pure.

I had died and come back, and something irreplaceable in me had changed. I was no longer entirely myself, but I didn't know what I might be instead. Even for someone who was used to wearing different forms as casually as most people wear their clothing, this alienation was profoundly unnerving.

I remembered the ache of the monster's hunger, and my wings twitched.

Somewhere in the field below me, a hare bounded across the grass. I nearly banked, to hurl myself at my prey. But I was human enough to know I could not stop now, so I flew onward, my wings pulling me past the silver ribbons of the Tisza and the smaller streams cutting across the *puszta*.

I flew past the plains outside Pest, then over the miniaturized city, pausing to rest briefly in the hills beyond Buda Castle. There I shifted into human form to survey the damage from Hadúr's attacks. The memory of the stars still stung, but I couldn't find the scars on my arms.

That was new.

Always before, injuries had chased me from one form to the next—even after my death. What had I done, when I let the tree nudge me into dragon shape? Chilled by this new strangeness, I flung myself back into falcon form and threw myself at the skies. By late afternoon I had reached the curated woods around the palace at Eszterháza.

My first order of business was to find clothes. It was not so much that *I* minded being naked when I resumed human form, but other people seemed to.

My second was to find food.

I crept cautiously through the woods behind the palace until I reached the stables, where I supplied myself with a blanket. Long gone were the days when the Eszterházys had employed stable boys that I might filch clothes from. My horse, Holdas, whickered at me.

"Soon," I promised. Wrapping the blanket around me with as much dignity as I could muster, I walked to the house.

I imagined the look on János's face when he discovered I was not, in fact, dead. His eyes would widen with shock, he'd sputter, and then he'd well up—for all his gruffness, he was surprisingly softhearted. The image made me smile.

Someone needed to weed the courtyard, paint the trim, mow the gardens beyond the palace—and probably oil the hinges on the gate. I'd nearly forgotten the cacophony of needs at Eszterháza. *St. Cajetan, but I loved the old place.*

The middle-aged maid who opened the door to my knocking was a new one. She surveyed my blanket and obvious nudity beneath with disfavor.

"Master János is busy at the moment," she said.

"I can wait for him."

She pressed her lips together. "He will likely be occupied for a long time."

"I don't mind."

"If you've come to beg money, we've none. If you've an issue for the magistrate, it's the squire you should be seeing, not Master János."

"I've no business. I'm his nephew, Mátyás."

If I'd expected a warm welcome at that, I was mistaken. Her nostrils flared, two white lines appearing beside them. She looked me up and down once sharply, then said, "Master Mátyás is dead these eight months, and I find your joke in very poor taste!"

She slammed the door in my face.

Fool. I should have foreseen that reaction to my announcement. I retraced my steps, returning to the overgrown gardens behind the palace.

Two of the glass-paned doors opening into the garden were boarded over and nailed shut. But the third proved unlocked. I made a mental note to tell my great-uncle not to be so trusting of strangers and let myself in.

I went slowly, alert for the maid or anyone else who might be moving through the rooms. A rattle of nails on the floor forewarned me of Noémi's vizsla, and I ruffled Oroszlán's ears when he bounded toward me. After leaping up to lick my face, he settled into pace beside me.

I climbed the stairs to the second floor, circling around a narrow courtyard. I paused briefly in my old room to find a plain linen shirt and trousers. After a moment's hesitation, I fished my father's signet ring from a drawer—the griffin rampant, bearing a sword and flowers, winked up at me. Then I passed down the corridor toward the salon where János liked to hole up. As it turns out, I'd correctly interpreted the maid's "busy" as "sleeping": János was slumped peacefully in his favorite chair near the ceramic stove, an unfinished tray of pastries on the low table before him.

I shut the door silently behind me—and started.

János wasn't alone.

The Lady sat beside him, watching him with that un-fathomable gaze of hers.

I must have made some involuntary sound, because she looked up at me, a smile softening her mouth.

"How did you—?"

"You forget I was once a goddess. I have eyes every-where. As fleetly as you travel in falcon form, I can travel faster."

"But what are you doing here?"

She didn't answer me immediately. Instead, she turned back to János, reaching out to stroke his weathered cheek. "It is hard on him, to grow old. He hates the gout that plagues him, that keeps him tied to these drafty halls when he would rather be of service to his kingdom. Did you know?"

I had guessed as much, though János did not like to speak of it. But I could not guess where her comments were tending.

"He looks so peaceful now. It would almost be a shame to wake him. I find it curious, even after millennia of watching you humans, how sleep is such a vivid semblance of death. It would be so easy to slide from one to the other. Painless too. Your great-uncle might welcome it. Surely many spirits wait for him on the other side." Her eyes filled with a kind of ferocious tenderness.

Chills crawled down my back that had nothing to do

with the room, which was unseasonably warm, just as János liked it. Affecting a nonchalance I did not feel, I said, "Likely he would welcome death, as you say. I only came for my horse—and anything portable I might sell."

I held my casual posture for a long, breathless moment as the Lady scrutinized me. The troubled set to her mouth suggested she did not quite believe me, but she did not stop me as I plucked a small gold ormolu clock from the mantel and left the room.

I let out a sigh of relief as I retraced my steps down the corridor. I hoped my deception had been enough to convince her to leave my uncle alone. I did not think the Lady was evil, but she had a kind of single-mindedness that could be ruthless. And I did not think former goddesses were prone to weigh human lives as I did.

I stopped in a few more rooms, gathering small portable valuables to lend truth to my lie. I swung by the kitchen, empty at midafternoon, and filched a loaf of bread, some cheese, and some wrinkled apples from last fall's harvest.

My heart was stone-heavy as I made my way across the weed-congested lawns to the stables. János had been more father to me than my own father, who had not shown much care for me when he lived, and even less when he took his own life and left us penniless. I might not agree with János's politics, but he had shown my sister and me a rough, casual affection we hadn't known before, and made us the best home he could in his awkward, confirmed-bachelor way.

One of the few regrets I carried with me from my death was that I had not been able to say good-bye to János or my sister. Now I could never do so. If I sought out Noémi, even Anna, I would only signal to the Lady that I might be moved by threats against them.

I'd be confounded if I let the Lady force my hand. If caring for people meant endangering them—very well then, I would care for no one but myself. Selfishness was an art form I was rather good at.

I let myself into the stable, squinting in the dim light. Only two of the once proud fleet of Eszterházy horses remained. Holdas whinnied a welcome from his stall. Cukor, that fat, stupid gelding, took up another mouthful of hay without the least interest. I took down a saddlebag from the wall and stuffed the food and other pilfered items inside it.

I saddled Holdas, murmuring softly to the horse when he rolled his eyes at me. Clearly, no one had dared ride him since I'd left. I hoped, at least, János had let him out to run in the fields, or this was going to be uncomfortable for both of us.

I couldn't resume my old life—someone was bound to recognize me and tell Noémi, and she'd only be hurt that I had not sought her out. Worse, she'd find me and force a confrontation, and I didn't think I could pretend to hate her to her face. There was always the possibility that no one would believe it was me—I *was* supposed to be dead. But I could not risk it.

I would have to disappear. Become nothing and nobody.

Not Eszterházy Mátyás.

Not táltos.

No one.

CHAPTER 12

I left Eszterháza slowly, lingering over the familiar haunts of the Hanság marsh, skimming the southern edge of Lake Fertő, and then heading east.

I spent the first night in a small *csárda* not far from Kapuvár, where I'd sold the ormolu clock. After tossing all night on the rough mattress, I was happy to settle my bill and leave with first light.

The empty, solitary hours of that second day weighed on me. I hadn't realized quite how much I had depended on the Lady and the grey women for company as I'd recovered from dying. I tried talking to Holdas, but he flattened his ears and attempted to knock me from his back. Only the fact that I felt his irritation before he showed it saved me from falling.

I stopped for lunch in a farmer's field, breaking off a chunk of rapidly drying bread. A crow settled on a branch near me, cocking his head to one side and fixing me with an intelligent black eye. I could feel his curiosity like a shiny coin in my head.

I like crows. They're smart, and while a raven is perhaps more magnificent, crows are more approachable. Less conceited, maybe. I blamed this preference on my mother, who had named me after Hunyadi Mátyás, the great Renaissance king, also known as Matthias Corvinus or the Raven King. Legend had it that when young Mátyás was to be crowned king to end a protracted civil war, his mother signaled for him to return to Hungary from Prague by sending a raven with a ring in its beak.

My mother no doubt intended that my namesake should inspire me to great things: she died disappointed. And as it felt presumptuous to adopt Mátyás's ravens, I'd chosen their lesser cousins instead.

I tossed a piece of bread to the crow, who caught it in his beak and swallowed it in one gulp. "Not quite as tasty as carrion, but it will do in a pinch, eh, *varjú*?"

The answering caw sounded like laughter as the crow shook himself, then lifted into the air. I watched him go. *Perhaps I should follow him.* I could stop being Mátyás entirely, embracing nothing but the hunt and the flight.

A little recollection convinced me otherwise. Besides the obvious energy it would take to shift all the time, the entire lack of human contact and conversation might kill me.

The next night I spent longer than was wise in the taproom of another *csárda*. A passing Frenchman was running an informal faro bank, and the sight of the tiger-backed cards sent electricity racing through me.

How long had it been since I'd held cards in my hand? A lifetime. I joined the group of punters at his table, alternately winning and losing. A barmaid perhaps ten years my senior began to join me in between her rounds, cheering me on when I won, regaling me with gossip when I lost. I let most of her chatter wash over me, enjoying the way her plump hands moved when she talked, the way her cheeks flushed when she hit something particularly salacious.

At the end of the evening she kissed me. And while it was clear she would have welcomed more—I found, abruptly, that I had no taste for it. I put her off politely, and she shrugged philosophically. I counted up my remaining chips and discovered my losses had outpaced my earnings, carving a sizable dent into the funds I'd earned from selling the clock.

I also shrugged philosophically.

Another crow found me the next morning, winging behind me as I rode down a narrow dirt road. Following an impulse, I pulled Holdas off the road to let him graze, shifting quickly and pumping my wings to follow the crow. We tore through the sky, tumbling and wheeling, joined by the other members of the crow's family. At length I returned to my own form, feeling more like myself than I had since dying. Gambling and shapeshifting—if I could only patent the combination, I'd make a fortune.

When night fell, creeping slowly across the still-warm air, I was nowhere near a village large enough to boast an inn. I found a farmhouse that looked tidy, the woven rushes in the roof neatly patched, the walls whitewashed.

The round farmwife who answered my knock was not

willing to let me into the house—and spying the half dozen or so children tumbling across the floor behind her, I doubted she had room for me in the house even if she wished it—but she offered me a spot in the adjacent barn.

As it had already begun to drizzle, I accepted gladly. She sent one of the older boys to show me to a stall where I could house Holdas, and then to the corner of the barn where they kept fresh hay.

I'd slept in worse places, certainly—most memorably the night William and I had gotten spectacularly drunk in Pest and spent the night sleeping on the cobblestones just outside the *kocsma*. At least the barn was clean. The boy who'd led me to the outbuilding reappeared a few minutes later with a pile of blankets, and I settled in for the night.

The steady drum of rain covered most of the animal noises, the lowing of the single cow, the whickering of Holdas and a pair of draft horses in neighboring stalls, even the handful of chickens roosting along the far wall.

I was nearly asleep when a crack of lightning shot white light through slits in the walls, and thunder boomed moments later.

In the brief illumination, I saw that the door of the barn was open, and someone stood in the doorway. The cow bellowed like a crazed thing, banging against her stall and trying to get away.

I couldn't see why the cow was so wound up. It was only a girl in a white shift, which was clinging damply to a shapely figure. Her dark hair hung in wet clumps around a pretty, if narrow, face.

A second bolt of lightning lit the sky behind her, and the

rain against the roof grew sharp and hard. Hail. The girl moved, darting forward with a strange, unjointed grace. She slid into Holdas's stall, and I groaned. Holdas tolerated fools even less willingly than I did. If I didn't warn her, she risked being trampled.

I slid out of my warm cocoon of blankets and floundered in the dark for my boots. I categorically refused to walk barefoot through a barn—I had no desire to clean manure from my feet.

"Miss?" I called out, approaching the stall. "I shouldn't stay there if I were you. My horse isn't very kind to strangers."

As if to underscore my words, I heard a sharp hissing and Holdas reared up, his eyes flashing red in the dim light.

I swore and ran forward, setting a hand on Holdas's neck and nudging his mind with a stream of calming thoughts. His hooves flashed down, narrowly missing the girl huddled in the corner, thin arms wrapped around sharp shins. She stared at me unblinkingly. Another flash of lightning illuminated her face: her eyes were wild and burning, with irises so dark they seemed to swallow her entire eye, leaving no whites at all.

"Are you hurt? How did you come here?" I didn't particularly relish the thought of a roommate, but I couldn't send her back into the storm, growing more violent by the minute. What would drive a girl out in a night like this?

She whispered something, a sibilant string that meant nothing to me. The hiss of her voice seemed to crawl beneath my clothes, burrowing into my bones. *What* was she? She couldn't be entirely human.

Voices caught my attention above the rising clamor of the storm: many of them, and they were angry. I moved to the door of the barn, blinking as a mix of rain and hail stung my cheeks.

Light flickered in the field beyond: a half dozen lanterns, by my guess. The next stroke of lightning showed that the assembly was much larger. A dozen men and a few women, all armed with farm tools: scythes and hoes, pitchforks and axes. A pair of dogs howled and raced back and forth beside the leaders. My gaze flickered back to the girl.

Damn it.

I'd no wish to be part of a mob hunt. I'd even less wish to stand against them, risking my neck for someone who might, for all I knew, actually have been guilty of something. But if the mob caught up with her here, they'd spook all the animals, and there would be no rest for any of us.

"Here." I crossed back to the stall to keep Holdas from mauling the girl and held out my hand. She lifted her face to me just as another flash of lightning threw brilliance across it. Something dark stained her lips, and I did not think it was late berries she'd ransacked from some larder. I hesitated, wondering what kind of crime I was abetting. But those big, nearly black eyes did not seem dangerous or evil, only frightened, and the hand that clutched convulsively over my arm was so thin as to be almost translucent.

I led her across the barn to where I'd been sleeping, directed her to lie down on my blanket, and threw the second blanket over her, hoping she'd have the sense to stay put.

Then I went back to the entrance of the barn.

The mob was at the farmhouse, banging loudly on the

door. I saw a light flicker inside, then a tall, stringy man appeared. He shook his head, then gestured to the barn, and the mob surged toward me.

I leaned, deceptively casual, against the door frame. As soon as they were within hailing distance, I said, "Here's a *hűhó*. What's amiss, my friends?"

A big burly man with a white-flecked beard lifted his torch and scowled at me. "We're hunting one of those thrice-damned praetheria. Made off with my prize ewe."

A sheep. I nearly laughed in relief. It was only a sheep that she'd stolen—and, probably, eaten.

"Have you seen her? Looks are deceptive—looks like a slip of a girl, butter wouldn't melt in her mouth. But she's dangerous. Killed the sheep with her bare hands like it was nothing."

A narrow woman beside him added, "You'd best be on the watch. Handsome thing like you, she'd have you for breakfast. One of them Fair Ones, you know. Seduces then eats her lovers."

I brushed away a twinge of irritation. I needed to tread carefully. These people may have read too many fairy stories—and had too much to drink—but they were no less dangerous for being irrational. Maybe more. The only thing I believed of the girl was that she had stolen a sheep.

"I've seen no one," I said. "And I'd like to go back to sleep, if you don't mind."

"You've been sleeping? Then you'll pardon us if we search the barn behind you. We know she came this direction."

"I tell you, there's no one else here. And you're disturbing the animals."

The dogs were sniffing at the doorway of the barn, whining eagerly.

The burly man's gaze swept my plain clothes. "You talk like a Luminate but wear the clothes of a peasant. I don't trust you. The dogs say she's been here."

I couldn't hope to outmatch the entire crowd, and I had no real wish to. I sighed, moving aside as the mob crammed through the open doorway. I went back to my bag and blankets, putting one hand on top of the girl's head. "Stay still," I whispered.

I concentrated on the dogs, feeling the emotions tumbling through them: eagerness at the hunt, the distinctive sharp scent that insisted *here,* somewhere *here* was the thing they chased, a tiny curl of displeasure at their wet fur. I sent a thread of magic toward them, taking the edge off their eagerness and suggesting that no, this was not the scent they sought.

The dogs immediately lost their intensity, snuffling with interest at the different smells the barn offered, but no longer following a single scent. No one in the mob seemed to notice.

The crowd rushed into empty stalls, swept items off shelves even when it was obvious nothing so large could hide there, tossed through a barrel of feed. There was no real method to their search. I called out a warning when they reached Holdas. I'm not sure they believed me, but Holdas snorted and reared up, so they held back, only shining the torchlight into the stall.

The burly man who led the mob elbowed his way to the corner of the barn where I'd been sleeping. His eyes fell on my mounded blanket.

"You hiding something here?"

"Please don't touch my things," I said. "There's nothing to see."

With a dismissive sneer, he lunged for the blanket and whipped it off.

The doleful eyes of a russet vizsla, much like my sister Noémi's, looked up at him. The decision to shift the girl had been spur-of-the-moment, when I touched her head earlier. I was still surprised the spell had taken. I could sometimes shift things if I touched them, but usually only small things with a superficial resemblance—a stone into a blade, a hair into a thread. I had only once before succeeded in transforming something major, outside myself, and that was when I had shifted Anna's soul, just before I died. Cold prickled down my spine. Was this another instance of my táltos gifts expanding?

The man swore and flung the blanket back; the dog-girl flinched away from the rough movement.

"There's naught here. Let's move on, before we lose her trail completely."

The men, women, and dogs moved back into the storm. The dog-girl quivered on the blanket for a long moment. When I was sure the others were gone, I set my hands on the finely shaped skull and shifted her back. My stomach curled in on itself, more ravenous than usual from shifting the girl.

"I'm sorry," I said. "It was the only way I could think to save you without hurting anyone."

Those black, blank eyes scoured across my face. "Thank you," she said in Hungarian, her voice hissing across the sibilants. *"Köszönöm."*

"You should probably stay here tonight—I don't think the mob will be back before morning."

I wasn't sure how much she understood, but she curled back on my blanket, her eyes sliding shut.

"That wasn't—" I sighed again, abandoning my blankets to the girl. I kindled a small Lumen light and inspected the rest of the barn. I restored some of the fallen items to their shelf, though there wasn't much I could do about the feed scattered across the floor. In the opposite corner, I found a rough horse blanket. I spread it out, lay down, and pretended to sleep until morning. Mostly, I listened to my stomach complain and calculated if it would be worth the extra expenditure of energy to shift into something that could eat the spilled feed.

Sometime after dawn, I fell into fitful dreams. I saw Noémi at a fancy Viennese ball, dancing with a man whose golden eyes glinted through slits in the mask he wore. A clock chimed, and the masked man released my sister to untie his mask. But as the mask slid down, Noémi began screaming: her hands were fountaining blood, and the face behind the mask was mine.

I woke gasping, my neck aching from a night spent on the ground. The lanky farmer stood nearby, cussing as he made his way through the barn.

I scrambled to my feet. "It wasn't me." A quick glance to the far side of the barn showed my blankets were empty. The Fair One, if that's what she really was, had already vanished.

The farmer shook his head. "I know. Weren't your fault the mob traced the monster here. Saints be praised the Fair One didn't find us and murder us in our beds."

I spent the better part of an hour helping him put his barn back in order. His wife insisted on sending me off with a hearty farm breakfast: sausage, bread slathered thick with butter, milk with a frothy layer of cream. I fell on it like a man who hadn't seen food for the better part of a week.

Heaven, I am convinced, can contain nothing more divine than freshly cooked farm bread with sweet butter melting into its light-as-air heart.

"Eat more if it tastes good." Though the invitation was standard hospitality, the good farmwife did not sound as though she meant it. I could almost see her calculating in her head how much this morning's meal would set her back.

I made sure to press some extra coins on her before leaving. Then, my head still light with lack of sleep but my stomach pleasantly full, I set off again, the intermittent sunshine a halfhearted blessing on my head.

CHAPTER 13

I tried to put the mob's pursuit of the praetherian girl out of my mind: I had my own troubles to worry about, not dwell on a thin white face with black eyes. The Lady had warned that the major danger threatening Hungary came from the creatures—but surely such small, hunted things couldn't be a threat. And she had also said not all the creatures sided with the Four.

I shook myself. It wasn't my business.

It took Holdas and me two days to reach the Duna River. The ferryman charged me extra to bring my horse across, as Holdas refused to let anyone else on the ferry with us, and so the ferryman had to make an extra trip.

"You're a brute," I told the horse. He snorted at me, wholly unrepentant.

For three days we traveled eastward at a leisurely pace, seeing nothing otherworldly, passing only a few farmers and their families on the road, and spotting the blue-and-black-clothed *gulyások* driving their herds of cattle in the distance.

In another day or two I'd reach Debrecen, the largest city in the eastern part of Hungary and a good place to disappear. There was a university there, which meant a large student population that was constantly shifting, opportunities for employment, and a chance to further my studies if I chose to stay that long. Plus, my funds were dwindling more rapidly than I had anticipated, and I'd need to find work if I wanted to feed myself.

I crossed the famous nine-arched bridge across the Hortobágy River. A low, whitewashed *csárda* rested near the crossroads, a few smaller cottages scattered close by. I stopped for paprika-spiced fish stew and bread, then resumed my journey.

The wind was strong that afternoon, blowing a thick dust up from the road and kicking dirt across the fields. I tied a handkerchief across my nose and mouth to keep from breathing the worst of it. I nearly turned back to the *csárda,* but winds were unpredictable, and I'd encountered worse.

Not two miles from the crossroads, a glossy black carriage was pulled to the side of the road. I scanned the carriage wheels for signs of accident but saw none. Perhaps the wind had unsettled or spooked the horses.

I drew nearer. The horses were grazing placidly enough on the grass they could reach from their harness. Where was the driver? The riders? The windows, when I tapped at them, brought no answer from inside.

A shriek rang out from the field beyond the carriage. I squinted to find three men standing in a knot together, poking at something on the ground with a stick. Probably just a rabbit. Distasteful, but not my concern.

The shriek sounded again, and I frowned. I probed gently in the direction of the sound with my táltos sense. My mind brushed up against the creature's, and I recoiled sharply enough that Holdas sidestepped uneasily beneath me. That was no rabbit. Under the heavy weight of its terror, the animal—whatever it was—was nearly sentient.

Damn it.

I nudged Holdas forward. I reminded myself I was out-numbered, and I was not responsible for how a trio of spoiled, bored noblemen chose to spend their time. (Never mind that not so very long ago *I* had been a spoiled, bored nobleman—and I had never resorted to tormenting ani-mals.)

Wisps of the creature's terror and anguish trailed after me. We made it perhaps a dozen steps before I sighed and turned Holdas around.

We rode straight at the three men. They didn't scatter, as I'd half expected. I'll give them that much.

Following some devil—perhaps inspired by the hand-kerchief I still wore—I said, "Stand and deliver!"

One of the three squeaked and flung his hands up, ex-posing a spotted cravat and a brightly colored waistcoat so tightly cinched I wondered how he could breathe. A second began sifting through his pockets. He plucked up a gold watch and thrust it at me.

I tried not to notice the creature on the ground, a small,

thin, knobbly thing, slowly creeping away. I didn't want to draw attention to it.

The third man eyed me dubiously. He was dressed more plainly than the other two—probably their coachman. "He ain't armed." He brandished a long, braided whip at me. "There's three of us to his one; we can take him!"

He cracked the whip and Holdas reared back. It took all of my calming attention to settle him down, and the man was still advancing. Now the other two had gathered what little courage they possessed and were following behind him, carrying the same sticks they'd been using to torment the creature.

I could have simply ridden away—but let it never be said of me that I was so rabbit-hearted. (Or so sage.)

I desperately wanted a drink.

If I was to drive them off, I needed something that would make a statement. I sent my mind out, seeking the faint electricity of living things nearby. *There.*

"I shouldn't come nearer if I were you," I said. Already, the dark specks along the horizon were speeding closer.

"Yeah? Who's gonna stop me? You? And what army?" The coachman raised his whip arm—then screamed as a crow descended, ripped the whip from his hand, and dropped it on the top of his head. A second crow followed, diving at the trio, and then a third. Crows are quite social, and the entire murder descended on my would-be attackers.

"Who are you?" the first man asked.

"Luminate!" the second screamed.

I grinned, and the handkerchief I wore stretched across

my cheeks. *"Rex Corvus."* The King of Corvids—rooks, ravens, crows—if one was literal-minded. Or a nod to Matthias Corvinus, if one preferred the historical.

The first of the men, the foppish one, goggled at me. I could almost see rusty wheels churning in his brain, converting his grammar-school Latin. "The King of Crows?"

Close enough.

The second man dodged the swooping crows. "Call off your demon-birds! We'll give you what you want, only leave us alone."

A small mental nudge and the birds dispersed, though a pair remained behind, circling lazily over our small group to remind the trio what they faced if they challenged me. The two noblemen threw a small purse of coins at me, followed by a couple of jeweled rings. Then they raced back toward their carriage, the coachman in hot pursuit.

One of the crows, drawn to the shiny gems, swooped down to snatch up a ring. "Fair enough," I said, dismounting to collect the coins and the remaining ring, and by the time I'd remounted, the carriage was already trundling along the road toward Debrecen.

I tracked back across the field, following the faint trail of pain left by the injured creature. I found it at last, by the river's edge.

"Are you all right?" I asked.

The creature curled more tightly into the fetal position.

"I won't hurt you." I wished Noémi were with me. Though we had both belonged to the Luminate order Animanti, I had never been adept at the healing rituals. As a point of fact, I had never really been adept at any of the spoken rites and rituals of the Luminate: most of what I did—the shifting, the animal persuasion—I did by instinct. I had used the rituals, of course, because I'd no wish to draw the Circle's attention, but I had never really needed them. I suspected the Lady would say this was part of my being born táltos.

The creature did not respond, and having no wish to torment it further, I left a gold coin on the bank beside it, then returned to the road. Holdas was reluctant to give up grazing for riding, but eventually he climbed back onto the road, and I pointed him the way we had come. My desire to reach Debrecen had been superseded by a desire *not* to overtake the men I had just robbed.

That night I slept in the stiff spare bedroom of a farmer and his wife, beside the formal, unused bed still piled high with the embroidered pillows and blankets the wife must have brought to the marriage as a dowry. I left them another of the gold coins as payment, and the wife kissed my cheeks heartily while her husband glowered at me. I made a rapid escape, before the husband could read his wife's response as affection for *me* rather than for the gold.

The spring air was mild and sweet, and birds sang across the prairie grass as I rode back over the nine-arched bridge and past the crossroads.

I whistled, pleased with myself and the world at large.

And that, naturally, is when a well-aimed rock knocked me from the saddle and into the dust of the road.

Ж

When I came to, I found myself tightly trussed to the trunk of a tree. Judging by the sun overhead, I'd been out for an hour or more. A handkerchief had been stuffed into my mouth, and when I tried to speak, the three strangers in the grove with me turned with one movement to face me.

One of the men held the small velvet bag I'd confiscated from the noblemen the day before; another held the larger saddlebag, where I kept my purse and the few remaining items from Eszterháza. *Such is life.* I'd inherited my father's attitude toward money: what came effortlessly could be lost just as easily.

Still, the whole encounter stung. Not because I'd lost my money, but because I'd never even seen it coming.

One of the men, half a head shorter than me with a long, luxuriant black mustache, approached me. "I'm going to untie your gag. If you try to shout, I will shoot you in the knee."

I nodded to show my understanding, and he stripped the cloth from my mouth.

I smacked my lips, trying to get the dryness and the slightly sour taste of the cloth from my tongue. "I don't suppose you have any water?"

"We talk first, then give you water. Maybe. If we don't kill you."

I shook my head. "If you're trying to intimidate me, it won't work. If you meant to kill me, you'd have done it already."

He slugged me in the gut, and I doubled over.

My damnable tongue. Even János had said it would be

the death of me. When I could talk again, I said, "All right. I believe you."

I knew he meant for me to be intimidated, frightened even, but somehow I could not muster the energy. He might have a gun, but I figured my odds of shifting before he could finish aiming were pretty good, and there were plenty of creatures small enough that he'd have a hard time getting a bead on me. I was more curious than anything.

"You're not from here," black mustache said. "You're carrying goods worth more than the clothes on your back. I think maybe you stole them."

"And now you've stolen them from me. I don't think I'm seeing your point."

"We're looking for someone. Calls himself the King of Crows. Robbed a bunch of noble boys on the road yesterday. You know him?"

"Never heard of him. I'm sorry—but why do you care anyway?"

"This is my territory. Other gangs don't operate here."

"And you are?"

He fingered the tips of his mustache. "Fekete László." László the Black. He announced the name as though he were someone I ought to have heard of, like Rózsa Sándor.

"Ah. Of course! Well then, now that we've cleared that bit up, if you'll kindly return my horse, I'll be on my way. You can keep the money," I added generously.

The redhead standing beside László the Black said laconically, "Can't give you the horse. We shot him."

A beat of silence. My ears began ringing. I couldn't seem

to feel my toes or the tips of my fingers. Holdas was a brute, but he was the only family I could still claim.

The redhead burst out laughing. "Your face! Your horse is not dead. Followed us here, in fact—though I think he might be possessed. Nasty creature."

The relief was solid as a punch. With the shock of the announcement no longer blunting my senses, I could, in fact, sense Holdas faintly from a field nearby. "Ha-ha! You bluff excellently well—I don't suppose you play cards?"

"Naturally." The redhead grinned. Fekete László eyed me critically. "You talk like a Luminate. Probably there's someone somewhere who would pay good money for your safe release."

"I wish that were true! But my parents died some five years ago—my father by his own hand after squandering all our family fortunes. All my earthly goods and all I hope to inherit are in that bag there." I nodded at the saddlebag László held.

László frowned.

"Do you think I'd be traveling in these clothes if I were lying?" I used my chin to gesture at the outfit I'd worn daily for the past week or more. Despite admittedly haphazard efforts at cleaning them, my shirt and trousers were less than pristine, and probably smelled a bit too. Though not, I'm happy to say, as much as my captors.

"You *are* Luminate, though? Any magic?"

I shrugged. "Not to speak of."

"A lot of Luminate lost their magic after the Binding broke," the redhead said. "He's probably telling the truth. Might as well let him go. We can blindfold him and take him back to the crossroads."

The third bandit, a dark-haired, dark-complexioned boy with a long scar across his right cheek, said nothing, only rolled my father's signet ring from one hand to the other.

László frowned up at the sky. "That'll take you an hour or more—and then the time to come back. I can't spare you so long. Take him far enough from here that he can't track his way back and let him loose on the *puszta*. Mayhap he'll live; mayhap he won't."

"Callous," I said, tsking.

"I'm beginning to dislike you." László fingered the hilt of a knife at his belt.

"Only beginning to? I've clearly failed, then."

The redhead shouted with laughter. "I like him, László. He's quick, fearless—or possibly just stupid—and he's clearly not above the law. We could use someone now that Feri has gotten himself hanged."

I tried to ignore the kick of excitement in my gut. Were they asking me to be a *bandit*? Hungarian *betyárok* were all the rage these days—the romance of the untrammeled life, the lure of illicit encounters and daring escapes.

László folded his arms and surveyed me once more. He glanced back at the scar-faced boy. "Bahadır, what do you say?"

Bahadır. That was not a Hungarian name—or Austrian either. I eyed the boy with interest. There was a story here.

Bahadır shrugged. "Why not?"

László waved at the redhead. "Go ahead, then, Ákos."

"What do you think, stranger? We work long hours and the pay isn't great, but you get a share of anything we do get. We're not violent either, if you're squeamish about that—killing your mark is as good as asking the army to come after you. Long as we're mostly peaceable, they don't hunt too hard for us. Course, if we get caught, it'll mean the noose."

I thought for a glancing second. I needed to disappear, and I needed to find work—if this wasn't quite *honest* work, it at least promised to be *interesting*. I could always leave if it got old. Besides, they had my father's ring—and I wanted it back.

"Deal. Now, if you'll untie my bonds, we can shake on it."

Anna

CHAPTER 14

The June evening light broke in shafts through the trees surrounding one of the main thoroughfares in Prater Park. Noémi and I strolled arm in arm, a dozen paces or so behind Richard and Catherine. After a lengthy sermon and even longer dinner, we'd collected at the park to see and be seen. In one of the fields a little way down the road, the Furstenfeld family was holding the first of many fetes for the Congress. The roadway was thronged with people: wealthy Viennese merchant families, Luminate nobility with soul signs glimmering like fireflies in the waning light, peasant men and women in traditional lederhosen and dirndls, a pair of Serbian girls with cloth wound around their heads.

It was Whitsunday, the seventh Sunday following Easter, though apart from the extra touches of red flowers and birch branches at the altar of St. Stephen's Cathedral, no one seemed to mark it but me.

"This time last year I had only just arrived in Hungary," I told Noémi. "Do you remember the dreadful stories you told to frighten me?"

She laughed. "Oh yes. How I hated you when you first arrived: rich and spoiled and utterly oblivious. I meant to terrify you. Did I?"

Her stories hadn't, but that night I had seen shadows that were not shadows crawl between trees.

That night I had met Gábor for the first time.

That night everything about my life had begun to change.

"Only a little. I'm made of sterner stuff than that."

Noémi hugged my arm. "I'm glad. And glad I was wrong about you too."

A flash of red caught my eye and I turned. Some distance back, a pair of Dragović's soldiers stood beside the road in their distinctive uniform: a short brown jacket with red braiding, white trousers with blue-and-white stockings, wide yellow sashes over which hung a curved ornamental sheath and a long pistol with an inlaid butt. Though the night was warm, both wore their distinctive red hooded cloaks, from which they drew their name: Red Mantles. The soldiers' heads hung close together in conversation. One, to my surprise, was a girl, her dark hair in two neat braids. She saw me looking at her and glared, one hand going to the hilt of the knife she carried at her hip.

I felt her eyes burning into my back as I walked away.

I forgot about the girl-soldier as we reached the fete. A loose perimeter had been marked with gauzy fabric strung between wrought-iron posts, gold lights playing around the gently swaying wall. A pair of uniformed footmen greeted the guests as they approached, allowing the Luminate and the wealthier merchants entry but turning others away. Those turned away lingered in the roadway, watching us enter and murmuring, or roamed along the margins, staring with wide eyes at the spectacle beyond.

An arched bower of wisteria just beyond the footmen welcomed us into the fete. Someone—an Animanti, probably—had crafted smaller flowering vines to weave in and out of the wisteria, resulting in a profusion of delicate colors and floral scents. Silver bells sounded on the early night breeze. WELCOME TO A NIGHT IN FAERIELAND, proclaimed a banner over our heads.

"Oh," Noémi breathed, and I smiled. My cousin had a distinct weakness for pretty things.

The first of the faerie "realms" we came to was a dazzling world of colored glass. Some Luminate charm (Lucifera, probably) set glass beads of all shapes and sizes hovering independently in the air, and they danced around us, forming and reforming an impossible variety of patterns. Tiny Lumen lights followed the glass, giving the impression of walking through a rainbow.

A few paces farther brought us to Titania's bower, cunningly illusioned so the flowers—cowslips and bluebells and daisies—stood higher than our heads. I put out my hand to one of the bluebells, and my fingers slid through the illusion. At the center of the bower we found Titania herself, accompanied by a page in silk robes with a short, feathered turban on his dark curls.

I froze. Titania was not, as I had expected, some

Luminate woman spelled to look more fey. She was, in fact, praetherian—tall, attenuated, her tan skin gleaming under the enchanted lights, and gossamer-thin wings beating at her back. Fine silver shackles strung with bells hung on her wrists, chaining her to her bower.

I swallowed against sourness in my throat.

"What's your name?" I asked her. "Are you all right?" The inanity of the question struck me as it left my lips. She wore chains. She was not all right.

She did not answer me, only looked through me with clear silver eyes—eyes so limpid and sad I began to ache in sympathy. I knelt, inspecting the chains, but there was no enchantment on them that I could break, and when I tugged at them, they did not give.

"Anna!" Noémi said. "What are you doing?"

"She shouldn't be here." I tugged at the chain again.

"You don't know her situation. Perhaps she's been hired to be part of the tableau," Noémi said, though she sounded uncertain.

"Miss!" a man in a dark suit shouted, jogging toward us. "Please don't touch. You'll disturb the creature—and the other guests."

"Why is she chained?" I asked. "Can't you let her free, if she must be here?"

"The chains are only a precaution against her glamour. Now move along, young ladies, there are others here to see Titania."

Noémi and I moved on reluctantly. My cousin gripped my arm as I glanced behind to see "Titania" watching me, those great eyes unblinking.

The third realm we entered was grimmer, better suiting my mood. Here the trees seemed heavier, darker, and a low laugh echoed out from them, raising the hairs on my arms. Leaves bobbed on the wind, swirling together to form a shape that was almost a man, then blowing apart. I nodded reluctant approval: the juxtaposition of the dark and the light seemed very Shakespearean to me—Titania in love with an ass-headed Bottom, Puck dancing with the fairies.

"Anna, are you sure this is part of the fete?" Noémi asked.

A shadow moved between the trees, and I peered into the gloom. A tawny-bodied creature with the head of a boar roared, black wings flexing behind him, and I stumbled backward, releasing my hold on Noémi. A creature very like that had charged me at Eszterháza, after I'd released the praetheria from the Binding spell.

The boar-man sprang forward—only to catch against his own chains. He shook the chains at me, and I realized the strange guttural gurgles might be laughter. I shook my skirts, patted my hair, and pretended I had not been nearly frightened out of my wits. Noémi cowered behind me.

Three tiny light-flecked creatures flew past me. One of them snagged the hair I had just straightened, yanking it hard enough to bring tears to my eyes. I watched them flit away, and a chill slid through my stomach.

Those praetheria, whatever they were, were not chained as the others in the fete were.

Whitsunday.

Noémi had told me once that creatures from folklore

were more powerful on nights like this, when the Binding stretched thin. Even if the Binding was gone, praetherian power was not. I remembered the shadow-on-shadow sleekness of the fene that had chased me a year before and shivered. Who had thought it a good idea to mimic a faerie kingdom on such a night?

"We should go," I said, turning back to Noémi.

But Noémi was gone.

The rest of the fete had disappeared, swallowed up by the heavy-limbed trees surrounding me. I could hear the noise of the party—the laughter of children, the tinny jangle of bells, the murmur of voices—but they were distant, as through a veil or a wall.

Illusions, I thought. Whose?

I spun around, studying the trees and shadows around me. Even the boar-man had vanished. The wind hissed through the branches, and the grasses stirred at my feet.

Then I saw it: a praetherian more tree than creature, with dark eyes that glimmered in the dusk, crouched around the roots of a tree.

"Mine," it said, watching me intently.

"I beg your pardon?"

"You," it said. "Mine."

"I don't think so," I said firmly but politely. I turned to leave and found that my feet were rooted to the ground. Grasses snaked across my shoes, anchoring me. I met the creature's eyes. They were flat like mud. "Let me go. Please."

"Mine," it said again.

It was like arguing with a small child.

"I am *not* yours. And my friends will be looking for me."
As if to underscore my words, I heard Noémi's voice in the
distance, calling my name. "Here! I'm here!" But my shout
seemed muted, as if it met a hidden ceiling and bounced
back.

"Mine."

"You've got to let me go. There will be trouble if you
don't." Forcing myself to calm—telling myself that this
ridiculous creature could not mean me harm—I tried to
concentrate on the spell it was using to hold me. I closed my
eyes, extending that peculiar second sense, something I had
not consciously done since I had broken the Binding. *There.*

The spell buzzed dully. My shadow self skittered inside
me, angry and frightened. For a fleeting second, I was inside the Binding again, holding the magic of that spell-
world for a fire-filled moment before Mátyás died.

Shaking myself, I shoved the fear down and concentrated
on the anger, using it to funnel my focus, and plucked at
the spell. A faint resistance, then a snap, and my right foot
lifted.

"MINE!" the creature roared, and, with a slurping
sound, my left foot sank into the ground, all the way to
my ankle.

Unable to keep my balance, I lost the thread of the spell
and toppled over. Another snap, this one accompanied by
agony blazing up my left leg. I cried out, my hands going
to my ankle, now bent at an awkward angle. What could
the praetherian want with me?

I reached for the spell again, but the haze of pain in my
head made it hard to focus.

"Borevit!" A soft light stole across the clearing, and the wood creature flinched. Vasilisa followed the glow, her hands on her hips in an almost human gesture of impatience. A faint jingle of bells accompanied her. "Let the girl go at once. We've talked about this. When your master agreed to help Svarog, he agreed to abide by our rules. You are to leave the humans alone."

"Mine," it said again, but weakly, and the ground released my foot.

Vasilisa turned to me. "Can you stand?"

I shook my head, and she knelt beside me, laying long, impossibly cool fingers on my swollen and throbbing ankle.

"Don't," I said, abruptly sure that I did not want to be in her debt, though I could not have said why. "My cousin will be here soon enough. She's a healer."

A shadow flickered across Vasilisa's face. Her fingers tightened, and fire shot through my leg, followed by a wave of ice so bitter cold I choked on a scream.

She stood, brushing her hands on her silvery skirt, before reaching down to pull me up beside her. Other than from a phantom ache, my leg was fine.

The wood creature was gone.

"What was that?" I asked.

"A foolish mistake," Vasilisa said. "Do you not recognize a faerie trap? That creature was one of Chernobog's—in another ten minutes he would have sucked you underground entirely."

I swayed a little, picturing it: the slow suffocation, soil pressing around my chest, my face. The smell and taste of dirt my last memory.

Vasilisa smiled, but her smile had a malicious edge. "Oh, you might not have died at once. He might have saved you for his master, and that would have been entirely worse."

"But he shouldn't have been here—soldiers have patrolled Prater Park for weeks, and the others were all chained. . . ." I broke off at the look in Vasilisa's eyes.

"And why should we not be here? You believe it is okay for humans to use us as decorations for a *party*?" She held up her wrist, where a pair of delicate silver bells hung. "In *chains*? When you treat us so, you cannot be astonished when we change the rules of the game."

I rubbed my arms, chilled despite the evening's warmth. Vasilisa was not wrong. Between the humans and the praetheria, it was not the praetheria who should be ashamed of the night's work.

"Miss Arden!" An unfamiliar voice rolled across the grass, followed almost immediately by the dark-haired girl I'd seen earlier, one of Dragović's Red Mantles. "Are you all right?"

"She's fine," Vasilisa said. "She stumbled and I helped her."

The girl pressed her lips together as if she did not believe us. "You ought to be careful, Miss Arden. I do not like this fete, this flaunting of praetheria feels dangerous to me. There are things out there—" She stopped, her gaze flickering over Vasilisa and pausing for a beat on her bells. "You ought to choose your friends with greater care."

"I suppose I ought to thank you, but my affairs are not your concern," I said, my cheeks heating.

The girl tossed her head and whirled, the tips of her

braids spinning out behind her, and marched away. Not far past her, Noémi and Catherine had spotted me.

"She is right," Vasilisa said. "You ought to be careful. And less stupid. You may be powerful, but where I am from, stupid is dead. If I had not come, you might have died. You must master your magic, if I have to teach you myself."

"You . . . what?"

She pinched my chin. "Listen. I will not repeat myself. I will teach you to use magic, and not because I am kind or generous. I will teach you, because you and I both need that power."

She released me and vanished, and I was still rubbing my chin when Noémi and Catherine caught up to me.

CHAPTER 15

The invitation to tea came two days after the Whitsunday outing to Prater Park. Catherine read through it at once at breakfast, then shrieked, leading both Richard and me to spring from our seats to peer over her shoulder.

"The archduchess has invited us to tea! At the Hofburg!" She held the invitation to her heart as though it were a small child, then turned to me with a sly look. "Perhaps her son has put her up to this."

I found that unlikely, particularly after the mull of things I had made at the Congress. But Catherine continued to fuss about the proposed tea until I was heartily sick of the topic. When she disappeared to make house calls after luncheon, I was profoundly relieved.

I settled into a bronze chaise longue with a sigh, opening a new volume of poetry that had just arrived: John Stanyan Bigg's *The Sea-King*. The early afternoon stretched blissfully empty before me.

The epigraph, from Robert Southey's *The Curse of Kehama,* tugged at me: "her heart was full / Of passions which had found no natural scope." How many women could claim such feelings? Noémi, with all her natural healing gifts, pressured into a society marriage with a man twice her age. Myself, with power I would not use and a voice I could not use. And what of Catherine's passions for magic, her ambition to join the Circle? Where and how had she buried such longing?

I brushed such gloomy thoughts away and read rapidly, devouring the story of a Norse maiden with a dark past and a darker obsession:

> *Strange tales were told of that lady bright,*
> *And stranger of her pedigree;*
> *'Tis said she would go in the stormiest night*
> *And sail about on the terrible sea:*
> *And lash the fierce waves when they mounted on high,*
> *To storm the gates of the ebon sky.*

So caught was I by the story that when the butler interrupted with a brusque "A visitor, miss," the book tumbled from my hands onto the plush Turkish rug.

"Says her name is Vasilisa," the butler continued.

The hair on my neck lifted. I ignored it and retrieved my book. "Please show her up."

The butler remained for a moment, eyebrows pressed together. "Are you certain, miss? The woman seems not entirely . . . safe."

What had Vasilisa said to the poor man? "I'm certain. I'll come to no harm."

Vasilisa appeared moments later, sweeping her eyes around the room dismissively before settling them on me. Then she smiled. "You are nervous? Good." She stripped off her gloves and set them on a side table. "Come here."

Eschewing a greeting as Vasilisa had, I set the book on the chaise longue and stood. "What are you doing here? What happened to your bells?"

"They did not suit me at all." She shrugged. "I hear it is customary to call upon friends."

I waited.

"Fine. I am here to teach you magic, as I said. So you will not die in foolish traps." She pointed a finger at a mirror framed by an ornate curl of roses and lilies. At her gesture, the gilt dripped from the flowers like blood; the lilies shriveled and morphed until the entire frame was crawling with worms and maggots. I shuddered, my heart thumping. Vasilisa waved her hand again, and the frame was restored. "You see? I will it, and it is so. As a human, your will is not so strong: you use rituals for such spells.

"Magic comes from life force. Magic is not soul, but soul fuels magic. The stronger your soul, the stronger your magic. Humans are fools to think praetheria have no souls. It is because we have big souls, old souls, that we have such powerful magic. And you, because you are chimera, you have two souls. You could have great magic, if you were not afraid."

She knew what I was. She had said as much, when she first met me, but I had hoped she was mistaken. Mouth dry, I shook my head. "That hardly matters if I cannot cast spells. My souls repel the magic."

"But you have drawn on that magic before," Vasilisa

said. "When you broke the Binding. You used that boy's own soul-magic as he died."

"Mátyás," I said, choking. "He had a name."

"It is a pity humans forbid blood magic. The death of a soul can release great power, like the breaking of a very great spell," Vasilisa said, looking cross. "Some of my finest work—" She broke off. "Never mind. Those were different times."

I dropped my eyes to the carpet so Vasilisa could not read them. There had been a hunger in her face that made me think Vasilisa would welcome a return of those different times.

"Now, show me what you can do." Vasilisa summoned a Lumen light, though hers glowed green rather than the usual blue. "Here's a simple spell: break it."

"No," I said. "I don't want to do this." My spell-breaking was unpredictable, too destructive. I couldn't use it for mere sport or because Vasilisa asked it of me. I could feel the spell, though, a faint frisson like scraping along my bones. *If you were not afraid . . .* Vasilisa's words echoed, taunting, in my head.

"No?" Vasilisa eyed me thoughtfully. Then she whipped her hand forward.

A bolt of lightning seemed to shear me in half, knocking me to the ground. Pain sparked through every part of my body, including the back of my eyes, blinding me. I lashed out with the desperation of a wounded thing. A tiny *pop!* sounded, and when I could pry my eyes open without gagging at the pain, the room was still whole.

Well, mostly. The mirror on the wall had shattered,

shards of glass raining down on the floor. The empty eye of the mirror frame mocked my consternation.

I scrambled to my feet. "What did you do?" My body ached in places I had not known it was possible to ache. "You might have killed me!"

"But I didn't. Again."

"No." I stepped back and folded my arms across my chest. "Not until you explain to me what in *hell* you are trying to do."

"I'm teaching you to be chimera." Her grin flickered, her teeth dagger points in the gold light filtering through gauzy curtains. "We can resume this lesson in hell, if you like."

"What if I don't wish to use my gift?"

"That is not a choice you have. You will break spells, whether you wish to or not. The choice you have is only if you will control your gift or be controlled by it."

She was right, though that was small comfort when the very thought of breaking spells sent my pulse hurtling through my body. "Why did you attack me?"

"You're chimera. You have two souls: you break spells by pulling the magic into *both* souls at once, and the souls pull the spell apart. But to call the spell to you, your souls must be united in will. Powerful anger can sometimes do this. Or fear." She bared her teeth at me. "Or pain."

I flinched. "So how do I control it, aside from bringing someone with me to throw rocks at me every time I need to be violently angry?"

She waved her hand at me. "You do not accept your chimera self, and so it is hard for you to bring your souls together."

173

"I know what I am."

"Knowing is not the same as accepting. You do not like what you are."

I did not answer. I had made peace with my shadow self before I broke the Binding, but I had not fully unleashed her since. Vasilisa crowed at me. "See? I am entirely right." The green light, which had blinked out, kindled again in her palm. "Now. Break the spell."

I closed my eyes and reached out with that extra sense, looking for the buzz of the spell. I imagined myself as a cage, opening to let my shadow self out, to let my anger and pride and black-curdled grief fly free. I arched my back, imagining I had sprouted wings like my chimera self. For the first time in months, I was weightless, my souls buoyant and light.

A spout of fire smacked me in the face, dragging me back to earth. Heat blazed across my forehead, swam down my cheeks. I choked on the acrid scent of burnt hair and flesh and screamed.

I'd nearly forgotten Vasilisa. I batted at the flames with my hands, the heat of them searing my palms and fingers. How *dare* she?

With the small part of me not occupied with putting out the fire on my face, I found Vasilisa's spell and cracked it open.

But I didn't stop there. I followed the lines of magic back to their source in Vasilisa's heart. I gathered the loose threads of power and shaped them into a blade and then shoved them home with all the force I could muster.

Vasilisa gasped and crumpled. The fire in my face blinked

out, the mild spring breeze blowing in from the open window cooling my cheeks with its kiss.

My fingers crawled along my hairline, over my eyebrows. Nothing was crimped or singed or blistered. It had all been an illusion.

With the memory of heat only in my palms, I knelt down beside Vasilisa.

As the horror of burning receded from me, a new kind of horror filled me. What had I done? I had been angry. I had acted without thinking. Worse, for a moment I had enjoyed it.

Had I killed her?

I set shaking fingers to her neck. Nothing.

A shuddering breath lifted her rib cage. Vasilisa groaned and sat up. I rocked back on my heels, bracing myself for her rage or recrimination.

Instead, she laughed. "Well done, my chimera. We may make a weapon of you yet."

The tension fled my body, leaving me weak with relief. "I thought I'd killed you."

"You? You've not enough strength or will for that. You surprised me, is all." She lifted one hand to me, and I hauled her upright. "But one thing you did well. When you break a spell, the magic goes free. You did not let the magic escape: you shaped it."

"But why didn't *that* shaping get broken by my two souls?"

"Instinct," Vasilisa said. "Your kind *can* cast spells. But to cast is different than to break: to cast a spell, you must separate your two souls, and use only one soul to hold the magic and shape it. With practice, you can do this. But you must know yourself well, to know what is soul and what is not."

Was it possible Vasilisa was right? At once I was back in the Binding, sending an ecstatic profusion of lights into the air, the only time in my life I had been able to cast a spell. What would I sacrifice to feel that untrammeled joy again?

"But I used no rituals."

She shrugged. "You do not need them, if the will is focused enough. Most humans cannot do this, so there are rituals. But you were very angry."

I sighed, imagining Catherine's reaction to the suggestion that rage gave me strength.

"Again," Vasilisa said, brushing her hands together.

I hesitated, my resolve wavering. A yearning to feel the pleasure of spell-casting warred with common sense. I had not killed Vasilisa, but it was her strength and not my intent that had saved her. In that fractional moment I had wanted to hurt her. To kill her, even. Until I could master *that* impulse, I could not trust myself with spells. "I think you should go."

)(

Vasilisa had not been gone more than a few minutes—just long enough for a maid to sweep up the broken glass from the mirror—when the butler was back.

"Another caller, miss." Disapproval drew grim lines about his mouth. "A tradesperson, I think. Calls herself Borbála Dobos."

I had been on the verge of telling the butler to send the

176

caller away, but at the name, I changed my mind. "Will you send her up?"

Borbála tucked herself into one of the Biedermeier chairs, crossing her suited legs and setting a top hat on the floor beside the chair. "Thank you for seeing me."

"It's my pleasure. But I'm afraid you can't stay long. My sister will be home soon."

"Ah." Borbála's thin mouth turned down. "Your sister does not approve of the working class? A familiar hazard in my line of work, I'm afraid. And my penchant for men's clothes does not help."

"My sister is wary of anyone she thinks might give me ideas," I said.

Borbála laughed. "I should think you were capable of that without help."

I grinned at her.

Taking that as an opening, Borbála flipped open her ever-present notebook. "I heard that you were attacked by a praetherian in the park this Sunday past. Is that true?"

While this was true, it was not a story I wanted the press to run with. I did not think the actions of one rogue praetherian reflected the praetheria as a whole. "It was a misunderstanding."

She lifted one eyebrow and scrawled something. "A misunderstanding that required you to be rescued?"

"Why does it matter? I'm safe, and the misunderstanding was resolved."

"It matters because an entire Congress of nations has gathered to decide how the praetheria are to be treated, and we know next to nothing about them—their habits, their goals, their own laws and customs. It's the job of journalists to know these things, to keep governments in check when they may be on the verge of a catastrophic mistake."

"They're not dangerous," I said, ignoring the small prick of conscience at the mild lie. "At least, most of them are not."

"I'm inclined to agree with you. But I don't think we can do justly by the praetheria or by ourselves until we understand whom we are dealing with. I am still hoping to speak with your gold-eyed friend from the lecture."

"Hunger?"

"That's the one." The scrawling pen stopped, and she looked at me, her dark eyes piercing. "Curious how the praetheria seem to trust you. It begs a question: how has a well-bred young lady earned their trust?"

That line of questioning might lead to other, more dangerous questions. I settled for another partial truth and a diversion. "Perhaps because they saw me during the fighting in Buda-Pest. Are you familiar with the poet Petőfi Sándor?"

She brushed aside the diversion. "I doubt that is it. They say Zrínyi Pál, the Hungarian with the Russian delegation, is your uncle. They say also that he's the most likely suspect for the broken Binding spell. Perhaps they respect you for that connection?"

I let out a tiny puff of relief. If she thought the question of the Binding settled, she would not interrogate me on it. "That seems likely. Can you tell me something? If the Binding was so important, why has nothing happened to my uncle? Why is he still at liberty in Vienna?"

"The tsar has cast his protection over your uncle, and no

one is willing to risk offending the tsar. Yet. Your uncle plays a dangerous game in coming here—if he should lose that shield, I would not for the world wish to be in his shoes. Without the tsar's protection, Viennese society will eviscerate him."

I shivered, pressing my hands into my skirt.

"I beg your pardon," Borbála said. "That cannot be pleasant to hear. I meant to tell you I heard your speech at the Congress the other day. I thought you spoke well."

"Thank you," I said. "But it doesn't matter. No one else seemed to heed me."

"Speaking your truth always matters. Don't be afraid to be different—sometimes those very differences are what lend your voice strength."

X

Catherine was not impressed at arriving home to find the broken mirror. It had been one of her bridal gifts. When I pointed out that the maid had already been in to clean up the broken shards, her brows knit together.

"I am not worried about that," she said. "I am more concerned about the impulse behind its breaking. Was this your work?"

"I'm sorry. It was accidental."

"How?"

"I was practicing magic. . . ." I saw at once that this was the wrong thing to say.

Catherine shook her head. "You have no powers: you are Barren, remember? And Mama forbade you—"

"Mama is not here!" I said, anger coiling in my gut.

"And she was wrong. I am not Barren. If I were, I could not break spells. And that, dear Catherine, you know I do rather well."

Catherine flushed red. "It's not kind of you to remind me. But that was only a fluke. If you truly had power, I'd have seen other evidences of it."

"I am *chimera*, Catherine." Rage made me incautious: I only wanted to shock her. "I have two souls. And I can break spells greater than even you can cast."

I stopped, clapping a hand to my mouth before I could tell Catherine any more damning facts. I had nearly told her about the Binding. I had already told her too much.

Her eyes were wide. "Chimera?" One hand fluttered down to her stomach. "Are you dangerous?"

At once the anger whooshed out of me. "Not dangerous. Not on purpose, in any case." I brushed past my open-mouthed sister and fled to my room.

In all the years we had lived together, I had seen many things in Catherine's eyes: anger, disappointment, irritation, hurt, and betrayal. But never fear.

But just then my sister's face had mirrored the expression she had worn when the praetherian had been shot at the ball: the look of someone confronting an unimagined monster.

I hurled myself onto my bed and wrapped my arms tight around my torso. *Was* I a monster?

Being chimera did not automatically make one monstrous, no more than being born praetherian. One's birth was not a *geas*—it was not a curse that predetermined one's fate or one's choices. Actions, not soul (or souls) or physical makeup, made one a monster.

But.

My ankle throbbed with remembered pain, and I saw again the creature in Prater Park, sucking me slowly into the ground. Vasilisa's still face after I attacked her flashed through my mind. Beings who were not innately evil could still be destructive, myself no less than the wood creature.

Catherine's broken debut spell, Gábor's niece, the spell Pál had cast against the Romanies, all the lives lost in the wake of the broken Binding (Grandmama, Mátyás, Herr Steinberg, others I could not name)—all my responsibility for a gift both terrible and great. I still didn't know how to process everything, how to separate the good I had done from the hurt I had caused.

Vasilisa had shown me I needed greater control over my ability, even if I chose not to use it. But what price would I be asked to pay?

CHAPTER 16

The footman pushed open the door of a salon wallpapered with pale green and white stripes, deeper green furniture sprinkled across the room. As he announced my name, my heart lifted—I had missed my unguarded conversations with Noémi, and Catherine's agreeing to set me down at the Eszterházy palace while she completed some errands was an unlooked-for gift.

I stepped onto the threshold—and stopped.

Noémi wasn't alone.

But she wasn't sitting with her intimidating aunt, the princess Maria Theresia Eszterházy, who had been one of the formidable patronesses of Almack's in London thirty years earlier, or with her cousin Miklós's English wife, Lady Sarah, or even one of the small grandchildren.

No, the eyes fixed on Noémi gleamed gold in the morning light, and the low laugh that rang out reverberated in my bones. A maid sat sewing in a corner, but I scarcely marked her.

"Noémi," I said.

Noémi jerked upright as if shot. Hunger merely uncoiled himself from the settee and smiled at me. "Good to see you too, Anna Arden."

"What are you doing here?"

"Must I have some ulterior motive to want to spend time with a beautiful, amiable woman?"

"Yes," I said.

"That's unfair, Anna," Noémi said. "I asked him to call on me."

My body flushed, then went cold. "Please tell me you didn't ask any favors of him."

Noémi wouldn't look at me. I glared at Hunger, who returned his most limpid look.

Hunger plucked up his top hat. "I've overstayed my welcome. I wish you good day, Miss Noémi. Anna."

He lingered on my name, as if he enjoyed the feel of it in his mouth. Blood burned up my cheeks, and I cursed him in my head. "Good day."

Noémi rose with him, pressing one of his hands in both of hers. "Thank you. For coming today. For listening to me."

"The pleasure," he said, "was all mine."

I took the place Hunger had vacated on the green settee. Noémi sat somewhat stiffly beside me.

"What did you ask of him?"

She shrugged. "We talked, merely. He asked about my brother."

What had Hunger told her about me? About Mátyás? "And?"

"And—Anna, I love you like a sister, but I don't see that my conversation with Hunger is any of your concern. After all, you are the one who champions the praetheria. You should be pleased that I have befriended one."

"Befriend him if you will—but don't trust him. Anyway, let's not argue. It's been so long since I've had you to myself."

"Yes." Noémi fell silent, staring at a white rose drooping from a vase on a lace tablecloth. Belatedly I noticed the purple smudges under her eyes.

"Are you all right?" I asked. "Have you been dreaming again?"

"Always," she said. "Sometimes it seems to make no difference whether I'm dreaming or awake. The dreams curl up like smoke in front of my eyes, clearer than anything I see in my waking world. Mostly I dream of war: praetheria and Hungarians and Austrians all tangled together in a mass of bodies."

My skin prickled. "Do you think the dreams are visions?"

"I don't know. Do *you* dream of war?"

I squirmed. My dreams were an embarrassing mixture of humiliating moments—appearing before the Congress in only my undergarments—and, most recently, passionately kissing Gábor in a field of primroses, before being caught by the archduchess. "No."

"I saw Mátyás again," she said. "He carried a bow and a knife, and he was hunting something—rabbits, maybe—on the *puszta*. A pair of crows circled overhead. He stopped to talk to someone I could not see. He was angry." Noémi traced the lace pattern with her finger and looked at me, her spectacles gleaming. "I think the dream means something. I think he's alive. We should go look for him."

"You won't find him on the *puszta*," I said. "He's gone."

"But you can't know that. And you can't know that my dreams are just dreams unless we try." Noémi crossed her arms over her chest. "I'd not thought you lacking in courage."

"Oh," I said, laughing a little helplessly. "I'm all for wild quests. But there must be some purpose to them."

"So you won't help me? Or my brother?" Noémi stood up.

"I want to believe you," I said.

Noémi paused at the edge of the table, one fist holding up her skirts. "You want too many things, Anna. Your problem is that you don't *do* enough of them."

※

The day of the archduchess's tea dawned dull and dark, the sky heavy with sluggish clouds. But by midmorning a stiff breeze had pushed the clouds from the sky: the work, I guessed, of a master Elementalist. Even the weather dared not defy Archduchess Sophie.

Catherine's coachman delivered my sister and me to the party, held on the sprawling grounds of Schönbrunn. After leaving us at the front doors of the palace, the coachman drove around to the carriage house to wait for the end of tea. A footman in the gold-and-black livery of the Haps-burgs escorted us through the glistening halls of the palace and into the gardens beyond, where tea was set up on an emerald lawn facing the labyrinth hedges. The archduchess swept around the lawn, greeting incoming guests. She looked like a flower herself: a dark-haired iris in a slim green sheath.

Catherine smiled out across the gardens, but there was something wistful in her look that tugged at me. She exchanged pleasantries with the other young wives as they passed by, though she did not make the rounds herself. There was no ecstatic clasping of hands, no elaborate cheek kissing.

"Catherine," I asked, leaning toward her. "Are you happy here?"

"Of course I am. As you see, we're invited everywhere, and I can scarce cram another morning call into my schedule." As if to prove her point, she sprang up and glided across the grass to a group of matrons, but I had not missed the twin spots of color high in her cheeks.

Troubled, I watched her go.

A pair of young women approached me, arm in arm to emphasize their closeness, and I lost sight of Catherine. We chatted for several minutes, but I could not shake the feeling that behind their light words and compliments on my gown, I was being weighed on some invisible scale—and found wanting.

I was relieved when the tea was finally brought out on shiny carts, and I could assume my place beside Catherine at one of the small tables dotting the lawn. But before I could do more than take one bite of a delicate pastry, one of Archduchess Sophie's ladies-in-waiting was standing beside me, dipping a curtsy.

"Miss Arden, Archduchess Sophie would be honored if you would join her."

Catherine made shooing motions with her hands, so I stood and followed the lady-in-waiting.

Archduchess Sophie sat a little apart from the other women, at a small table with two place settings and a magnificent vase of creamy white flowers. I took my seat, conscious of the surreptitious glances of the other women present. The archduchess opened the conversation mildly, asking about my family's health, my impressions of the city, and the Congress.

In truth, the two sessions I had attended after that initial, volatile confrontation between Hunger and the others had been disappointing: only endless arguments without ever coming to any kind of agreement about the praetheria.

"I am . . . learning a great deal," I said cautiously.

The archduchess sipped her tea, her eyes flicking past me to settle on an ordered grove of trees. She set her cup back on its saucer. "I find I am fascinated by illusions, the way a trick of light or shape can change one's impressions. At a ball, illusions can transport one to another world—or at least, hide one's mundane reality. In politics, illusions can allow one to wield power without appearing to—or encourage a precarious peace to flourish."

When I didn't answer, she sighed, as though I had some-how disappointed her.

"You are too direct, Miss Arden. You seek to blunder

through and force change where a more subtle hand might be needed. Take my son, for instance. He very much admires you."

Heat rushed through my face, and I grabbed my teacup with more energy than was strictly necessary. Had Franz Joseph set his mother up to this? I hoped not: I could not like a man whose mother did his courting for him.

The archduchess continued. "I trust I do not offend you when I say that, as a mother, I was initially dismayed by his interest. For one, he is much too young to be thinking of marriage. For another, I had hoped that when the time came, he might settle on one of my sister's daughters. But no matter. As I thought on it, I began to see the advantages of such an alliance."

I nearly choked on my tea.

"You must know that appearances are deceptive. For all the illusions of peace presented by the Congress, we are nearly at war. Tsar Nicholas professes friendship to my uncle and my son, but he would be ready enough to turn our weakness to his advantage. And even as we speak, armies are massing in Croatia and in Romania, ready to turn on Hungary."

Mátyás is dead; justice is gone. If my world dissolved into war, what was Mátyás's death worth? We had broken the Binding to prevent a rebellion from escalating into greater violence. "Can't the emperor simply tell them not to fight? Hungary is still a state under the Austrian Empire, and Croatia and Romania profess allegiance to the Hapsburg crown."

"If only women ruled the world, it would be easy, would

it not? We would resolve things civilly, over tea. But how can you tell an angry people not to fight? Would your student friends have stopped at a word?"

Despite the tea and the warm spring morning, I shivered.

"Don't look so dismayed," Archduchess Sophie said. "There *is* something you can do. The Hungarians adore you, and you belong to one of their highest families. Now, more than ever, Austria and Hungary need to present a united front. If you allow my son to court you, the hope of a nearer alliance between our countries might quiet some of the louder critics. And that same alliance would make the Croatians hesitate to attack. Their quarrel is with Hungary, not with us."

I plucked at my own napkin, smoothing it across my knees. "I do not know how to answer you. I *want* to help. But I cannot lie, or pretend an interest I do not feel. Your son is lovely, but I've no wish to be empress."

"Perhaps you prefer a Romani tent?"

My head shot up. There was no anger in the archduchess's face, but I was afraid nonetheless.

"There is very little I do not know about you, Miss Arden. I know about your friend, the one who works for Kossuth. I know your brother-in-law's career is new and still fragile. The smallest breath of scandal could hurt all of you. Think of the distress to your sister—not to mention yourself—if you were to be cast out of proper society."

The fragrance from the cut flowers on the table was overwhelming. I could not seem to draw enough breath. "I am not afraid of your threats."

189

Archduchess Sophie laughed. "The young are so charmingly naive. They still believe that weapons are the only ways to hurt people. But I'm hardly threatening you. I'm merely giving you information you might find valuable. If you'll recall, we began this conversation speaking of illusions: I do not care what your true feelings are, but if you value stability between Austria and Hungary, I suggest you do what you can to maintain it. You may start by encouraging my son."

A warmth began to buzz through me, washing from my face down my spine.

The archduchess held my eyes with hers, unblinking. "Think how very wise you should be to listen to me. A little pretense, harming no one, and you might save three countries from war."

She was right, of course. And she asked such a little thing. . . .

The buzzing grew louder in my head. My shadow self twitched uneasily, and I blinked, breaking our eye contact.

The buzzing—the subtle but persistent indication of a spell.

The archduchess hadn't sought to persuade me with words alone, she was trying to *charm* my agreement.

"It would be best for everyone, don't you agree?" the archduchess asked.

I won't be compelled. My shadow self swooped up, trailing sparks of anger. Without a thought to the consequences, I reached out for the thin line of her spell and snapped it. The residue from the spell washed over the flowers. Creeping brown stained the edges of the white blossoms.

Archduchess Sophie's eyes widened. Her nostrils flared almost imperceptibly, and cold shot through my spine. I had been incautious. I ought to have resisted the spell, not broken it. If the archduchess had not already known I broke spells, she knew now.

My teacup rattled as I replaced it. "I will think on your offer. May I be excused to return to my sister?"

The archduchess nodded shortly, her lips tight. I fairly fled across the lawn, dropping back into my seat beside Catherine with considerable relief.

"Anna," Catherine sighed. "You were not shocking, were you?"

I was not sure who had been more shocked: the archduchess or me. Catherine eyed me doubtfully but let me return to my tea and cake, dense layers of chocolate and apricot jam. The sweet cake was bitter on my tongue, and my pulse still thundered through my body.

As soon as politeness allowed, Catherine and I took our leave, following another liveried footman back through the halls to the front door. Just as we reached the entrance, Franz Joseph emerged from a nearby salon so promptly I suspected he had been watching for us.

"Miss Arden!" The young archduke's face lit up. If he was playacting at his mother's insistence, he was very good. "I'm so glad I was able to catch you before you left. I hoped I might escort you home."

"My sister . . . ," I began, and Catherine pinched me. "That is, we'd be delighted for your escort."

Catherine and I climbed into the carriage, waited as a groom brought a horse around for the archduke, and then proceeded back to the heart of Vienna. Franz Joseph rode beside the open carriage.

"I trust you enjoyed your tea?"

"Oh yes. The pastries and cake were remarkable." I smothered a laugh at Catherine's relieved expression. What did she think I would say? That I found his mother terrifying?

He bowed a little. "I'll convey your compliments to the kitchen."

A snarl in the traffic took his attention away for a moment as he navigated his mount around a stopped cart. He turned back to me.

"I wish you would tell me more about your family. I should like to know everything about you."

I fought the urge to glance at Catherine, who was pretending to be engrossed in the scenery on the other side of the carriage. Flirting lost all its charm under my sister's observation.

I told him about my childhood, riding horses and watching birds in Dorset. I told him about James, who was finding his place as a scholar at Eton. Franz Joseph listened with a quiet intensity that I liked, and then he told me of his own childhood, riding and hunting in Tirol in the fall, falling asleep to orchestral music during summers at Schönbrunn.

It should not be so easy to like a man who would someday be emperor. Particularly when his mother knew enough to ruin me.

)X(

A small, silk-wrapped parcel lay on my pillow when I reached my room. I untied the ribbon and the silk fell away to reveal a small wooden stork, painstakingly carved and painted, its great wings raised. I ran one finger along the wings, flooded by a warm rush of memories: storks circling the woods near Eszterháza, the toneless clatter of their call as dusk fell.

Hungary.

Home.

I picked up the small card accompanying the carving.

Every wish for joy and happiness on your birthday—Gábor

In the excitement over the archduchess's tea, my birthday had been completely eclipsed. Only Gábor remembered.

I held the card tight between my fingers and forgot about the archduke's flattery and his mother's threats. I thought only of Gábor: I had to see him again.

CHAPTER 17

The gates of the Hofburg were already thronged with people when Catherine and I arrived, three hours before the start of the famed Corpus Christi procession. The day had dawned clear and bright, and the sun now beating upon my head was unrelenting. The day could not have dawned otherwise, as the procession, dubbed "God's Court Ball" by the elite Viennese, was perhaps *the* event of the social season, even more so with the Congress in session.

I did not entirely understand the fuss, but Richard assured us that the imperial family took the holiday very seriously—everyone who was anyone was expected to attend.

Despite the deflating influence of the heat and the crowd, my heart expanded like a hot-air balloon. It was not so much the parade I anticipated (though that promised to be splendid), but the aftermath. Thanks to Catherine's close watch, I had not been able to speak with Gábor in the past two weeks, but surely I could slip away for a few moments in the commotion of the procession. Two days earlier, Ginny had taken my carefully worded note to the Hungarian embassy and returned with Gábor's answer. He would meet me after the parade, in the Burggarten behind the imperial residence. He thought it likely that he could gain entrance to the Hofburg with other members of the Hungarian embassy.

The palace was closed to those without tickets; in another hour, the gates would be locked to everyone. After waiting in a brief line, Catherine handed our tickets to a guard, and then a footman led us through an immense atrium and up several flights of stairs to a richly ornamented salon overlooking the street below.

Catherine dropped onto a gold-and-white-striped sofa, pulling a fan from her reticule. The June afternoon was close and sultry, and only a thin breeze stirred the heavy crimson curtains near the open window.

There were others in the room with us, courtiers I recognized from various social events but was not on speaking terms with. I sat down beside Catherine to wait, anxiety making me sweat even more than the day's heat. What if I were not able to slip away? What if Gábor were denied entrance, despite Kossuth's patronage?

I took a deep breath, wiping my clammy hands on my skirt. It would work. And if it did not, we would simply have to try again.

Servants circulated through the room, bearing trays with tea and light refreshments. A murmur of conversation rose around us.

"And your cousin's friend was held up, in broad daylight?"

one of the young ladies asked her neighbor, fingering a glossy chestnut ringlet. "How perfectly terrifying."

The other girl, with drooping yellow hair and a drooping mouth, nodded. "By a magician, no less! The highwayman called himself the King of Crows and spoke, my cousin says, like a Luminate born and bred."

"Nonsense." The blonde's companion, a narrow older woman, took a precise bite of cake. "Not all magicians are Luminate these days. Not since that mess with the Binding. Doubtless just some brigand with a bit of magic."

The brunette said, "I could fancy being stopped by a dashing Hungarian highwayman."

I smiled a little. I could fancy that too.

"If he's a highwayman, he's likely to be middle-aged and dirty," the companion said, and both girls sighed, disappointed.

A maid stopped beside me, and I waved her on. I could not bear to eat anything. She bobbed a curtsy. "Beg pardon, miss, but I've a note for you."

She dropped a small square card in my hands, and my fingers fumbled with the seal. Gábor must have sent further instructions for me.

But the handwriting was not Gábor's at all.

My compliments to you and your sister. I hope your viewing accommodations are comfortable. If you should find yourself in need of anything, you have only to ask. If it is not too great an inconvenience, I should like to convey my compliments in person following the processional. —Franz Joseph

I pinched the card tight between my fingers. How was I to find Gábor and still be present after the processional?

With any luck, Franz Joseph's high position would delay him.

Catherine arched her eyebrows at me, questioning. I folded up the note and tucked it into my reticule. "The archduke sends his compliments," I said.

After a lengthy wait, the processional began. Musicians, priests, court chamberlains and dignitaries, privy counselors and court nobility paraded before us—Catherine pointed to a very smug Richard. Everything gleamed and sparkled: jewels sewn into collars, gold threads, the richest clothes the courtiers possessed.

The Russian delegation, including Count Svarog and my uncle, marched down the street, followed by Tsar Nicholas in military uniform, a red coat with gold decorations and white breeches. As I watched, Pál lifted a hand in salute to my window, though he could not possibly have seen me. The hair on my arms lifted.

The Russian soldiers just behind the embassy delegates, marching six by six, began to shimmer oddly, as though a fog had settled on them. Or an illusion . . .

When the shimmering resolved itself, it was not soldiers who marched in the street below, but praetheria, in six neat lines. The bells most of them wore jangled in the air.

Catherine gasped. Similar cries of alarm echoed around the salon. In the street below, the crowd shifted, stirred by some strong feeling.

Vasilisa glided at their head, a crown of gold laurel leaves on her hair. Hunger marched beside her, resplendent in black lined with gold. The others I did not recognize, but they too glittered in ways that outshone the Austrian court:

light played across hair and fur and feathers, one creature wore a coat of frost and diamond-bright ice, another wore a tunic fashioned entirely of iridescent feathers.

A line of Russian soldiers followed them, making it clear that the praetheria were an invited part of the Russian delegation, even if their participation had been hidden until they reached the palace.

Furious whispers erupted across the room.

The praetheria passed out of sight, but the jubilant air that had hung over the procession was gone. I did not know what the appearance of the praetheria in league with Russia (and my uncle) betokened, but it could not be good, for the Congress or for the praetheria.

The last of the court nobility marched down the street, and the archdukes appeared. Even at this distance, Franz Joseph stood out from the crowd. Behind the archdukes came the golden baldachin, followed by the emperor himself, hatless in a sign of humility. The emperor's guard marched behind him, then the royal ladies of the court. But the glitter and glamour that might have impressed me earlier was spoiled by a vague sense of disquiet.

As soon as the emperor was out of sight, I turned to Catherine. "I don't feel well. I just need a bit of fresh air. I'll nip down to the gardens and be back directly."

Catherine looked dubious. "I'll come with you."

She could not at any cost come with me.

Before I could say anything, my sister stood in a fluid movement but spoiled the effect by grasping the back of her chair.

"Are you all right?" I peered at her more closely. She

seemed pale. "Maybe you should stay here and rest. I won't be long."

Catherine dropped back into her seat with a long sigh. "Very well."

Feeling only slightly guilty about leaving Catherine, I made my way down the stairs and, after asking a passing footman for directions, to the imperial gardens.

I did not see Gábor at once and wasted a few precious minutes hunting around the flower beds. Then he stepped out of the shadows beneath a tree.

He wore a fine lawn shirt beneath a silver-embroidered dolman, and my heart lifted, a balloon buoyed by warmth and joy. I raced toward him as fast as my dainty high-heeled shoes would allow.

"I have missed you," Gábor said, by way of greeting.

"And I, you," I said, taking the hands he held out to me and drawing him back into the shadows. No sense in making it easy to be seen.

For a long moment we said nothing, only looked at one another. His eyes traced over my face as though memorizing it. My gaze dropped from his dark eyes to his lips, then back up again. Though his face was nearly as well-known to me as my own, I never tired of seeing it. I wanted him to kiss me, but we hadn't much time, and Gábor would not rush this.

So I leaned in, and Gábor, releasing a tiny sigh, bent to meet me.

His lips were warm and familiar, but there was nothing particularly *safe* about this kiss. Heat burst through me with mingled excitement and a painful sweetness. The kiss deepened, his tongue brushing lightly against the tip of mine, his hands tightening against my back. I ran my fingers up the embroidery on his sleeves before tangling them in his hair, feeling his warmth even through my gloves.

I could have stayed there forever, in a cocoon of kissing and murmured endearments, but I did not know how much time we had. Catherine would surely send a servant for me as soon as the archduke showed up.

I pulled away, conscious of a throbbing in my lips, and asked, "Were you able to see the processional?" As though this were an ordinary moment, a conversation between mere acquaintances and not two people who had been intimately wrapped up in one another only moments before.

"Some," he said, curling his fingers around mine. "Those of us who were not in the processional were crammed into a servant's room with only a single window and an angled view on the street."

I thought of the well-appointed salon I had sat in, attended by servants, and felt a pang of guilt and frustration. Why was society so intent on maintaining its social hierarchies?

Gábor continued. "The others were not happy about the praetherian presence—they believe Russia is building toward some independent action, regardless of the Congress."

"What do you believe?"

He sighed and released one of my hands, shoving his fingers through his hair. "I don't know. Every time I approach certainty, I find myself with more questions. I think I told you that Kossuth wanted me to speak with Dr. Helmholz?"

I nodded.

"I have been assisting the doctor a little, with his research, when Kossuth can spare me. Mostly writing out his results in a legible hand, but also learning more of scientific methods. I don't believe Congress can deal with the praetheria unless they understand them."

"Must they be 'dealt with'? Can't they simply live among us?"

"I don't know. I wish I could believe, as you do, that the praetheria are not dangerous. But I saw the aftermath of that battle in Buda. The creatures make dangerous enemies."

"We *make* enemies of them when we treat them so poorly."

Gábor rubbed his thumb against the back of my hand almost absently. "I don't disagree. And I don't mean to argue with you. Only, some of Dr. Helmholz's results are troubling, and I cannot be certain of his methods. I think his research may not be entirely ethical. He refuses to let me into his laboratory."

"Have you told Kossuth?"

"I've tried. But Kossuth doesn't want to introduce further complications when the Congress is already so fraught."

I knew I should feel troubled that Gábor was so worried about the doctor's research, and a part of me was, but a greater part of me was singing. That Gábor, always so careful of his thoughts and feelings, should share with me meant he trusted me—and that trust meant more than an open declaration from most men. "If it disturbs you, I know someone who might be able to discover more," I said, thinking of Borbála Dobos.

"Thank you," Gábor said. He tucked my arm through his and smiled down at me. "And you? Are you well?"

I thought fleetingly of the archduke coming to meet me in the salon where Catherine waited. I could give Gábor a quick answer and make my way back upstairs. That was, no doubt, what I ought to do. But I wanted to return his trust with my own, and anyway, I'd rather be in the gardens with Gábor than any number of fine rooms with any number of archdukes.

"I'm afraid," I said. "I worry that the Congress will shut away the praetheria, that Hungary will be engulfed by a civil war, and that everything we fought for, that Mátyás died for, will be lost." Gábor slid his arm around me, and I leaned into his shoulder, finding comfort in the steady *thump-thump* of his heart. Already, the anxieties of the past week sloughed away, and I had the curious sense that the world was righting, after spinning awry on its axis for a very long time. This is why my heart kept returning to Gábor, despite our disagreements—because when I was with him I felt stronger, more sure of myself, than when I was alone.

"I know now why I break spells. I am chimera. I have two souls, and those souls rupture charms. But I still don't understand my abilities. If I'm honest, they frighten me. I cannot control the degree of destruction I unleash."

Gábor was silent for a moment, but his silence was not judging. His eyes were gentle, thoughtful, and I loved him for listening, for not rushing to find me a solution or to talk over my fears. "I would not want anyone, least of all you, to fear who they are. Your powers may be destructive, but *you* are not."

"I wish I could be so certain."

"I wish I could give you some of my faith." He hesitated. "You don't have to save everyone, you know."

I thought of the praetherian, shot dead in the ballroom, of the horrible helplessness that had gripped me. "Someone has to try."

He shook his head. "Most people don't want someone to save them. They want the resources to save themselves. You shouldn't assume responsibility for people who haven't asked it of you—no one can bear that weight." He dropped a kiss on my hair. "Not even you."

From anyone else, I might have felt patronized. But all I felt from Gábor was a vast well of concern. I shifted, turning toward him and raising my face for another kiss.

"Miss Arden?" Franz Joseph's voice rang through the garden, and I broke away from Gábor, my cheeks burning. I stepped forward into the light beyond the trees, Gábor close behind me. The archduke scurried toward us. "There you are! Your sister said you were not feeling well?"

"The room was a little close," I said, conscious of Gábor watching me, a question in his dark eyes.

"I beg your pardon," the archduke said, registering Gábor behind me and drawing up his chin. "I did not know you were with someone."

"A friend from the Hungarian delegation, here to see the processional. He was in the gardens when I came down,"

I said, wondering if my hair was still neat or if I looked as though I'd been illicitly kissing someone. Which, of course, I had—but while being well-kissed was delightful, *appearing* to be well-kissed was disgraceful. "Kovács Gábor."

Gábor bowed, then murmured his excuses. I fought the urge to watch him walk away and turned my attention to Franz Joseph. The archduke took my gloved hands in his, kissing each in turn. His military costume was nearly overwhelming this close, the high collar encrusted with gold and glittering medallions at his breast.

I waited. The archduke had not yet released my hands, and his fingers tightened around mine as though he were agitated. I was suddenly very conscious that we were essentially alone and wished I could pull my hands back.

"I do not quite know what to say." Color flooded the archduke's face. In that moment he appeared much younger than his eighteen years, and I lost some of my nerves. "When I sent my note earlier, I only wanted to see you for a moment. But now . . . You saw the parade, did you not? And the Russian delegation?"

I nodded.

"There is so much unrest in my country. The common people in Vienna are restless, wanting freedoms we cannot give them. Croatia and Romania pull at their leash, wanting to be free of Hungary, perhaps of the empire itself. Hungary has already broken most of her old ties. The empire is not what it once was—and now this. If the praetheria do indeed throw their lot in with Russia, we cannot withstand that army."

My heart recognized the look on his face—that aching sense of responsibility. *You don't have to save everyone.* "The unrest affects all of us. May the Congress have the wisdom to guide us."

Franz Joseph shook his head, one brown curl falling over his brow. "I don't know if the Congress can act soon enough—and there are too many competing interests and alliances. Hungary sides with Britain and Poland, the Ottomans want to preserve their neutrality, and the German states, though ostensibly on Austria's side, are not strong enough to support us. France is on the verge of its own civil war, and the Italians hate us for what we did in Lombardy."

"Surely if it came to war, Hungary would side with you? We are still part of the empire. And Britain cannot want to see a stronger Russia."

"Perhaps. I don't know. All I know is that I must do *something.* I have a proposition for you. You are well-respected in Hungary, and the common folk here see you as something of a people's hero. More than that, the praetheria seem to like you. I believe if I were to align my fate with yours—that is, if we were to marry—it would calm much of this unrest. At the least, an engagement would buy us time to find a peaceable solution."

I fell back a step in astonishment, my blush rising to meet his, and the archduke released my hands at last. An actual marriage had played no part in his mother's talk of illusions. "You want to marry me? Surely this is not what your mother wants for you."

"She has encouraged me to seek you out, though she

does not know I am here now. But I have thought a great deal about this and have concluded it would be good for my country—and for me. The Russian actions today only confirmed my inclination. You are everything I should like in a wife: intelligent, spirited, passionate about justice."

"But you do not love me."

His blue eyes met mine, unwavering. "I esteem you greatly. And I have not ever expected to marry for love."

Gábor. My heart pinged. I knew it was not common among my class, but I *had* hoped to marry for love. Much as I liked the archduke, I did not love him. I could not marry him.

Not even for a kingdom? I might be an archduchess—an empress, even.

My chimera self stirred, responding to possibility. A part of me should like that very much. Too much.

Not even to stop a war? Was it selfish to want to marry for love, if not doing so could prevent a catastrophe? Surely there were other ways to avert war.

Franz Joseph stepped closer. "Miss Arden—may I call you Anna? I—" He broke off, scanning my face with curious intensity.

He dipped his head toward me, and I registered his intention too late to forestall him. I turned my head, and his kiss landed on my cheek: a butterfly-soft touch of flesh on flesh.

The archduke drew back, his face scarlet, his hands falling to his sides. "I'm sorry. That wasn't—I mean, I didn't—"

His incoherence touched me. Had he ever kissed a girl before?

"You don't need to apologize, Your Highness. You do me honor."

A spark lit his eyes. He looked as though he might attempt another kiss. I held up my hand. "But I do not think now is the time or place."

Franz Joseph glanced around the garden as though belatedly recalling where we were. "You're right, of course," he said with dignity, as though I were not the worst kind of hypocrite for kissing Gábor in the garden and then implying it was bad manners for the archduke to attempt to do the same. "I have shocked you. Please don't answer now— think on my offer. Together, we might stop a war."

I nodded, not trusting myself to speak. I could not possibly say yes, not with the memory of Gábor's kisses so fresh on my lips—but I could not bring myself to say no either.

CHAPTER 18

Catherine was waiting for me at the edge of the garden. My body flushed hot and then cold. How much had she seen? How much had she heard? She did not seem particularly elated, so she could not have heard the archduke's proposal. I allowed my stiff shoulders to relax a fraction.

Then she spoke. "I saw you, Anna. I came down with the archduke, but he asked that I grant him privacy to speak with you. I saw that boy."

"He has a name. Gábor."

"And who is his family? What are his prospects? An *archduke* is interested in you. You have opportunities now that I—that most women—would be overjoyed to have. Do not throw this away because you think you might be in love. That love will be cold comfort when you find society closed to you and you struggle to make ends meet."

I had no good answer for her, not when my heart and

head were currently warring over Franz Joseph's surprise proposal. I knew what I wished to do, and what society would say I ought to do. But which of those two things was right?

When I didn't answer, Catherine threw up her arms. "If you won't look after your interests, I must. Mama left you to my care. Until I've had a chance to consult with her, you will stay home."

"Am I to be barred from everything? What of the Congress?"

Catherine pressed her lips together. "Very well. Church, the Congress, outings involving the archduke." She ticked the items off on her fingers. "But nothing else."

And just like that, my world, which had seemed so expansive only moments before, contracted with a bang.

)(

The morning after the Corpus Christi parade, I sent a note to Borbála Dobos with Gábor's address, indicating that my friend knew something of Dr. Helmholz and his praetherian research that might interest her. And then I waited.

I spent the week at home, the picture of insipid young womanhood, setting dreadful stitches in my embroidery and reading torrid poetry that put me in an even more wretched mood. I rambled around the flat at all hours of the day in a vain attempt to shake the tightness from my skin. I fantasized about breaking out of the house: tying my sheets together and escaping through my window as I had once before, or climbing onto the roof from one of the tiny attic rooms where the servants had their quarters and jumping onto the neighboring building and making my escape by rooftop. I might have snuck out in earnest, but I did not want to give Catherine more ammunition without good cause. More than once it crossed my mind that if I accepted Franz Joseph, Catherine could not keep me so confined.

Evenings were punctuated by quiet family dinners, just Catherine, Richard, and myself. Most days Richard returned from the embassy looking increasingly grim.

"The Russians are talking of pulling out of the Congress and opening their borders to the praetheria," he said, spearing a bite of quail. "Ponsonby thinks it will mean war. Perhaps I should send you both back to England while I still can."

"I spoke with Mama via the embassy's mirror conduit," Catherine said, almost defiantly, as though I might question her for borrowing one of the embassy's powerful mages for such a domestic errand. She wrapped her hands across her stomach. "She thinks you should return."

I couldn't seem to swallow. "Please don't send me back. She'll marry me off to the first country squire she can find—in Yorkshire, if she can manage it. I'll never have the chance to do anything that matters."

"You'll have children," Catherine said. "And the affairs of the estate."

A slow death by stagnation, then. The children I would not mind so much, but I wanted it to be *my* choice. "Please. I know I've made a mull of things. But what is happening here with the Congress matters. I want to be part of that. I want to be something for myself before I have to be everything for a husband, for children. Surely you can understand that?"

Catherine went very still.

"If it matters to her so much, surely we can afford her another chance," Richard said, and for the first time I could see why Catherine might have wanted to marry him. I could have kissed him myself. "Besides, I don't think the archduke would like it if you took Anna away so soon."

Catherine sighed. "Very well. But *one* more mistake, Anna . . . I want your word you will be careful."

"You have it," I said.

Anything was better than going back to England. If I crossed my fingers in my lap, I took care to do so where Catherine could not see me.

Ж

Ginny brought me a note the next morning: it had been given to her by a boy on the street as she emerged from the archduchess's school. My name was scrawled across the front in Gábor's writing. I snatched the note from her and buried it in a small pocket in my skirts.

"Did you tell Catherine?"

Ginny moved past me to plump the pillows and smooth the counterpane on my bed. "And have I worked for you these six years and more without you learning this about me? I don't tell tales, Miss Anna."

I ducked my head, chagrined. "I know. Truly, I do. It's just—this confinement is fraying my last nerves."

Ginny looked at me with some sympathy. "Your sister only wants your happiness. She just believes it will come in a different form than you do."

"I wish she would trust me to know my own mind."

"And do you?"

I brushed her question aside. "How are your lessons?"

Ginny's eyes brightened, and she launched into an explanation of what she had been learning, ending with a small demonstration of a new light illusion that sent daisies sprouting across my room. "It's wonderful to belong to something, miss, something bigger than what I do here. *You* know that. It's like a bit of wine, it is. Makes you feel warm and strong together."

"Yes," I said, wondering what else Ginny was learning at this school of hers. It struck me that Ginny's life would not always be intertwined with mine: magicians were in high demand. She would be a fool, when her schooling ended, to stay as a lady's maid. I knew I should be happy for her, for the opportunity it afforded, but as Ginny bundled up a dress of mine for brushing and bustled out, I already felt the cold of her absence.

I shook myself and fished out Gábor's letter, retreating to my window seat for better light.

Thank you for sending Fräulein Dobos to me. She has been both sympathetic and helpful, though I cannot say that what we have learned has eased my conscience any. I hope to tell you more of what we learned when next we meet. Yours, Gábor

I read the letter again, searching for—I'm not certain. Some words of love, perhaps, rather than gratitude. I read the signature over and over, tracing my finger over the *Yours,* wondering if Gábor meant it, or if it were simply a conventional closure. I had not spoken to him since Franz Joseph had interrupted him, and I could not help torturing myself with imagining he had witnessed our conversation just as Catherine had. What did his brevity mean here—that he was simply busy, or that he was trying to put some distance between us?

X

Sunday evening, after a brief reprieve from my confinement to attend church, I had just drifted off to sleep when I was awakened by a loud crack against my window. I lay blinking for a moment, trying to ascertain *what* I had heard, when a second crack sounded. I stumbled out of bed to the window, which faced the mews behind the town house.

A pale face floated in the darkness just beyond the window. After the initial shock faded—was I still dreaming?—I recognized the face as Vasilisa's and wrenched the window open. Oddly, it did not occur to me to wonder how she was flying: it seemed a perfectly reasonable thing for her to do.

"I need you to come with me," she said without preamble, "as witness."

I gaped at her, my mind still slurred by sleep.

"Do not stand there looking witless. Come!" This last was said with an imperious hand thrust at me. Vasilisa was not wearing bells tonight either.

I glanced down at the narrow street below my second-story window. "I can't fly."

"Then it's lucky I can. Come!"

213

"Where?"

"I must show you something. It is a matter of life and death to us."

Something in her urgent voice tugged at me. "I'm in my nightclothes." A more formidable challenge presented itself: "And my sister should flail me alive if I left the house right now."

A spark lit Vasilisa's eyes. "No, would she?"

"I mean, not literally, but she would send me—"

Vasilisa lost interest in Catherine. She flapped her hands at me. "Go and put clothing on, then come."

A powerful burning lit me. I had been confined to the house too long—I only needed a cause worth risking Catherine's wrath. I stripped off my nightdress and pulled on an older frock. Vasilisa slipped a small stone bowl into her pocket—it looked like a mortar and pestle—and drifted into the room to help me fasten the hard-to-reach buttons at the middle of my back. I tried not to shudder when her cold fingers brushed against my spine, lingering a beat or two longer than was necessary.

I followed Vasilisa to the window. She stepped onto the sill and I followed, crouching on the frame beside her. She grabbed my hand, and we stepped forward into the air.

My stomach floated up as we dropped. I imagined Catherine's shocked expression as the servants were called to scrape my broken body from the road. Then Vasilisa hauled me up behind her, with a strength I had not known she possessed. She wrapped my numb arms around her waist, and we flew through the warm summer air over the silent streets of Vienna, past the shuttered stores of the shopping district, over fountains glimmering in the half-moon light. St. Stephen's Cathedral kept quiet watch in the distance.

After the first rush of fear, I forgot myself in wonder, watching the miniature streets flash past, feeling myself in a fairy story. An old, remembered longing surfaced: the powerful ache I'd felt after seeing the world of the Binding for the first time. Hunger had shown me that world; now Vasilisa, Vienna.

She set us down in an unremarkable street: a glance around the dimly lit space disclosed a series of darkened shops, a few medical establishments. Two figures waited beside an unmarked door: Borbála Dobos—and Gábor. My heart began thumping, and not simply with anxiety at being dragged from my bed and flown across the city.

Vasilisa lifted her hand, and a pale light illuminated the door. She set her hand against the wood, and the lock clicked; then the door swung open.

"What is this place?" I asked.

"Dr. Helmholz's laboratory," Gábor said.

"Come," Vasilisa said. "You three must witness this for me. The Congress will not believe the report of a praetherian."

I followed her into the lab, wondering what the penalty was for breaking and entering. Suppose someone caught us?

Gábor slipped beside me and took my hand. I clutched it, grateful both for the warmth of his presence and for the reassurance that whatever I had been reading into his silences was the product of my own fevered imagination.

"What are we doing here?" I asked as the door swung shut behind us.

"You'll see," Borbála said, her voice grim. "We think the doctor has been going outside the law in his research."

Vasilisa kindled a small light for us to see by. Her eyes glittered as she led the way deeper into the lab.

In the front were several small rooms: a stale and stuffy sitting room with empty teacups still resting in a ring on a low table; a couple of rooms buried in paper and diagrams, books stacked haphazardly upon every surface. No wonder Dr. Helmholz had needed Gábor's assistance: his writing was atrocious.

At the end of a narrow hallway, we found a larger, much tidier room that smelled strongly of lye. A pair of plain tables marched down the center. Closed cabinets lined the walls, and an assortment of glass beakers and vials occupied the shelves above the cabinets. Some undercurrent in the air pricked my nose; even without being able to identify it, the smell set my teeth on edge.

Vasilisa frowned at the work space and stomped back down the hallway to the nearest office, sifting through the documents until they snowed down around her in a paper blizzard. Gábor and I followed. The pages settled on the floor in drifts: nearly illegible scrawls in German, a half-finished drawing of a gnome, a more polished sketch of a vila that made me blush. I could not tell, from the pictures, whether Dr. Helmholz pursued his study of the praetheria because he despised them—or desired them. But some strong emotion had prompted the dark lines scoring the paper, nearly tearing it through in spots.

"Bah," Vasilisa said, dropping another sketch, this time of a creature of beast aspect, heavy lips curled back to reveal scimitar teeth. "I should burn this place down, but then we would not find what we seek."

"I think there is another door, in the workroom," Gábor said.

Vasilisa did not respond, stalking back into the large workroom again. She began inspecting the room, opening the unlocked cabinets, pushing at the locked ones, tugging at the shelves. I feared she would overset one and rain down glass debris on us, but she did not. Gábor released my hand, and he and Borbála began tapping at the walls between the cabinets. I hovered behind them, still not entirely certain what we were looking for.

One of the cabinets groaned open at Vasilisa's tug. I jumped, and a section of the wall gave way.

The smell reached me first: strongly chemical, and underneath it a metallic note and the sickly sweetness of rot. My stomach knotted. I did *not* want to follow Vasilisa into that room. *To witness,* she had said.

"Come," she said, and the compulsion was back, tugging at my legs and my heart.

I took one step forward, then another. Half a dozen more, and I was standing on the threshold of a secret room, fighting back stinging bile in my throat. Gábor and Borbála pressed into the opening beside me.

Five tables, ordered in a line. And atop each of them a praetherian. Dead. Surgically neat incisions split them open, rib cages (or what passed for ribs) folded back to display the organs inside. Some tree-creature, with rings and cavities instead of organs. One of the light-creatures I had seen at the ball the night the praetherian was shot, its skin now dull and lightless. Its shape was androgynous, its torso narrow where it met the arms and broadening to softness above the hips. A smaller shape was laid beside it, curled around itself like a newborn kitten. A baby.

I staggered back from the doorway and fell to my knees, gagging. I knew, dimly, of unsavory scientific sorts who resorted to cadavers from grave robbers to study anatomy. But it had always seemed like a story one would tell to frighten children. This, I suspected, was much worse: where would one come upon praetherian corpses in the city? They would be difficult to find, far easier to create.

Dr. Helmholz presented his findings to the Congress. This was the man the world trusted to give them objective information about the praetheria, so they could feel justi-fied in shutting them away. He was not a scientist. He was a murderer.

Vasilisa knelt beside me, her fingers digging into my chin, her bone-pale eyes piercing mine. "Witness," she said again, insistently. A thin sheen covered her eyes— rage, or grief, I couldn't tell. I suspected both. She dragged me down the row, stopping before each of the bodies in turn. *"Witness."*

"Yes," I said.

Mátyás

CHAPTER 19

A trickle of sweat ran down my neck, itching between my shoulder blades. I fidgeted in my saddle, and Holdas snorted at me. Nearby, László shot me a look that might have killed a lesser man. I puffed out my cheeks, then released the breath slowly. A crow landed in the trees nearby and cocked its head at me. *Not now, Varjú,* I sent at it irritably. The crow had taken to following me the last morning or two, but I doubted László would approve of my new pet. The crow cawed loudly, making László flinch, before fluttering off.

We'd arrived in the copse of trees when wisps of early-morning fog still hugged the grasses. Now the only hugging being done was the infernal heat wrapping around us as the sun crested overhead. A scout had brought word just after dawn of a rich carriage lumbering our way, but it was taking an eon for it to reach us.

A new epitaph: *Here lies Eszterházy Mátyás. He couldn't wait.*

At last, like heavenly choirs singing, we heard it: the distant thudding of hooves, the dull creak of wheels.

At a signal from László, we erupted from the trees, screaming and firing pistols into the air. The horses pulling the carriage shied back. The driver swore, then threw his hands up.

László waved one of his men toward the carriage. The man yanked the door open, argued with the inhabitants, and then rode back to us, a purse fisted in each hand and a triumphant smile on his face. We returned home on a wave of energy.

That night I joined a few of the others and László in a game of twenty-one. We played at the sturdy wooden table dominating the kitchen of the farmhouse where László currently camped. As the cards began to fly beneath a flickering lantern, my blood thrummed through me. It wasn't the prospect of money, though the jangle of coins in my pockets whispered their own kind of lure. It was the game itself, the thrill of risking everything on a single card.

I downed a shot of vodka purchased by that day's spoils and thought perhaps the life of a bandit suited me after all. There was, besides the camaraderie, the thrill of riding up on a carriage—the heady sense of risk, of unknown challenges, the need to think quickly on my feet.

It was very much like gambling.

※

I woke late the next morning to a pounding skull and an eerie quiet.

I stumbled out of my bedroll and into the kitchen, where Bahadır sat alone at an empty table, reading.

"There's bread in the cupboard and tea on the stove." Bahadır's Hungarian was soft and gently accented.

"Where are the others?" I poured some tea into a green-glazed ceramic mug and lifted it to my lips.

"László sent some out scouting. Some of the others have gone to church. I believe it's Whitsunday."

A flash of memory: hurtling across the fields on Holdas to win the Whitsun King crown, Noémi's and Anna's smiling faces as I crossed the line. I'd died before I could collect on my winnings: a full year's free drink. I wished, with a furious, futile intensity, that I could be at Eszterháza again this year, riding Holdas in the race, quarrelling with the squire, teasing Noémi. I would never have that life back.

I finished my tea and a thick slab of bread, then eyed Bahadır. The morning stretched long and empty before us. "Do you know what happened to the ring you took from me?"

"László has it. I don't know where he put it."

"Hmm." I scratched my cheek, thinking. The Lady had kept me clean-shaven while I slept, but already a short beard had taken over my chin. The hairs were coarse against my fingers. "Do you play cards?"

The boy set his finger in his book to mark his place. "Not often. My faith forbids gambling." I had seen him a couple of times, early in the morning and at other times of the day, at his prayers.

"What if we play without real stakes? How does whist sound?"

Bahadır shut his book. "I know the rules. I will play you for a story."

The boy's eyes were dark, his scar livid against his cheek. He surely had stories. And me? What stories would I tell if I lost? Would I tell him how I'd flown down from the world tree, where the Lady had brought me back from death? Perhaps I'd tell him how my cousin and I split the world wide with a spell when I died.

Though the morning outside was bright, inside the farmhouse it was cool and shadowy.

My stories were not safe. My blood began humming. "For a story," I said.

⚬

I won the first several hands, and Bahadır told me his story. Or rather, he told me *one* of his stories. Even as his words spelled out one version of himself, of his life, I wondered what stories he was not telling—what other Bahadırs might coexist inside this slight, even-spoken boy.

"My father was an *ağa*, a leader of the Janissaries. Do you know them?"

I nodded. My history lessons had covered the Janissary soldiers, the magical-military arm of the Ottoman Empire. As the Islamic faith barred the practice of magic, non-Muslims (mostly Christians) with magic had been conscripted into the Janissary forces to help guard the empire against Luminate forces.

"The Janissaries were nearly abolished in 1826, after re-

224

sisting military reforms by the sultan. Cannons were fired at the barracks and thousands died. But not all of them. The sultan could not afford to destroy them completely, not with Russia looking for reasons to expand into Ottoman territory. My father was one of the men appointed to train up the new ranks, to keep them in line."

From the haunted look in his eyes, I could guess at what happened next. "He failed?"

Bahadır nodded. "He was blamed for a failed coup and executed. As his son, I was to share his punishment, but I ran." His fingers brushed the scar on his cheek.

"How did you come to be a bandit?" I asked. "Isn't thievery against your faith?"

He met my gaze evenly. "Isn't it against yours?"

I laughed. "Touché."

Bahadır studied me a moment longer. "I was young, alone, hurt, and starving. It was winter when I reached the Hungarian *puszta,* and I lay down alongside the road. I hoped I would sleep and not wake. I did not think I had anything to live for. Ákos found me, gave me food and a place to sleep, money to send to my mother and sister. That was more than anyone else had done, so I stayed."

Ж

One of the men did not return that night. At first László was irritated—the man had a wife not far from Debrecen. Probably he had taken unasked-for leave. He'd pay a small fine when he returned, and László would think no more of it.

When another of the men reported that the missing man

had been in company with them as far as the nine-arched bridge, László only laughed. "The fool probably stopped for a tankard or three at the *csárda* there. He'll be home in the morning."

I could not shake a curious disquiet. *Whitsunday.* I had not forgotten what happened to Anna last year: she had been followed by the fene across a moonlit field. At the time, I had dismissed her stories as a girl's wild imaginings, but I had learned since that Anna was not that sort of girl.

I was not the only uneasy one.

"It's not a safe night to be out alone," Ákos said, tugging at a red curl by his ear.

"It's a clear night, three-quarter moon," László said, pouring himself another shot of vodka. "But you want to search for the blockhead? Do as you please."

Ákos was already standing, Bahadır right behind him. I sighed. I'd much rather stay in—drink some of László's vodka, challenge him for my father's ring. But my bones would not settle right.

"I'll come with you."

※

The *puszta* stretched empty and white beneath the moonlit sky, a wind making the grasses tremble like waves on a lake. We'd ridden back to the *csárda* and found a crowded taproom but no sign of the man we sought. Now we were riding a widening circle around the farmhouse.

A silent-winged owl swooped through the air near us, and Bahadır startled. For once, Ákos did not laugh.

"This night is full of ghosts," Ákos said.

We rode onward.

I'd kept my animal sense alert, feeling through the air around me for anything out of the ordinary. Most of the movement I caught was mundane: mice and other nocturnal creatures moving through the brush, the glide and sweep of owls hunting. But something wasn't right. There was an absence, some distance to our left, where no animals stirred.

I nudged Holdas toward the absence, and the others, after a shared silent look, followed.

"Did you see something?" Ákos asked.

"Call it a hunch, rather," I said.

As we drew closer, the sense of not-rightness intensified. There was something else too: something not quite animal. Not human either, as my animal sense didn't register them. Something sentient.

Holdas stopped abruptly, snorting.

A wave of evil slammed into me: toe-curling, stomach-curdling, throat-pinching. I'd never felt anything like it.

The other horses seemed to sense it too, halting behind Holdas and pulling uneasily at the reins.

"What is it?" Bahadır asked, peering across the plains before us.

Whatever it was, I couldn't see it yet, only feel it. I unholstered my gun, and saw Ákos do the same. "This way," I said, nudging Holdas forward.

The tightened muscles beneath my legs told me Holdas was not happy with me, but he complied.

A few more feet, and I could see what I had not seen

before: a mass like an old seamed rock, shadows shifting and eddying around it in defiance of natural laws of light. Beneath it, something very like a human hand, lifted in supplication.

My blood froze.

A shot cracked beside me, and I whirled to see Ákos, his face set in unnaturally grim lines. The monster shifted—not rock so much as ancient and massive, lengths of corded arms and legs uncoiling as it rose. *Guta,* I thought, the name lining up with stories my nurse had told. It turned slowly and spotted us, and the whole world seemed to halt.

Even the wind stopped.

The monster stepped forward, and the earth trembled. I could feel the shock even through my horse. Another step, and the guta picked up speed, barreling toward us.

Ákos and Bahadır were both firing now, but guns weren't going to stop this.

I cast my animal sense out, shaking awake the rooks nesting nearby, the roosting falcons and cranes, calling in all the hunting owls.

The birds flew in across the *puszta,* an avian cloud gathering strength as it came.

The monster was closer now: I could see its eyes, black and curiously unreflective.

Hurry.

Ákos's horse reared back, throwing the bandit to the ground and charging briefly forward as it arced away. But the monster was faster, intercepting the horse. It wrapped its massive arms around the terrified animal, and the loud crack of bones shattered the night. The guta dropped the horse and lumbered forward. Only a few meters of prairie grass stood between it and Ákos, already scrambling back to his feet.

I reached for the monster, trying to calm it, but I couldn't penetrate its mind. Beneath me, Holdas screamed a challenge. I yanked my attention from the monster, narrowly preventing my horse from charging the damned thing. The birds were almost here.

Bahadır bent in his saddle, extending his hand to his friend. "Come!"

"No!" Ákos shouted. "Run!"

Bahadır hesitated, and Ákos slapped the rump of Bahadır's horse. "Go!"

The horse took off. The redheaded bandit whirled back to the monster, a handful of steps away.

Now.

The birds descended like a curtain—a shrieking, cawing whirlwind of feathers. The guta swung at them, and I felt a gut wrench as his blows connected, knocking my birds from the sky.

Eyes. At my command, the birds converged on its head. The guta howled, an unearthly shriek that battered the air, and began its lumbering run. Away from us, thank St. Cajetan.

I reached out and hauled Ákos up behind me. We swerved wide around the guta, toward the lump of a human body.

The man was clearly dead, his face smashed in. Ákos swallowed hard.

I didn't want to touch the blood-soaked, misshapen body. But I couldn't leave him either. After Ákos was done being sick in the grass, we hefted the body over Holdas's saddle.

The guta was almost out of view now, the birds still swirling around him. I told them to release the creature when he was far away from any habitation, and we began walking back to camp.

"The King of Crows," Ákos said, looking at me and carefully avoiding the body. When I didn't answer, he added, "I won't tell László."

"I don't know what you're talking about," I said.

Ákos snorted, then we headed after Bahadır.

CHAPTER 20

Minus the rare monster attack and illicit activity, being a bandit was very much like revisiting my student days in Buda-Pest: long periods of waiting about, enlivened by cards, gossip, and too much to drink. A great deal of talk about women, but scant evidence of prowess in the form of actual women.

Most days László would send a few men to scout along the major roadways crossing the *puszta*. If they spotted anything promising, they raced back to camp and we plotted the ambush. The road from Debrecen to Buda-Pest was generally the most lucrative, though not the only one we'd hit, as László insisted we vary our routes. We didn't stop coaches every day either—sometimes nearly a week would pass between holdups.

"Predictability," László said, "is the sin of small minds. Besides being likely to get us killed. If the soldiers can't catch us, they can't hang us either." A week or two into my stint with them, we moved camp, this time to a slightly larger farmhouse with a barn. The farmer was gone, visiting his son in Buda-Pest for a few weeks, so László had commandeered it.

Some days we were unsuccessful: sometimes the scouts failed to report the presence of Luminate magicians (László refused to engage magic, seemed to have an almost pathological fear of it). Sometimes the armed guards were stouter than they looked, and we'd retreat empty-handed.

Most times we were successful enough. Fekete László had built a fearsome reputation that worked to intimidate fat, blustering merchants and elderly travelers. For younger women, he took to sending me with Ákos.

Such was the romance of the highwayman that a handsome young *betyár* could relieve a coach of its valuables with very little effort, and every sign of pleasure on the part of those being robbed. Only a day or two earlier, Ákos and I had stopped a carriage with a trio of women. The mother had passed out from shock, but the daughters fluttered with excitement.

The younger daughter pulled her gloves off slowly and slid a seed pearl ring off her finger. She held her hand out, the ring in her palm. As I reached for it, her fingers closed around the ring.

"You'll make good use of it?" she asked. "It has sentimental value."

I grasped the bare hand and kissed the closed fingers. She gasped, pink flooding into her cheeks. "If it has such value, you should keep it. Surely you have something else you can spare?"

Cheeks still burning, she pulled a small coin sack from the reticule beside her. I kissed her hand again, and she giggled.

Guessing from the cloudy expression on the older sister's face that she was feeling neglected, I made a show of kissing her hand as well.

Ákos mocked me as we rode away, kissing his fingers to me. "You kiss like a king."

I grinned back at him. I'd far rather kiss a pretty girl's fingers than fire a gun at her. "I do try. I've got a reputation to uphold."

)(

Summer rains kept us trapped inside the farmhouse for nearly a week in late June. We played cards, mostly: twenty-one and whist, piquet and trente et quarante. Sometimes dice. After four days of this, tempers were running high.

Following a lengthy losing streak, László flung out of the farmhouse into the drizzle. One of the other men chased after him, trying to soothe his temper. Varjú, my adopted crow, cawed from the roof of the barn.

The rest of us continued to play in silence. I watched the door warily, waiting for László's return and subsequent eruption.

But when the door at last burst open, László was smiling. "We've found some rare sport—come and see!"

Cards fluttered unheeded to the floor as the others burst up and out the door. The rain still fell, but few of the men paused for a wool mente. I ignored them, certain that whatever László thought "rare sport" would be deathly uninteresting to me. I didn't move, even when harsh shouting floated out from the nearby barn a few moments later.

This was none of my business.

The door banged open again, and the men tramped back in. László and another of the men wrestled something small and dark between them. It was squat and manlike, with a furry, bearded face and deep-set eyes. Sentient too, as I could feel nothing of its thoughts like I could with animals.

I didn't recognize the language it was shouting: something Slavic, at a guess. But it was clearly a language, and the monster was equally clearly terrified.

"Here," I said, standing. "Let the poor thing go. It's done nothing to you."

"But see," László said, poking the creature in the back with a stick and setting it howling again. "It speaks! We want to see if it will dance as well."

The men pushed the heavy wooden table against a wall, clearing a narrow space in the room. László flung the man-creature onto the floor and pulled a whip from his belt. He cracked the whip just beside its feet, and the praetherian shot up, jumping from one foot to the other. The men roared with laughter. Ákos, his freckles standing starkly against his pale skin, bolted from the room. After a moment, Bahadır followed.

I stayed, my frown lowering. Why hadn't these creatures sense enough to stay away from László and his ilk? And why must *I* inevitably end up involved? *Walk away,* I told myself. *Leave them to their game.*

Instead, I heard myself say, "That's enough. Whatever this is, it wasn't set on earth for your amusement."

László's face turned ugly. He sent the whip snaking in my direction, so I had to jump before it lashed against my boots. "Perhaps you want to take its place, Matyika?" He used the child's diminutive of my name as if it were a curse word. "The praetheria aren't human."

I took a long breath, exhaling through my nose. My palms tingled, my fingers already curling into fists. *Don't be a fool,* I told myself.

Too late.

I marched onto the floor, sweeping the creature behind me. Its matted fur, when my hand brushed against it, was chilled. No doubt it had only hoped to wait out the rainstorm in the barn.

"You're out of line, boy," László said, the whip sizzling through the air toward me. By now the others were crammed up against the wall, as far from the reach of the braided leather as they could get.

I flung up my arm to block the whip, and let it coil across my forearm. I gasped at the sting, then shook it loose. The second time László let fly, anger got the better of me. I caught the end of the whip and whispered a word. At once the long cord shifted, the braid smoothing into scales, the wooden handle in the bandit's hand elongating into a deadly and elegant snake head. The snake hissed, fangs bared, and László dropped it.

"Shit!" László shook his fingers as the snake slithered across the floor and disappeared through a crack beneath the door. His eyes narrowed at me. "You've been holding out on us, demon spawn." He glared around the room. "Everyone, clear out! And get that hellish creature back where it belongs. Matyika and I are going to talk."

The other bandits fled. I crouched down so that I was eye level with the creature. "I don't know if you can understand me, but I'm sorry for what's been done to you. I'd suggest you get away. Find somewhere safe, far from humans."

The creature nodded, as if he understood the gist of what I was saying, if not my actual words. He put his palm, curiously naked in contrast to the rest of his furred body, against my cheek. It was shockingly cold, so cold it sent prickles of pain across my face, radiating down my spine.

But then the creature was gone, scrambling through the doorway, disappearing into the wet grasses and brush of the *puszta*.

I turned back to face László.

"I don't like liars," László said, folding his arms across his chest. Rain dripped from the eaves outside the window.

"Well, you never particularly liked me, so that's fair," I said affably. "I'm happy to move on as soon as the rain clears."

"Not so fast. I could use someone with magic."

I rubbed my hand where the whip had stung it. "I'm afraid my abilities aren't for sale."

"You don't know what I'm willing to offer. Double your share."

"Not enough."

"Triple, then."

I thought how I had run from the Lady for asking too much of me. I was good at running. It was staying to disappoint people that I struggled with. I shook my head. "I'm sorry. I'll be leaving in the morning. And don't worry: I won't betray you. I'm not a cheat."

"Hmm," László said, as though his mind were already elsewhere. "Well, you needn't decide at once. Think on it."

There was nothing to think on, but I nodded, and László stalked out of the farmhouse, heading back toward the barn.

)(

László seemed unusually agitated that night as we ate our *gulyás* stew, cooked over coals in the kitchen. Instead of eating, he picked at a bit of bread and paced the room, weaving around the closely packed *betyárok* as if he did not see them.

After we scraped away the last of the stew and piled the dishes in the washbasin for some unlucky soul to wash later, László spoke.

"My friends," he said, waving his arms expansively at the company. "My band of brothers. We've been through hard times together—and good times. I've been lucky to call you my friends as well as my men."

Ákos and I exchanged a look. It was unlike László to wax grandiloquent. What was he building toward?

"We've won ourselves a reputation on these plains. People know not to cross László the Black. But I've a task that will win us a reputation all across Hungary, and beyond!"

Misgiving settled in my gut. A local reputation wasn't a bad thing: it meant people were more likely to give up their goods without resistance. But a national, even an international reputation? That only meant the crown would be sending hussar soldiers after you, and soon.

Ákos said as much.

László waived his concerns aside. "If you're afraid, you can stay behind. This isn't a task for the fainthearted. I've gotten word from a reliable source that a very expensive shipment is coming this way. Bound for the Ottoman sultan—to be sent from Debrecen through Transylvania and across Turkish Wallachia."

"What's in the shipment?" I asked.

"Gold, most likely. Jewels, possibly. The shipment is contained in four wagons reinforced with metal locks. Three armed guards ride with each wagon."

Ákos looked up in dismay. "We'd be outmatched. We can't take on trained guards."

"Of course we can. We're good shots, all of us. And we've got something they don't." László looked at me.

St. Cajetan, grant me wit.

"If the shipment is so valuable, you can guarantee that a couple of guards are trained magicians. I doubt I could take them, even if I was willing," I said.

"You can change a whip into a snake—surely you can do the same for their weapons."

I wondered how exactly László thought that scenario would play out. I had to touch things to shift them—what was I supposed to do, walk up to a guard and say, *Excuse me while I turn your firearm into a serpent?* They'd shoot me before I got to the second guard.

"It doesn't matter what I can do—I'm not doing it. I already told you I'd leave in the morning."

A dismayed buzzing broke out between Ákos and Bahadır and some of the other men.

László's eyes flicked over me. "You're scared."

"I'm not. Merely uninterested."

"I can practically see your knees knocking together." László's sneer twisted his mustache. "And only a coward would leave his friends so easily."

Bahadır's tan skin was chalky behind his lurid scar. Guilt twinged through me. László didn't care much whether or not the boy survived. Still, if I were gone, maybe László would give up this sudden obsession with an unobtainable shipment.

I shrugged. "They say there's no honor among thieves. I've had a good run; it's time to move on."

"Care to wager on it?"

I froze. "What?"

László lifted his chin. "Play you for it. A game of rouge-et-noir, best of three. You win, and we let you go with that ring you've been wanting—even send you with some coin in your pocket to speed your way. I win, and you stay. Help us one last time."

A curl of excitement stirred in my gut. *Madness.*

"All right," I said.

✕

Ákos acted as dealer, shuffling together several decks of cards at the head of the table. László and I sat on either side. Play was fairly straightforward: Ákos would deal two rows of cards, one "black" and one "red," and the winner was whoever called the row with a total closest to thirty-one, but less than forty.

"Black," László said, setting my father's signet ring on the table.

That left red for me. I called it and set a handful of coins on the table opposite the ring.

The first hand was a draw, with both rows tying at thirty-four. The watching bandits made derisive noises and passed around a bottle of plum brandy.

"Black," László said again.

Ákos dealt the cards once more, counting first the black. "Thirty-three," he said, laying down the last card. Then he began on the red. "Twenty-seven," he said, laying down a five. *Four*, I prayed, brushing my fingers against a silver filigree cross we'd taken during a raid. Another five in a pinch. Outside, my crow called in the trees. *Wish me luck, Varjú.*

Ákos set down a king. "Thirty-seven."

László crowed and slapped the table. "Who's king now, Matyika? Again."

The third time, black went for thirty-six and red for thirty-four, and László glowered at the table. Ákos sent me a small, sideways smile. My heart thundered in my ears, energy pounding through my blood.

A fourth time. Black: twenty-two, twenty-nine, thirty-two. László slapped the table again. "Beat that, my crow king."

I took a shallow breath. Another row of cards and I could be on my way, money in my pocket and my father's signet ring back on my finger. Each red card laid sent my heart rate spiking. Eighteen. A queen. *Twenty-eight.* A two. *Thirty.* The silver cross dug into my fingers. I needed an ace to win.

Ákos flipped over the final card. A five.

Thirty-five.

I didn't hear what László said, though I watched him scoop the money and the ring into his pocket. I stared at the scarred table and scattered cards. I'd given László my word: I was committed to whatever idiocy he planned.

Here lies Eszterházy Mátyás. He took a gamble and lost.

CHAPTER 21

"Anything?" Ákos whispered beside me.

I shook my head.

We'd been in position for what felt like an eternity, though was probably only a little more than an hour, waiting with our horses in a tiny thicket of trees providing some of the only cover in this part of the *puszta*. Behind us, the grasslands rolled out to the horizon like a scroll. Sweat trickled down my spine, and I rubbed irritably at my nose. Holdas shifted restlessly beneath me.

"Here they come," Bahadır said, edging beside me as we watched the first of the iron-banded box wagons roll into sight. The guards surrounding the wagon wore mostly black, their guns held tight in their hands. They scanned the road before them and the surrounding plains.

I groaned inwardly. These were no poorly paid and bored security guards. They were trained, professional, alert. An older woman sat on the wagon box beside the driver, her hands tucked in her lap. I would bet a year's wages that she was Luminate.

We watched the first carriage pass, then the second. The third was our target. I couldn't see the fourth, which meant the first part of László's plan had gone off without a hitch, and the fourth carriage had been delayed on the road. Our first task was to separate the wagons, then attack. Ahead of us, another group had staged an artful accident with the youngest of our troop, relying on the guard's compassion to at least slow the wagon.

Our turn.

"Now," I said, reaching out with my mind. Obligingly, the horned viper I'd found earlier slithered up onto the road, hissing. Simultaneously, a flock of starlings burst from the brush nearby, wheeling through the sky in a vast, synchronized sheet.

The horses reared up, tangling their leads and backing the carriage off the verge, just as we'd hoped. The driver swore and clambered down from his perch, rushing to inspect any damage to the wagon. The two guards jumped down as well, going to the horses' heads to calm them.

We waited for a moment, scanning the road for signs of reinforcements. Nothing. The guards on the previous carriage hadn't yet noticed the accident—or if they had, they weren't stopping.

The starlings dipped low over the carriage, spooking the still-tangled horses and occupying the guards. Even the magician was distracted, her hands moving in a complicated Wind charm to blow the starlings off course.

That was our signal.

We charged the road. Ákos dropped the coachman with a well-placed blow to the head. The first guard swung his gun at me, but I grabbed the barrel and shifted it to a snake in his hands, just as László had suggested.

The man screamed and threw his hands in the air. I charged the wagon where the magician and the driver sat. The woman was a bigger threat—but if she was like most Luminate, she couldn't perform magic without her hands free for the ritual. I grabbed her ankle and a bit of her dress with it, and as she began muttering a second spell, I shifted the fabric of her dress so vines sprouted from the lace at her wrists, curling and thickening as they grew, weaving a dense mesh that trapped her fingers.

A shot fired, nearly hitting my ear. Damn. I'd forgotten the driver.

A second shot answered the first, and the driver tumbled from his seat. Ákos stood beside me with a still-smoking gun.

Bahadır rounded up the four victims: two guards (one unconscious), a driver (bleeding sluggishly from a shoulder wound), and the lady-magician (spouting words no proper lady should admit to knowing). He bound them together with rope, and then we waited for László to find us.

A cloud of dust on the road ahead of us resolved into two of the guards from the second carriage riding our way. Someone must have spotted that the accident wasn't entirely accidental. Behind them, the second carriage was laboriously turning around in the road, following after its guards.

Three bandits on horses raced across the fields toward the road. One of them—I guessed László—raised his gun and fired. The coachman toppled off the second wagon, and the horses sprang forward, running unchecked toward us.

The guards returned the fire. László bent low, riding nearly sideways on his horse, in the plains style, with the horse's body shielding him from gunshot. The third man gave a gurgling cry and then slid under his horse, dropping onto the field.

I needed to help. But shifting to something monstrous enough to stop the guards would only frighten the horses further.

I reached out again, a calming, soothing brush. The guards' horses stopped beneath them, and when the guards tried to spur them into flight, the animals twitched and bucked and it was all the guards could do to stay in their seats. By the time the horses quieted, Ákos and Bahadır had joined László, and the guards surrendered.

"Where are the others?" I asked.

"First carriage got away—our men weren't fast enough, and the guards shot them. Two dead, one wounded. The last carriage is on its way now."

As he spoke, I glanced down the road and saw that he'd reported truly: two of our bandits were riding on the seat of the fourth wagon as it trundled down the road.

"Now we see," László said, rubbing his hands together, "what kind of treasure it is we've won."

One of the bound guards spat on the ground. "I'd not open the carriage if I were you."

"Why? You hoping to keep the gold for yourself?"

"It's not gold."

László shot the man in the leg. "Don't lie to me. Give me the keys."

The other guard, eyeing his companion's bleeding leg nervously, tossed the keys to László.

Something inside the wagon slammed against the walls, shaking the entire frame. I froze, glancing at Ákos, who looked equally horrified. László didn't pause. I'm not even sure he noticed. He fitted the key to the lock, then wrenched the door open.

That moment is etched in my mind: the blue sky arching above us, the wind hissing through the grass, the sweat matting my shirt to my back. Normal things, normal sensations. Nothing to hint at what was to come.

László opened the door, and the world seemed to explode.

Women spilled out of the wagon. Young women, their limbs long and lithe, their faces so lovely it burned to look at them, their hair every shade of fire: most were the yellow white of a fire's heart, but also deep red embers and the faint blue you sometimes get at the bottom of a candle flame where the fire meets the wick.

For a moment we all stared dumbly, our mouths open in shock. Whatever treasure we had anticipated, it was not this.

Then a kind of hunger burned through my body, sizzling across my brain and wiping away whatever thoughts I'd had.

A wave of pleasure crested through me, so intense I saw stars for a moment. Then I lunged forward, my only conscious thought to reach the women before someone else did. I narrowed in on one, a tall, queenly thing with orange hair and eyes that danced. I would give her everything— my body, my heart, my soul, my life—and it would be worth any cost. Even pain at her hands would be better than the most exquisite pleasure of anyone else's touch.

The men we'd bound together were moving too, snarling at each other as they struggled despite their bonds to reach the women. Even the magician was trying to shout spells. One of the guards tripped, falling to the ground, and the others screamed and kicked at him. The other guard freed a knife from his boot, and as I stumbled past them, he slashed through the ropes that bound them together. Freed, he turned the knife on his companions, stabbing the Luminate woman in the throat and the driver in the eye before springing toward the wagons.

Blood sprayed my arm, tiny pricks of heat that wakened a horror somewhere deep inside me. Varjú swooped around my head, cawing anxiously at me. The flutter of feathers distracted me. Dimly I registered that the horses were mostly oblivious of the turmoil the women had unleashed, and some instinct in me responded.

I shrank down, my arms spreading into black wings. In crow form, I fluttered to the top of the wagon. The strange frenzy bled away from my brain.

The carnage rocked me. A heist that had been mostly bloodless (excepting the men László had shot) had somehow turned into a bloodbath. All the guards but one were dead, and that one now knelt before a blue-haired maiden, offering her his bloodstained hands. She grasped them, licked the blood from them with a delicate pink tongue, and smiled.

At least two of the bandits were dead, and László was limping, blood streaming from a wound in his thigh and another in his shoulder. One arm clamped around his gut, and I suspected he might be wounded there too. But two of the girls danced around him, brushing their fingers through his hair, across his black mustache, and his face quivered with ecstasy. Their movements seemed to grow stronger and more sure as they danced, fire flickering along their brightening hair. László wavered for a moment, then dropped to his knees.

Ákos advanced on Bahadır with a sword. Bahadır's hands were empty, and he seemed oblivious to the threat, his whole attention focused on the praetheria.

The smart thing would be to leave now: to leave Laszló and the surviving guard to their fate, to wing off across the *puszta* and never come back, to let the women disperse into human settlements as they pleased.

But I'm not particularly good at doing the smart thing.

I watched the women for a moment longer, studying their supernatural grace. The orange-haired woman I'd spotted earlier moved to the second wagon with a key. She unlocked the door, freeing more of her sisters. They embraced her as they sprang free, stroking her brightening hair, and something about the familiarity of that movement gave me hope. And an idea. The women were careful to avoid the iron bands around the wagon as they emerged, and it wasn't until they were well free of the wagon that their brightness flared.

I flew toward the orange-haired woman who seemed to be the leader. I shifted back into human form, tensing my entire body against the onslaught of desire. But I allowed myself only a moment in my own shape before grasping a bit of her hair and shifting again, this time assuming her mirror image.

I concentrated on hair between my fingers, ignoring the otherworldly thrum of blood in my veins, the sense of the world itself as a thing bright and burning. I held the image of the iron bars in my mind and pushed it outward. Metallic grey began creeping up the fire-gold hairs, bleeding from roots to tips, until it encircled the woman-creature in an iron crown.

I released the fistful of hair and the woman cried out, dropping to the ground. Her sisters gathered around me hissing, fire in their eyes. As their clawed fingers snatched at me, I shifted once more, sending iron bands snaking across my skin. The praetheria hissed louder and drew back.

The woman before me was weeping in pain now, her hands fluttering toward the iron strands on her head and then jerking away.

"I yield! I yield!" Her German had a coarseness to it, as though she had not used it in some time.

"Call off your sisters. Tell them to contain their glamour."

She nodded, then whispered something in a liquid language that snagged at my heart, though I couldn't understand the words.

At once the brightness of the women dropped away, like

a fire extinguished by a bucket of water and nothing is left but the smoke. The final guard stumbled to his feet, glanced at his bloody fingers and back at the still bodies of his companions. He was briefly sick in the grass before staggering away. Ákos dropped the sword he carried at Bahadır's feet.

I shifted back to myself and touched the iron band in the woman's hair. It vanished, and she struggled to her feet, tears still tracing silver fire along her cheeks. Ákos stripped off the light wool dolman he wore and handed it to me without comment. I wrapped it around my waist.

"Who are you?" she asked.

"Nobody important," I said. "More to the point, who are *you*?"

"My sisters and I are samodiva." A breeze picked up, and the woman rubbed her arms, shivering. Gallantry briefly warred with modesty—should I offer her the dolman Ákos had just given me? Gallantry lost.

"How did you come to be here?" Powerful as they were, I could not imagine what trick it took to capture them, though the iron had worked to keep them secure.

"A foolish mistake. It doesn't matter now. What will you do with us?"

László said the carriages were intended for the Ottoman sultan. Were they a purchase, I wondered, or a gift? I might be looking at a thinly disguised assassination attempt. "You can't stay here. But I can't in good conscience release you either. You'd decimate every household in the *puszta*."

"We know the rules of your world. We don't gener-

250

ally hunt humans. But we have been bound for many days without food, and we were hungry." Her eyes flickered back to the bodies littered on the ground.

I knew that kind of hunger, as though my stomach were an endless chasm and my whole body could not stretch thin enough to contain it. In fact, I was beginning to feel the start of that hunger now, the inevitable effect of shifting too much in close succession. Familiar heat rose to my head. In a moment I'd be too light-headed to concentrate well.

"If I set you free, what guarantee have I that you won't attack humans?"

"We've no death wish," the samodiva said. "We just wish to return home." Her voice caught with a sigh on the last word.

A girl with ember-red hair edged next to her. "I'll stay as security. If you hear word of my sisters causing havoc, you can kill me."

"We can't ask that of you, Zhivka," the orange-haired samodiva said.

"I'm not ready to go home," the girl said. "I'd like to see more of the world. And . . ." She dropped her voice lower, stepping near to me. "I know who you are. I've heard the rumors: the King of Crows, hiding on the *puszta* and saving praetheria."

"I'm not anyone's savior."

"But you are the King of Crows? I saw your crow form. And you saved a Fair One from a mob. We all heard the story."

How could they know that? The other samodiva were

nodding now, their eyes alight with interest. I stepped back a pace, unnerved by their glowing intensity. "Glamours restrained," I reminded them, and their glowing dimmed a notch.

"All right," I said, because my head was starting to buzz and I could not afford to show weakness before the samodiva. "You may stay. Your sisters should leave, though, before anyone else comes down the road."

The first samodiva nodded. "Not all our sisters are free." As though that were a signal, the women seemed to melt away, running fleetly along the side of the road, flashing in and out of sight among the few trees spotting the roadside. Fire in the pasture, I thought, and knew a moment's pity for the unwary guards manning the first carriage that had escaped us.

I turned back to Bahadır and Ákos. The ground around them was strewn with bodies, including László's.

I supposed someone would have to bury them.

I swayed.

I needed to get away before I collapsed.

"Ákos," I managed. "Put the bodies of our men into the wagon, then bury the others. Bahadır, go up the road and see if you can find any wounded. If there are bodies, hide them." The girl—Zhivka?—watched me, waiting. "You—stay here. I'll be back as soon as I can."

"Where are you going?"

Away, I thought.

But I only made it to the other side of the thicket where we had hidden that morning before passing out.

CHAPTER 22

I woke to the tang of metal and salt on my tongue. I jerked upright, sputtering. A red-haired girl with cheekbones like a scimitar's edge, curving and deadly, sat inches away from me.

I scuttled backward, cursing, then wiped at my mouth. My hand came away bright crimson. Blood. There was blood in my mouth.

"What have you done to me?"

"I have not harmed you," Zhivka said, drawing her arms around her chest.

"Then why am I bleeding?"

"You fainted. Your pulse was very thin. You needed sustenance." She held up a mottled rabbit, its neck slit wide, blood matting the fur on its belly.

I gagged, bile and blood biting at my throat. She hadn't been entirely wrong—the blood *had* given me some of my energy back, though I was still ravenous. I eyed the dead rabbit. I couldn't eat it raw in human form, but my crow could. Though it probably wasn't worth the energy of shifting.

"Where are the others? I thought I told you to stay."

Her mouth turned down. "I did stay. For a little while. But it was boring. And lucky for you I did come. You needed my help."

"Fair enough." I stood on shaking legs and whistled. Holdas came tromping through the brush, shaking his head. There was hard bread and a chunk of cheese in the saddlebag. I pulled it out and tore into the bread. Within moments, the food was gone, and I felt more myself, though still hungry.

I glanced at the rabbit again. "Can I have that?"

She smiled, and my heart thumped. Even without her glamour, she was devastating. I should have to remember that her looks were a weapon.

I tucked the rabbit into the saddlebag and swung into the saddle, then pulled Zhivka up behind me. We rode back to the road to collect Ákos and Bahadır and a pair of wounded bandits who had been farther up the road and thus escaped the samodiva.

"We buried the guards," Bahadır said. "What do you want us to do with the others?"

"Ask Ákos," I said. I'd be damned if I took over for László.

After a long, measured look at me, Ákos said, "Bring the wagon. We'll take the bodies back to camp and send word to their families."

We followed directions and rode silently back to the farmhouse. As soon as we reached it, I built up a fire and stuck the rabbit on a spit.

※

Dinner that night was a sober affair. Of the dozen or so *betyárok* who had ridden against the caravan, only five of us remained. And Zhivka.

It had probably been a mistake to let her stay. Ákos and Bahadır were terrified of her, though Bahadır hid it better, even managing to offer her salt for her soup. Their terror didn't worry me. It was the others who did—their clipped words and sharp body language told me they had not forgotten the destruction the samodiva had wrought that afternoon. But their eyes spoke differently. Their eyes kept drifting back to Zhivka, brushing across the curves of her cheeks and lips, lingering on the generous lines of the body beneath her dirty white dress.

I made a mental note to give her some of the men's spare clothing after supper—and to give her the room László had occupied, the only room in this farmhouse with a lock.

"What now?" Bahadır asked me.

I shrugged. "Ask Ákos."

"We stay," Ákos said. "This is all the home and family I've known these past three years."

"There's a price on my head," Bahadır said. "I've nowhere else to go."

"Will you stay?" Ákos asked me.

My debt of honor to László was paid, and I'd retrieved

my father's ring from among his things; I could be a free man, if I chose.

"Please stay," Bahadır said. "We are stronger with you."

"I wager," Ákos said, "that you can't last two weeks in László's place without getting someone caught."

I shook my head. "I'll not fall for that so easily." I thought of leaving, tracking across the *puszta* with only Holdas for company. There was freedom in the picture—but loneliness too. I found I did not want to leave the others, frightened and vulnerable as they were. Not yet. I'd become infected with honor in my old age.

"I'll stay." Only until things felt secure—then I'd leave.

X

The next morning something scratched at the door just as dawn bled grey fingers into the room where we all slept.

A few of the other men groaned, then rolled back over to sleep. I punched the pillow beneath my head. It was a branch, I thought. The scratching sounded again, too insistent to be accidental.

Cursing beneath my breath, I scrambled from my blankets and sidestepped bodies to reach the door.

I flung it open. The hairy creature I'd saved from László stood on the doorstep. He said something and spread his hands wide.

"I'm sorry. I don't understand. Do you speak German, perhaps?" I asked in German, then switched to English. "Or English?"

"He offers his service," Zhivka said at my ear, and I jumped, stubbing my toe as I landed.

"What kind of service?" I asked.

"He is domovoi. He can protect your house, so long as you treat him kindly."

Ákos came up beside me. "Might as well let him stay. It was only after we drove him away that we had such ill luck."

Zhivka said something to the creature, who bobbed his head and shuffled across the muddy courtyard to the stables. "He will sleep in the barn," she said. "And you should like him. He is a bit like you, táltos."

How did she know that? Wary, I said, "I don't know what you mean."

She seemed amused rather than offended. "I think that you do. The domovoi can shift. Small things, you understand, like a dog or a cat."

"Or a crow?"

Her smile glimmered, and my throat seized up. "Or a crow," she agreed. "Though not so good-looking as you."

Ákos laughed. "I like this one, Mátyás. She knows how to keep you in your place."

I mumbled something and took refuge in the kitchen, under the pretext of warming water for some pilfered tea.

The domovoi was only the start. Within the next week, a motley assortment of creatures found their way to that isolated farmhouse: a small, knobbled brown man; a pair of craggy-faced, moss-covered treelike creatures; and late in the week, a giant, towering a good two heads above me. He seemed a bit simpleminded, and harmless, and Zhivka wept when she saw the burn scars along his arms, tokens of his most recent encounter with humans.

Their arrivals unnerved me. Not because of the

praetheria themselves, but because each arrival was followed by a small side-glance from Ákos, as if my reaction decided the matter, not his. At first I thought the creatures would shelter for a night or two, then move on. But as the days passed, it became clear that they meant to stay.

"They come for you, King of Crows," Ákos said to me at the end of the week, sitting beside me as I shuffled through a deck of cards. "But I don't understand why they seek you out."

The Lady sent them, I was nearly positive. But I had not asked outright, because if I knew for certain, I should have to do something about them—accept the role she gave me as protector or send them away. Innate laziness suggested the best action was to do nothing. However, at Ákos's nudging, I crossed the dirt-packed courtyard to the barn. Zhivka trailed behind me, in case I needed help translating.

Inside, the air was thick and musty, rank with the familiar odors of livestock: horse, cow, a fat pig in the far corner. But under the familiar smells were foreign ones, something sharp and bitter that made the hair on the nape of my neck stand up.

The creatures seemed peaceable enough. The giant had taken up refuge in an empty stall, and the two tree-creatures had planted themselves in the corner opposite the pig. The others clustered around a pile of hay, burrowing into the dry strands for warmth, as the summer morning had come on misty and chilled.

"Why are you here?" I asked.

Holdas, hearing my voice, whiffled a greeting. The creatures, however, didn't answer. The domovoi hugged his knees and rocked back and forth on the ground.

"You frighten them," Zhivka said.

"*I* frighten *them*?"

She arched one thin eyebrow. "You stink of magic."

I tried to take a surreptitious whiff of my armpits. I stank? I could smell nothing above the usual odor of cotton and wool and skin that was, perhaps, due for a washing. "Well, I mean them no harm."

"Do you mean them well? The two are not the same."

"I—" I broke off, scowling. "I'll ask the questions, if you don't mind."

Zhivka smiled, pleased at successfully nettling me, and as always, her smile sent prickles that were equal parts pleasure and terror down my back. She looked at the creatures and spoke, her lovely voice lilting and reassuring. Even I felt my hackles softening and smoothing out.

"They have heard this is a place where they might be safe."

Alarm tingled across my skin. "How do they all know where to find us? Is it so widely known where we are?" If a small horde of praetheria could track us, what did that say of the hussars in Debrecen? Perhaps we were at risk. I'd talk to Ákos later about moving camp.

She laughed, a light trickle of water across stones. "No. I think you are still safe. They say the Lady told them."

Each word pierced me. The Lady meant to goad me into taking on the role of protector, whether or not I wanted it. Irritation built in me, fanning into a flame. "Tell them they cannot stay here any longer. I'm willing they can shelter here for the rest of the day, but they must be gone tomorrow."

Zhivka looked at me, shadows gathering in her eyes. "But, Mátyás . . ."

"I haven't given you leave to use my first name. I want them gone by morning. Tell them!" I stalked to Holdas's stall and flung myself onto his back, not bothering with the saddle. Without looking at Zhivka or any of the others, I rode out of the barn and into the rain that misted across the endless plains.

By the next morning the barn was empty of all except the livestock and the domovoi, who insisted that this had been his home before we had arrived and only the master of the farmhouse had the right to turn him out. If I caught fleeting glimpses of the others in the grasses that afternoon as we made plans to stake out the road the following day, the glimpses were brief enough that I was never sure what I had seen. And no one else complained.

That night, the rain came down in heavy sheets, and lightning cracked across the sky, followed by thunder booming over the grasslands. When the others huddled into their blankets to sleep, I crossed the courtyard to the barn, to ensure the animals were not savaging themselves in terror. Varjú called unhappily from the roof of the barn and fluttered down to follow me.

My hair was plastered to my forehead before I was five steps from the door; by the time I reached the barn, I was soaked through and shivering. I whispered a Lumen light into being when I crossed the threshold—and stopped.

A dozen pairs of eyes blinked back at me. Gathered

before me were all the creatures I had sent away—and a few more. Near the wall, a healthy space between her and the nearest praetheria, I spotted a tangle-haired creature I hadn't seen before, with blood-dark lips and clawed fingers, her shapely legs ending incongruously in goose feet.

My breath caught. Lidérc. Even I knew this one, the creature of nightmares.

I wasn't heartless enough to send the others out into a rainstorm, but this one, she couldn't stay.

"You need to leave," I said, my body tensing in anticipation of a shifting. If she fought me, I'd need something more powerful than my human self to drive her out.

"And where should I go?" She did not seem defiant, only defeated. "This used to be my homeland, but there is nowhere here for me. Everywhere I go I am met with hatred and suspicion. And yet I helped free you: I fought with the soldiers near Buda Castle after the Binding was broken." Her eyes flickered, though the light I held was steady.

"You helped free the Hungarians?" I had not heard this story.

"The girl who broke the Binding asked for an army. We gave her one. And for this we are driven out of your borders."

Anna.

The lidérc curled her arms around her chest, a narrow black tongue licking at her dark lips. "I would have died for her, had she asked it."

Her words reverberated through my bones, a soul-deep kinship. I *had* died when Anna had asked it. In that, we two were alike.

Weariness slammed over me. I wiped my hand across my face. I knew, then, that I could not send the lidérc away—or the others, for that matter. Whatever they had done, however they had come to be here, we were bound together by some force I was only beginning to understand.

"Stay, then," I said. "But I must have your word—on whatever you consider sacred—that you will not harm my men, or any other human for that matter, unless your life is at stake."

A murmur of agreement swept through the barn. In the morning, I'd bring Zhivka, and we'd have them formally swear. For now, I called to Varjú, who had settled in the rafters and was shaking water from his wings, telling him to warn me should any of the creatures try to approach the farmhouse during the night.

X

Three weeks after László's death, Ákos announced another raid.

I lifted my eyebrows. I was not certain we were ready for that—Bahadır and another of the *betyárok* still jumped at anything that sounded like gunfire. But I was not the leader, and we did face the problem of providing for our growing menagerie, though the creatures mostly took care of their own needs—Zhivka and the lidérc went out to hunt every day at dusk. I did not ask where they went or what they hunted, and they did not tell me. But sometimes Zhivka would come back with a duck or a brace of hares for our pot.

In the end, it was just me, Ákos, and Zhivka. We rode down the single carriage, its gold coat-of-arms gleaming against the maroon body of the vehicle.

Zhivka had turned up her glamour a little. Riding across the grasses, her ember-red hair streaming behind her, her beautiful face focused as a blade, she looked like something out of an old story. Emese, the mother of the Árpád dynasty, storming across the plains with the first Hungarian tribes. Or the British Boudica, riding on London to burn it to the ground.

She was dazzling, even to me, who had begun to grow accustomed to her.

The coachman had no chance. As soon as he spotted her, he pulled up on the reins. His gun entirely forgotten, he gaped at her. And when Ákos and I reached the carriage to demand they stand and deliver, the inhabitants of the carriage were similarly so smitten that they handed us their jewels without any protest.

Back at the farmhouse, my men toasted Zhivka with home-brewed ale. She shrugged, as though it were no great thing, but I saw the secret smile hovering in the corners of her lips. After that, we talked of ways to use the other praetheria: the lidérc to terrify the wealthy into submission; the two horned tree-men with the blue-green, bark-textured skin (they called themselves leshy) to grow their branchlike limbs across the road and block passage; the giant to threaten to break an axle if they would not pay him for safe passage.

But we had not yet done more than talk. Bahadır pointed out that using the praetheria too often would only draw attention to our group. Already, the slow trickle of prae-theria coming in search of us meant that our group was too large to stay safely at the farmhouse.

We began moving the camp from night to night, stopping at the farmhouse only if the weather was inclement. Sometimes we'd return to the farmhouse to find that owners of outlying farms had stopped by in our absence, leaving us cakes or vegetables or hay for our horses.

The first time this happened, I asked Ákos why.

"They want our blessing and protection. A strong *betyár* means that the farms are not so open to attack by rogue bandits. Isolated praetherian attacks on livestock have dropped since so many have joined us. And they know that come winter, if they are starving, we will give them what we can spare. Part of the *betyár*'s code of honor."

"Isn't it dangerous that so many know where to find us?"

"They won't betray us."

I wished I could be so certain.

Anna

CHAPTER 23

At the next meeting of the Congress, I found I could not concentrate: all I saw, as the members discussed what to do with the praetheria, was bodies splayed out across a table.

Witness, Vasilisa had said, but I did not know how. The men in the room had not listened to me before: why should they listen to me now?

The Congress began much as usual, with each of the main parties arguing their position. Ponsonby urged strenuously that an independent kingdom of Poland be established and a sanctuary be formed there for the praetheria, funded by British coffers and by the Congress. The Austrians, predictably unwilling to relinquish their territory in Galicia, refused, counter-offering a reserve in Austrian lands. The German confederacy and the Hungarians favored the British plan; the smaller kingdoms, like Saxony, favored the Austrian plan, as did the Turkish delegation, which sought primarily to preserve neutrality and prevent Russian aggression into their territory.

Across the room, my uncle Pál whispered something to Tsar Nicholas, whose face purpled. The tsar shot up, shouting at the room in French. Beside me, Richard murmured a translation.

"Bah! You are all imbeciles, afraid of what is stronger than you. You seek to curtail my power and influence. You want to cage the praetheria like beasts, because you fear them too. You need only send them to me. Russia will welcome them, and I will keep all of Europe safe."

Lord Ponsonby snorted and muttered, "I dare say. After the Russian armies conquer the rest of Europe, it *might* be safe. But at what cost?"

The tsar cast a long look around the room. "We do not need this Congress. If you will not agree to support us, we will withdraw our voice and open our borders to the praetheria." He sat down, arms folded across his chest, as arguments broke out all across the room. Beside him, Pál smiled.

It was some time before order was restored in the room. At length, Emperor Ferdinand rose, and the quarrelling members fell silent.

"Where is Dr. Helmholz?" he asked. "The man said he had vital information for us regarding the praetheria."

For a long moment no one answered. Then Borbála Dobos spoke, from the back of the room. "I tried to speak with the doctor at his rooms this morning. His housekeeper said he has not been seen for two days."

A string of images shot through my mind: the doctor abandoning his lecture to dance after a group of vila, the fragile curved shape of a dead praetherian baby, Vasilisa's face as she asked me to witness. I shivered. Was his disappearance only an accident?

Dragović stepped forward. "I believe I know what Dr. Helmholz meant to share. The praetheria have been difficult to study because of their variety, but Dr. Helmholz believes he has found one thing that unites them: excess life force. I understand this means that most praetheria have more magic inside them than the average human."

Vasilisa had told me as much, but it was only now, surrounded by a Congress more interested in their own security than the well-being of the praetheria, that I saw the implications. No wonder the praetheria had been held inside the Binding for nearly a millennium. It was not simply that the Binding spell had been fueled by their magic—it was their *excess* magic that made them a prime target for such a spell in the first place.

I was not the only one to see this link.

"It hardly seems reasonable," a fat man near me objected, "to let such creatures roam free when their independence directly threatens our own."

"How?" I burst out. The man ignored me. Richard shook his head warningly.

"Without the Binding, our own magic suffers." He pointed at his soul sign, a pale, flickering lion. *A weasel, more like.* "Why should we suffer a curtailment of our own powers just so creatures who despise us can be comfortable? I vote we reinstate the Binding—or something very much like it. Such power should be returned to the Luminate, where it belongs."

A murmur of agreement swept the room. Lord Ponsonby

said to Richard, "At all costs, we cannot let Russia take them."

Anger built steadily in me, driven by the crowd's disregard for the praetheria, their willful ignorance of the Binding's price. In my head, a faint echo of Vasilisa's voice from a long-ago ball: *What you could be, Anna Arden, if you were not afraid!*

I shot upward, ignoring Richard's frantic grab at my sleeve. "Why? So you can abuse your power as the Luminate have done before? Tell me what *crime* these poor creatures have committed other than existing. If you and yours had been enslaved for nearly a thousand years, you also would long for freedom."

Voices rose in protest, but I brushed them aside. If some of the praetheria *had* killed children, hadn't we done the same to them—hadn't we precipitated it? I could not condone the killing, but humans had to share that blame. "You don't know what you ask. The Binding was a dangerous spell—it was forged in blood and broken in blood. Its existence poisoned society, created gaps and divisions where none should have been."

All the eyes in the room were pinned on me, a mixture of contempt, derision, and amusement. For a moment I could not seem to breathe, the room fading before me and Mátyás appearing in its place, his eyes steady on mine as I drove a dagger home. *No.* We could not repeat that.

I took a slow, shuddering breath and found Gábor, seated unobtrusively at the back of the Hungarian delegation, watching me with clear eyes. His quiet intensity calmed me, and I plunged onward.

"You decry the praetheria as empty, soulless killers, but some of them have been my friends. It's true that some of them may be evil—but so too are some humans. And yet we do not lock up all of society as a result. Do you know how your Dr. Helmholz found his results? By capturing and murdering praetheria who had done nothing to him."

Richard was standing beside me now, his hands on my shoulders, trying to turn me from my seat and propel me from the room.

"Do. Not. Touch. Me." I don't know what Richard heard in my voice, but he dropped his hands as though stung.

"Beast lover!" Dragović shouted, turning to the room at large. "She's been tainted by their faerie glamour. She's no one, nothing. We should not listen to her!"

My anger burned white hot.

"You think because I am a girl, I am weak. Because I speak for those who are given no voice here, my voice should matter less. You are wrong, on both counts. I am not weak." I focused on Dragović's soul sign, a narrow red dragon crawling about his collar. "Has no one told you who I am? The archduchess herself called me the darling of Hungary—and do you know why? Not because I set a prison full of men free, though I did that. Not because I helped spark a revolution, though I did that too. But because I broke the Binding. I made a bargain with the praetheria, and an army followed me out of the spell and destroyed the finest soldiers Austria could throw at us. I am not afraid of you."

I paused for a moment, feeling the buzz of small spells

all across the room. With that fine inner sense for magic, I reached across the room and snapped the thin line of the spell holding Dragović's soul sign in place. As a shocked hum of conversation swelled across the room, I closed my eyes and tugged one by one at all the narrow threads of magic filling the room. Two dozen soul signs disappeared in a blink—and the illusion of hair from the heads of at least two elder statesmen. As each spell broke, I caught the tiny release of magic, my fury helping me focus.

Tiny daggers of pain started at the base of my skull, but I was not done yet.

"I have sacrificed too much already for the praetheria to be free—you will not re-enslave them. If you try, I will break whatever spell you set against them and turn it against you." I released the gathered magic in a rush, letting it take its own shape, and a wind rushed around the room, tearing at hair and scattering papers like fall leaves.

I swept an angry glare across the room, and most of the men recoiled from my stare. The sense of power filling me then was immensely satisfying.

What you could be, Anna Arden . . . This. Confident, powerful—even terrifying. But I wasn't frightened.

This is what I was meant to be.

The shocked quiet lasted only a moment before the archduchess's clear voice cut across the room. "Well, that was an impressive little stunt. I think we are done here today."

Her chilly tone doused some of my indignation, and fear settled in its place. What had I done? I had blurted out my secret about the Binding and threatened the most important men and women in Europe.

And for what?

A middle-aged man I did not know charged across the room toward me.

"Do you know what you have done, you minx?" His accented German was thick with fury. "My family has lost the magic we have held for centuries. What arrogance, what arrant selfishness, to think you could arrange the world to suit only yourself. Your father ought to beat you." He spat at me, the cold globule striking my exposed collarbone, before Richard urged him away.

A crowd had surrounded us now, shouting at me, shouting at Richard, calling me names so filthy my ears burned, suggesting I be whipped, beaten, hanged, and worse. I did not know where to look. No one had ever dared speak to me so before. I rubbed the spittle away with a handkerchief, but my fingers lingered on the spot. Some invisible protection had been stripped from me, and I was naked, exposed, in its absence.

This was not at all how this scene was supposed to play out. In novels, when heroines finally make a stand against evil, it falls before them.

Lord Ponsonby spoke to Richard over the din. "This is a bad business. You'd best send the girl back to England!"

Being sent back to England was mild compared to the suggestions currently being hurled at me. I caught Gábor's eye across the room: he looked nearly as anguished as I felt. But he couldn't reach me. The press of bodies was too great.

The crowd pushed closer. I'd thought the Congress made up of civilized—if self-interested—men. But there was nothing civil in the faces surrounding me, nothing genteel in the hands reaching for my sleeves, shoving me back against Richard. I couldn't breathe.

A pair of soldiers shoved through the mob. "Miss Arden? You're to come with us."

CHAPTER 24

The soldiers led me, not unkindly, from the hall to a small sitting room on an upper floor. Richard followed closely behind. Once we were inside, the soldiers took up position just outside the door.

I paced back and forth before the window, watching the other delegates escape the building and wishing I could join them. The air inside the room was only marginally cooler than the warm air outside, and wisps of hair stuck to the sides of my cheeks. How could I have been so foolish? Why hadn't I kept a better leash on my tongue?

Richard was silent for a very long time, sitting on one of the chairs and tracing patterns on the carpet with the toe of his shoe. "I don't need to tell you that your behavior today was reprehensible. A young lady of quality to set the Congress by its ears! Had you no thought for me or for your sister, for the damage your behavior—not to mention your claims—might do?"

I had rather he shouted at me.

"Did you in fact break the Binding?"

I nodded.

He dropped his head in his hands. "God help us."

Hesitantly I said, "I am sure Lord Ponsonby and the others will not blame you for my actions. You were not in Hungary when it happened. How could you have known?"

Richard lifted his hands and looked at me for the first time, his blue eyes piercing. "I am not so worried about the cost to my reputation as I am about the danger to my family. To your sister—and to our child."

For a moment I could not speak. "Catherine is expecting? Why didn't she tell me?"

"She did not think you cared to know."

I turned away from Richard, wrapping my arms across my stomach. Had my behavior in Vienna suggested I was so self-centered as that?

"I would never hurt Catherine's child." I saw again the almost translucent limbs of the praetherian baby and shuddered.

"Can you swear, with such a power as yours, that you have never inadvertently hurt someone?"

I returned the only answer I could: silence.

Before Richard could say anything else, the door swung open. The archduchess, followed by Dragović. Archduchess Sophie sat in a high-backed chair and gestured to the one facing her. "Please sit."

I sat.

"Your behavior today was most unwise, Miss Arden," the archduchess said. "Your defense of the praetheria was to be expected, but you might have kept the Binding out of it."

I gaped at her. "You knew?"

She brushed at an invisible speck of lint on her skirt. "Let us say I strongly suspected. Our intelligence network is not completely useless, and after your little trick at my garden party I was virtually certain. But now that you have made a public announcement, we shall have to do something about it. About you."

"She broke no law," Richard said.

"In a strictly legal sense, this is true. There was no law made prohibiting breaking the Binding, because no one thought it possible. But social custom is a powerful rule, and Miss Arden violated that expectation. She upended a significant social order. She must be held accountable."

"She is a British citizen," Richard said, and I realized that, in his quiet way, he was trying to defend me. "Queen Victoria should decide her punishment, if punishment is needed."

The archduchess tapped a finger against her cheek. "Very well. There are a few things about the Binding that still bear investigation, but I give you permission to make plans to send her back to England. In the meantime, I strongly suggest you keep her confined at home. I will not be responsible for what angry Luminate might do to her."

※

Catherine was hovering in the entryway when we returned. Studying her now, I could see the curved line of her stomach, almost hidden by her corset. "You are late! I expected you this half hour past."

Richard dropped a kiss on her cheek. "I am sorry we made you anxious. I will tell you everything later. Perhaps you can have a tray sent up to Anna's room? She will be staying there some time."

Catherine turned wide eyes on me. "Anna?"

My throat was tight. "Richard told me your news. I want you to know I am very happy for you. And I'm sorry. For everything."

I fled to my room and lay down on my bed, flattened by the weight of all I had lost that morning: Richard's and Catherine's trust, any possibility of helping the praetheria at the Congress, my secrets.

I did not cry. I was afraid once I began, I should never stop.

Catherine came midafternoon with Ginny and a tray with tea. Ginny set the tray down and disappeared, and Catherine sat on the bed beside me. Her hand brushed my hair lightly, and then withdrew, as if she were not certain of her actions.

"Richard told me. I am sorry. I know this is not what you wanted."

I tried to smile. "I won't be your burden much longer. You must be happy about that, at least."

Catherine frowned, tucking her hands around her stomach. I had not realized how often she did that. *A baby.* A wonderful and terrible change in her life.

"You must not think you are a burden." A smile ghosted her face. "A pestilence and a pain, but you are my sister and

I have been more glad to have you here than not. And I—I think you have been very brave, to chase what you think is right despite everything." She gripped my hand and kissed it before slipping out of the room.

⋊

I stared at the words on the page, the letters blurring together as my eyes lost their focus. Late-morning light illuminated a small patch on the windowsill and the fringe of my book as I sat on the window seat.

"A visitor, Miss Anna," Ginny said, poking her head around the door. "It's Mr. Gábor."

Questions of why he was here and why Catherine had allowed him entry would have to wait. I paused before my mirror only long enough to pat my hair down and pinch my cheeks. I clattered down the stairs to the drawing room and found Gábor there with Catherine, both of them conspicuously not looking at the other.

"Your friend has come to say good-bye," Catherine said. "I thought, under the circumstances, it only fair that he say it in person."

My heart stuttered. "Good-bye?"

Catherine withdrew to a corner of the room, allowing us some privacy. Gábor stepped forward, hands extended as though he'd take mine, but then his eyes flickered to my sister and he dropped them. My own hands grasped empty air. We both remained standing.

"I'm afraid I have to leave Vienna. Kossuth has given me a mission and I cannot delay. I came to see that you were well—I was worried for you yesterday, until word reached the embassy that you were not kept at the palace, but allowed to return home."

"They're sending me back to England, to face Queen Victoria's judgment," I said, unable to keep a note of despair from leaking into my voice.

"Then I will pray for you, that the Queen be merciful." Gábor's beautiful eyes were troubled, and there was a rigidity in the way he held himself that made my heart beat hard and quick.

"Will you come back?" *Will you find me?* I swallowed the words before Catherine could hear them. What would happen to us, now that Gábor was leaving and I could not stay in Vienna? Could friendship and affection—even love—span so much distance?

"If I finish my errand before the Congress finishes, then yes, I will return to Vienna." His voice lowered. "But that is not what you are asking, is it?"

I shook my head, and Gábor sighed.

"I have been thinking of this ever since I saw you in the garden with the archduke. We do not inhabit the same worlds. If our paths sometimes cross, it is only a trick of our orbits. Yesterday, when you rebuked the Congress, you were splendid—and perfectly at home. You belong to that world, filled with diplomats and movers of nations."

You kissed me, I wanted to say. *Were those kisses like candy, all sweetness and no substance?* "I am about to be banished. I will influence no one when the Queen and my mother are through with me. I will be an outcast among my own class."

Gábor shook his head, his eyes still intent on mine. "Maybe for a few years. But I know you, and you will not be restricted long. But if you pledge yourself to me, doors that are open to you now will be closed."

Catherine had said the same, but Gábor's words sliced deeper. "I don't care."

"Not for yourself, but if there are children? You've seen how my sisters and my brother and I are treated. Do you want that for your sons and daughters?"

My cheeks grew warm at the thought of having children with Gábor, and I looked away. "The world is changing."

"Not quickly enough. There are other barriers too. Your family would not welcome me any more willingly than mine would you. My mother and grandmother want me to have a Romani wife. Could you turn against society and your family as well?"

I met his eyes again, though a prickly thorn had lodged itself in my heart. "Why are you making this so hard? None of this matters if we love each other. If you do not care for me that way, then say so. You do not need excuses."

At once his careful façade cracked, and I saw the anguish in his eyes. "If I did not care for you, I would not be here. It is *because* I love you that I have to let you go."

I forgot that Catherine was listening, forgot everything but the fact that Gábor was drawing away and I could not stop him. "I don't want you to let me go! It is my life too— you do not get to make this decision alone."

Gábor took a step back, his hands behind him as though he did not trust himself not to reach for me. "I've already made my decision." He bowed once, then fixed his hat back on his head. "May God grant you every happiness." His voice broke on the last word, and he left the room.

For once, Catherine did not say anything. As the room reverberated with Gábor's absence, my sister simply folded me in her arms and let me cry until I had nothing left.

)(

Two days later, just as I had finished pushing some uneaten toast around on my plate, Ginny scratched at the door.

"Miss Anna?" she said, opening the door to peer in at me. "You have a visitor."

My heart jumped, thinking it might be Gábor again, but Ginny shook her head. "It's not your young man."

"He's not mine anymore."

Ginny helped me pull a brush through my hair and twist it up into a simple knot. She made me change out of the gown I'd worn since the previous day and pinched my cheeks for some color.

I could not see that it mattered.

My visitor was familiar to me, though I had not spoken above a dozen words to Noémi's austere uncle, the prince Eszterházy. He held a folded and sealed square of paper in his hands that he turned over and over again. Catherine sat knitting in a nearby chair.

When I entered the room, he smiled at me, though the gesture seemed forced. He held out the paper. "This is for you, from my niece."

I felt only a flash of astonishment that he should carry out such a lowly errand, when he continued.

"If you do not mind, I should very much like to know the contents of that letter, Miss Arden. You see . . . Noémi has gone missing, and I am hopeful that she may have told you something of her destination."

Noémi missing? I remembered how Noémi and Hunger had sat talking, their heads close together, and misgiving seized me. I took the letter and opened it.

Anna—

Perhaps I should not be writing this, as angry as I am, but I fear the words will burn me if I hold them in any longer. HOW COULD YOU? Hunger told me what happened in the Binding.

I nearly dropped the letter. *No.* After Mátyás died, Noémi had been my bulwark, more sister than friend. I had just lost Gábor. I could not bear to lose Noémi too. Why had Hunger told her? How could it possibly benefit him?

Hunger claims Mátyás's death was necessary. I am not sure I believe him. In any case, why would you not tell me? Why have you lied to me all these months? I feel as though I have lost my brother again. I am certain I have lost you. You were never the person I thought you were.

You say Mátyás died in the Binding, but I cannot believe it. The dreams I have of him are too real, too vivid. That you tried to kill him, I am certain. But I do not think that is the end of it.

The duke of Rohan has come calling again and

asked for my hand, finding my poor eyesight and
poverty no impediment given my family connections.
Or perhaps he thinks I should be grateful. I cannot
stay and marry him, so I have gone to find Mátyás.
If my uncle brings this to you, tell him not to worry
for me. Do not come for me yourself—I do not ever
want to speak to you again.

I refolded the letter, my fingers slow and precise as if that precision might give me some control over a life that seemed to be spinning rapidly out of my grasp.

For so long I had guarded all my secrets, about the Binding, about Mátyás. Now, within a span of days, they had all been spilled.

"Well?" Prince Eszterházy watched me closely, his brow slightly furrowed. "Has she told you where she went?"

"She has gone." I tried to swallow, but my throat closed up. "She has gone to find her brother. She does not believe he is dead."

"Her brother?" The prince was astonished. "I was sure she had sent word of some romantic elopement. A pity, since the duke would have made her a comfortable husband."

"Comfortable, perhaps, but not what she would have chosen."

"Then why did she not tell me? We are not fiends, to force her into a distasteful match."

"I do not know." And the galling thing was, I didn't. What other things had Noémi kept from me? What had I failed to notice in my crusade to save the praetheria? I knew she had been obsessed with her dreams of Mátyás. Why had I not tried harder to stop her—or told someone what she believed?

"Does she say where she has gone?"

"No," I said. "She may have gone to Eszterháza, to see her uncle." Noémi was competent enough, but to travel alone seemed foolhardy for any young woman. I sent up a small prayer for her safety.

"Is there anything else in the letter?"

Only betrayal. But as I could not see how that would help anyone now, I lied. "No."

He sighed. "I had hoped you might help us. Well, I have sent men after her. I hope they can find her before she comes to harm."

X

My world had never been so circumscribed as it was just then. Even in England, when Mama had kept me from society, she had allowed me out: exploring the fields, visiting the village, shopping in the markets. Catherine and Richard allowed me nowhere.

I prowled the limits of my room, taking books off the shelf at random and replacing them. Even my beloved poetry books could not hold me: they were mere words, "a tale told by an idiot, full of sound and fury, signifying nothing," as Shakespeare's Macbeth had said.

Words were not enough. Once I thought they would be—if I found my voice, if I found the right words, I could compel people to hear me. But it wasn't enough. One needed more than the right words; one needed a platform from which to be heard. A king might lack eloquence, but he would be heard. A guttersnipe, no matter how facile with language, would struggle to find an audience beyond those who shared her gutter.

But I could not simply give up. I could not go back to England. I had seen a world shatter inside the Binding; I had seen a revolution begin to change the world. I wanted to be part of that change. I wanted to matter.

To do that, I needed more than my bare self. Joan of Arc had persisted in telling the truth of her visions until someone had given her an army. Like Joan, I simply needed an audience—and a powerful ally.

I sat at my desk and pulled out a sheet of the finest parchment I owned, the Arden phoenix crest emblazoned at the top, and began to write.

CHAPTER 25

Listening to Catherine and Richard's carriage rattle away from the house, I felt like Cinderella, left behind as the world gathered for a ball. The masquerade that night at Schönbrunn promised to be a crowning event of the Congress season. Instead of a costume, I wore a nightdress; instead of a glittering ballroom and throngs of people, I was alone in my bedroom.

Catherine had been adamant I stay behind. "Richard and I must make an appearance, but we will not stay above a few hours." She eyed me. "And do not think you can sneak out. I've given the staff orders that you are to be confined to your room. Someone will be watching your door at all times."

When the tumult in the house died down, I peeked out my door. A footman was slouching against the wall of the hallway. He stood to attention as my door opened.

"Beg pardon, miss, but you're not to leave."

I sighed. "I know. Could you send one of the maids to the kitchen to see if Cook has any of the plum cake left?" When he nodded, I let my door fall shut. I closed my eyes and leaned against the wall.

I had heard nothing in response to the letter I had sent to Franz Joseph, asking for an audience. Likely, he regretted his proposal. But he had made the offer, and a man of honor did not go back on his word. Much as it would gall me to betroth myself to a man who no longer wanted my hand, I could not see I had many options. Gábor was gone—and I would not think of him. (Not above a dozen times a day.) I would not receive my inheritance from Grandmama until I reached twenty-one—or until I married. And if I could not find a powerful ally, Catherine would ship me back to England, to face the Queen's justice.

I had no reason to say no (saving, perhaps, some moral squeamishness), a dozen reasons to say yes.

And if I could not, after all, bring myself to say yes, I could use the threat of that proposal to enlist Franz Joseph's aid. If anyone could successfully intercede with the Austrian emperor or the English Queen, it was a future emperor.

But none of my plans would matter if Franz Joseph did not respond.

A sound in my room sent my eyes flying open. My wardrobe door was wide, dresses soaring past it onto the floor and my bed.

My first thought was that it must be Ginny—but no. I had given Ginny the night off, at her request. There was no need for her to be confined to the house simply because I was. And she could not have slipped past me unobserved. "Who's there?"

A head emerged from the wardrobe: Vasilisa.

"What are you doing here?" I supposed she had climbed through the window again.

She waved her hand. "I am here because you are not at the ball, and I wish you to be there."

I could not help it: I laughed. "So you are to be my fairy godmother?" She looked the part, I'd grant, all pale loveliness. Though she had a hard, feral edge I'd never pictured when reading *Cinderella*.

Her answering smile showed all her pointed teeth. "If you like."

"And shall I win the prince?" I asked, only half jesting. If Vasilisa was in earnest, this would afford me an excellent opportunity to talk to Franz Joseph.

"I hope you break his heart." Vasilisa surveyed the discarded gowns with distaste. "You have nothing that is suitable. We shall have to use magic." She plucked up a pale blue gown and shoved it at me. "Put this on."

Though it was hardly a costume, I thought the dress was rather lovely, lace dripping over a pale blue satin underskirt. Still bemused by this new turn of events, I watched as Vasilisa tapped her lips, then flicked her hands toward me.

My amusement vanished as silver threads began growing up my hands like a living thing, a delicately sharp pattern like hoarfrost on the window in January. The dress too began to shift around me, spikes springing from the collar like an Elizabethan ruff to encircle my head and throat. The skirt slimmed and lengthened, a long pool of palest whites and blues, shimmering in the last fade of evening light.

"You shall go as the Queen of Winter, the ice at the end of the world. I want all the court to see you as you are."

"The court *has* seen me. Surely you heard that I confessed to breaking the Binding."

She snorted. "I want them to see you as something more than a foolish girl."

Another flick of her narrow wrists, and something heavy settled on my head. Lifting my hands, I found a glass crown, the points sharp enough to draw blood.

"Look," Vasilisa said, turning me to the mirror.

Instead of the mask that was de rigueur at masquerades, the frost from my gloves continued up my throat, spreading in swirls across my cheeks, biting across my lips. By some glamour, Vasilisa had enhanced my purely average prettiness, until the face that peered back at me was like snow in moonlight: beautiful, terrible, deadly. A face to break the hearts of men and women alike.

I was not certain I liked the girl in the mirror.

"This is how you see me?" I asked.

"As you could be—were you not afraid."

I stared at my reflection for another long moment, wondering if it was fear that set my pulse pounding or anticipation. The door to my room was still securely shut; the guards did not suspect anything.

"Stop mooning at yourself," Vasilisa said, pinching my arm above the frost gloves. "We have work to do."

And then she pulled a cloak of darkness across the two of us, opened the window on the sweet-smelling summer evening, and flung us into the sky.

꙳

It was nearly midnight when we reached the sprawling Schönbrunn estate some miles from the walls of Vienna. The massive sweep of the baroque façade blazed with lights. Vasilisa set us down behind the main palace, on the gravel walkway near the labyrinth hedges. I rubbed my hands together. Though the summer evening was warm, the flight above the city had left me chilled and vaguely unsettled. I was not supposed to be here. Catherine was unlikely to recognize me in my costume, but should she return early and discover me gone . . . I would find Franz Joseph, then leave as soon as I could.

Behind the main building, the formal and informal gardens were decorated with blue and green lanterns. Elementalist magic sent sprays of water tumbling through the night air, above guests strolling the gardens. Silver and turquoise lights played across the walls of Schönbrunn in rippling waves, while footmen decked in shells and coral, white lace foaming down their trousers, passed with trays of food and drink.

We'd come down in an underwater kingdom.

Vasilisa and I climbed the stairs behind the palace to the ballroom, the massive French doors thrown open to the night breezes. Inside, the ballroom stopped my breath. In daylight, the rococo exuberance and the painted friezes were lovely, if a bit opulent for my taste. But at night, with Lumen lanterns casting blue lights on the polished floor and sparkling off jewelry and ornamented masks, the gold leaf on the ceiling seeming somehow to burn, the room transformed into something from legend. The undersea theme continued in the ballroom, a circulating breeze carrying the faintest hint of salt and sand; illusions of waves crested along the walls.

All those years that Mama had kept me home, I had had a lurking sympathy for Cinderella's desperate yearning for the ball—if not the prince. But as I stepped through the doors, a hush seemed to fall over the assembled dancers. As the dancers turned to stare at me, eyes widening with fear-tinged awe, I wondered if the story was not about something more than the desire to escape. If it was not, perhaps, about that moment when a girl, previously scorned, overlooked, and made to feel small, sweeps triumphantly into a room where she is the sole focus.

I confess: I liked it.

Then Vasilisa stepped beside me, as striking in bronze and green as I was in my ice and silver, and their attention fractured. The musicians struck up again, the dancers resumed their swirl, and the party moved on.

I was thronged, nearly at once, with a dozen young (and not so young) men wanting to dance with me, and a few of their sisters, wanting the name of my modiste.

"Such a stunning gown," one said. "And such gloves! Wherever did you find them?"

"My fairy godmother made them," I said, laughing.

I put off my prospective partners with a pretty word or

two and a loose promise to be available later, then plunged into the crowd.

It was oddly liberating. No one knew who I was—I might be anyone, which meant also that I might be utterly *me*. But that same anonymity meant others were also difficult to recognize behind their masks—though I saw Catherine, dressed for her royal Russian namesake, and gave her wide berth.

I caught snatches of gossip as I went: that Kossuth had returned to Buda-Pest to raise an army against the emperor (unlikely), that Dragović had dispatched his lieutenant to Croatia to mobilize their own army (probably true—and terrifying), that the secretary of the treasury's niece had been seduced by a golden-eyed praetherian (I refused to have an opinion on the likelihood of Hunger's actions). But the last bit of gossip brought me short:

"They say it was a girl who broke the Binding, not that Hungarian lord with the tsar. Practically a child!"

"I don't care if she was a babe in arms. She ought to be shot for what she's done. My Lukas has not been the same since he lost his magic."

"Shooting is too merciful. She should be hanged."

Dizziness gripped me, bringing a wave of heat into my face. I did not think I should ever grow accustomed to people wishing for my death. I stood still until the faintness passed, then moved on, grateful that Vasilisa's illusion hid my real self.

Stopping had been a mistake: before I had quite caught my breath, I was surrounded again by men, young and old, all wanting something. A dance, a turn around the garden, a word. Though none of them touched me, I felt their needs as an almost tangible, smothering weight.

"No," I managed. "No, I'm sorry." Beyond them, I spotted a slim, young man dressed as Alexander the Great, his brown hair shining above a black mask and laurel-leaf crown. By his profile, I guessed he was the archduke. "Excuse me." I cut through the crowd around me, cringing as I pressed between two guests, feeling their breath on my hair, the heat of their bodies in their clothes. The room was too close.

Alexander broke off his conversation as I approached and turned toward me.

"Madam, do you seek me?" I had guessed right: he was the archduke.

I curtsied. "I should like a word with you, if you please."

He hesitated the barest fraction before nodding and offering me his arm.

"The room is very warm," I said. "Would you show me the gardens?"

The archduke's blue eyes glittered behind his mask, but I could not read his expression to tell if he recognized me or not.

An elegant woman in sea-blue satin, dripping pearls and wearing a diamond-encrusted crown, started after us, but the swirl of dancers pressed too close, and we reached the gardens safely.

Franz Joseph led me across the lawn toward a copse of trees. A few other couples strolled in the lanes, illuminated by fairy lights and the full moon overhead.

He turned to face me and pulled off his mask, his blue

eyes scanning my face. His fingers settled, light as down, against the patterned whorls on my cheeks. "Illusion?"

I nodded.

"You are heartbreaking tonight, did you know that?"

I hope you break his heart. Why had Vasilisa brought me to the ball?

"You know who I am?"

He nodded shortly. There was a constraint in his posture, in his silence, that sent my heart plunging.

"I have given a great deal of thought to your flattering offer." I paused for a moment, waiting for some sign: a lifting of his lips, a warmth in his eyes. Nothing. I took a deep breath, squashing my scruples, and plunged on. "I should like to accept."

I caught the merest flicker of surprise in his face before his expression smoothed out and he gripped my hands. "Miss Arden. You do me great honor."

A breeze stirred around us, pricking gooseflesh on my arms.

"I . . . A gentleman should never go back on his word, I know," Franz Joseph said. "But your confession to the Congress—is it true that you broke the Binding? Mother says it is, but I cannot believe it."

I dipped my head, wondering as I did so why Franz Joseph would rather believe I had *lied.*

"Why?" His voice emerged unexpectedly high, cracking at the end. I began to feel as though my hands, still clasped in his, were no longer my own.

"Because my friends were going to die if I did not and Hungary would continue bound to laws that were not her own. Because the Binding was inherently unfair. Why should some have magic and others not, only because the Circle deemed it so? Why should the praetheria be condemned to spend their life supplying us with magic?"

"Why indeed?" He dropped my hands at last and stepped back. He pressed a fist to his lips. "You could not have known."

"What did I not know?"

Franz Joseph's shoulders sagged. For a moment he looked lost, bereft. A boy who had mistaken his way in a crowded market. I stepped toward him, my hand outstretched, but he retreated a pace, and I let my hand fall.

"The Hapsburgs have never been powerful Luminate—less so after the Binding. When you broke the Binding, you took away any magic I had." Franz Joseph opened his fist and inscribed a circle in the air. "Lumen."

A spark so faint I might have imagined it nestled in his palm before snuffing out.

No. A cloud scuttled across the moon, throwing the gardens into sudden darkness.

"But your mother—" I began.

"Is not a Hapsburg by blood. Have you not wondered why Count Grünne is always with me? He casts spells for me, so no one suspects. What future emperor could rule a magical people without magic himself?"

"I am sorry," I whispered.

"Are you? Would you have left the Binding unbroken if you had known?"

I looked away, unable to meet the pain in his eyes. Of course I would not. Not for him, not for a hundred like him. I had not left the Binding unbroken, even to save Mátyás.

I ran my tongue along my teeth, trying to wash away the bitter taste in my mouth. "I won't hold you to your offer."

"I did not say I did not wish to marry you." Franz Joseph stepped closer to me at last, cupping my cheek with his hand. "I don't know what I wish. You are—you are impossibly lovely tonight. You have so much passion for life. For justice."

That dizzy heat swept up me again, and I wavered. Franz Joseph caught me in his arms, his lips inches from mine.

"You are intoxicating," he whispered, a strange light filling his eyes.

I had only a moment to wonder at his mercurial shift, from cold and distant to close and warm, before he pressed his lips against mine.

I closed my eyes, ignoring the chill that shot through me. This was what I wanted.

He slid his tongue between my lips. I waited for the kick of excitement in my gut, but felt only a breeze slithering around my bare shoulders.

Franz Joseph pulled back. "We may have to wait until I reach my majority. You do not mind, do you?"

I did not mind. But aside from a slight relief that I would not be sent back to England at once, I did not feel anything, not even fear at his mother's reaction. It struck me that this deadness ought to concern me, but I pushed it aside and said, "Can we keep this between us, just for a little while?" Those who wanted to see me hanged would not be pleased with the news just yet.

"Of course. May I tell my mother, at least?"

"If you must." I shivered.

"You're cold. Let's go back to the ballroom."

X

I did not hear what it was Franz Joseph said to his mother—he left me with Count Grünne while he broke the news to her. The count thought it his duty to dance with me, so I caught only glimpses of Archduchess Sophie as they spoke, and her iron countenance did not change.

After the count there was a string of other partners, and I lost sight of Franz Joseph for a time. I felt oddly unsettled: it was excessively careless for a girl to misplace her potential bridegroom within half an hour of her betrothal. I was, in fact, looking for him when someone caught my hand and swung me into a waltz.

Hunger's gold eyes gleamed down at me.

I tried to pull away, but his grip was steel-strong. "Why did you tell Noémi about Mátyás?"

"She asked if I had witnessed his death. Did you want me to lie to her?"

"Yes! Or at least steer the conversation away. Noémi may never forgive me."

He peered at me with interest. "And this matters to you, her forgiveness?"

"Yes, of course it does. She is my best friend."

"Humans are so odd—so caught up in vindication and vengeance, absolution and atonement. You are forever caught in the past, forever looking to the future. When do you live in the now?"

"Unlike you, I cannot separate my past from my future, or from my present."

"I did not say my past had no bearing on my present." Some dark undertone in his words seemed to rasp against my skull, sending my heart thumping.

I changed the topic. "Did you seduce a secretary's daughter?"

The gleam grew brighter. "Should you care if I had?"

"It is not, of course, any of my business—only perhaps you don't know that it is not the socially acceptable thing to seduce unmarried women of good families."

"But the married women are fair game?"

"I did not say that!" My cheeks burned. "Never mind. I don't wish to speak of your conquests at all."

"Very well. Let us speak of yours. The archduke seems well and truly caught. Did I not promise to make you a queen?"

I stopped dancing, and the couple behind us nearly stumbled over me. *You are intoxicating,* the archduke had said.

"Did you arrange this? Is that why Vasilisa insisted I come here tonight?"

He shook his head. "I helped the archduke see you in a way he might not otherwise have done, is all. Anything more is your doing. Did Vasilisa dress you?"

I saw myself suddenly as a doll, bowing to Vasilisa's whims, moving to the strings Hunger pulled. There was a sourness in my mouth, and I tried to pull away.

"Not yet," Hunger said, holding me fast.

The waltz came to flourishing conclusion. Hunger laughed and released me to Franz Joseph, who stood waiting nearby.

"Has that man been bothering you?" the archduke asked. I shook my head. "How did your mother take your news?"

"I did not tell her yet. She is preoccupied with other concerns at the moment. The timing did not seem right." He hesitated. "Anna, you may not like this, but—"

He broke off as the archduchess marched into the middle of the ballroom. A powerful glow enveloped her, and a thin wind seemed to curl around her feet, rustling the hem of the sea-gown she wore. She looked regal, powerful—and utterly terrifying.

"My dear friends, you honor us with your presence this evening. Thank you. We have an announcement to make. You are all aware of the Congress that has been meeting in Vienna these past two months, deliberating over how to best integrate the praetheria into our society, following their release from the Binding spell. The deliberations have been long and arduous. But early this morning, accord was at last reached."

A chill settled in my breast. My hand closed convulsively around Franz Joseph's. "This morning? But I was not informed . . ." I fell silent, hearing the ridiculousness of my words as I said them. Of course I was no longer part of the Congress.

"Though we mean the creatures no harm, too many of them are dangerous or unpredictable. They cannot be allowed to roam free. A temporary holding camp is being established for them near Melk; they will be sent to a more permanent site once it is completed."

No.

"No!" someone else shouted. I spun, looking for its source. The tsar stood a few paces away, my uncle Pál beside him.

Pál caught me looking at him and smiled that thin smile I so disliked. He was *enjoying* this.

"The sequestration is effective immediately. Dragović!" Behind the archduchess, a dozen or so Red Mantles fanned out across the room.

"No!" the tsar shouted again, in French, then German. "The creatures are *mine*! You shall not have them. You shall not weaken me like this. Praetheria! Men at arms! To me! To me!" A dozen or so men with the erect bearing of soldiers drove through the crowd toward the tsar. Beside the tsar, the golden-haired Count Svarog seemed to flicker—his face splitting apart for the briefest of moments to reveal four heads, each grimacing at the crowd around them. I blinked, and the man's face was restored, handsome beyond anything I had seen.

What kind of illusion was that? Who *was that?*

A tall, willowy man with bark-textured skin and branching antlers, wearing the gold-and-black livery of the Hapsburg family, dropped his serving tray and bolted toward an open door onto the balcony. A Red Mantle seized the tree-man just as he reached the door, then released him with a screech.

"He shocked me!"

The archduchess lifted both hands. Doors on either side of the room opened, and dozens of men and women entered, wearing the black and gold of the emperor's household. But they did not carry themselves like servants, and as I watched, a short, grizzle-haired man began weaving his hands in the air and murmuring. I felt the slightest buzz of the spell as it passed, and then the tree-man halted, halfway out the French door, before tumbling frozen to the ground.

I dropped Franz Joseph's hand and began to move—to challenge the archduchess or help the tree-creature, I was not entirely certain which. But he caught my arm.

"Anna, don't! Your compassionate heart does you credit, but you'll only injure yourself if you try anything now. The Congress has decided: nothing you do can change the fate of the praetheria. Wait."

But would waiting change anything? For that matter, would *acting* change anything? If I helped a creature escape now, would that prevent its capture later?

It was hard to think clearly, and I had so little time.

Another praetherian shed its human aspect, and a serpent slid from empty livery as it fell to the ground. It streaked across the floor, accompanied by shouting. One of the black-and-gold figures pointed at it, and it writhed and knotted before the archduchess, then fell still.

All around me, the room was in chaos: ordinary men and women scrambling for the doors, the Red Mantles surrounding the praetheria, the black-and-gold figures flooding across the ballroom, the buzz of their spells all around me.

I shook free of Franz Joseph and crossed the floor to Archduchess Sophie. My gloves began unraveling as I walked, the illusion melting away like real frost before warmth. My dress too was reverting: titters followed me.

I did not know what this meant, if Vasilisa had been captured or had burned up her magic trying to escape.

I hoped she was flying free across the night.

Pál caught my arm as I passed him. "It's not too late to join us," he said. "Come with me, and the tsar will protect you."

"I don't want your protection," I said, and continued my march to the archduchess.

She looked at me coldly. "Anna Arden."

I curtsied. "Your Majesty, please, don't let this happen. Some of the praetheria have served you well—and they cannot help their birth. They deserve better than this."

"You presume too much, Miss Arden. Life is not fair," the archduchess said. "Not for you, not for me, not for anyone. You will be happier if you accept that."

"You are the most powerful person in this court: if you were to set your will against this, you could stop it. Please. I have done everything you asked. I have let your son court me. I have tried to smooth relations between Austria and Hungary."

She raised her eyebrows. "Have you? From where I stand, I have seen only a foolish girl who sets herself against everything and everyone."

"Anna." Franz Joseph tugged gently on my arm. "There's nothing you can do."

"Not now," I said. "But someday I will have the power to stop this."

At that, Archduchess Sophie's face did change, the tiniest curl of a smile lifting her lips. "Did my besotted son propose to you? Dear, what impulsive children you are."

"I will be my own man soon enough," Franz Joseph said. "I can make my own choices."

"But you will not marry to disoblige me, or your country, my Franzi. Listen carefully, Miss Arden. Your beloved Hungary is facing a civil war. Already Croatian soldiers march toward Buda-Pest, and Romanian soldiers will follow them."

"And you allow this?" I asked the archduchess.

"We do not officially sanction insurrection."

But the smile playing about her lips told me another story. The conversation I had overheard ages ago came back to me—the archduchess complaining about the ignominy of submitting to a mess of students, Dragović promising to set it right.

"Within a year, likely less, Hungary will be brought firmly back within the Hapsburg Empire, where it belongs. Any value you might have brought to marriage as an alliance builder is lost completely. Not to mention your disastrously unpopular decision to break the Binding—and publicly announce as much."

Her words hammered against me.

"Perhaps there is some value in your ability to break spells—but it seems a mercurial ability, and unreliable. Besides which, I have had a most revealing conversation with one of my foremost Luminate historians. He verifies what you charged at the Congress the other day, that the original Binding was forged with blood magic—what we now would call death magic. He tells me, also, that it is highly unlikely such a spell could have broken without similar magic."

Though the fringes of the room were still in turmoil—praetheria fighting to evade capture, Russian men flanking their tsar—a small bubble of quiet formed around us. Catherine stood nearby, gripping Richard's hand. William waited just beyond them, his gold mask pushed up onto his red hair, leaving his pale, freckled face exposed. My entire body was stiff with tension, my bare hands rubbing anxiously at the lace overlay of my skirt.

"Is this true, Miss Arden? Was someone killed to break the Binding? Did *you* kill him?" Archduchess Sophie asked.

I could not seem to swallow. I did not want to lie, to diminish Mátyás's sacrifice. But I could not tell the truth either. Death magic was forbidden, a capital offense.

"You needn't answer me. Your face betrays you."

Franz Joseph lifted a hand toward me, then let it fall. "Anna?"

I could not answer him. He wanted me to swear my innocence, and I was not innocent.

"If it were only a matter of the broken Binding, we might have sent you to England for trial, as you broke no formal law. But this is another matter entirely." The archduchess caught her breath, but there was no triumph in her eyes. "Miss Anna Arden, for crimes against the crown and against human dignity, for willingly taking a human life in support of your dark magic, your life is hereby forfeit." She nodded at Dragović. "Seize her."

Mátyás

CHAPTER 26

The scream curdled in the air of the camp, leaving a sourness in the dense July warmth.

I sprang up from my maps with a muffled curse. Screaming seldom presaged anything good—besides which, the day was damnably hot, my sweat-soaked shirt had dried prickly and itchy against my back, and I wanted nothing more than a stiff drink and a long nap in cool shade. *Not* breaking up another of the interminable squabbles in camp. And especially not poring over maps of the *puszta*, planning yet another raid—something that should have been Ákos's responsibility, but which he had breezily delegated to me.

You made me leader—I nominate you to do my work, he'd said.

Where was the bastard now? Sound asleep, under a tree. I ought to upend the remains of the dishwater over him.

A second scream chased the first. Ákos would have to wait.

I found the culprits some few hundred meters from camp, a couple of the younger bandits cornering the lidérc, teasing her about her webbed feet until she spat at them and screamed. I sent the lidérc back to camp—if she had a name, she had not yet disclosed it—and sentenced the others to scrub the accumulated laundry and to clean up after the horses.

Then I made Ákos gather everyone together. A heat haze shimmered over the *puszta*, turning the grasses to water where the ground met the sky. Gnats hummed around my face, and I swatted them absently.

Ákos looked at me, and I sighed. I'd no wish to play leader. But something must be said.

"I do not ask that you like each other," I said. "But I do ask that you respect each other. You've all come here seeking a kind of sanctuary—an escape from the hatred of a mob, from poverty, hell, maybe even from boredom. I don't care why you've come. But you WILL respect one another, or you will leave."

The men and creatures grumbled, but they quieted. Boredom was at the root of some of their quarrels, I knew that, but there were only so many tasks we could set them to do.

As the *betyárok* dispersed, Ákos sent our best hunters—the lidérc, Zhivka, a few of the men—out to the plains to find meat for our supper, with strict instructions that they were *not* to bring home livestock belonging to the *puszta* farmers who eked out a living even poorer than our own.

Or, heaven forbid, a dog or two, as the lidérc had done when first sent to hunt. *Meat is meat,* she had said, mystified by my efforts to explain that for us, dogs were companions, not food.

When everyone was safely occupied, I exhaled and walked to the makeshift corral where Holdas grazed with the rest of our horses. I saddled him and rode a wide circle around the perimeter of our camp, looking for our scouts. Varjú followed, floating on invisible air currents.

A light breeze skimmed across the grasses, but even that could not make the heat tolerable. It closed around me like bars, a trap of stale air and stagnating warmth. I met with the scouts, who assured me all was clear—no sign of hussars hunting us, or of potential marks either—and I returned to the camp.

As I drew closer, I pulled up short at the sight of Bahadır, the leshy tree-men, and our giant just outside the camp. As I watched, Bahadır bowed low to the praetheria, who followed suit, though the giant nearly lost his balance and pitched forward. Bahadır steadied him at the last minute.

The tree-creatures put their hands together, raised them above their heads, and then spread their arms and fingers wide. Bahadır mimicked their actions.

"What are you doing?" I asked, bemused.

"I am teaching them how to behave politely to humans," Bahadır said, "and they are doing the same for me. This"—he demonstrated the move I'd just observed—"is a standard leshy greeting that means, I think, to bless with sun and rain so your roots and branches may flourish."

The tree-creatures nodded gravely. I was still learning to

read the different praetherian expressions, but they seemed pleased. I dismounted and repeated Bahadır's movement, and the two of them hummed low in their throats.

"Well, carry on," I said, leading Holdas past them toward the corral, carrying with me a buoyant hopefulness at such dissimilar creatures trading knowledge with each other, as though there might someday be a world where such things were normal, and not a curious exception.

Ж

I found Zhivka bathing in the long gold sunset, lying on the prairie grass and rubbing her hands across her arms in the fading light, her face beatific.

A twig cracked under my foot, and she shot upright, her frantic eyes easing as they came to rest on me. "Did you need something, my lord?"

"Mátyás," I said.

"I was told not to use your given name, my lord."

I groaned. "How long do you plan to hold my incivility against me?"

"As long as it amuses me," she said, patting the ground beside her. "Come, join me. This is a good place for thinking."

I settled on the grass. "What do you think of, when you come here?"

"Fire," she said, gesturing at the distant sun. "My sisters. I miss them."

"I miss my sister too." When we had lived together, Noémi had seemed more nuisance than anything else and we fought frequently, but now I'd be overjoyed to be the subject of her scolding again. I wondered how she filled her days in Vienna, if she ever thought of me. If she was well. "I hope you know that the agreement I made with the samodiva does not have to hold you here. You're not a prisoner. You're free to go, if you wish."

Her eyes lit, incandescent. I was not sure if it was a banked fire inside, or just the reflection of the fading sun. Then her chin drooped. "I must stay. But I thank you for the offer."

Why? I wondered, but the peaceful moment made me disinclined to ask. I remained a little longer, talking of minor camp gossip, before reluctantly rising again. The sun had already disappeared, only a wash of light against the sky marking its passing. I wished I could linger, but there were too many tasks already calling for my attention.

$$\chi$$

The brief interlude of peace in camp was destined not to last.

A few days later I returned from a scouting venture to find a visitor. By the time I loosed Holdas on the grasses, Ákos had already welcomed her and settled her on a rock that passed for a chair. Her back was turned to me, but the dark hair flowing like velvet down her shoulders was familiar. Far above, dark shapes circled over the camp. Turul birds.

The Lady had returned.

I stopped when I recognized her, rooted to the ground

just outside the circle of our tents. As I watched, others began drifting toward her: some of my most hardened *betyárok,* the lidérc, the domovoi. Even Varjú, curse him, kept sidling along a branch overhead to get closer. Ákos sat by her feet, his face rapt. She stroked a hand across his cheek, and he blushed—Ákos, whom I had never seen so befuddled, not even by Zhivka at her most enthralling.

I stalked toward the Lady. If the others fell back at my glowering approach, the Lady merely smiled. "What are you doing here?"

Her gaze didn't waver. "My birds bring me reports of your movement, but I thought it time I spoke with you again. You have wrought well." She gestured to the clearing around us, the crowd equal parts praetherian and human, all pressed close together.

"This wasn't done for you," I said.

"No? But it was done all the same. These men and creatures would follow you into death."

No. My heart burned cold. "I won't ask them to. All I want is for us to live our lives unmolested."

"That is all most of us want. But few will have that chance. Do you think the Four will curtail their plan because you want to be left alone? Do you think the Austrian emperor, who even now sends money to Croatian troops to invade our borders, cares what a band of outlaws thinks about living in peace? If peace were so easily won, I would welcome it, but it will not be. Will you not reconsider?"

I shook my head. "This is not our fight."

"It will be."

A low murmuring gathered around me. Did they judge

314

me for saying no? Let them. I'd already taken on more responsibility than I had ever wanted.

"If you will not assume your role as táltos, at least let me
teach you to master your powers."

"I don't need help with my powers. I've enough."

She shook her head, her hair sliding down her shoulders like water. Someone sighed: it might have been Ákos.
"You've not touched the powers of your rebirth—only
those powers you had in life, your shifting and your animal
persuasion. But you've so much more, powers of which
you've barely tapped the surface. A táltos who dies and is
reborn becomes a shaman, capable of taking on any shape,
able to send his soul from his body in dreams."

When I shifted, there was always a moment in a new
form where I felt alien: where the skin or fur or feathers I'd
assumed seemed disconnected. I felt that way now, without shifting, as though I had suddenly become someone
unrecognizable to myself. I scratched at my forearm.

"And what should I do with this power?"

I had not forgotten the monster I'd become when I'd
shifted at Hadúr's provocation, that all-consuming hunger. "If you've watched me at all, you must have seen that
I'm lazy, venal, selfish, rather cowardly. If you make me
a god—who will stand against me? How will you ensure
that I do not destroy the very people and country you mean
to save?" I broke off, breathing hard, as if I'd run a race.

The Lady closed the distance between us, setting her
hands against my cheek. Her touch was cooling in the
heavy summer air. She smelled of lavender and vanilla, the
same scent my mother had worn when I was young, and

for a moment my craving for the past thrust me so forcibly into the mind of my six-year-old self that I wanted to cry.

"I know you," the Lady said. "I have known you all your life."

The way she looked at me with those clear eyes, I wanted to believe her. I wanted to be known like that, with a clarity that saw me for my faults and strengths all together and did not judge. More than that, in the moment she looked at me, I wanted to *be* the person she saw.

But I was not that person. I did not think I could be, no matter what she thought she saw or hoped to convince me of.

"I have served under weak leaders and they are dangerous. But you are not weak," Ákos said.

"Et tu, Brute?" I asked. When Ákos only stared at me, I sighed. "Not you too? Besides, I'm not even the leader here."

"Are you not?" the Lady asked.

Ákos grinned at me. "My leadership consists mainly of handing any real work to you. You've done a marvelous job."

A pokolba. He was right: every major decision recently had been mine. Ákos only confirmed my orders. I'd stepped into a role I didn't want without realizing I'd done it.

"My answer is still no," I told the Lady.

"Your powers may hurt more than you if you leave them untouched."

"They've done nothing so far," I said. "Let them stay buried."

She nodded once. "I will go, then."

"That would be best."

At once a chorus of outcry arose, and I moved back to allow the others to press around the Lady, petitioning her to stay. She floated from one to the next, setting her hand on their cheek or head or shoulder, leaving her blessing.

"I am sorry, my friends, but I have other things I must do, others I must be watching. Do your best to persuade Mátyás to help me, and I may come back."

If it had not been for the fact that I'd never seen a glimmer of mischievousness in the Lady, I'd have sworn that the smile she sent me was dulcet, hiding an edge. She had effectively trapped me. She might do as I asked and not petition me further, but it did not matter: the others would pester me for her.

Already, the lidérc was inching toward me, her fey eyes flickering. "Why won't you help the Lady?"

I only shook my head and did not answer. I stalked toward the horses. If Holdas was surprised to be ridden out again so soon after coming in, he didn't show it. We raced beneath the low-slung thunderclouds until the rain came on, and then raced some more. Varjú sped after us, wheeling in the sky.

The *puszta* spun all around me, an ocean of grass. I reached a spot where there was nothing, no landmarks to break the endless flatness where the land kissed the sky. I could lose myself here. Holdas and I could keep riding and never go back.

But I knew too well how it felt to wait for someone who did not return. I had sat vigil with my mother the long day after my father did not return, until nightfall, when someone brought us word that he was dead, shot by his own hand in one of the private rooms at his club.

The *betyárok* were not my family; they were not a fifteen-year-old boy waiting for their father. A tug of responsibility pulled me back anyway. I had not asked to lead them, but they had given me the role. I could refuse it still. But I couldn't bring myself to. The responsibility sat heavy on me, but it was not entirely uncomfortable. It felt . . . *right*.

It felt damned terrifying.

I spat all the curse words I could think of at the lowering sky, rain stinging my face like tears.

Then I rode back to camp. To my *betyárok*. My own clan of bandits.

CHAPTER 27

The soldiers were gathered in a dim *csárda,* flickering yellow light from a smoking fire washing across their distinctive hussar uniforms, glinting on the hilts of their sabers, catching in the feathers of the shako hats now discarded on the table and floor before them.

I watched them from the shadows, with only a vague recollection of how I'd come to be there: flying across moon-dark fields.

"The *betyárok* must be stopped," one said, touching his hand lightly to his pomaded hair. Even at this distance, I could smell the hog lard used to grease it. "They've grown too powerful."

"And they've too many of those damned monsters. It's a perversion." Another spat on the floor.

The first pulled out a map of the region, unrolled it on the table. "Our report sets them about here," he said.

"We'll scour the area and pin them down. When we've found them, we'll wait till nightfall."

"Are we to kill or capture?" a third asked.

The leader shrugged. "It's all one to me. But their King of Crows you will leave to me. I will gut him and use his own entrails to hang him." He lifted his head from the scrutiny of the maps and looked directly at me, his eyes dark and small like a rat's.

Everything in me seemed to fly apart, and I woke, choking and thrashing in the dark.

A dream. I tossed my blanket from me and stood. It was only a dream, a nightmare born of secret fears.

But my leg muscles cramped, and my heart still pounded as though I'd run in from the plains.

In the morning the domovoi sidled up to me as I tried to wash my face.

"We would fight with you, táltos. With the Lady." His rough Hungarian had improved in the weeks since he'd joined us.

"I don't want to fight," I said.

The domovoi stroked his long beard. "If war comes to you, you do not choose."

I pictured soldiers pouring into camp, slaughtering *betyár* and praetherian alike. What had the Lady said about my dreams? "Have new guards been set about the perimeter yet?"

He shrugged.

"Make yourself useful and tell Ákos to see to it." Lingering unease from the night's dream still prickled along my spine.

Midmorning, the guards brought me a prisoner, blindfolded as I had been when László caught me. The man's hair was dark, his face mostly obscured by the handkerchief. Still, something about the way he stood seemed familiar.

"Why have you brought this man here?" I asked, pitching my voice so it sounded gruff and determined. A voice to take seriously.

"He was asking at the inn about the King of Crows," Ákos said.

I turned to the prisoner. "What is your business with him?"

"That business is with the bandit king himself."

That voice . . . I closed the distance between myself and the prisoner and pulled off the blindfold. "Gábor?"

My old friend blinked at me. *"Mátyás?"* A frown pulled his eyebrows together. "But Anna said you were dead."

"I *was* dead." I sighed. "It's a long story. Are you in a hurry? We haven't much, but we can offer you some *gulyás* stew." I untied the ropes fastening Gábor's hands together, watching as he rubbed his wrists.

"Are you the King of Crows?" Gábor asked.

I ducked my head, conscious of Ákos suppressing laughter nearby.

Gábor groaned. "I might have guessed as much."

I sat with Gábor as he polished off a bowl of stew. While he ate, I explained what I knew, how the *Boldogasszony* had brought me back to life after the Binding spell broke, and I had fallen in with a group of bandits.

"But if you're alive—why do Anna and Noémi think you are dead?" I could feel Gábor's eyes on me, steady and measuring. He saw too much, damn him.

"Because the *Boldogasszony*—the Lady—wants me to save Hungary. And she will threaten anything she thinks I care for to make me play her role. She nearly killed János to force my hand. I cannot let her think I care." I scanned the sky and nearby trees, listening for birds that might be the Lady's eyes and ears. For the moment, we were safe.

Gábor rubbed his chin. "I'm afraid I've come to ask a similar favor. Kossuth sent me to find you, to ask your aid for the Hungarian troops. And not just Hungary—the Hapsburgs have passed a law that the praetheria are to be sequestered, and Russia has opened their borders to them, in defiance of the Congress."

My throat dried. "Are Noémi and Anna safe?"

"They have powerful friends and family. They are as safe as anyone." He looked at me curiously. "Why won't you help the Lady? You were a hero once."

"All I had to do was die! There's no way to fail at dying. But this—there are so many ways to fail that it makes my head ache just thinking of it."

Gábor must have sensed my reluctance to say more, because he changed the topic, glancing around the camp at the praetheria: at Zhivka trailing bits of light, and the domovoi riding on the shoulders of a tree-man. "I heard the *puszta* was a safe place for the praetheria."

"Safer than other places," I agreed. "They deserve better from us."

⅄

That night, over a dinner of stew and *pogácsa* biscuits that Ákos managed to make light and flaky despite the limitations of a camp stove, Gábor told the others about the Congress in Vienna and its decision to put the praetheria in camps.

"Humans have always feared us," the lidérc said, baring her pointed teeth and stretching her goose feet toward the fire. "And we are already outlaws. We will stay here."

"To be fair, you are terrifying," Ákos pointed out. "I'd not want to wake and find your face above mine!" He grinned at her, to show he meant no malice.

"You should dream of being so lucky."

"And what news of Hungary?" Bahadır asked. "Is there to be war?"

Gábor ducked his head. "I am afraid so. A Croatian army marches on the Banat. There are already border skirmishes in Serbia, and the Romanians in Wallachia observe us closely for signs of weakness. When I left Vienna, Kossuth Lajos was preparing to return to Buda-Pest to ask the government for money to raise troops."

"I would fight," Ákos said, his words echoed by most of my *betyárok*.

I looked at him in surprise. "Why? You're not trained soldiers. And—there's a price on your head."

"We love our country," one said.

"And we can hold guns and ride horses. That is as much as most new recruits know," said another.

"Besides," Ákos added, "they'd have to pardon us, don't you think, if we were to fight?"

This patchwork family that I'd begun to build was disintegrating before my eyes. I'd no wish to see them die, but I would not stop them if they wanted to fight.

"I too would fight," the lidérc said.

When everyone stared at her, she shrugged one shoulder beneath her tangled hair. "Hungary is my home too. And I do not dislike you enough to want to see you die."

Touched, I said, "This isn't your war. You don't have to fight."

"The Lady said we shall all have to fight," the domovoi said.

Bahadır asked, "Why would you fight alongside the same people who want to lock your kind away?"

"It is not so simple," Zhivka said, staring at the fire, her hands weaving shapes that were echoed in the flames. "This fight is not just Hungarians against Croatians and Serbians, or humans against praetheria. There is a bigger war brewing, about the kind of world we wish to live in. The Lady will fight for Hungary and for many of the praetheria, for a world where humans and praetheria can live together."

She fell silent for a moment, her eyes troubled.

"And their enemy?" Bahadır prompted.

"The Four will drive a human army against Hungary and the Lady, and when that army fails, they will send praetheria to destroy the rest." Her words were slow, reluctant.

"And that world?"

"The praetheria will rule. What humans survive will live as the praetheria lived for centuries in the Binding: as chattel."

"How do you know this?" I asked. "How do you know the Four are not a story the Lady tells to shape the world to her own design?" If the stories were true, then of course

I should fight. But I would fight as a soldier, not as a leader of soldiers.

The others looked at me as though I had spoken blasphemy in the nave of a church.

"You were only a story," Gábor said, "until I found you."

"If they were only a story," Zhivka said, "then I would not be here."

X

The attack came without warning.

I had been dreaming, flying across the *puszta* in crow form, following the ribbon of the road toward Buda-Pest. Then, between one wingbeat and the next, I was skimming the tips of a forest. I dropped low, pulled by some powerful instinct into the mouth of a clearing. A girl sat cradled between the roots of an old, mossy tree, her blond head resting on her forearms, which were propped upon her knees. Her dress had the look of something once fine— some shiny, crimson stuff—that had been dragged through mud and a briar patch.

My dream self had shifted to human form—clothed, unlike my waking self—and the girl lifted her head.

Noémi's entire face lit, a sun emerging after a long gloom. "Mátyás!" She sprang to her feet and would have come to me, but her wrists were bound with daisy chains and creeping vines.

I ran toward her, arms outstretched—and a scream shattered through the clearing, cleaving through my dream self and pulling me back into my own body.

Even awake, the scream still echoed in my ears. No, not

an echo, I realized—someone was in fact screaming. More than one someone. I sat up. A bullet cracked past my face, plowing into the ground where my head had rested only a moment before.

I scrambled up, adrenaline burning away the last heaviness of sleep.

We were under attack.

A wood witch darted past me, a soldier close behind her, blood already dripping from his drawn saber. *Whose blood?* And where were the guards—Ákos and one other—who were supposed to have sounded a warning?

No time to think about that now. I scooped up the gun lying near my pillow and whirled, senses already reaching for Varjú nesting in the trees nearby. He was awake and waiting.

The crow swooped low just as another gunshot exploded.

I dove away from the exposed clearing toward the scanty shelter of a copse of trees. The camp was in chaos, uniformed hussars trampling through bedding, stabbing viciously at anything that looked like a body. Other huddled shapes, motionless on the ground. A few of my *betyárok* grappling against their attackers. One of the tree-men swinging a hussar up and over his head before releasing him to the sky.

Zhivka, lit like a torch in the night.

"Zhivka, no!" Her glamour might be potent against a handful of men, but without her sisters she couldn't take down the mass of soldiers swarming through the camp. She'd be a target before she got far.

Too late. The crack of a gun from a soldier I couldn't see, and Zhivka crumpled like a burning rose.

I sprang toward her, clubbing a hussar who stood in front of me on the head, shooting another as he took aim at Bahadır.

I was reaching through the night for roosting crows and falcons when pain sliced through my leg and I stumbled, losing the thread of my magic. The curved saber withdrew, then flashed toward me again. I hurled my gun at him, which had the advantage of throwing my attacker off guard, but the distinct disadvantage of leaving me without a usable weapon.

As the hussar lunged a third time, I finally shifted into crow form and flung myself up in the air. While the soldier gaped, I dove toward his face.

He screamed, clasping his hands over his eyes, and I swooped low, plucking up his dropped saber. As I lifted into the air, straining against the weight, something caught my injured leg. I let go of the sword, to a satisfyingly pained grunt below, and the pressure eased off. I fluttered to a nearby branch, my heart sprinting and my leg aching.

"Surrender!" one of the soldiers in the center of the camp called out. I focused on the voice and ruffled my wings in shock. I knew that face: he'd stepped out of my dreams. The leader of the soldiers I'd seen drinking in a *csárda*. Had it been more than a dream? I should have paid more attention when the Lady spoke of my reborn gifts. "We've come to take the praetheria to Vienna, the rest of you to face the justice of the land."

There were too many bodies on the ground, more *betyár*

than hussar. Some were wounded, but some did not move. My giant lay slumped on his side against the earth, and I clacked my beak in dismay. The soldiers had approximately half again our number, and they'd taken us by surprise.

But if they took us prisoner, we'd face trial. My life would certainly be forfeit, possibly my men. I wasn't worried about myself—I hadn't met a prison yet that could hold me—but the others made me hesitate. Bahadır might die simply because he was foreign. The others would likely be hanged for a demonstration. And the praetheria would be imprisoned for life, at best.

We could not surrender.

I screamed a challenge and shot skyward, the crows and falcons I'd summoned winging through the night, sleeping horses now awake and stampeding toward the camp.

I was feeding the animals images of the hussars when a bullet shattered my wing, dropping me from the sky. I had a moment of despair, etched in sharp lines of fire and pain, before slamming into the ground. Agony burst through me like a firecracker and then, mercifully, nothing.

Anna

CHAPTER 28

Two Red Mantles seized my arms. I tugged and kicked, but their grip was implacable.

No. There was no spell here for me to break, only human strength—and I was powerless against it. I cast a desperate glance around the ballroom. The throng leered at me, black masks hiding glittering eyes, costumed hoods casting monstrous shadows against the wall. The light spangling off the mirrors was bright and hard and cruel. It seemed impossible that the archduchess had just given the order for my death.

Catherine wept quietly into Richard's shoulder and would not look at me.

"Anna?" Franz Joseph said again, his voice thinner this time, like an echo.

The guards began hauling me forward, across the floor. William ran toward us, blocking our progress.

"You can't take her like this, not without a trial!" William said, his hand going automatically to his hip, where an ornamental scabbard hung, part of a pirate costume.

His fingers hadn't even closed around the hilt of the sword when the guard on my right shoved a wicked, curved Turkish knife into William's gut.

William doubled over, his hands clutching his stomach, blood blossoming around his fingers.

"William!" I screamed, but already I was being dragged past him, my sight obscured by the black-and-gold magicians streaming across the room, driving the praetheria before them. A curl of anger tightened inside me, my shadow self stirring with it. I jabbed my elbow at the guard who had struck William. He merely grunted and tightened his grip.

I started thrashing between them, fighting hard enough to stop our forward momentum. "If he dies, I hope you rot in hell!"

My left-hand guard released me, and I thought for a moment that I might pull free, but he yanked his pistol from his belt and slammed it into my skull.

The room went black, then flared white. Pain rang through me, echoing down my spine and pinching my fingers. Before I could catch my breath, the guard had grabbed my arm again and we were moving.

My blurred eyes caught on a familiar face, frozen in the sea of motion: a girl a half dozen years older than me, her face pale beneath her freckles, her arm raised before her as though to ward off a blow—or cast a spell.

Ginny.

The colors of the room swirled around me, melting together like water-paints on paper.

"Miss Anna," Ginny cried, dropping her hands and running toward me. I remembered: she had asked for the night off.

"Did you know about the praetheria?" I was still being hauled toward the doors of the ballroom. My shoulders throbbed from the uncomfortable angle; my wrists burned where the Red Mantles gripped me.

"They said it was an exercise," Ginny said. "Lord Ponsonby sent a message from the embassy that any British students were to lend aid. I didn't know it would be like this. I didn't know you'd be here."

"Then stop. Don't do this." How could Ginny help the magicians, knowing how I felt about the praetheria? After seeing the archduchess denounce me? Given a choice between betraying the ambassador's order (and the British crown) and betraying me, she'd chosen me. My head throbbed with the aftereffects of the soldier's blow, and I fought not to vomit right there in the ballroom.

I thought I heard her say "I'm sorry," but the sound was lost in the chaos of the room. The air around me was dense with noise: the distressed cries of ladies of quality, being discreetly herded from the room; the shrieks of praetheria, less discreetly herded by magicians and soldiers alike; the murmur of spells.

Then, at once, I felt it: the magic woven through the air like fog, the faint buzz along my bones. My captors used no spells, but the room was rife with power.

I only needed to break a single spell. A small magic

would suffice to distract my guards and break free, though where I would go, God alone knew.

I dug my heels against the floor. My captors grunted at the extra resistance, though they did not slow noticeably. Closing my eyes, I reached for the magic as I had when Vasilisa struck me, letting the pain in my arms focus me. I nudged my shadow self, and she bloomed upward, her rage burning through me. I would not die for trying to do the right thing, regardless of the law.

I snagged a spell in the making from a student as we passed, grimacing through the pounding in my head. By the time the caster reacted with a muffled curse, it was already too late. I snapped the strands of the spell and pulled the released magic to me. The power pummeled me, seeking release, so I acted almost instinctively, shoving the magic into the floor at my feet, through the parquet-patterned wood and down to the stone foundations.

Months before, when I had broken the Binding spell, I had used a trick Gábor had taught me to let the magic take its own shape, rather than shape it with my will. Now I had only a little magic, but perhaps the same tactic would suffice. The rocks beneath my feet were unnatural—hewn into a form that was not their own, made to hold a shape and a structure not found in nature. I tried to feel something of that grounding, a stillness beneath the wildly churning ballroom.

"Be as you were," I whispered to both the magic and the stones, ignoring the wrenching ache in my arms, the rapidly approaching door.

A breath, and then the floor shifted, the rocks churning in their foundation. My guards and I tumbled to the floor. I recovered soonest, having expected *something,* and scrambled to my feet. I darted across the room, toward the doors leading into the garden.

The wood beneath me lifted and fell like an ocean wave, and all across the room people shook. Some managed to keep their feet; most toppled. When the wave reached the far wall, everything seemed to pause for a moment. Then the marble pillars quivered, the windows rattled in their frames, and glass rained down.

Screams echoed across the room. Some part of me winced, but the greater part felt a savage kick of satisfaction. *Let the archduchess try to misjudge me again.* A few praetheria limped through the open windows, and I cheered them silently.

I dodged fallen masqueraders, trying to keep my feet as a second wave rolled across the floor. A curious low grinding sounded, and then a massive section of the outer wall collapsed, dust and rock falling into the ballroom amid more screams.

A gust of air filled the room. A gold-flecked, black dragon flexed its impossibly long wings in the new opening, his enormous shadow falling across the crowd. He shook, and the walls nearest him trembled, then crumbled down, broadening the opening I'd triggered. A pair of praetheria scrambled through it. When a soldier attempted to follow, the dragon blocked him with wide, sharp wings.

I knew that dragon: Hunger, in his sárkány form. Hope flickered briefly inside me, just as a long draconic arm shot in my direction and claws curled around my torso, plucking me from the ground.

All around me marble and mortar lay strewn across the

floor; people and praetheria were tangled together in knots, a few struggling to rise, many motionless. Soldiers—some in the red-lined capes of Dragović's men, some wearing the red and gold of the Hapsburg guards—raised rifles to fire.

In the center of the room, unscathed and furious, the archduchess stood watching. She shouted something, but I couldn't make it out. A faint buzz tickled my skin—a spell, seeking after us. Ignoring the pain pulsing through my shoulders and tightening my scalp, I reached for the spell. Dark spots dancing in my vision, I concentrated for a moment on the fine lines I could sense stemming from somewhere in the center of the room, then I snapped them. I grasped for the released energy, but in my pain-fogged state, I missed. The newly released energy stirred up a vortex around us.

Glass shards stung my cheeks, and I threw my arms up to protect my eyes. Hunger roared again and surged upward, lifting me from the floor in a sickening lurch and swirl. I swallowed hard, and then we were through the wind and the glass and soaring through the gap in the wall toward the distant pinprick of stars.

I am not certain how long we flew: the air was cold, this high above the ground, and the seconds stretched out infinitely. At some point I passed out from pain. When I came to, we were far away from the city lights, flying over patchwork fields illuminated by the full moon.

At last Hunger set down in a wooded area. When he released me, I staggered before sitting abruptly on the ground. My dress was torn and dirty, but it no longer seemed to matter. My life was forfeit. Mátyás and Grandmama were dead, maybe William too. Noémi and Gábor were gone, my father and James so far away they might as well be on the moon. Catherine despaired of me, and Ginny had betrayed me. I could not go back to Vienna, or to England. I might go to Hungary, but the archduchess might claim that harboring a fugitive justified an Austrian invasion.

I was briefly sick in a bush. When I straightened and wiped my mouth, Hunger was back in human shape, his gold eyes resting on me with something akin to compassion. Unlike my cousin, he emerged from his shifting fully dressed—a small mercy for which I was grateful, even if it was only an illusion. My frayed nerves could not handle another shock.

"Thank you," I said, "for rescuing me."

"I seem to have made a habit of it."

Despite my injuries, I stiffened. "I am not a damsel in distress."

Hunger laughed, then winced. "It is not weakness to need help. Even the most powerful among us need allies." I saw now that he was wounded too: small gashes across his cheeks and hands; a larger cut, bleeding sluggishly, across his thigh.

"You're hurt!"

"It's no matter. We've healers among our number. Come." He held out a hand to me.

I crossed my arms across my chest. "I've not forgiven you yet."

"I neither need nor want your forgiveness. But don't be foolish. You're half sick with pain."

At that, I let Hunger help me rise, though I swallowed

another scream at the lance of fire that shot through me when he tugged on my arm. My head throbbed in time with my halting steps, the cost of spell-breaking compounding my physical injuries.

Hunger led me into the gloom. As my eyes adjusted to the dimmer light under the trees, I began to realize this was not a randomly chosen destination: among the trees were clear signs of habitation. Small huts woven of grass and moss nestled in the roots of great trees. I thought, at first, they might be children's playthings, but eyes glimmered at me from shadowed doorways. Farther in, the huts grew larger and more intricate. I passed a carefully planned structure of mud and twigs, with smooth river stones forming whorls and waves along the walls and thick straw plaits for a roof. A few paces more and I spotted a sod room carved out of a hillock, daisies springing up around the wooden doorway.

"What is this place?" I asked, but Hunger didn't answer. I guessed it to be some kind of praetherian camp—but these homes had not been thrown together in a hurry. Whoever lived here had been here for some time.

Hunger set me down on a moss-covered hollow at the base of a tree. The moss seemed to shift to better fit my form, though I might have imagined that: my body ached so fiercely that the moss felt like the best of down pillows. I closed my eyes, trying to will sleep to wash away the burning in my head and arms.

When Hunger returned a few moments later, I blinked up at him to find *things* crawling across his hands. They looked like a curious cross between a moth and a grub:

wingless, but with the soft covering of a moth and wide, feathered antennae. He plucked them one at a time from his hands and placed them on my shoulders. I tried not to cringe or cry out—Hunger's amused eyes told me he clearly expected *some* reaction from me. Only my gloved fingers tightened into fists. Two of the grubs began creeping down my arms, snuffling at the skin below my sleeves. A third began climbing the nape of my neck. As the fourth slipped down the collar of my dress, an entirely involuntary gasp escaped me.

"Get it off!"

"Give them time to work."

At that, I stopped attending to the crawling sensation across my skin and tried to observe the deeper impact. Where the grubs' snuffling anterior touched my skin, it warmed briefly and then the pain lost its sharpness. It was a slow, agonizing process—made worse because the longer the creatures climbed across me, the more I yearned to tear my skin off. But at last the pain had eased enough that I no longer felt like retching every time I moved. Hunger, reading something in my face, pulled three of the creatures off me and set them in the brush beside the tree, where they vanished.

I insisted that Hunger let me remove the fourth creature myself—the one beneath the bodice of my dress. The grublike body was soft, and not unpleasant, but I was glad to be free of it all the same. Exhaustion washed over me.

A short, squat praetherian, as much mushroom as living being, waddled up bearing a wooden bowl filled with steaming broth and vegetables. I reached for the bowl before remembering I was in a praetherian camp—and I knew what happened to folk who ate faerie food.

Hunger watched me impatiently. "There's nothing in it to hurt you."

My definition of "hurt" and Hunger's might be vastly different. A spell that would hold me in thrall for the rest of my life might not technically hurt me, but I wished to avoid it all the same.

"I'm not hungry." My stomach growled. I *was* hungry, but at that moment I craved sleep even more than food.

"You're a terrible liar." He sighed. "You must eat something. Vasilisa would insist I force-feed you, but I haven't quite her vindictiveness. I'll send someone for apples— from human orchards, so you needn't look at me like that."

"Thank you," I said meekly.

Hunger disappeared again, and I lay back in the moss-covered hollow and curled my arm beneath my head. I had meant to wait for the return of the apples, but a soft, honey-scented breeze wafted over me, and I closed my eyes and slept.

I woke periodically in the grey half-light before dawn, blinking at the creatures marching past: shining vila, hirsute giants, more of the tree-men with their craggy faces and moss beards, a dire wolf with frosted shoulders. They walked in and out of my dreams, blurring the line between sleeping and waking.

It was not until the sun washed fully across my face that my mind woke. Someone had covered me with a cloak woven of leaves and flowers during the night. As praetheria continued to pass me, I realized I had not dreamed them. Many of them were armed. Some with clubs and rocks, others with bright swords and steel-tipped lances, one or two with guns.

The archduchess had only made her announcement regarding the praetheria the night before. Had the creatures armed themselves so quickly? Or had they anticipated such a move?

Alert now, I rose, letting the flowered cloak drop at my feet. I followed a centaur to a clearing in the woods where perhaps two dozen praetheria had gathered. I watched for a moment as the centaur rode among them, directing first one and then another how to hold the weapon they carried.

They were preparing for war. I could not blame them—I had seen the corpses in the laboratory; I had heard the archduchess's orders in the ballroom. But my heart quailed at the thought of more fighting. Of Catherine, pregnant and vulnerable in the city.

Hunger materialized beside me. "I warned your Congress that we would not go peaceably into another cage."

"Could you not simply flee?"

Hunger's eyes caught mine, holding them for a long moment until I flinched and looked away. "Would you give up your own home so easily?"

I imagined the rolling green fields in Dorset and smelled the salt tang of the sea; I saw cranes circling the fields near Eszterháza. "No." Chill settled around my heart, ungainly as the cranes I had pictured.

Hunger was silent, watching a pair of the mushroom-like creatures swing clubs at one another, both missing before falling on the ground in giggles. Then he said, "We have not lived in this world for a long time. It does not remember us, or perhaps we do not remember it. The praetheria are weak—weaker than they should be, as weak as they were when the Binding spell sapped our power. We need roots to this world to return our strength. In two generations, maybe, if we could be left in peace, we could establish our own roots. Sooner, through blood sacrament, through the consummation of marriages with humans who are rooted in this world.

"If we had time, we might attempt that. But your kind will not give us time. So we will establish those roots through war. If enough blood is spilled—yours and ours together—we can remake this world for praetheria."

"And where will humans fit in this world of yours?" I set my hand against a nearby trunk, picking at flaking bark with my fingers.

"Where have we fit in your world?"

That was no answer. "I am human. Nearly everyone I love is too. Most of them are innocent. Would you kill them too?"

"Most of us were innocent too. That did not save us."

I had only once been truly terrified of Hunger—when his veneer had slipped inside a bloody garden in the Binding, and he had tried to keep me there. But that terror was a snowflake compared to the ice spreading slowly through my body. I had watched the praetheria slaughter Austrian soldiers in Buda-Pest last fall: Hunger would visit that same destruction on everyone and everything I knew.

"You promised me a favor if I spoke for you to the Congress. Please, won't you show mercy?"

He smiled, a feral slash of teeth and lips. "And who defines mercy? The victor or the victim? Is it merciful to spare human lives and let generations of praetheria die?"

"There has to be another answer."

"I don't think there is." There was a curious note in his voice—in anyone else, I would call it regret.

I looked away from Hunger, away from the clearing and the creatures preparing for war. Somewhere nearby, late linden trees were blooming, their distinctive honey-and-lemon scent as bright as the sunlight filling the small meadow. It was the smell of Eszterháza in summer—the smell of home.

I can never go home again.

The centaur cantered up and bowed his head to Hunger, murmuring something in a language I did not know, with rounded syllables, vowels drawn out and liquid. Hunger answered him in the same language, and then the centaur bowed again and trotted off.

"I should go," I said. "I'm of no use to you—and right now I'm only in the way. I might even be a danger. The Red Mantles will be hunting me."

"They will not take you from us."

Something in the hard edge of his voice gave me pause. I had begun retreating from the clearing, but at that I stopped. "I do not belong to you."

"I saved you. You owe me a debt."

"No. These past months I have put myself at risk for you, defending you before the Congress. My life is forfeit because I set you free! There is no debt." There must be somewhere, far enough from the Hapsburg influence and

343

politics, that I might be safe. Egypt. Or Arabia. Perhaps India.

Hunger nodded shortly, his gold eyes glinting. "Very well. No debt. But you will stay." My skin shriveled away from the strength of the order. He must have seen that in my face, because he softened his next words. "You are safe here for now."

But I knew his words for a lie:

I was not safe anywhere.

CHAPTER 29

For a people in hiding, the praetheria were not as cowed as I might have expected. That night, as the sun fell and shadows crept across the earth, the praetheria set aside their weapons and their defensive plans. There were no instruments that I could see, but the wind soughed through the tall grass and leaves shook overhead and dry branches clattered together and something like music emerged.

Not all the praetheria danced—the centaur stood vigil at the far edge of the wood, and several times I caught the rasping overhead of heavy wings. But enough did: fae no larger than my handspan spinning through the air in globes of light, the tree-men swaying to a tune only they could hear, a little man with a fox face whirling with a squat, toadish creature.

Hunger invited me to join, but I refused him. Already my longing for my quiet room in Catherine's town house overwhelmed me: I wanted Noémi and Gábor and even Catherine. If Hunger touched me, I might dissolve into salt tears.

I munched on an apple and watched the dancers. At the far edge of the dance, a woman with hair limned gold by the firelight rocked gently to the music. Her back was turned to me, but something about her—the way her hands moved carefully and controlled through the air— reminded me of Noémi.

I looked away, the sweetness of the apple gone sour in my mouth. I dropped the half-eaten core on the ground and retreated to my moss-covered hollow.

I meant to sleep, but sleeping proved elusive. Thoughts chased through my head, each one sharper than the last. I wondered where Noémi was, if she had found anything but mirages in pursuit of Mátyás. I hoped she was safe. What would she think, when she heard of my fate? That I had been imprudent, that I deserved it. My thoughts drifted to Gábor.

He had claimed he loved me, but he never asked me what *I* wanted before cavalierly deciding my future for me. My anger warmed me briefly before turning wistful. Where had he gone on Kossuth's errand? Did he miss me at all? Was he well?

I pictured Catherine alone in her sitting room, her hands on her belly. Did she mourn me? Was she angry that I had so intemperately risked her social status? Or was she merely grateful not to have to witness my execution? I thought of William bleeding on the ballroom floor. Did he still live? And Vasilisa—where was she, if not here?

So many questions, none of them comforting.

All I had wanted was to matter: to salvage Mátyás's death and do some good in the world. I had broken the Binding and failed to save the praetheria I set free. Everything I touched seemed to crumble: the tentative peace between Hungary and Austria, my friendship with Noémi, my romance with Gábor. And Mátyás, dead in the gap between our world and the Binding.

I had used my chimera gifts to shatter the world and then recoiled from the aftermath. I had suppressed who I was— and that had not saved me. I had been condemned for what I had done as chimera anyway.

I had nothing left, no reason to hide what I was. If I ever managed to escape to safety, I would embrace my chimera self—the pain and the glory of it, all together.

X

I woke to voices sometime in the silver-lined hours of middle night.

"Tell the others we leave when I give word," Hunger said. "And remind them we must be careful. This must look like an isolated rescue, not part of anything larger. The humans must believe we're frightened, incapable of planning any large coordinated attack."

I opened my eyes to slits, but I could not see him. He must be somewhere just beyond the screen of trees.

"I'm sick of hiding," another voice growled.

"It will not be long," Hunger said. "If we go to war now, we might win, but at a cost we cannot afford. The

Austrians are already set to invade Hungary on the heels of the Croatians, and Svarog has the tsar convinced that if he but waits for Hungary and Austria to ravage each other, he can rule half of Europe. Once the human armies have decimated each other, we will act. Within a year, our home will be ours again."

Fully awake now, I rubbed the gooseflesh along my arms. *Svarog.* That was the name of the golden-haired count always with the tsar—and Pál. At the ball, his face had seemed to split into four. I had thought it an illusion, but what if the impossibly beautiful human face were the illusion and the four-headed creature underneath the reality? For months a praetheria had held the ear of the tsar.

A thin wind hissed through the trees, blowing grit against my cheeks.

I pressed my knuckles against my lips, my head spinning. All this time in Vienna I had misread the praetheria. I had liked them, sympathized with them, defended them, nearly given my life for them. I had not liked the idea of praetherian violence, but I had understood it as defense against human cruelty.

But this.

This was no reactionary war in self-defense. Planting one of their own in the Russian court spoke of long planning, perhaps from the moment I had set the praetheria free. All these months, while the Congress droned on, oblivious, the praetheria had spun their own plot, the archduchess and Dragović playing right into it. Not all the praetheria, surely, but enough.

"Nothing is certain until it happens," Hunger said. "We

will use stealth. Ba—Vasilisa would not forgive us if we betray our strength in rescuing her."

I swallowed down nausea and curled on my side, my arms pressed tight against my stomach. Beneath the covering of moss, the knobs and whorls of the tree roots rubbed raw against my ribs.

I had counted Vasilisa and Hunger as—well, if not exactly friends, something like that. Allies. And yet, looking back, it was Vasilisa who drove my sympathy until I betrayed myself to the Congress. *Witness,* she had said—and I had, my own tongue witnessing my crime. And Hunger had driven the wedge between Noémi and me. Had he also said something to Gábor? I could not seem to breathe.

"And the girl?"

"She comes with us to Vienna. We may need her."

They had never wanted to help me, only to use me. And now they planned to destroy nearly everything I cared about.

The faintest sound of footsteps, and then Hunger's moon shadow fell across me. I did my best to stay limp as he lifted me into the air.

Any understanding I thought I had dissolved in the night air, the footing beneath me like grasses in a marsh—solid until I stepped forward, then unable to support my weight. I had never wanted the praetheria in the sanctuary Congress proposed—still did not wish that—but what was I to believe? All my efforts these past months had been toward a mirage, to build a future out of a present that never existed.

From the midst of my aching uncertainty, only one thing

seemed clear: I could not let the praetheria overturn my world. As an abstract moral equation, for praetheria to kill and enslave humans as they had been killed and enslaved might seem fair and just. But I could not live according to moral abstractions, not when my family and friends were involved. I would fight the praetheria if I had to. Warn the human governments what they planned.

But first I had to escape.

It was an instant's work for Hunger to transform, after shaking me awake, his shape billowing upward and outward like an ink spill in water. His sárkány self was sleek in the moonlight, all dark lengths and muscle, with gold lining his scales. His wings, webbed like a bat's, unfurled once before he tucked them at his sides and knelt, so I could climb.

Another of the praetheria secured a harness and light saddle between the joints of Hunger's wings, and then backed away, waiting for me. When I hesitated, one of the demi-giants waiting in the clearing simply plucked me off the ground and set me on the saddle, my dirty skirts hiking up past my knees. The scales beneath me were surprisingly smooth.

I glanced around at the rescue team. A griffin, his beak savage in the moonlight, looking as though he'd stepped out of the Eszterházy crest. A pair of giant eagles. A winged horse with a long, wickedly curved horn. A lizard-like creature with the head and wings of a rooster. I had a nagging uneasiness that I ought to know what the last was.

The others were airborne first. Hunger whipped his head around to stare at me, his golden eyes slitted beneath a knobbed ridge, perhaps assessing the harness. Satisfied, he sprang aloft to join the others. My stomach merged with my heart in my chest.

The woods and waterways below us were a miniature crafted by a master, tiny shapes carved by moonlight, shadows crossed by silver ribbons. The wind rushed past me, and I gripped my hands tight around the harness. I could not entirely suppress a flicker of excitement, though I suspected I ought not enjoy a flight like this on the back of my enemy.

My enemy.

I could feel the bunch and release of the great muscles powering Hunger's wings just beneath me. I had not ridden astride since I was a small child (and Mama caught me at it), and it felt at once powerful and exposing. Despite everything I knew of Hunger, of his odd sense of humor, his quicksilver moods, his amoral outlook on the world, I could not seem to understand his betrayal.

It was not long—perhaps a half hour—before I spotted the walls of Vienna rising in the distance. Hunger barked something at the others, and they lifted higher, until the city was so small I could have cupped it in my hands: a ring of wall surrounding the inner city, the rest splayed wide beyond the glacis. This high, the air was clear and cold and thin. Dizziness rushed over me, and I leaned in low toward Hunger, praying I would not fall.

A second barking order and they descended, dropping so suddenly I let out a small screech, and Hunger rumbled beneath me.

The wind shifted, bringing with it the smell of smoke.

A searching glance across Vienna revealed orange flames devouring rooftops all throughout the inner city. Black-and-grey billows smudged the horizon where the cityscape met the night sky. My fingers tightened around the harness. *Was Catherine safe?* An unchecked fire could gut a city in a night.

The fire was densest just ahead of us, near the prison set south and east of the glacis, beside the army barracks. As the praetheria descended into a quiet courtyard, I could hear the toll of warning bells and the thunder of carriages, probably part of a fire brigade.

"What's going on?" I asked as Hunger landed with a muffled thud.

"An uprising in the city. Not our concern." Hunger's voice emerged deep and gravelly from his dragon throat.

The timing seemed awfully convenient. It would only take a little praetherian glamour to convince already rest-less students and citizens to take to the streets. I rubbed my cold arms, then pulled myself out of the saddle and slid down. It was a long way to the ground: I had to drop the last few feet, and the impact reverberated up my legs.

The rooster-lizard creature stalked to the heavy wooden doors leading to the street beyond and set its wing against the wood. The wood flashed to stone, then crumbled apart.

"Don't look directly at her," Hunger advised me, and I realized what the creature was. *Cockatrice.*

I edged closer to Hunger. He might have betrayed me, but at the moment a familiar danger seemed infinitely safer than an unfamiliar one. Hunger shifted back into human shape.

The praetheria crept out into the street. Feet pounded the pavement nearby, soldiers streaming down an adjacent road. Called away to the fire, no doubt. *Let Catherine be safe. Let the city survive this night.*

I thought of the soldiers on guard in the prison, already distracted by the fire, utterly unprepared for the small army approaching them. Death stalked them, and they did not know it.

Shadows from the close-pressed houses seemed to pull away from the walls and gather around us, cloaking us from view. Our footsteps too seemed unnaturally hushed against the cobblestone street. I glanced around at the intent faces of my captors, all of whom seemed focused on the task at hand, and slipped backward two steps. I had to make sure Catherine was all right.

Without looking in my direction, Hunger reached back and snagged me, his fingers closing over my arm like a vise.

"Stay with us," he said. A smile crawled across his face. "I promise you will not like it if we have to hunt you down when this is over."

We reached the prison moments later. I did not see what happened to the guards who stood sentry, but I heard the half-voiced cries and swallowed hard. Poor devils.

"Be vigilant," Hunger warned. "These guards are only commoners, but they are sure to have spell-casters posted nearer to Vasilisa."

We entered the building, the cockatrice folding her wings close, the griffin compressing his large body in the curiously flexible way cats have of moving through tight spaces. The Shadowing and Muffling spells continued inside the stone building. Lumen lights glimmered along the wall, proof of the presence of magicians.

We startled a sentry, whistling as he walked. I looked away, not wanting to see which of the praetheria took him down, or how. I heard the crunch of bone and was nearly sick, but Hunger hauled me forward.

"You cannot be ill here."

I glared at him. How, precisely, was I supposed to exercise that degree of control over my stomach if they were going to slaughter people?

It crossed my mind to scream, to warn the guards and give them a fighting chance. But as soon as the thought occurred, I dismissed it. I did not know if the Muffling spell would stifle my scream—but if I drew attention to myself, I'd only find myself silenced in ways I did not like: trussed up like a Christmas pig. Or killed.

Instead I followed silently, hoping that when we at last found Vasilisa, I might discover some route for escape.

Another twisting corridor and then a third. Finally, a wider hallway crowded with men, their voices reaching us even before we'd turned the corner.

As the first curl of shadow stretched down the hallway, one of the guards pulled a whistle from his pocket. At the shrill sound, the others sprang to attention. There were only a half dozen or so—either the Hapsburgs did not rate Vasilisa a great threat, or the others had been called away to the fire.

"Stay," Hunger commanded me, and I did, my feet freezing in place. I tried to feel for the threads of the spell, to snap them, but I could not seem to grasp them before the fighting was over.

The cockatrice led the attack, her eyes flashing. The first of the guards rushing to meet us, hands waving wildly in a spell, halted suddenly. His face seemed to freeze, eyes unblinking, before he toppled over, quite dead. The griffin followed the cockatrice, his beak slashing and tearing. The winged unicorn speared another guard as casually as I might slide a needle into silk. Unicorns were supposed to personify peace and purity: the red blood now staining its horn and dripping to the floor had the sick wrongness of an orgy in a church. Half the guards were down before they had time to do much more than draw their swords.

One of the guards broke away and raced down the hallway, likely for reinforcements. With a snarl, the griffin followed. Another raised his hand above his eyes, his saber held awkwardly before him, the flat side reflecting the cockatrice's fowl aspect. The cockatrice screamed only once before charging at her reflection. Hunger called after her, but she ignored him, eyes fixed on the crested beast seeming to challenge her. A scant foot from the guard she stopped, frozen, a cold grey creeping across her body.

The hussar lowered his saber, trembling, and Hunger ran him through with a sword salvaged from a dead guard. As the soldier dropped, Hunger tossed the blade aside, then crouched over each fallen guard in turn, searching through their pockets. After a moment he stood, clutching a narrow ring of keys. He tried two in succession in the lock of the rather plain door before one gave.

Hunger wrenched the door open, then leapt back, swearing.

He glanced back at me, irritation plain across his features. "Come here, Miss Arden. I need your help."

The spell binding my feet released me, and I stumbled forward. "Why?"

"Because the room has been spelled against any kind of praetherian influence: running water, iron-washed walls, garlic strands, holly root, and a devilishly complicated spell that I haven't time to pick through right now."

"You want me to break the spell?"

The crease between his eyes deepened. "Not unless a simpler approach fails. Just walk through the door and carry her out. The Hapsburgs didn't plan for human aid when they set their prison."

"If I help you, will you release me?"

He bared his teeth at me. "If you help me, I might not let the griffin eat you. Besides, I know where your cousin is."

"Noémi?" What had she told him before she fled? "If I help you, you'll tell me where she is?"

Hunger dipped his head.

Still, I hesitated. If Hunger and the others were willing to risk exposing their plan to rescue Vasilisa, she must be critical to its completion. How much would this rescue cost those I loved? On the other hand, if I did not do as they wished, I would likely die—and then who would warn the others? There was Noémi to think of as well. Better to free Vasilisa, then try to escape.

I walked into the cell, conscious of a curious pulling sensation, as though my skin were too tight on my body. A narrow walkway ran the perimeter of the oblong room. In the center, on a small stone island surrounded by its own moat of flowing water, crouched a woman.

It was not Vasilisa.

This woman was old, so old the wrinkles in her cheeks had their own runic system. Her back was hunched a little, but she did not seem particularly weak, only ancient, her white hair straggling along her spine obscuring part of her face.

"I think this is the wrong room," I said, retreating from the doorway.

Hunger gave me a little shove, back into the room, and I had to wave my arms to keep from tumbling into the water. The water appeared normal, but I could not be sure the guards hadn't slipped something poisonous into it.

"That's Vasilisa. The spell prevents her from using her magic, so she's lost her glamour." He laughed at my surprise. "You thought a creature who has existed for hundreds of years inside your Binding spell has always been so young and lovely?"

"I did not think she was so old," I muttered, but in truth I had not thought about it very much. I had accepted her at face value—at her own valuation. A mistake, I began to see, I had made with a great many people. Who was she, really?

"There," Hunger said, gesturing at a wooden plank near the door. "Use that."

I set the plank across the rushing water and crossed carefully. Vasilisa's eyes were closed, and she crooned to herself, as though she were cocooned in her own world.

"Vasilisa?" Was that even her true name? I braced myself against some irruption of her quicksilver moods.

But her eyes only flashed open, and she stood, reaching out to stroke my cheek. "You always were a delicious child. Thank you."

I stepped back a fraction so her hand fell away. I was not entirely certain she meant *delicious* as a compliment. "Can you walk?"

"Of course I can walk. Though not, precisely, across the water." She sighed. "I had hoped a thousand years was enough for people to forget *that* particular weakness of mine. You shall have to carry me."

My heart sank. Still, Hunger was watching. I turned my back to Vasilisa and crouched. Her wiry arms slithered across my neck like gallows rope. She was heavy, much heavier than I'd expected of someone so old and slight, and when I tried to stand, my thighs burned and I nearly pitched us both forward into the water.

"Careful!" she screeched, hauling back on my hair as though it were the reins of an unruly horse.

Clasping my hands underneath her knees to keep her steady on my back, I crept forward across the plank. It groaned beneath our combined weight.

"Quickly!"

"If I go any more quickly, I'll fall off the plank."

She grumbled and pulled my hair for good measure but did not complain again until we were across the water.

Hunger had not been able to cross the threshold, and I suspected Vasilisa could not do so unaided either. Though my arms burned and my legs trembled, I did not set her down but plodded forward toward the door.

At the doorway, something seemed to catch us, nearly wrenching Vasilisa from my back.

"You'll have to break the spell," she said.

I wondered how far I would make it if I dropped her and ran. Glancing at Hunger's intense face, I suspected it would not be far.

Sighing, I resettled Vasilisa on my back. Plunging toward the doorway again, I slammed into the same catching sensation, as though I were a child who had mistaken a glass door for an open doorway.

This time, though, I could feel the buzz from the magic. Burdened as I was, the spell seemed to bend and twist around me, evading my reach. At last, however, I grasped a thread of it and pulled it toward me, bracing myself for the release of magic. A momentary flash of heat, and then a blaze of light as the spell snapped.

I caught the magic as it slithered free. I imagined it as a wall and shoved it away from me. The spell was not particularly elegant, but the force of the magic sent Hunger and the others sprawling on the corridor floor.

I dropped Vasilisa on the threshold of the room and ran.

Following the path I thought I remembered through the prison, I reached a door to the outside within moments. It was not the door we had entered, so my recollections had not been entirely accurate, but I was out of the building, and I was free.

My side burning from the unaccustomed exercise and the corset too tight about my ribs, I stumbled across the street toward one of the dark alleyways.

I had nearly reached the shadows when something coiled around my ankle and jerked. I fell, scraping my hands across the cobblestones and banging my elbow. Pain sizzled up my arm.

Hunger hulked behind me, back in dragon form, two claws of his powerful foreleg wrapped around my ankle.

Vasilisa hobbled up behind him, cackling. "You should never run from immortals, child." She helped me stand, but I jerked away from her touch as soon as I was upright.

So close. I wanted to weep.

Hunger barked twice, sharply, and after a few moments, the griffin and the winged unicorn emerged from the prison. The great eagles, who had circled above the prison keeping watch, fluttered to the ground beside us.

Hunger repositioned his claw around my waist. The saddle and harness went to Vasilisa, who was still weak from her time in the prison. When she was secured, Hunger gave the signal, and we lifted into the air.

A string of epithets chased themselves through my head. Some of them may have escaped my lips, because Vasilisa laughed from her perch on Hunger's back. My legs dangled above the cobblestones, and I swallowed a bubble of panic. Hunger had only to lose his grip and I'd plummet to my death.

I was well and truly caught.

Why was Hunger so insistent that I stay with them? If he were worried about my betraying the location of the praetherian camp, he might have killed me after Vasilisa was free. He must have wanted something else. My shadow self whispered, chimera.

I pushed that thought away, to attend to when I wasn't dangling a hundred feet in the air, and the street exploded in light.

The griffin fell with a terrible shriek, its feathered wings a conflagration. Hunger's claws tightened reflexively around my waist, their cruel tips digging through even my corset. I screamed too, but he did not seem to hear me.

The spell-casters had come at last. A half dozen men and women stood on the streets below us, shooting spouts of flame and ice into the smoky air. A blast hit one of Hunger's wings and he flinched, sending a shower of ice shards onto my head. He swung up, out of range, and my heart shrank.

If the praetheria escaped, my own escape would be harder. If they did not—the Hapsburg magicians would deliver me to the archduchess's execution.

Something enormous rose up behind the spell-casters, a creature of metal and fire. Likely it was powered as William's mechanicals had been, by magic and machinery. The vast wings pumped once, twice, and, with a squeal of metal on metal, it lifted up. Electricity buzzed across its body like a miniature lightning storm as it careened through the night air toward us.

Hunger's own wings sliced down, whipping my hair into my face. He was more maneuverable than the machine, but he was hampered by his live passengers. He dove, trying to drop beneath the machine's trajectory, but the metal monster clipped his enormous, thrashing tail.

Vasilisa shrieked, though she sounded more angry than terrified.

Electricity burst across Hunger's back, triggering pulsing shocks through me. Hunger writhed midair, and his claws opened.

I dropped like the free weight I was.

A second metal monster shot into the sky like a star, but I barely saw it. The ground was rushing up to meet me, and all I could feel was a great blaze of anger.

This was how I was going to die? The injustice of it burned through even the bitter taste of terror.

I slammed into something solid. Pain crackled through my body with breathtaking intensity. Everything went dark.

Mátyás

CHAPTER 30

They say you learn new things every day.

I learned that my shifted form does not hold when I fall unconscious, as I woke to find myself human—and naked—my hands trussed behind my back. The pain was so intense that black spots swam in front of me, and I wished I were still insensible. The gunshot in my forearm still wept blood, and I was fairly sure the bone beneath it had shattered. My leg burned with the saber wound, and I could not breathe too deeply or my ribs—broken or badly bruised, I couldn't tell—sent spikes shooting through me. My right ankle had swollen to twice its normal size. I could scarcely see from my right eye.

Here lies Eszterházy Mátyás. He was too stupid to live. (Again.)

Bahadır groaned beside me, blood dried and crusting around a hole in his shoulder. Like me, he was tightly bound. Also like me, he could not seem to sit upright. Unlike me, he still possessed his clothes.

"Hold on," I murmured, though I was not entirely sure if I was speaking to Bahadır or myself. Louder, I said, "Have you a doctor?"

The leader grunted. "If I had, I'd not waste him on you. If you die, you'll save us the trouble of killing you." He nudged the fallen giant with his toe, an expression of distaste on his face. "So rumor was right: you've assembled a misbegotten band here."

"They're living creatures, same as—" I began, but one of the soldiers cuffed me across the chin with the butt of his gun. I reeled back, pain shooting up my jaw, radiating into the rest of my broken body.

Varjú croaked overhead, chiding the soldier. Another hussar sent a casual shot into the tree, and Varjú lifted off in a flutter of feathers and leaves. *Go home,* I sent at him. It wasn't safe here.

"I don't believe we asked you to speak," the soldier continued. "You're a criminal. We'll take you back to Debrecen to hang soon as we've dealt with these creatures."

"What will you do with us?" The lidérc's voice was uncommonly subdued, muffled a bit by the blood still trickling from her nose.

"All praetheria are to be interned in a camp near Vienna."

"Another Binding?" The lidérc spat on the ground. "I'd rather you shoot me now."

One of the soldiers lifted his rifle. "That can be arranged."

Gábor's voice sounded near my right ear, though I could

not turn far enough to see him. "Stay calm. You'll do your friends no good if you antagonize the soldiers."

"And the rest of my men?" I tried to keep my voice flat, nonprovoking, showing nothing of the growing dread that threatened to choke me. Still, I flinched when the soldier with the gun mock-lunged toward me. The soldier laughed.

"Hanging's good enough for them," the soldier with the gun said. He patted his hip, where a coil of rope swung by his side. "Happen to have the goods right here."

"They're due at least a trial," I said.

"How about a trial by noose? We hang 'em—if they live, they're innocent." The soldier laughed again.

"And you," the leader said, stepping close. "I'll string you up with your own guts." He kicked me in the side, and I lost the rest of his words.

I curled around my burning ribs, pain pulsing through me in waves. I'd dreamed he'd say as much—had that dream been a prophecy? Or something else? I fought through my agony: I still had to try to save my men. "You cannot simply hang us," I gasped, pulling on my haughtiest, plummiest accent. "I am an Eszterházy—hang me without trial and there will be a public outcry."

For the first time, the leader looked vaguely uneasy. "Why would a Luminate be leading bandits on the *puszta*?"

I shrugged. "Why does any spoiled nobleman do anything? I was bored, of course." I grinned, forcing a lightness I did not feel. "It's quite a rush."

"Damned Luminate," the leader muttered.

"He's lying," the gun soldier said.

I started to shrug, then stopped—it hurt too much. "I suppose that is a risk you take. I'm wearing my father's signet ring, if you doubt me." I wiggled my fingers, feeling the weight of the griffin ring.

"Better not risk it," the leader said. He nodded at a pair of his soldiers. "Bind the creatures together, then the men. We need to get moving."

The soldiers began hauling the surviving praetheria upright. One of them pulled Zhivka to her feet, and I let out a slow, hissing breath. I had not known she survived the night. Her face was pale and scratched, her side smeared with dried blood where a bullet had grazed her, but her chin was high and her shoulders back. The soldier put a dirty hand to her cheek and bent close to whisper to her.

Zhivka bit him. He released her with a snarl, shaking his fingers, and she darted to the center of the camp. The fire in her hair brightened, her features taking on the incandescent sheen of her glamour. My heart seized.

The last time she'd tried her glamour, she'd been shot. They wouldn't be so gentle this time. Already, the hussar leader was swaying toward her, his eyes glazing. The soldier who'd been bitten dropped to his knees before her, holding his gun out like an offering.

"Cut me free," she whispered, her words hanging in the wind like a caress.

Bound and broken as I was, I strained forward in response to the appeal in her words, even though the movement set every cell in my body on fire.

A high, far-off birdsong hung in the still air. The sun, just cresting above the limitless horizon of the *puszta,* shafted the world through with gold.

A gunshot cracked through the camp.

Zhivka's face blazed with inhuman brightness—and then the bullet struck her knee, spraying bits of blood and bone into the grass beneath her, and Zhivka's glamour vanished like a snuffed candle. She dropped to the ground with a cry.

The leader shook his head and stalked toward the fallen samodiva. "What have we here? The camp whore?" His eyes traced over her face and body in a way that made me itch to punch the teeth from his smug grin. He bent to brush a fire-red curl from her face. "Praetherian? A bit of a perversion, but I can see the temptation. Put her on my horse and tie her down. Wrap some iron around her wrists to be sure."

Two of the soldiers obliged, hauling a shrieking Zhivka between them. It took a moment for her screams to resolve into a word: *Mátyás*.

The hussar leader's gaze slid back to me. "It's a long, lonely ride to Vienna. I'll need something to keep me warm at nights. The praetherian's good enough for that, and if I use her a little too roughly—well, no one will care."

I'd meant to wait for a better moment to shift and help the others escape. Preferably after dark. But at the leader's words, something snapped inside me. My pain morphed into anger, and I began shifting, responding to an impulse I barely understood, my body swelling upward and outward, my skin darkening and hardening, leathery wings sprouting from my back. A massive pain seized me, as though my head were splintering into a million pieces, and then I was seeing from seven pairs of eyes, from seven draconic heads. Already, my shattered bones were healing, a gift peculiar to this shape. The shape I'd taken when Hadúr challenged me was primal and powerful beyond anything I knew.

And it was ravenous.

I plunged down, one of my mouths bared wide, and bit the leader in half, cutting off his terrified scream. The snap of bones and tang of blood in my mouth only set the craving for flesh and blood flaring higher.

Tiny bullets pinged against my hide.

Gábor's voice echoed in my head: "Mátyás, don't! Come back to us." But then his name fuzzed in my mind, drifted away like smoke. The sense that some of the humans below were familiar—even beloved—receded, and I was left only with a yawning need burning through me, wiping out any sense of who I was or had been.

The ache of that need drove away my lingering pain. I seized three or four of the scattering, screaming beings below with my heads, and their blood ran down my tongues and spilled across my chins. Some of the blood was warm and salt and copper: human blood. Some of it was cooler, sour with a faint floral note.

All of it fed my appetite.

Fire burned up my leg, a bright note piercing me even through the blood haze. I looked down, determined to devour the author of my pain, and saw a girl, incandescent with flame, holding fast to my ankle.

Her name darted into my heart.

Zhivka.

I came back to myself in a rush, halting the heads, letting

them melt back into one, letting myself shrink back into my own body.

I blinked, and my hands were human again, with blood beneath my nails. I wiped my arm against my wet mouth, and it came away scarlet. All around me were bodies. Most were soldiers, but one of the tree-creatures lay halved before me, and I dropped to my knees and vomited across the grass.

I gagged until there was nothing left, until my empty stomach wrung itself out, but the sour taste of what I'd done lingered.

"Thank you," I gasped to Zhivka, who'd let the fire flicker out and now sat on the grass beside me, one hand to the back of her head. "Where are the rest of the soldiers?"

"Dead." Gábor rubbed his hand against his forehead, leaving a streak of black gunpowder. He held a knife in his free hand. "Or fled. What you did—it was terrifying."

I looked around. The tents of our campsite were flattened, the cauldron over the fire upturned, the fire itself out and smoking. Only a few of us remained: Bahadır, nursing his shoulder; the lidérc, meeting my gaze with an almost defiant one of her own; the domovoi weeping, rocking back and forth beside a fallen tree.

"And ours?"

"Also fled."

"Maybe you should go too." Pain rattled through my skull; horror made my blood run sluggish.

Zhivka shook her head. "You are táltos, as the Lady said. And where should we go?"

I waved my hand. "I don't know. Find the Lady. Find

shelter elsewhere, with someone who won't—" I gagged again, remembering the bitter taste of the leshy blood.

"You will learn control," she said.

But to learn control meant summoning the Lady again, meant swallowing my pride. Though that bitterness could be nothing compared to the guilt that threatened to swamp me.

※

We spent the next few hours seeing to the wounded—though not before I had scavenged some clothes from a dead soldier.

Gábor knew enough of medical science to dig the bullet from Bahadır's shoulder, and Zhivka helped cauterize the wound.

Gábor and I together wrapped Zhivka's injured knee, and Gábor used a bit of magic to set the shattered bone.

When the most dire wounds had been tended, I devoured a full loaf of bread and a dozen eggs. Zhivka offered me a slab of meat, but the sight of it had set my gorge rising. The demon hunger had left me, but I was weak from the aftereffects of shifting.

The dead we laid out in state, for burial in the evening when it had cooled. The tree-creature I had slain had already been claimed by his partner, who had taken the body away to bury the roots and set the rest adrift on water. I did not know if the leshy would return, but I doubted it. I could not blame him: I did not want to stay with myself either.

I would have moved camp, if I could—no one wanted to spend the night where so many had died. But I couldn't risk moving those who were injured. When we'd dealt with the most pressing needs of the living and the dead, I went to find the guards who had not returned. Already, my heart was weighted down with what I feared I'd find.

Bahadır struggled after me. "Take me with you."

"But your arm—"

"Will not interfere with my ability to walk. Please."

I walked onto the grasslands prepared to search for some time, ready to shift if we could not find them quickly. But in the end we needed neither time nor shifting. A clutch of vultures circled over our camp—a few of their brothers drifted lazily to the south. When I focused my animal sense on them, I could feel the shivered excitement of a find.

We found the other guard first. He'd been shot by the soldiers in his stomach and leg, wounds that would not have been immediately fatal. I hoped it had not taken him long to die.

I watched Bahadır closely. His face had frozen, as though he were preemptively steeling himself against what we might discover.

Ákos we found slumped near a small trickle of water, with a single bullet to his forehead. He was still smiling, as though he'd been taunting the soldiers when he'd been caught.

I knelt on the ground beside him and gently closed his eyes. Then I sobbed, as I had not done since my mother died.

CHAPTER 31

The night after the massacre, I slept poorly. I kept jerking awake to stare at the stars, wishing I could be as distant and impartial as those shining bodies. Instead, I ached with grief, my eyes raw with rubbing and tears. Not exactly the dignified look for someone with the lofty title of "King of Crows."

Most times I woke to weeping, usually Bahadır, curled in a tight, miserable ball on the far side of the fire. Even after seeing my mother and Noémi through mourning after my father's death, I still didn't know what to do with grief (mine, or others'). But as I lay there, practicing my usual trick of ignorance, I heard Gábor's murmuring voice and Bahadır's soft reply.

Gábor and Zhivka and I traded watches that night, on guard against the soldiers' return and ensuring that none of the wounded worsened during the night. I had the last watch, and though sleep was fitful, I kept returning to it, knowing the next day would be hard enough without being sleepless.

Less than an hour before my turn as sentry, I fell back into a troubled sleep. I dreamed of flying across the grasslands to a stand of trees beside a river snaking through the *puszta*. In the distance, the vast spread of the world tree unfurled against the sky. A small pack of wolves hunted, urged on by a young woman with pale hair and wood-rot eyes.

Lords and ladies might use dogs to hunt boars and deer—what would one hunt with wolves? My curiosity piqued, I flew onward, trying to spot their prey. The plains were mostly empty, but far ahead someone walked alone, a pair of falcons winging overhead.

I swooped lower, and the whole earth slid sideways.

"Mátyás!"

I opened my eyes to Zhivka's white face. She was shaking my shoulder.

"Fires burn bright," she said, releasing me. "I thought you might be dead."

"I was only sleeping."

She shook her head. "You weren't. Your breath was so shallow I was not sure you lived. And you were so still, your face so empty, as though you had gone very far away inside yourself."

"I was dreaming," I said, less sure than before.

"Before the Binding," Zhivka said, "being a táltos was not so rare. Some were dream walkers, able to travel with their spirit from one dreamer to the next, or simply send their soul out as they dreamed. Are you sure it was only a dream?"

In that moment I wasn't sure of anything. I'd dreamed of hussars hunting us, and they had come. I'd seen Noémi in chains. And who was it the pale-haired woman hunted? If my dreams were truth, then it had not mattered that I'd stayed away from Vienna to protect Noémi—she was imperiled all the same.

 ⚬

We packed up camp the next morning before the soldiers could return. Gábor worked alongside me, folding blankets and stuffing them into canvas bags for transport. The wounded we dispatched to sympathetic farmers nearby, with funds to cover their care.

"Where will you go?" I asked Gábor.

"With you," he said. "Kossuth sent me to find you and bring you back to Buda-Pest."

The landscape of the kingdom was changing. Gábor had said war was already at our door in the south. From what I knew of Austria, I suspected it would not be long before she joined in, desperate to reclaim Hungary. I was, and always would be, a patriot. But—

"I can't go back. Not yet." I could not continue being the King of Crows, a highwayman who occasionally performed along the roadside. That life was gone. These soldiers might have left, but there would be others.

And the praetheria. I had told the Lady I did not mean to be a hero, but I could not stand by and see them dragged off to a camp without trying to help—a camp that I suspected would be little better than a prison. I'd seen how the majority of humans treated the creatures: as though they were something monstrous, something better destroyed than left alone.

If being táltos was my destiny, it was not something I was eager to embrace. But maybe it was time to stop running from it. Maybe if I had not refused to learn what I could do, I would not have lost myself to my dragon shape. I would not have killed indiscriminately. If I had understood my dreaming, perhaps I would have known the soldiers were coming, and Ákos and the others would still be alive.

I refused to live in the past. That had destroyed my mother.

I would mourn Ákos and the others, and then I would move on. The stories said the world tree was hidden from the eyes of most men, but I was not most men, and I would find it again. I would find a way to swallow my pride, if I choked on it, and beg the Lady to teach me what I needed to know.

I might fail.

Probably I would, since my luck seemed to have run out of late.

But I could no longer live with doing nothing.

"I mean to find the Lady. I need to know more about what I am than I currently do."

"I'll come—" Gábor broke off at a high keening that soared through the camp.

I did not look up at first: the *betyárok* and the praetheria between them had dozens of ways of mourning, and the sounds of someone sobbing had marked time ever since the soldiers had come.

This time, though, the keening did not rise and drop off. This time, it continued to escalate, joined by more and more voices, a wave that crested toward us.

I looked up.

The second of the tree-creatures had come back. He carried something pale and drooping in his arms, and his voice sounded in a long, hollow cry like wind tearing through a mountain valley.

I did not recognize her at first. Her face was colorless and still, without the beatific glow she usually wore. But when the tree-creature drew closer, her features resolved into something familiar.

He carried the Lady in his arms. When he reached me, he laid her gently on the ground—some high, holy sacrifice laid before a priest.

But the Lady was not a sacrifice I had wanted, and I was no saint.

Gábor knelt beside the still form, his fingers brushing her pulse. He looked a question at me. "I can't feel anything. Who is she?"

"She is dead," the tree-creature said, breaking off his mournful howl. "Her light is gone. I cannot feel it."

Horror made my tongue stiff and clumsy. "She was the *Boldogasszony*," I said. "Mother-goddess of Hungary." She had chivvied me and set me on an impossible task, and I had hated her for it. But I had also welcomed her belief in me, just as one welcomes the secure belief of a priest in his faith, even as one finds their own faith faltering.

Now she was dead, and I felt unmoored, unanchored, lost. Who—or what?—could kill an immortal?

The heavy summer air clung to the hair and skin of everyone in the camp. All of us turned toward the Lady, who had once walked among us, drawing worship from those assembled as easily as one might draw water from a full well.

"Who could have done this?" Gábor asked, echoing my own question.

"Only another immortal," the lidérc said. Her tongue flickered between her lips.

The shock of the Lady's death kept radiating through me, a drop of water followed by increasing ripples. I had spurned her help—but I had always felt her offer there, waiting if I chose to take it up. Now it was too late. Even if Hadúr could teach me some of what the Lady knew, her loss was like a familiar trail covered with snow in an avalanche, a comfortable landscape made strange and treacherous.

We buried the Lady on the *puszta,* beneath a mossy old oak, standing solitary sentinel. Far overhead, I could sense her turul birds circling, their distress clear even at this distance. *Go home,* I thought at them. *Tell Hadúr.*

The leshy who had carried the Lady into camp sang, a long, wordless melody that curled through my bones. Though the summer afternoon was warm, my hands were cold, the tips of my fingers white. My rebirth had been defined, in part, by running away from the Lady. With her death, what was I?

As we walked back to the camp, somber and silent, I saw again my dream from the night before, a pale-haired girl hunting near the world tree. What immortal had killed the Lady—and why?

"Gábor, Zhivka, do you know of any praetheria who look like a young girl with hair the color of old bones?"

"Anna has a friend, Vasilisa, who looks like that," Gábor said.

"Have you seen her?" Zhivka asked, her eyes dilating. Beside her, the lidérc shifted her weight from one goose foot to the other.

"In a dream only," I said. The cold ripples from the Lady's death grew deeper, wider. "She is friends with Anna?"

"I think so," Gábor said. "I saw them frequently together. Why?"

"We need to go back to Vienna." Later, I would find Hadúr, ask him to teach me what he could. But for now, I needed to know that Anna and Noémi were safe.

Anna

CHAPTER 32

Sunlight streamed bright and thick across my face, like a small child demanding my attention. I blinked at it irritably and shifted onto my side. Pain screamed through me, just as memory returned. Breaking Vasilisa from the prison, attempting to escape.

Falling.

I should have died.

I could not waste time on wonder—how I had lived, how I had come to be in a bed, wherever this was. I had to ensure Catherine was well. I had to leave warning about the praetheria.

I had to run.

I wrested myself upright and flung the bedcovers away from my legs, coughing at the smoke fumes still heavy in the air. Someone had removed my dress from the night before—it lay in shredded ribbons on the floor—and replaced it with a large nightshirt. I swung my shockingly bare legs down, stood, and nearly fell back on the bed. The whole room swam, a swirl of black stars and colors.

The door opened, and a young man with dark hair, a robust mustache, and military trousers peeked in. "Ah, capital! You're awake."

He looked exhausted, the dark circles under his eyes a pointed contrast to the cheer in his tone. I wondered if it was his room I was occupying—and if he had been the one to disrobe me. I pushed the thought aside. I did not have time to indulge in embarrassment.

"The fires?" I asked.

He rubbed a soot-stained hand across his forehead, his eyes flicking briefly to my legs. "Contained, for the moment."

Thank God. I pulled the blanket from the bed and wrapped it around my lower body.

"There is still fighting by the university barracks. Bloody students never know when they're beat." He coughed. "Are you well? Those creatures damned near carried you off. Lucky our spell-casters were able to drive them away."

"Yes," I murmured. "Very lucky. Look, I'm afraid I must be going. Can you find me some clothes?"

He frowned. "Er, this is a soldier's barracks, ma'am. The hospitals were full last night with burn victims. I'm afraid we don't have the kinds of clothes you require. Only tell me who to summon to fetch you home."

I thought of Richard's face at the ball, white with shock, of Catherine weeping. Catherine might worry for me, but it was not the worry this soldier expected.

"Then bring me men's clothes. Those will do just as well, and really it's quite urgent."

His frown deepened. "That would hardly be suitable, Miss . . ."

"An—" I began, "Anikó Kovács." I couldn't give him my real name—doubtless the soldiers all knew about my sentencing at the Schönbrunn ball. Though I could have come up with a different surname than Gábor's. My cheeks burned. "Is there any food to be had?" I switched tactics, wondering how much I might play upon the boy's sympathies. "I've not eaten much in several days. I was captive, you see."

His face darkened. "Those blighted praetheria. My commanding officer will wish to speak to you later, about what you know of those creatures and their current camp."

Realization slammed into me so hard it left me breathless. *You will not like it if we have to hunt you down when this is over,* Hunger had said. The praetheria would return for me—the question was not if, but when. Perhaps they were already winging their way back to the city.

I paced the room, restless. "Tell your officer that Austria must not be drawn into war with Hungary and Russia. The praetheria are waiting for that—they mean to attack when the armies are weak."

He snorted. "I should like to see them try. Don't worry—you'll be safe here. We drove them away last night, didn't we? And our magicians broke your fall just in time."

Only because the praetheria didn't wish a pitched battle, and Hunger had been injured.

I had to get away and find someone who would believe me.

I clasped my hands together. "Some food, if you please?"

"Oh yes, of course!" The young man disappeared at last.

I allowed myself one sigh of relief, and then I sprang into action. I pulled open the drawers from the narrow chest near the bed. Underthings were tossed untidily together, and I slammed the drawer shut. The second drawer proved more promising, with a couple of folded shirts. I snagged one and then opened the wardrobe. Regimentals lined neatly along the single bar. I didn't want a uniform: I'd be far too conspicuous. At the back of the closet I found what I was searching for: a pair of everyday trousers.

I slipped on the shirt and trousers, absurdly conscious of how thin the shirt was, particularly without my chemise beneath it. The shirt was too big and the pants were too wide, but I only needed them to get me to Catherine's house. The single pair of boots I rejected as far too big. Better to go barefoot. I braided my hair awkwardly—I had not done this since I was a child, and then for Catherine's hair, not mine—then knotted it at the back of my head before leaving the room.

I peered cautiously around the doorway, looking for posted guards. The corridor was empty, so I eased myself out. Perhaps my polite host *was* my guard. Or perhaps the guards were sleeping off their exhaustion from the night before.

The second corridor was likewise empty, but a pair of soldiers were lounging in the third, and they saw me.

"Hey!" one shouted.

I began to run, casting a quick glance over my shoulder. That was a mistake. My braid tumbled down, and they both laughed.

"Someone was lucky last night, I see," one hooted. "Damn. Wish I'd thought of that instead of fighting fires all night."

"I'd fight *that* fire!"

My cheeks flamed. They thought I had spent the night with one of the soldiers. Well, let them. Better they thought me loose than a fugitive. I ducked out a door at the end of the hallway. The daylight was filtered orange; smoke still stained the sky above the city walls.

It was not far to the glacis—only a few streets. I fled across the road toward the city wall, feeling horribly exposed by all that open space. A shadow passed over me and I flinched. *Hunger.* But it was only a cloud momentarily blocking the sun. I huffed a shaky laugh and continued, a little more gingerly. A blister was beginning to form beneath my big toe.

The guards at the gate stopped me, frowning at my boy's clothes and bare feet.

"It was the fire," I said. "My home was burned, and I had to borrow my brother's things. But my mama is still in the city—I must see if she's all right." Desperation lent a convincing air to my lie.

The guards waved me through. Once I was inside the walls, it took me some time to get my bearings: this was not a part of the city I frequented. I might have asked someone, but in my borrowed clothing I was hesitant to draw too much attention to myself. I looked, at best, like a vagabond. At worst, I might be taken for a runaway. Or a prostitute. I gripped the waist of the pants in my hand to keep them from falling down and forged onward.

A burst of pigeons from one of the churches thronging

the streets made me squeak in alarm. All those wings so close to my head reminded me of the great eagles circling Hunger as we launched upward from the prison. Some two blocks from Catherine's town house, the blister under my toe burst, and new ones were forming. Every step hurt; every breath burned from the lingering smoke. I passed several blackened houses, and my heart beat faster.

I did not know if Catherine was all right—or if she would welcome me into her house.

I knew what my odds would be if she did not. I had no money, no shoes, only a few pieces of men's clothing. I would not make it far without better supplies. And if the praetheria did not find me, the soldiers would.

As a point of fact, there *was* a soldier waiting in the street before Catherine's house, possibly guarding against looters, probably watching for me. But it was not this that made my breath hitch. The façade of the town house was black and blistering, along with its neighbors. Down the street, I could just glimpse the inky bones of a crumbling building. *The fire.*

For a moment I could not move, overpowered by the memory of returning to a similarly blackened home to find Grandmama and Ginny hurt, leaving Lady Berri dead behind me. What would I find here?

I couldn't enter where the soldier waited, so I limped around to the mews and crept in through the servants' entrance. I put my sleeved arm up over my nose to filter the worst of the smoke and made my way upstairs.

The house was like a mausoleum. I'd never seen it so empty and still. Everywhere there were signs of a rushed leave-taking: fallen chairs, tea dishes left untouched on the salon table, clothing dropped in the hallways near the bedrooms.

Where was Catherine? Was she all right? Was her baby all right?

My room was equally ravaged. Most of my dresses and all of my jewelry were gone. I didn't know if Catherine had taken them herself, or if servants had. Or perhaps looters had come before the soldiers arrived.

I limped across the room to the wardrobe. Removing a petticoat, I began to tear it into strips. I'd seen Noémi bandage wounds a few times: how difficult could it be?

Several long minutes and a few unmentionable words later, I'd managed to wash my poor feet with the remaining water in my vanity table pitcher. After dabbing the open blisters dry, I wound the petticoat strips around them. My feet were now unsightly messes, twice their normal size, but the blisters were no longer exposed. I had some vague sense that I needed to keep them clean or infection might set in. I hoped I'd done enough.

I hobbled back to my dressing table and peered into the mirror. My doubled chimera faces peered back before merging into one. I looked awful: pale and drawn, dark circles beneath my eyes, sooty grime ground into the pores of my face. I plucked at my fraying braid.

I'd be safer traveling as a boy. The soldiers were looking for a young woman of quality, not a farmer's son. And a young woman traveling alone opened herself up to insults. I removed the baggy linen shirt and wound some additional lengths of petticoat around my chest, binding it as tight as I could to obscure the swelling of my breasts, feeling as though I had unmade myself. I was soft and loose through my core, where I had been used to support from my corset, and tight through my chest.

I went back down to one of the salons, searching for my sewing basket. Retrieving my sewing shears, I returned to my room.

I took one last, long look at my hair, rippling in dark waves over my shoulders. I loved my hair, both worn long or in a crown around my head. Drawing a deep breath, I hefted the thickness in one hand and began to cut, scissors sawing through my hair.

The long locks rained down around my feet like dead things. I blinked, hard. After everything that had happened, everything I had lost, I would *not* cry over a paltry thing like shorn hair.

Surveying myself in the mirror, I saw a stranger: a boy of average height and average looks, with bewildered dark eyes. And though I knew it was necessary, knew I must disappear, I could not help feeling lost. This Anna Arden who stared back at me in the mirror with the hair of a boy: who was she?

Before I left, I ransacked the house. Nearly everything of value was gone, but I found some smoky bread, hard cheese, and a small knife in the kitchens, and a pair of boots large enough to fit my bandaged feet in a servant's room.

Back in my room one last time, I took a sheet of paper from my desk. I held the pen for a long moment before setting it to paper. There were so many things I wanted to write: accusations against Franz Joseph for being too cowardly to stand against his mother, a defense of my actions, an apology to Catherine. But I limited myself to merely describing the conversation I had heard in the praetherian camp. I signed the letter and sealed it.

I carried the letter to the Hungarian embassy. It was a delay I could ill afford—every minute I spent in the city increased my risk of being found—but I could not flee without sharing what I knew. I hoped too that I might hear something of Catherine. Or William.

Approaching the gate, I ran through possibilities in my mind. I might leave the letter with one of the guards outside the embassy. Or perhaps with a servant just inside, if the guards would let me pass. But as I weighed my options, a carriage pulled up, and a well-dressed couple emerged from the embassy.

My mouth went dry. Catherine—and Richard.

My sister looked well, if pale. Richard held her arm solicitously, murmuring something to her. Her gaze swept across me, unseeing—then flicked back. I managed a minute wave. Her eyes narrowed in confusion, then settled on my face. They widened a fraction.

Richard ushered her toward the carriage, but she paused. "Dearest, would you see what is taking my maid so long? I thought she'd be down here by now."

Richard said something I did not catch. Catherine shook her head, and Richard went back into the building.

Catherine watched him walk away, then turned to me and beckoned. "Boy, will you carry a message for me?"

Obediently I edged toward her. When I was near

enough, Catherine whispered, "What has happened to you? You look . . ." She trailed off, and I touched my hair self-consciously.

Catherine continued. "I'm leaving Vienna. Richard doesn't believe it's safe, not with the fire and riots and rumors of war—he's sending me home to England. He'll be back in a moment with my maid. We haven't much time—and you must go. Somewhere safe. If Richard knew I had seen you, he'd report you himself." There was a curious thickness to her voice. Her fingers reached for me before she caught herself and pulled them back. Was my sister *crying*? My own lip began to tremble. Catherine could not cry: if she began crying, I might never stop. There was nothing for us beyond this moment but good-bye.

"I'm sorry," I said. "For making a mull of things, for never thinking of how my actions might affect you, for trusting where I should not have."

She drew back, swiping at her cheeks with the back of her hands. "You do not get to hoard all the blame. Since you disappeared I have been thinking. Of you. Of my baby. How I should feel if it were my child and not my sister who acted as you have done."

She took a slow, shuddering breath. "I may not agree with everything you did. But I believe you acted from your convictions, and I respect that. I am sorry I did not support you as I ought to have. Had I been more understanding, you might have confided in me sooner. Had I been less jealous of you, for coming here and trying to change the world after I had exchanged all my Luminate ambition to become a wife, I might have kept you safe."

"I do not think even you could have saved me from my-self," I said, my voice wry, and Catherine gave a choking laugh.

I took a deep breath. The guards were beginning to notice us, the fine lady talking too long to a street urchin. "Will you take a message to the Hapsburgs for me? Tell them the praetheria are engineering a war—they want us to fight one another, and they'll attack when we're weak." I handed her the letter I had written.

"Are you certain of this?"

I nodded.

"I will ensure Richard and Lord Ponsonby know." Catherine rested her hands on her stomach. "You are not alone, you know. The people who have loved you, love you still. And there will be others, wherever you go, if you look for them. We are not meant to be alone. Promise me you will search for people to help you."

I nodded, though my heart was not in it. I had already lost everyone who mattered: Grandmama, Mátyás; now Noémi and Gábor. By day's end Catherine would be gone too. Whatever Catherine believed, that loneliness was sharp and piercing—and it was my life.

My sister took a small purse from her reticule and pressed it into my hands. "Send us word when you are safe."

By the time Richard emerged again from the building with the truant maid, I was already scuffling my way down the street, on my way out of Vienna at last.

If I could but evade the Hapsburg soldiers and the prae-theria long enough, I might begin to figure out how to reconstruct the shambles of my life.

CHAPTER 33

Strong emotions are nearly impossible to sustain for any length of time. For the first few hours after leaving Catherine, I walked with my nerves on high alert, scanning the sky overhead, braced for the sweeping shadows that meant Hunger had come back for me. By the time the close-clustered houses of Vienna had given way to sporadic homes and sprawling farms, exhaustion and cramping pain in my feet had dulled some of my watchfulness. I stopped in the shade of some alder trees not far from the road and pulled out a hunk of bread and cheese wrapped in brown paper.

I leaned back against the trunk, sighing a little. The tight knot in my stomach refused to loosen, so I picked at the bread and listened to the insects buzzing in the meadow behind me. The slowly descending July sun slanted through the trees, warm against my bare hands—and wrong.

One's first day of exile should be a gloomy thing: heavy,

lowering clouds. Thunderstorms on the far horizon—a fitting presage of one's life. To have sunlight instead seemed somehow a mockery. I supposed I should have been grateful I didn't have to walk in the rain, but I couldn't summon the energy.

I needed a goal, some destination other than simply *away*. I couldn't stay in Austria or in Hungary, and England was out of the question. Where had Noémi gone, following her dreams of Mátyás? To the Hungarian plains, I thought. It was as good a direction as any. Perhaps I could find her and put to right one thing in the muddle I'd made of my life. Then I could disappear.

I tried not to examine too closely the thought that Gábor had also headed toward the plains, looking for the King of Crows.

Hooves pounded down the road before me, a cloud of dust rising in their wake. I sat up straighter, the green-with-gold-piping uniforms visible even through the haze. The distinctive crested helmets marked them as Austrian cavalry, rather than the friendlier Hungarian hussars. I squashed an impulse to hide—it was too late; they had surely seen me, and hiding would scream my guilt more loudly than anything else.

Most of the troop rushed past, but one of the soldiers pulled up beside me.

"We're looking for a young lady, possibly traveling alone or in the company of monsters. Have you seen anyone matching this description?"

Yes. In my mirror this very morning. I shook my head. "Is she in trouble, sir?" I pitched my voice low.

He laughed shortly. "She *is* trouble, more like. There's a

price on her head. Look sharp now, lad; there's a reward if you find her."

I fumbled a salute, and the soldier dipped his head before riding after his mates. I collected the remains of the crumbling bread and stowed it in my knapsack, my heart still thudding. I had been careless, but I would not be so again.

I left the road, heading east across the fields.

⟩⟨

It took me five days of trudging to reach the reedy fringes of a lake, sleeping in inns when I could afford them (though the small supply of coins Catherine had given me dwindled rapidly)—in the fields or barns when I could not. A grey heron lifted into the air at my approach. I dropped to the ground and watched it disappear against the sky, my hands clasped loosely in my lap in something akin to prayer. I knew this lake: Lake Fertő, or the Neusiedler See, which spanned the border between Austria and Hungary. I was not far from the Hanság, not far from Eszterháza.

Not far from home—though I might never know home again.

It was dangerous to come here, where I had lived all last summer, where I had met Gábor, where Grandmama had died. Anyone who knew my past might look for me here.

But I had seen no soldiers in forty-eight hours, I had been alone for longer than that, and the hunger for something familiar was so strong I could nearly taste it.

I walked along the outskirts of the lake, far enough out

to avoid the marshiest spots, close enough that the glint of sunlight on the water was always in sight. Twice I stopped to hide at the sound of voices, but it was only ever hunters, intent on their prey and not the least interested in me. My feet burned with the constant rub of new blisters, but I had become more adept at ignoring the pain.

I was not *entirely* foolish. I skirted through the woods near Eszterháza rather than following the road, and I spent the waning hours of afternoon watching the palace. No soldiers came or went.

When night fell, I found the door with the weak latch leading into the corner study on the ground floor and let myself into the house.

No alarm of any kind sounded. Though I had written to János *bácsi* after returning to England, I had not been brave enough to ask what had happened to his magic. I didn't know if the missing ward meant he had grown careless or he simply lacked the magic now. I crept up the stairs to the second floor, where I had seen a glow of light.

I was nearly to János's favorite salon when I heard the clatter of dog nails on parquet floor. *Oroszlán.* Noémi's vizsla rounded a corner and barreled toward me. I side-stepped just in time, having no intention of being buried by the dog as I had been the first time we met.

János stumped into the corridor. "Confound you, *kutya*, what has gotten into you this—" He stopped, brandishing his cane like a weapon.

"Get out of my house."

"János," I said, pulling off the cap I wore and ruffling my short hair. "It's me, Anna."

He squinted at me. Oroszlán snuffled around my feet.

"You look like a boy."

I sighed. "It's a long story."

"Well, you'd best come in and tell it to me."

I followed him into the room, where a small fire burned in the tile stove despite the heat of the late-July evening.

János sat in his favorite seat, and I took the one beside him, my heart pinging as I remembered how Grandmama used to sit here and exchange gossip with her cousin. He listened gravely as I told him about the Congress in Vienna, how I had tried to defend the praetheria who had helped us win the battle in Buda-Pest, how I had angered the archduchess and she had set a price on my head.

I did not tell him *why* my life was forfeit: that I had used Mátyás's death to break the Binding spell. János would hate me, just as Noémi did.

János poured me tea and handed me a sandwich, which I ate with more relish than it deserved. "I wish I could keep you here," he said. "I owe as much to Irína."

I shook my head. "Grandmama wouldn't want you to put yourself in danger for my foolishness. I'll be all right. But I could use a horse."

"Cukor is the only horse left in the stables, but you can have him if you need him. Mátyás's horse was stolen a couple months back."

"Stolen?" I asked, remembering the ill-tempered brute. "Who would want it? In any case, I cannot take your last horse, János *bácsi*. What if you should need it?"

"I can come by another one easy enough. And I don't travel so much as I used to."

There was nothing to do but thank him, though Cukor was only marginally faster than a creek in August, dried to a trickle.

"This is a bad business, though. First Noémi, now you." At my startled look, he explained. "My cousin sent a letter with one of his men when she disappeared. Thought she might have come here."

My heart dipped. "Then she has not been here?" Somehow I had been sure that Noémi would have come to Eszterháza in pursuit of Mátyás. Where had she gone? And where was she now?

A maid came in to remove János's tray, starting a little when she saw me. János said, "Please prepare a room for Miss—that is, Mr. Arden. He will be staying tonight. In the lavender room, I think."

Our talk shifted after that, turning to lighter questions about my time in Vienna, about the country summer in Eszterháza. When I started drooping above my teacup, János sent me to my old room.

The chamber still smelled of lavender and sage, and the familiarity of it brought tears pricking to my eyes. I stripped off my clothes and scrubbed a week's worth of grime from them in the washbasin as best I could before draping them across the windowsill to dry.

I had not been clean for nearly a week—or safe in much longer.

But sliding between the cool, dry sheets, I felt, briefly, both. Some inner bulwark shifted and cracked, and as I rolled onto my stomach to sleep, warm salt tears speckled my pillow.

Sometime in the small hours of the night, a howl split the air. I shot upward, my heart thumping, my breath shallow. I could not tell if I had been dreaming.

A commotion sounded in the courtyard, hooves clattering on stone. I tumbled out of the bed and scrambled to the window.

The courtyard was awash with torches held aloft by soldiers, the flickering light shining on their curved leather helmets, glinting off the metal hilts of their swords.

I had been so very foolish.

I didn't believe János had contributed to the trap, but I could not stay here to see him caught up in it.

I pulled on my still-damp trousers and shoes and raced down the hallway as quickly as my sore feet would allow, taking the servants' stairs to the lowest level of the house and then darting outside. Wood cracked loudly somewhere nearby, followed by the lighter tinkle of glass. They'd broken down the main doors.

I ducked into the stable. Starlight cast thin light into the dim.

Cukor drowsed noisily in his stall, but at my approach he awoke with a huff. I threw a blanket and a light Hungarian riding saddle on him, then the saddlebags someone had had the forethought to pack and leave near the wall of the stall.

Bless János.

I pulled myself up into the saddle, settling into the unfamiliar astride position.

This would be the tricky part: I had to lure the soldiers away from the estate, so they would leave János alone. I did not want him to fight and die for me out of some misguided chivalry. And Cukor—the sweet, stupid, placid beast—was no match for the long-legged elegant horses the soldiers were riding. I should have to be clever—more clever than I felt with my eyes still thick with sleep and my heart pounding through my throat.

I rode Cukor around the sweeping wings of Eszterháza to the wrought-iron gates. There I hesitated. The soldiers were already spilling into the palace through the wrecked doors; I needed to draw their attention. I kicked Cukor harder than he merited, and the poor horse screamed.

The soldiers nearest me spun around. I waved merrily, and urged Cukor into the fastest jog he could manage, riding back around the palace walls to the maze of trees and gardens behind it. I could not lose the soldiers in the fields spreading around Eszterháza, but I might have a chance in the woods.

Cukor and I had just reached the cover of the woods when something electric jolted me, nearly knocking me from the saddle. I doubled over, gasping, recognizing too late the buzz of a spell.

The archduchess had sent spell-casters with the soldiers.

The night lit with a flash, as though the sun had accelerated over the horizon. I glanced behind me to see a ball of fire shooting toward me.

Fighting through panic, I closed my eyes, ignoring the brilliant orange painted against my eyelids. Fire and electricity meant Elementalist and Lucifera, whether two magicians working together or one with both gifts, I didn't know. I reached for the faint buzzing of the spell and found its source near the corner of the palace. This was a larger spell than the soul signs I had broken in the Congress, larger still than the spells I had snapped at the archduchess's ball. It took a moment for my second sense to disentangle its threads.

The heat of the approaching fire seared my skin. Cukor bucked and screamed beneath me.

There. I yanked at the strands of magic, and the spell fell apart.

But anxious and jittery as I was, I wasn't quite fast enough to catch the magic as it exploded from the spell. When my eyes flew open, I saw that the fireball had split around me, forming a kind of fiery cage. And though the power behind the magic had faltered, the fire had already taken root where it touched dry ground, and the magic had only magnified the flame.

In a moment the magician would send another spell after us. Spotting a section where the fire was thinner, I urged Cukor through the flames. For once obedient, Cukor dashed across the clearing and away into the woods.

The fire widened behind us, obscuring my view of the palace. I whispered an apology to János for the destruction, though I could not help feeling grateful for the fire, which might at least delay my attackers long enough for me to escape.

A third spell, more electricity, followed after us. This time I caught the escaping magic and sent it back toward the magician.

After that there were no more spells.

Cukor and I rode into the fire-lit darkness.

X

Once we were safely away, Cukor slowed to an exhausted plod. I sprang down to walk with him, stopping to give him a handful of oats, rub him down, and water him. Our progress after that was slow, but steady, and we passed a tense day.

By early evening, I was forced to halt. Cukor could hardly move, and I was not much better—bleary-eyed from lack of sleep, footsore, and headachy from spell-breaking. I found a copse of trees some distance from any village, and we both tumbled into heavy sleep.

Cukor woke me sometime after midnight, pawing the ground nervously where I'd tied him a few meters distant. He whickered, then snorted, pulling at his ties as if eager to be away. I sat up in my thin bedroll, my pulse thrumming in my ears. I'd been dreaming of Mátyás, flying as a grey-faced crow above the plains.

The sky overhead was clear and sprinkled with stars, a fingernail sliver of moon. Wind stirred through the still-warm air, branches whispering together. In the distance, a tiny snap of wood.

I couldn't hear any cause for alarm, but Cukor rolled his eyes, and anxiety propelled me from my bed. I crept to Cukor, patting his neck reassuringly and whispering into his mane. He trembled beneath my touch.

Something was wrong. The clearing might be quiet, but the woods did not feel empty. They felt, instead, as though they were waiting, the quiet merely the hush of anticipation.

Acting on impulse, I wrenched Cukor's ties loose. Cukor sprang away, faster than I had ever known him to move.

Hide. The instinct crackled through me.

I sprinted toward the river, where I could hear murmuring in the distance. When I reached the shore, I stripped off my shoes and waded into the water, beginning to feel silly. Nothing dangerous had yet erupted from the trees. Probably, Cukor had alarmed us both over nothing, and I would have to spend the better part of the morning hunting him down—if I found him at all.

In the middle of the stream, I clambered up onto a boulder. I curled my knees beneath my chin, my heart still thumping madly. I would wait for a few minutes, to be certain it was nothing, then go back to my bed.

The wind tickled at my exposed toes and fluttered my hair around my ears. I gripped my knees tighter, waiting for my pulse to slow.

A scream split the night, the bellow of a terrified horse. *Cukor.* I started up, but then caught the faintest snarling, a thin yip. *Wolves.* I had forgotten there might be other dangers in the woods besides soldiers and praetheria.

But wolves belonged to more desolate regions: to mountains and wild woods, not to these small clumped trees scattered among settled villages.

Shivering now, though the night was warm, I slid down behind the boulder into the water. I peered around the rock, praying that the faint light of the almost-new moon and stars would not betray me.

But if there were wolves, they would not need the light. My scent alone would be enough, though perhaps the water could cover my smell. I sank down deeper, till only my eyes and nose were above the surface.

The water trickled cold fingers through my clothes, slapping at my cheeks. The wind pushed at the back of my head. *Upwind.* That, at least, was some mercy.

Something slid past my shin, and I swallowed a yelp. Only a fish, I told myself.

A dark shape appeared along the bank, followed by a second, then a third. Their eyes gleamed yellow in the faint light, and a pale luminescence clung to their fur. They were big, much bigger than I had expected, and they sniffed at the bank where I had gone in. A pair of them tussled over one of the shoes I'd left on the grass.

My heart beat so hard it hurt.

They ran along the bank, one of them putting his forepaws in the water before yelping and drawing back.

I let my breath out slowly. For whatever reason, the wolves seemed reluctant to cross the water.

Endless minutes stretched out as the beasts prowled the shore. My fingers grew numb in the cool water; my cheeks stung, pummeled by water and wind.

A hooded figure emerged from the trees behind the wolves, whistling to them. As one, they turned and padded back. The figure threw back her hood, exposing an unlined face and bone-white hair to the starlight. A kestrel rode her shoulder.

Vasilisa.

She crossed to the shoreline, and I drew back into the

shadow of the rock where I could not see her—nor, I prayed, be seen.

"Anna Arden," she called out, her voice shearing across the air, slicing under my skin. "Why do you hide from me? I mean you no harm." I heard the high, thin scream of a falcon, saw the dark shape of the kestrel rocket against the star-strewn sky as she released it. "I only wish to speak with you."

And yet you hunt me with wolves.

I took a long breath and then submerged myself in the water, hoping the kestrel would be far afield before I emerged. The wolves might not track me in the river, but if the bird spotted me, Vasilisa would know where I was. She would find a way to reach me, even if she could not cross moving water with her wolves. If her strength was back, she might fly.

Who was she? Hunger and his generals would not have gone to such lengths to free an ordinary praetherian, but despite all my childhood reading of fairy tales, I could not place Vasilisa among the strong, cruel women in those stories: Titania, the Morrígan, Melusina.

When my lungs began to burn, I surfaced, breathing shallowly through my nose. I peered around the rock, hoping my water-slicked hair and skin would blend with the eddying river.

Vasilisa still stood on the bank, scanning the sky.

Gooseflesh prickled along my exposed skin. I did not know how long she intended to wait, but I could not spend all night in the river. Though the July night was warm, the water was not, and I could die as surely from hypothermia as from the bite of one of her wolves. I studied the far shore, marking out a spot where a willow hung low over the water and the reeds bunched particularly close. If I could make it that far unnoticed, I might have a chance.

I took another breath and submerged, crawling along the stony bottom of the river. When I could hold my breath no longer, I turned my head to one side and raised it slowly, breathing just above the surface of the water before going under again.

My questing fingers closed around the reeds, and I slid among them, grateful for the wind that tossed them over my head and hid my passage.

On the far side of the river, Vasilisa had begun to pace, one of her wolves following behind her. The others had settled on the grass. I could not see the falcon, though its shriek sounded in the distance.

I pulled myself, dripping, onto the bank and slithered beneath the hanging branches of the willow. My head shouted at me to keep moving, to put as much distance between myself and Vasilisa as possible, but my trembling limbs would not seem to work. In any case, if I tried to run, I would only draw the attention of the falcon. I climbed into the willow tree, wedging myself against the trunk and curling my shaking arms around my knees.

Vasilisa did not come for me, and when I peered through the branches, I could see nothing—but she could not have gone far. Possibly only as far as the next bridge crossing the river. Everything but the clothes on my back was still on the far side of the stream—my pack and bedroll; my boots (though one, at least, had been shredded by wolves); all my money. And my horse—what was left of Cukor, anyway.

I sat unmoving as stars shifted overhead. I didn't dare go

back across the river for my things in case Vasilisa waited. I could more easily have faced Luminate magicians. Even if I snapped the spell securing the wolves to Vasilisa, I could not defend against their teeth and claws or her superior power. I couldn't go back to Eszterháza—János would be no match for her.

When thin gold fingers crawled across the sky, I uncurled my stiff body and slid down from the tree.

Then I started walking east.

CHAPTER 34

I walked through the July heat like a swimmer fighting upstream. The world felt strangely unreal, droning in a haze beneath the white spot of the sun. The sky overhead was impossibly blue; the hum of insects across the field was an invitation to find a dappled patch of shade and sleep.

But I could not stop to sleep. My eyes itched, and my body had the curious lightness of too little rest. My thighs chafed from the unaccustomed riding the day before; my bare feet were torn and bleeding. Cukor's final cry echoed continuously in my ears; before me, no matter the landscape, I saw glowing wolf eyes prowling the banks.

I kept moving east. I had gone beyond some vague idea of finding Noémi—I would only bring trouble on her if I did. Instead, a name haunted me, keeping time with the uneven stumbling of my feet.

King of Crows.

King of Crows.

Rumor held that he was powerful. That he was a bandit. That he had sheltered fugitive praetheria. If these were true, it meant he would not care that soldiers hunted me. He would not fear Vasilisa.

If there was sanctuary to be had in this world, he might be able to grant it.

Near midday I passed a low-slung thatched-roof farmhouse that seemed mostly deserted—the owners probably in the fields. I crept through an open doorway into a kitchen, the whitewashed walls lined with painted plates, a ceramic stove resting quiet in the corner. The cool of the room was a relief after the heat.

Just off the kitchen lay the customary unused spare bedroom, the fancy carved bed piled high with embroidered pillows and blankets that had likely been part of the bride's dowry. Carefully I eased a wool blanket from the bottom of the stack and curled it under my left arm. Farther down a narrow hallway, beneath a wardrobe in the bedroom, I found two pair of dress shoes, a woman's embroidered heels and a man's black boots. From their neat placement and general lack of wear, they were probably reserved for special occasions: church, weddings, fetes.

Hearing voices, I peeked out the window to see four people sloping across the field toward the house. Snatching the boots, as the woman's shoes appeared too small, I fled back the way I had come.

I sprinted down a narrow lane into the shadows of a grove and pulled myself up into a tree. When no one came hunting after me, I tore a few strips from the already ragged hem of my shirt, wrapped them around my aching feet, and stuffed my feet into the boots.

Just over a week ago I had captivated an entire ballroom—wealthy, admired. Today I was a fugitive, and a thief.

Sliding down from the tree and wishing I had grabbed something from the kitchen, I ignored my growling stomach and walked on.

)(

I walked for nearly a week to reach the Duna, stealing bits of food, eating half-ripe apples pilfered from orchards, sleeping in barns (when I could find them) and trees (when I could not).

Avoiding the major roads, springing like arteries from Buda-Pest at the country's heart, I did not see soldiers. Where had they gone, after that night at Eszterháza? Were they following false trails, or were they even now closing in on me? I hoped János hadn't been harmed for giving me shelter.

The black velvet night of the new moon came and went.

Twice, shadows moved in the brush at gloaming, eyes bright against the growing dark. But they were gone so swiftly I might have imagined them.

Eagles circled overhead, swinging wide lazy loops in the sky, but no screaming falcons followed me.

I tried—and failed—to shake the sense that Vasilisa was not so much hunting me as herding me. But *where*? And *why*?

Upon reaching the Duna, I persuaded a kindly farmer's

wife to take me across the ferry in her wagon, loaded high with produce, in exchange for helping her wrangle three squirming children. In truth, she probably did not need the help but only took pity on my half-starved and dirty appearance. She gave me a thick slice of bread, slathered with creamy butter and topped with fresh tomato slices.

The Hungarians call the tomato *paradicsom*—paradise. Licking the bright, sweet juice from my chin, I understood why Eve would have risked her Eden for a fruit.

Tiny, stinging insects hung in swarms over the water, but aside from that small menace, the day seemed calm.

I sang a song to the youngest of the children, a little girl who fidgeted restlessly on the bench beside me. My thoughts spun off, lured elsewhere by the warmth and the hum of music, when something large jostled the side of the ferry.

The farmer's wife screeched and clapped plump hands around her two eldest children. I hauled the youngest onto my lap.

A second bump, more forceful than the first, and the ferry tipped upward, sending everyone sliding toward the far side. A loud splash: someone had fallen off.

I peered at the water. It seemed placid, innocuous—only a few ripples skating across its surface. A large, dark shape hung just below the surface. As I watched, it shot toward the ferry. I tightened my arms around the little girl, just as a third jolt shook the boat.

A brief second where the shock jangled in my teeth, then a flash of blue, blue sky, and everything upended. The air filled with screams, and the cool water of the Duna swallowed the wagon and everything on it.

Water filled my nose and ears, a brackish taste on my tongue. The wagon dropped out beneath me, banging my hip as it went. I thrashed blindly for the child, grateful when my fingers closed over wet fabric. I pulled the child to me and pushed up to the surface, gasping in relief as the warm air kissed my cheeks.

The little girl in my arms was limp: I had to get her to shore and push the water out of her. I'd never done it before, but I'd seen a fisherman do it once, on a visit to the seashore when I was a child.

Something caught around my right ankle, hooking me back under the water. My arms tightened reflexively around the girl, and I blinked through the water to see a greenish masculine face grinning up at me. Bubbles escaped through gill slits at his neck.

Praetherian.

Panic spiked in me. I kicked at the face with my free leg, but he only laughed and caught my other ankle. I was going to drown, and the little girl with me. With a mighty push, I shoved the child up toward the surface, hoping someone would spot her and haul her out. Better the uncertainty than a slow death with me.

We were nearly at the bottom now, silt rising in small clouds around us, water plants pressing clammy strands against my legs and wrists. Black shadows crept across my vision and my lungs burned with the effort of holding my breath. My fingers spread wide in search of something I might use as a weapon, but the water plants broke off in my hands, and the fish that slithered around me were too small to hurt anyone.

The water was cool, welcoming. I might let go—release my breath, swallow the water, and wash away.

What would it matter, that I was chimera, that everything I touched crumbled to ruin, if I were dead?

Two things kept me from releasing my breath. One: a fierce stubbornness to *live,* even if I had nothing left to live for. Two: a small, cold doubt that the creature meant to kill me—he might intend to give me to Vasilisa. Or pull me into another world entirely.

Fire burned through my lungs, spreading through my head until I thought it might unmake me. What had Vasilisa told me, all those weeks ago? I was chimera: my dual souls ought to double my power, could I but accept them.

I was dying: there was no reason, here in the cool blackness with that fey face grinning up at me, to deny what I was.

My two souls, both frantic, swirled around each other. Reaching into the quietness at the very heart of myself, I tugged my souls together.

I needed something to startle the creature into releasing me. But the spell would have to be simple, and I knew so few of them. And it was so dark. . . .

Light.

"Lumen," I whispered against the water swirling around my lips, waving my hands weakly through the motions of the spell.

Brilliance exploded before me, as if the sun circling overhead had plunged into the river. The creature released my ankles, his hands shooting up to cover his eyes. I swallowed water and, choking, thrust myself up from the silt, swimming as hard as ever I had.

"There's one more!"

As I broke the surface, strong arms grabbed my flailing hands, pulling me steadily from the water even as clawed fingers scratched one last time at my trailing feet.

※

After I had vomited up the entire river—and then some—I lay on the sun-warmed grass, pulling in shuddering breaths.

When I could sit, I found that the others from the ferry were still gathered, crying and squabbling, on the bank. To my fervent relief, the farmer's wife and all her children had survived, even the littlest one I had shoved to the surface. Some debated whether anything was to be salvaged. Others spoke of sending for help to a nearby village. The farmer's wife said nothing, only sat on the verge and hugged her children to her, her cheeks still wet. The little girl sobbed in her arms.

I got to my feet, every muscle in my body feeling brittle as untempered glass. Pain shot through my vision, clustering at my temples. But I was alive.

As the others began dispersing, I stood apart.

One of the roads alongside the ferry landing stretched toward Buda-Pest. I wished I could follow it and dance at one of Karolina's balls and listen to students arguing at Café Pilvax, or attend a dramatic rendition of an ill-fated Hungarian king in the National Theater.

But I was not yet safe, so I turned east once again.

Water squelched defiantly in my boots as I went, the knotted laces still dripping.

X

I woke just before dawn to a rain shower, fat drops sliding down the leaves and into my face. I had slept wedged in a tree again, and my entire body ached. Sighing as I began my trudge in still-damp shoes, I wiped the water from my eyes. It could be worse: at least it was July instead of November. Or January. Though, as I tried to count backward on my fingers, it might be August now.

For three days I walked steadily eastward. The rain passed, the dark clouds rolling back across the sky like a scroll. The heat that set in was worse: my clothes stuck to every part of my body, and sweat stung my eyes. I smelled rank.

The flat horizon shimmered in the heat. Sometimes I thought I saw water in the distance, and I would hurry forward, desperate to replenish a canteen I had stolen and—if no one was around—to bathe and wash the filth from my clothes. But almost invariably the water was only a mirage. Once I thought I saw a castle, rising above the flat land, but it was only a fata morgana, one of those rare mirages that seem to float in the air. Generally, I found water when I wasn't looking for it—when an unwary step ended in a squelch rather than a firm tap.

The plains stretched as far as I could see, their expanse broken only occasionally by clumps of trees or, more rarely still, the uneven roofline of a village with its church spire piercing the sky like a stone prayer. Sometimes I would see cattle: not the domesticated cows of England, but a rangier, wilder sort with long, wicked horns. Usually a blue-and-black-garbed horseman rode alongside them, kicking up a cloud of dust, a pair of dogs behind him. Most of the herding dogs looked to be made entirely of rags, but once I saw a vizsla so like Oroszlán my heart contracted with homesickness.

I wondered where Noémi was, if she was safe.

I pictured my parents' reaction to Catherine's news of my disgrace, how Papa would grow silent and stiff and retreat to his study and Mama would weep, though more for the damage to her reputation than any real concern for me.

When I was tired, as day edged on toward evening, I thought about Gábor. Had he reached the King of Crows yet? Would he still be there when I arrived? What would I say to him? But these thoughts were more painful than the others, so I gave in to them only when exhaustion lowered my defenses: even if I found him, he would never truly be mine again. He had made that quite clear.

My thoughts brought me little comfort, but occasionally, elusively, when I stopped thinking and just moved, my feet finding their own rhythm through the grasslands, I was surprised by a kind of bone-deep peace. Hungary spoke to my soul, even here in her wildest, most desolate region. Or perhaps *particularly* in her wildest region.

I watched herons fly low across the fields, and a falcon circling high above. I listened to the wind sighing through the dry grass, and the tension that had chased me for so many days began to melt away.

I forgot to be vigilant.

At dusk on the fourth—perhaps fifth?—day since the ferry accident, I crossed a river much wider than the handful of smaller streams I'd crossed in previous days. Near the far side, a rock slid beneath my foot and I fell, banging my hip, still sore from its collision with the wagon, and soaking my clothes. I cursed and pulled myself onto the shore and into the shelter of a stand of trees.

I stripped down to my undergarments, glad for the warmth of the August night, and hung my wet clothes over nearby branches to dry.

My fingers ached from the cold water. I tried gathering a few fallen branches together and glowered at them for a moment. Then I forced my stiff fingers through the ritual of the Fire spell I'd seen my father and Catherine perform.

I had cast a spell only days before. I could do it again. As traumatic as my near drowning had been, there had been a moment of power and peace in the darkness of the river. When the first fire-casting failed, I tried again. And again. I sought for the clarity I'd felt when I held my two souls together, but it eluded me, and the wood remained stubbornly dry.

At last, exhausted, I drifted to sleep.

X

The party of songbirds above me was raucous, pulling me out of sleep. I yawned and stretched, reaching for my shirt.

My fingers closed around empty air. Thinking I had only aimed my hand poorly, I blinked to focus my still-bleary eyes.

I found myself staring into a face I recognized: a girl with two dark braids hanging down her back, a long hooded cloak lined with red around her shoulders despite the dawning warmth of the day.

One of Dragović's Red Mantles.

She handed me my shirt. In German, she said, "Get dressed. I am taking you back to my father."

"Your father?" I pulled my shirt on, then my trousers, watching her carefully. She was only a girl, if a soldier, and she appeared to be alone.

"Josip Dragović." She stood in a swift, elegant movement and dropped a mock curtsy. "Emilija Dragović, at your service."

CHAPTER 35

I stared at the girl, my heart thudding. "Dragović is your father?" I remembered how derisively he had looked at me for my championing of the praetheria, how eager he'd been to take on Archduchess Sophie's command for my arrest. And now he had found me. Or rather, his *daughter* had.

Well, I would not surrender so easily. I slipped my boots on and made a show of adjusting the laces. When I straightened, I charged toward Emilija, bending my head at the last moment so my crown struck her chest. Caught off guard, she dropped to the ground. Still a little dizzy with the impact, I ran past her, my feet crushing the dried grasses beyond the small stand of trees.

Emilija raced after me. She whistled once, and I heard, too late, the barking of a dog.

From the corner of my eye, I caught a blur of black and

white streaking toward me. I pushed myself to run faster, my lungs burning, but the dog plowed me down just as Emilija caught up with me. She was scarcely winded.

I spat dirt out of my mouth and tried to shift the dog from my back, but the low growl rumbling even through its paws persuaded me to stop moving.

Emilija fastened rope securely around both my wrists before calling her dog off. She yanked me up from the ground. The dog, a lovely Dalmatian, sat quietly at her side.

"I'm not sorry," I said.

"I should think poorly of you if you were," she said. "Come. We've some ways to go."

"How far?"

"My father's men tracked you as far as the Duna. They thought you had gone on to the Bükk Mountains, but I knew better. I tracked you alone." She sounded smug.

"Yes, but how far must we go?"

"My father said to take you back to Vienna if I found you. He has gone to the Balaton region to meet the Croat army coming up from Slavonia."

An army. Less than a year after I had broken the Binding and Hungary had broken away from Austria, and already my poor Hungarians were to be at war again. *This is what Hunger and Vasilisa want.* Would this girl believe me if I said as much?

Emilija led me back to where her horse was tied. She gave me a severe look. "You can either ride with me or walk behind my horse. Your choice. But if you wish to ride, you must cooperate when I help you mount."

My feet ached from the miles I'd come on foot. "I'll ride."

She nodded and cupped her hands together to make a step for me. I swung up onto the saddle, grasping the pommel with both bound hands. The mare twitched beneath me, and I had nearly tapped my heels to her flanks, to ride off without my captor, when Emilija said, "I wouldn't. Vatra is superbly trained. She would stop as soon as I called her, and then you should be forced to run behind us."

I stilled my feet, and Emilija swung up behind me. She seemed much more comfortable astride than I was.

We crossed back over the river I had forded with such difficulty the night before and rode for some time beneath the blazing sun, cutting across the rolling prairie grass like a schooner through the seas. I watched water mirages appear and disappear and plotted wild ways to escape, before settling on the most likely: waiting until she slept and then trying to work loose my bonds.

As a captor, Emilija was not unkind. She stopped at regular intervals for food and water (in truth, I ate better as a captive than I had as a fugitive); she allowed me to relieve myself in relative privacy, though she kept the long end of the rope binding my hands as a kind of leash.

She was not much of a conversationalist either. Though perhaps the fault was mine, for choosing poor topics of conversation.

"You know they mean to kill me in Vienna?"

"Yes."

"You feel no guilt for leading me to my death?"

"No. I am a soldier, and you broke the law."

"There was no trial—no proof!"

422

"You killed a man and used his death to power a spell."

I used his death to break a spell. I swallowed the correction. "I broke the Binding. It was an unjust spell, and I am not sorry for what I did."

I wondered if that were still true. I was not sorry the Binding was gone, but I wished Mátyás were not dead. I wished Grandmama had not died to allow me entrance to the spell. And now that Hungary was on the brink of war, and the creatures I had released from the Binding spell were preparing to incite even further destruction, a cold swell of doubt settled in my stomach. Had I done the right thing?

Yes, I thought, remembering Gábor and the soldiers we'd released from the prison, the celebrating in the streets when the Hungarians learned the head of the Austrian Circle had resigned. Whatever had happened after, I had been right to act. I was not responsible for what others had chosen in the aftermath.

Perhaps, if I could get Emilija to sympathize with me, she might let me free. At least, she might not watch me so closely. "They would have killed the man I loved." Pain wrenched through me at the thought of Gábor. I had loved him—loved him still, despite the anger that burned through me at the memory of our last meeting. We had not had enough time together for me to know if I could have sacrificed everything for him. I believed I could, if the love was deep enough, true enough, enduring enough. But Gábor had never given me the chance to find out.

When she did not answer, I asked, "Have you never been in love?"

"No," she said. "And before you pity me, you should

know I have never wished to be. I am a soldier, and a good one. I would not have broken the law, not even for love."

So much for sympathy.

But falling in love had never been a conscious choice. I had been well in it before I realized what was happening.

I sniffed. It didn't seem possible that all the energy and ardency I had thrown into the Congress, into protecting the praetheria, could end in this: capture by a girl-soldier and death—by gunfire, if I was lucky. By a noose, if I was not.

Perhaps I should have let Vasilisa take me. Then I might have survived long enough to escape again. Perhaps I should have let myself drown.

I shook myself. I would find a way out of this yet.

"Can you tell me," Emilija said, breaking in on my thoughts, "what it was that attacked you several nights past? I found the remains of the horse you had ridden and a pack with clothes and some money—at least, I believe it was yours. My dog certainly seemed to think so."

"Your father's men are not the only ones hunting me. The praetheria have been following me too."

"Your friends have turned on you so soon?"

Had they ever been friends? I had thought so, once. But Hunger, who had told Noémi the only secret I kept from her, was not my friend. Vasilisa, hunting after me with wolves, was not my friend.

I didn't answer.

We crossed a thin stream as ink bled across the sky, only a narrow band of gold on the horizon. Emilija drew to a halt and helped me dismount, securing the end of my leash to a tree before rubbing down her horse and turning it loose on the grasses. The Dalmatian flopped on the ground beside me, puffing happily. For a soldier's dog, he seemed entirely too good-natured.

A bird shot from a nearby tree and zoomed past, startling me. I caught only a glimpse of the banded face, the narrow falcon tail, and froze.

Emilija laughed. "Are you frightened? It's only a kestrel. They're common enough."

"I know what it is," I said, fear making me irritable. "But that bird—I think it belongs to the praetherian who's hunting me. We need to leave. Now."

In the grass nearby, Vatra pricked up her ears. Emilija's dog was on his feet beside me, fur bristling, his entire body vibrating with a low growl.

Emilija glanced from her animals to the disappearing speck of the falcon in the darkening sky. Her eyebrows drew together, and she tugged on the end of one braid. "You're spinning stories." But a note of uncertainty hung in her voice.

I shook my head. Vasilisa might not be kind to me, but she would not kill me. At least, I did not *think* she would. But Emilija—Vasilisa would let her wolves tear the girl apart and enjoy doing it. I didn't like the girl, but she was only doing what she believed to be her duty. She didn't deserve to die for it.

The kestrel screamed once, and Vatra shot across the field. Emilija whistled sharply, but the horse did not heed her. Her dog stood alert at her side.

Emilija swiveled slowly, squinting into the near darkness. "Who's there?"

No answer.

Then, some distance away, a faint howling.

The Dalmatian barked in answer.

Much nearer, a second howl pierced the sky. Then a third.

"We should run," I said again. "These aren't ordinary wolves."

Emilija set her lips. "I don't run." She untied her cloak, letting it fall at her feet, and lifted her gun from her belt.

I could not help admiring her bravery, even if it was foolhardy. That did not mean I felt the same. Everything in me screamed to run, but I was still tethered to the tree. I prowled around the leash, looking for a weakness in the knots. There was none: as Emilija had said, she was a good soldier.

Behind me, a shot sounded. I whipped back around; Emilija held the still-smoking gun, efficiently reloading it. One of the lead wolves had fallen back, limping, and the others hesitated around it for just a moment before leaping forward once more. Emilija fired again. This time, the wolves did not pause, and the two nearest her sprang at us.

I could just see Vasilisa, a pale smudge in the gathering shadows.

Vasilisa might spare Emilija if I surrendered. But could I go back to their camp and submit to being used as a weapon?

I had to get free. Maybe a Fire spell, to burn the ends of my leash. I tried to find that quiet center I had used to cast the Lumen light in the river, but my thoughts were too chaotic to settle. The wolves prowled closer.

Faster than I could track, Emilija exchanged her gun for

the saber at her side. The sword flashed down. One wolf, then a second, fell back, and Emilija retreated toward me, still swinging her sword. Her dog darted forward, snarling and biting at the nearest wolves. One of the wolves caught him by the throat and forced him down. Emilija shouted.

How was Vasilisa controlling them? The way the wolves obeyed her instinctively, without spoken commands, suggested a spell.

And spells, I could do something about.

I closed my eyes, ignoring the high, frantic pounding of my heart, trying to forget how vulnerable I made myself. I felt for a spell, for that faint suggestion of scraping along my bones. Nothing.

I opened my eyes again. Emilija was still holding her own against the wolves, though she was visibly tiring. The Dalmatian lay on the ground, its sides heaving red. Three of the wolves had abandoned Emilija and her dog and were now slinking toward me.

Vasilisa drew closer, her face glimmering like a shard of bone in the moonlight, her sharp teeth bared in a grin.

Her mockery fed a lick of anger. I shut my eyes again, determined.

This time I found it—the thin, almost insubstantial line of her spell, linking her mind in a kind of mesh to the wolf pack. I plucked at the main line of the spell, just as a tremendous weight nailed me against the ground, nearly jerking my arms from their sockets as the leash pulled taut.

My eyes flew open. Gold-brown eyes, lined in black, met mine. Hot, sour breath burned against my cheek and neck. *It won't hurt me,* I told myself, trying to recapture the thread I'd dropped on impact. *Vasilisa only means to capture me.*

Then the wolf's teeth tore into my left shoulder, and I screamed. Emilija shouted back, her own tortured echo. Pain lanced through my arm, burning away my focus. I flung up my bound wrists, an instinctive move to protect my face, just as the wolf's powerful jaws closed across my right forearm.

Vasilisa's laugh echoed across the still plains.

CHAPTER 36

The pain was unmaking me, unraveling my thoughts, undoing my will to stop Vasilisa.

Is this how I die?

I gritted my teeth against another scream as the wolf began worrying at my arm and sought for Vasilisa's magic one last time. I concentrated on the pain, allowing it to fuse my souls together as it had under Vasilisa's tutelage in my sister's drawing room. I reached for the intersection of threads I had felt earlier.

A blast of fire barreled over me. The wolf fell away, howling, and I collapsed back on the ground, the air seared from my lungs.

"Did you think I would not notice you tampering with my spells? I am not such a novice as that."

A grumbling roar filled my ears—probably the after-effect of the spell. I tried to pull myself upright, gasping at the pain in my arms. Vasilisa knocked me back with another blast of her hellfire. It did not burn me as a proper fire would, but the heat was a force all its own. Emilija lay unmoving on the ground a few paces away.

The wolves had abandoned us both to swarm at a tall, furred shape swinging massive paws in wild arcs. The wolves howled and darted forward and back, a strangely intricate and deadly dance.

I squinted at the shape. I had seen a bear just before, part of a traveling circus. I thought they existed only in the northern mountains in Hungary, not here on the grasslands. But if mammoth wolves could follow Vasilisa, why not a bear? Though the wolves seemed to be fighting it.

Vasilisa turned to the new commotion in irritation, sending an arcing crest of fire toward the bear. The creature howled, then seemed to blur and shoot upward, flapping out of reach of the second wave.

Vasilisa stopped, lips pursed and eyes brightening. "A táltos? I thought your kind were dead. But two prizes for the cost of one? I will not say no."

Táltos? A sudden hope crushed my chest. But I pushed it aside, using Vasilisa's distraction to grip the threads of the spell once more. One snap, then another, my shadow self gusting along the web of the spell like wind, breaking the fine control as it went.

The wolves, which had been yapping at the crow flying above them, fell still. Waiting. As the last thread binding them snapped, the largest wolf whipped around and disappeared into the night. The others followed almost at once.

I tried to catch the magic as the spell fell apart, but pain and hope made it difficult to concentrate.

Vasilisa whirled back to me. "You stupid girl. Do you know how long it will take me to collect them again?" She flung her arms upward, her hair standing around her. Electric energy crackled along her skin, lightning barely sheathed in her bare hands.

Terror spiked in me; then the world exploded in light and flame.

)(

I lost time for a while. Electricity zapped through my body, a river of pain gathering momentum as it roared along my limbs. I could not see through the white pulse that had blinded me: my world had shrunk to the burning ache defining my body. I wasn't a sentient being. I was agony, sharp and bright like a knife.

My ribs constricted and expanded, the muscles of my chest working frantically, but I could not breathe. I gasped at air, and the fire flowed into my lungs. My heart battered erratically at my chest.

I curled into a ball on the ground, the aching of my arm and shoulder blurring into the aching everywhere else.

It was over.

I couldn't fight Vasilisa. Not like this. Whatever strength I had, she was stronger.

Strange noises penetrated my self-absorbed agony: a heavy thud, the scream of a falcon, the cawing of a crow.

Rolling onto my side, I tried to spot the crow—the táltos. It was impossible, I told myself. There might be other shifters in the world, now that the Binding had broken.

And Mátyás was dead.

The crow was gone, replaced by something shaped like a bear, but with fur that looked more scaly than ursine. This could not be Mátyás. From stories Noémi had told of him after his death, I knew that he could only take on small animals, and only those he knew from real-world study. This creature had walked out of a storybook.

The ground around the táltos erupted, vines snaking around its ankles. It roared and tore free, and new vines slithered after the old, stronger and thicker. The bear-thing stumbled, falling face-forward on the grass.

I flinched, fighting the urge to crawl toward the creature.

The táltos shifted again, a snake slithering free of the creeping vines. A falcon circling overhead dropped down before I could give warning, snatching the snake into the air.

Something was wrong with my nerves. My body did not respond as it should; my lips would not shape the words in my head.

Another shift by the táltos, this time midair, and a crocodilian shape was plummeting back to the ground, pulling the falcon with it until, with a shriek, the bird disengaged. A crow surged up from the great lizard just before it hit the ground.

But Vasilisa had clearly been waiting for this. Before the crow could extend its wings a third time, she'd cast a net of stars all around it, a tightening noose that tangled around its wings until the crow fell.

No.

This táltos might not be Mátyás, but it did not deserve to share my fate. I closed my eyes again. The warm summer air played across my injuries. Vasilisa's spell was a bright spot behind my eyes, and I stretched toward it, closing invisible fingers around it and crushing the web of the spell. This time I caught the escaping magic, shaping it into a spear as I had once before in Vienna and thrusting it at Vasilisa.

If I had not meant the spell before, I meant it this time. Every bit of fear, pain, anger, and betrayal honed the point of the spell and aimed it at her heart.

She screamed, the net of stars bursting into a thousand blooms of light. The crow shot toward her, throwing massive bear arms around her before it had finished shifting. I heard bone cracking. Vasilisa shrieked again, her voice reaching a crescendo of agony.

A flash of light, and the bear-creature released her.

"We are not finished here!" She sprang into the air, her arms flung wide, and flew off, a pale shooting star against a dark night.

The edges of the bear wavered again, the great beast preparing to fly after her.

"Wait!" I called. "Stay, please. Help me."

I tried to move and found my nerves were responding again, if slowly, as though the signal took a very long time to reach them. I fixed my eyes on the bear and lifted my still-bound wrists, my arms trembly and weak as a newborn colt.

The bear melted down, revealing the táltos.

Revealing a boy.

A tall boy with broad shoulders, brown hair, and a mole beneath his left eye.

The round cast to his cheeks was gone, replaced by a

hollowness that made him both older and strange. A boy I hadn't seen in ten months. A boy who had died—I thought—at my own hands.

For a moment I could not remember how to breathe. Or how to speak. My heart jumped erratically in my chest.

Then: "Mátyás?"

A familiar dimpled grin. "You cut your hair."

A potent mix of exasperation and affection bubbled up in me, and I laughed, a movement that made all my injuries burn.

I registered, finally, that he was naked—an unfortunate side effect of shifting. Mátyás seemed to realize this at the same time, because he gave a strangled yelp and snatched Emilija's discarded cloak from the ground nearby.

I tried to push myself upright, gasping at the sharp twinge of pain. But by then Mátyás was already running toward me, the cloak making an awkward shield around his waist.

His hug crushed the breath from me. I did not mind—what were a few aches to having Mátyás back?—but I must have made some pained sound, because his arms loosened. He sat back.

"You're hurt," he said. Blood still oozed from my forearm where the wolf had gnawed on it.

"And bound," I said, holding up my wrists again.

"Right," he said. He touched the leather braid, and it became dried grass, fragile enough that when I pulled my wrists apart, it broke.

I looked at Mátyás. He looked at me. Abruptly we both began to laugh, as though the grass braid were the last thread holding us apart. And just like that, we were Mátyás

434

and Anna again—as if I had not killed him, as if he had not somehow returned from the dead.

X

Mátyás helped me stand, and I stumbled forward until I was beside Emilija, rolling the girl onto her back. Great gashes marred the smoothness of her cheeks, and she bled still, sluggishly, from cuts across her shoulder. A few inches to the right, and her throat would have been sliced wide.

There were other dark spots of blood along her arms and her stomach, but her chest rose and fell, and my frantic fingers brushed against a faint tattoo of a heartbeat beneath her jaw. "She needs help," I said.

Mátyás was already kneeling beside me, carefully ripping a swath from the bottom of Emilija's shirt. When he was finished, he handed me the wad of cloth. "Here. Hold it against the wound. Gábor and the others should be here soon. He'll know what to do."

"Gábor?" I repeated. After an evening full of shocks, I could not process this. "But he was looking for the King of Crows. How did he come to find you?"

Mátyás's blue eyes held mine. *Oh.* A burble of laughter escaped me. "Of course."

Gábor is coming. I will see him soon. I held that knowledge to me like a warm stone in a cold bed in winter. Then I turned my attention back to my cousin.

"But how did *you* come to be here? How are you alive?"

And as I tended to Emilija, and Mátyás gently picked up the wounded Dalmatian to lay at his mistress's side, he told me. How the Lady had rescued him and brought him back. How his táltos gifts had changed after his rebirth.

"I am still not entirely certain how it works," he said, "but I can travel in my dreams. We were already on our way back to Vienna to find you and Noémi, and I dreamed of you. I saw you sleeping near a river, a girl in soldier's gear"—he nodded at Emilija—"watching you. We figured you were in danger, so we came. I may have flown ahead of the others."

I smiled at him, reaching with my free hand to touch his arm, to reassure myself that he was here. Real. Alive. Then my smile faltered. *Noémi.* "Mátyás, there's something I—"

A loud rumble interrupted me. "What was that?"

"My stomach. I don't suppose you have any food?"

I shook my head. Anything we had was lost when Emilija's horse bolted. "I'm sorry."

He sighed. "I suppose I'll just have to wait."

"There's more," I said, and told him about Noémi, how she had gone looking for him and disappeared.

Mátyás listened to me gravely. "A bad business," he said. "Is this why you're here on the *puszta* with a boy's haircut and filthy clothes?"

For so many months I had kept my secrets close to me, afraid how they would change things if people knew. But I did not need to keep any of them from Mátyás, and that in itself felt like a small miracle. I told him everything. How the archduchess had ordered my arrest and the praetheria had rescued me. How I escaped from the praetheria—and why.

"We have to find Noémi," Mátyás said.

I nodded. "Yes. But there's a price on my head, and the praetheria are still hunting me. Hungary is about to be plunged into war."

"I know," Mátyás said. "Gábor wants me to go to Buda-Pest to meet Kossuth Lajos, who is trying to raise a *honvéd* army."

"I wish I knew how to stop the war. This is what the praetheria want—for us to destroy each other."

Now Mátyás nodded. "The Lady told me of the Four. She wants—wanted—me to help her fight them."

I stared at him. "I've never heard of them."

Mátyás waved a hand. "Four praetheria who lead the others. They've taken on curious names, out of Revelation or something. Death, Conquest, Hunger, War."

Hunger. And Vasilisa, I was nearly certain, though I did not know which name she bore.

"We have to stop them." Though heaven alone knew how. "Perhaps the Lady can help us."

"She's dead," Mátyás said.

His blunt words fell like stones, and I flinched. I remembered her touch, before I had gone into the Binding, like balm against a wound. I had believed in myself because she had believed in me. I blinked back the sting in my eyes.

"I'm sorry," he said. "I ought not to have put it like that. Only I'm still coming to grips with it myself. I think the woman who attacked you killed the Lady."

"Vasilisa," I said. "Though I don't think that's her real name."

Emilija moaned then, and we abandoned the conversation to attend to her, but she did not wake. When we resumed talking, it was of other things. Mundane things. János. My family. I told Mátyás about going riding with Franz Joseph, and he teased me for my royal aspirations. This enforced stillness as we waited for Gábor and the others was oddly luxurious, allowing me time to explore questions and answers without rushing onward to another event or idea. I had never seen time as an indulgence before—it was always something to be spent, not savored.

The "others" Mátyás had spoken of arrived—Gábor, of course, and an odd collection I had not expected. A soft-spoken boy named Bahadır. A flame-haired samodiva—Zhivka. A lidérc, whose appearance brought back my nightmares from my first night at Eszterháza, all those months ago. I remembered her grinning at me in the streets near Buda Castle during the fighting. If she had a name, no one seemed to know it.

Their presence in Mátyás's entourage was hopeful, a reminder that not all praetheria hated humans, a sign that it was not yet too late to forge a different future.

Gábor cleaned Emilija's wounds with fresh water and clean cloths, then he and Mátyás rigged together a kind of transport for Emilija behind Mátyás's horse.

While Mátyás and Bahadır settled Emilija and her dog into the transport, I followed Gábor to the river as he scrubbed his hands. The water burbled across the rocks, and I trailed my good hand through it, then splashed it across my heated cheeks.

I had rehearsed many times in my head what I might say if I saw Gábor again. *How could you? How dare you?* But watching his tired, thoughtful profile in the moonlight, I found I no longer wanted to accuse him. Instead, I wanted to settle on the bank beside him and watch the stars in companionable silence. Or murmur under the cover of darkness until the sun rose—strange how the night that just hours before seemed full of terrors only seemed comforting, now that Gábor and Mátyás were here.

"I did not think I would see you again," I said.

His eyes slid sideways, meeting mine. "I meant that good-bye when I said it. My time is not entirely my own right now. But—" He stopped.

I caught the syllable and echoed it back to him, my heart racing with the possibilities in what he did not say. "But?"

He ducked his head as though afraid to look at me and did not answer.

A thrill of power ran through me. Whatever he had said to me at Catherine's flat, he was not indifferent to me. In a little while we would ride to Buda-Pest, where Emilija could be cared for, and Gábor could discharge his duty to Kossuth Lajos by arranging a meeting with Mátyás. Then Mátyás and I would find Noémi, with the others if they chose. On our own, if we must.

Gábor and I would ride together. I had time, this night and the next and the next, to change his mind about our future. At the very least, to sow doubt about his single-sided decision.

"Let me see your arm," Gábor said, and I held my raw arm toward him. He did not flinch but set to cleaning the wound as gently as he could. When he had finished cleaning and wrapping my forearm, he did the same for my shoulder, and the tenderness in his face hurt nearly as much as my injuries.

Mátyás called us back toward the horses, and we

mounted. I settled into place before Gábor, leaning my head against his shoulder, feeling the steady thrum of his heartbeat like a blessing.

I should have been exhausted and terrified. But that night, riding through the vast, silent waves of grass beneath a starry sky, I was neither.

I stole glances at Mátyás, riding along beside us.

Mátyás is alive.

That he lived didn't entirely purge the guilt I felt at killing him—but the heaviness that had weighed me down since his death had cracked and fallen away.

Despite the uncertain future facing us, my heart was light for the first time in months. Armies might be marching on my beloved Hungary, soldiers might even now be hunting for me, there would be a price on my head in Buda-Pest, Vasilisa would doubtless be back and Noémi was missing, but in this moment I was safe, surrounded by two of the people who mattered to me most in all the world. Catherine had told me to find allies—and I had.

In that moment, it was enough.

AUTHOR'S NOTE

As historical fantasy mixes the real with the supernatural and I have drawn on both historical sources and my imagination for this story, I would like to note what is fictional and what is not in *Lost Crow Conspiracy*.

Many of the minor characters (and a few of the secondary) were historical individuals, though their behavior and roles have been fictionalized for the story. Emperor Ferdinand, Archduchess Sophie, Archduke Franz Joseph, Count Karl Grünne, Prince Eszterházy, and Kossuth Lajos all lived in the mid-nineteenth century. Archduchess Sophie was indeed called "the only man at court," a reflection on the way the court viewed the relatively weak Emperor Ferdinand. She is also rumored to have led a camarilla intent on undermining Hungary's independence. Prince Eszterházy served as the first foreign minister of Hungary, and Kossuth Lajos was initially minister of finance under Batthyány Lajos, but by the end of 1848, he was acting as president of national defense and generally viewed as the primary leader of Hungary.

Josip Dragović is loosely modeled on Josip Jelačić, who was, in fact, ban of Croatia, a loyal friend to the Hapsburgs, and a fierce opponent of Kossuth. However, because my version is fairly villainous and Jelačić is viewed as a hero by many people (though not, of course, many Hungarians or historians sympathetic to them), I opted to make him a distinct character. The Red Mantles also existed and were a highly trained and feared military unit—various historical records referred to them as Sereshans or Szeretshaners (possibly derived from *Saracens*) or Pandours, and the uniform described here comes directly from nineteenth-century reports. The military conflicts described in the book are mostly based on history: Serbians conducted skirmishes in southern Hungary as early as June, and Croatia invaded Hungary in the fall of 1848, officially on their own, but many historians believe they had the support and encouragement of the Hapsburg family. Less than six months after declaring independence in March 1848, Hungary was embroiled in civil war.

The Congress described here is obviously fictitious, as no praetheria were released in 1847. However, the format for the Congress is modeled on the fascinating Congress of 1814–15 following the Napoleonic Wars, where diplomats from across Europe (and elsewhere) convened to carve up Napoleon's former territories and haggle over treaty terms.

Franz Liszt retired from performing in 1847 to focus on composing; I've brought him out of retirement for my Congress.

The praetheria as described here are mostly drawn from Slavic and Hungarian folklore, though some of them (usually the unnamed ones) are my own invention. As is customary with folklore and oral tradition, there are competing versions of most creatures. I've tried to tread a middle ground with my descriptions, but some changes have been made for the sake of the story.

If I have not been strictly faithful to historical realities, I hope I have at least been true to the spirit of the time and place. Any mistakes are my own.

ADDITIONAL RESOURCES

Boyar, Ebru, and Kate Fleet. *A Social History of Ottoman Istanbul.* Cambridge: Cambridge University Press, 2010.

Curtis, Benjamin. *The Habsburgs: The History of a Dynasty.* New York: Bloomsbury, 2013.

Deák, István. *The Lawful Revolution: Louis Kossuth and The Hungarians, 1848–1849.* Phoenix, 2001.

Degh, Linda, ed. *Folktales of Hungary.* Translated by Judit Halász. Chicago: University of Chicago Press, 1965.

E.O.S. *Hungary and Its Revolutions from the Earliest Period to the Nineteenth Century: With a Memoir of Louis Kossuth.* Henry G. Bohn, 1854.

Hanioğlu, M. Şükrü. *A Brief History of the Late Ottoman Empire.* Princeton: Princeton University Press, 2010.

Hartley, M. *The Man Who Saved Austria: The Life and Times of Baron Jellačić.* London: Mills & Boon, 1912.

Jokai, Mór. *Hungarian Sketches in Peace and War.* 1854.

Kontler, László. *A History of Hungary: Millennium in Central Europe.* New York: Palgrave Macmillan, 2002.

Lázár, István. *Hungary: A Brief History.* Corvina, 1997.

Minamizuka, Shingo. *A Social Bandit in Nineteenth-Century Hungary: Rózsa Sándor.* East European Monographs, 2008.

Okey, Robin. *The Habsburg Monarchy.* New York: St. Martin's Press, 2000.

Shoberl, Frederic. *Scenes of the Civil War in Hungary, in 1848 and 1849: With the Personal Adventures of an Austrian Officer in the Army of the Ban of Croatia.* Philadelphia: E. H. Butler & Co., 1850.

Trollope, Frances Milton. *Vienna and the Austrians: With Some Account of a Journey Through Swabia, Bavaria, the Tyrol, and the Salzbourg.* London: R. Bentley, 1838.

Wenkstern, Otto von. *History of the War in Hungary in 1848 and 1849.* London: John Parker and Son, 1859.

Winkelhofer, Martina. *The Everyday Life of the Emperor: Francis Joseph and His Imperial Court.* Translated by Jeffrey McCabe. Haymon Verlag, 2012.

CHARACTER GUIDE

In Hungarian fashion, the surnames are given first, followed by first names, for the Hungarian characters.

*Denotes real historical person, though fictionalized in this story

Ákos (AH-kosh): a Hungarian bandit
Anna Arden: our intrepid heroine
Catherine Arden: Anna's older sister
Charles Arden: Anna's father
James Arden: Anna's younger brother
Mária Arden: Anna's mother
Bahadır Beyzade (buh-HA-deer BAY-zah-duh): a young Turk and friend of Ákos
Boldogasszony/The Lady (BOHL-dohg-AHS-sohnyuh) (the final component is voiced as a single syllable): The Joyful Woman; the former Hungarian mother-goddess
Ginny Davies: Anna's maid and friend
Dobos Borbála (DOH-bosh BOHR-bah-lah): Hungarian journalist working in Vienna
Emilija Dragović (eh-MEE-lee-yah DRAH-goh-vitch): Josip Dragović's daughter
Josip Dragović (YOH-seep DRAH-goh-vitch): ban (ruler) of Croatia and leader of the Red Mantles, a highly trained Croatian military unit
Eszterházy János (ES-ter-haa-zee YAH-nosh): Anna's great-uncle; Grandmama's cousin. (The family is most

445

commonly spelled Esterházy now, but in the past used both spellings. I opted for the *sz* spelling so it's consistent with Eszterháza, their Hungarian estate.)

Eszterházy Mátyás (ES-ter-haa-zee MAT-yash): Anna's third cousin; János's great-nephew

Eszterházy Noémi (ES-ter-haa-zee NOH-ay-mee): Mátyás's sister

*Eszterházy Pál, Prince (ES-ter-haa-zee PAHL): Noémi's uncle; Hungary's foreign minister to Austria, following the revolution

Fekete László (FEH-keh-teh LAA-sloh): "László the Black," a bandit living on the Hungarian plains

Richard Gower: Catherine's husband, a young diplomat

*Count Karl Grünne: Archduke Franz Joseph's valet

Hadúr (HAH-dur): the former Hungarian god of war

House of Hapsburg-Lorraine

> ***Archduchess Sophie of Austria:** Archduke Franz Joseph's mother, an influential woman in the Austrian court

> ***Archduke Franz Joseph of Austria:** Emperor Ferdinand's nephew and heir to the Austrian Empire

> ***Emperor Ferdinand of Austria:** head of the Hapsburg royal family; emperor of Austria and king of Hungary

Hunger: leader of the praetheria in Vienna; a sárkány (Hungarian shapeshifting dragon)

*Kossuth Lajos (KOH-shoot LAH-yosh): political reformer and leader of the liberal party in Hungary

Kovács Gábor (KOH-vatch GAH-bor): a young Romani man

*Count Pavel Medem (PAH-vehl MEH-dehm): Russian ambassador to Vienna in 1848

*Petőfi Sándor (PEH-toh-fee SHAHN-dor): a poet and revolutionary; considered by many to be Hungary's national poet and was influential in the March 1848 uprising

*John Ponsonby, 1st Viscount Ponsonby: British ambassador to Vienna, 1846–1850

William Skala (SKAA-luh): a Polish-Scottish revolutionary

Vasilisa (VAH-see-lee-sah): a young praetherian woman, undetermined variety

Zhivka (ZHEEV-kuh): a samodiva (woodland maiden with an affinity for fire); can pass as human

Zrínyi Irína (ZREEN-yee EE-ree-nah): Anna's grandmother, now deceased

Zrínyi Pál (ZREEN-yee PAHL): Anna's uncle; Mária's younger brother

PRAETHERIA

Some of the praetheria in the book are inspired by characters from folklore (predominantly Eastern European and Slavic), others are invented. Capitalized names belong to individual praetheria.

Borevit (BOHR-eh-veet): a wood demon, subservient to Chernobog

Chernobog (CHER-nuh-bog): the "black god" and a demon of the underworld

domovoi (DOHM-uh-voy): a protective house spirit, small, masculine, covered in hair with a long beard. Warm touch means prosperity ahead; cold touch means danger. Can be a trickster, but protects the house. Can shapeshift into small animals.

Fair One/Szépasszony (SEHP-ahs-sohnyuh) (the final component is voiced as a single syllable): a female demon with long hair and a white dress, often appearing during hailstorms and prone to seducing young men; might pass as human

fene (FEH-neh): a Hungarian evil spirit

guta (GUH-tah): a Hungarian demon who beats his victims to death; often associated with strokes, heart attacks, or sudden paralysis

leshy (LEH-shee): a Slavic forest spirit, often characterized by blue skin and a green beard, here described with bark-textured skin

lidérc (LEE-dehrts): a succubus-like creature with goose feet, believed to steal your breath while you sleep

samodiva (SAHM-oh-dee-vah): woodland maidens with an affinity for fire, sometimes having the ability to fly. Some can pass as human. Related to vila.

sárkány (SHAR-kahnyuh) (the final component is voiced as a single syllable): a Hungarian shapeshifting dragon; can pass as human

Svarog (SVAR-ohg): the Slavic sky god, often depicted with four heads (two male, two female); can pass as human

vila (VEE-lah): in Slavic folklore, fairy-like warriors, often believed to seduce or entrap unwary men. Sometimes related to samodiva.

vodanoj (VOH-dah-noy): a male water sprite, often held responsible for drownings (also *vodník, vodyanoy*)

GLOSSARY

a fene egye meg (uh FEH-neh EH-djuh meg): let the *fene*
eat it—"Damn it!"

a pokolba (uh POH-kohl-buh): to the hell; equivalent of
"Oh, hell!" or "Damn it!"

bácsi (BAH-chee): loosely "uncle," a term of respect for older
men

Buda-Pest (BOO-dah-PESHT): what we now think of as
one city used to be two separate cities (they officially joined
in 1873). Buda, on the west side of the Duna, was the home
of many of the wealthy elite; Pest, on the east side, was a
younger, more energetic city.

csárda (CHAR-duh): a country inn

Duna (DOO-nah): the Danube River

Eszterháza (ES-ter-haa-zuh): a formerly rich estate
belonging to the Eszterházy family, but largely neglected by
1847. The palace on the estate was known as the Hungarian
Versailles.

gulyás (GOO-yahsh): cowboy; also the name given to the
plains stew from which we get goulash

hajrá (HIE-rah): a Hungarian exclamation meaning roughly
"Onward!"

Hapsburgs: the imperial family of Austria-Hungary,
formally Hapsburg-Lorraine. In 1847, they were ruled
by Emperor Ferdinand. Today, the spelling "Habsburg"

is more frequently used, but "Hapsburg" was a common nineteenth-century spelling.

honvéd (HOHN-vaid): soldier; also the name for the 1848 Hungarian army

hűhó (HOO-hoh): hullabaloo

kocsma (KOHCH-muh): a tavern or pub

kutya: (KOOT-yah): dog

praetertheria (PRAY-ter-ther-ee-ah) or praetheria (PRAY-ther-ee-ah): scientific terminology used as a hold-all for any supernatural creature released from the Binding spell. Praetheria for plural; praetherian for singular and adjective.

puszta (POO-stuh): Hungarian plains

Romani (roh-MAH-nee): referring to Roma (Gypsy) culture and language, also to the people themselves

táltos (TAHL-tohsh): Hungarian shapeshifter and shaman

LUMINATE ORDERS

Animanti: manipulates living bodies. Common spells: healing, animal persuasion, sometimes invisibility. Less common: shapeshifting, necromancy.

Coremancer: manipulates the mind and heart. Common spells: truth spells, spell re-creation, persuasion, emotional manipulation. Less common: dreams and foresight.

Elementalist (formerly Alchemist): manipulates nonliving substances (light, weather, fire, water, earth, etc.). Most popular order. Common spells: weather magic, illusions, hidings, firestorms, water manipulation. Less common: firesmiths.

Lucifera: manipulates forces (gravity, space, time, magnetism). Common spells: telekinesis, portals, flight. Less common: temporal manipulation.

ACKNOWLEDGMENTS

Somehow, I can find the words for a novel, but struggle to find the right words to say thank you. This book is infinitely better for the smart and compassionate people who added their talents to mine.

Thanks to my superstar agent, Josh Adams, and my inimitable editor, Michelle Frey. And to the wonderful people at team Knopf, particularly Marisa DiNovis, Allison Judd, Lisa Leventer, Artie Bennett, and Dawn Ryan. Ray Shappell and Agent Bob once again created a stunning cover.

I would never have made it this far without my writing group, who are the sisters of my heart: Helen Boswell, Tasha Seegmiller, Erin Shakespear, and Elaine Vickers. Thanks are also due to my beta readers: Rebecca Sachiko Burton, Carlee Franklin Karanovic, Mara Rutherford, Summer Spence, and K. Kazul Wolf.

I am also deeply indebted to readers and friends who helped me with details of Hungarian culture and linguistics, Romani culture, Islam, and nineteenth-century Viennese history, including Kovács Ildikó, Szabó Katalin, Békefi Miklós, Glonczi Ernő, Dr. Elizabeth Jevtic-Somlai, Dr. Hussein Samha, Hadi Alharthi, and Dr. Blair Holmes. Dr. Dave Lunt answered my random questions about Latin, and Michael Bacera gave me great tips on climbing. If there are still mistakes in the story, they are mine.

So many more people offered encouragement in hundreds of small and large ways: Jenilyn Tolley, Karin Holmes Bean, Elly Blake, Stephanie Garber, McKelle George, Jeff Giles, Heather Harris Bergevin, Melanie Jacobson, E. K. Johnston, Emily King, Mackenzi Lee, Yamile Méndez, Jolene Perry, Joy Sterrantino, Erin Summerill, Katie Purdie, Becky Wallace, my Pitch Wars Table of Trust, Sisters in Writing, Class of 2k17, my fellow 2017 debuts, and the extraordinary book bloggers who have championed *Blood Rose Rebellion*, especially Krysti at YA and Wine and Sarah at the Clever Reader.

My family has my endless gratitude for their constant support, even if my youngest once responded to the appearance of my book on a store shelf with "Oh no, Mom. It's your book!" They've handled my deadlines with more grace than I have.

Lastly, to readers. This book wouldn't exist without you.

ROSALYN EVES grew up in the Rocky Mountains, dividing her time between reading books and bossing her siblings into performing her dramatic scripts. As an adult, she still counts the telling and reading of stories as one of her favorite things to do. When she's not reading or writing, she enjoys spending time with her chemistry-professor husband and three children, watching British period pieces, or hiking through the splendid landscape of southern Utah, where she lives.

She has a PhD in English from Penn State, which means she also endeavors to inspire college students with a love for the language. Sometimes it even works.

Lost Crow Conspiracy is the second installment of Rosalyn's Blood Rose Rebellion trilogy. Find out more at rosalyneves.com and on Twitter at @RosalynEves.